Dear Reader,

Welcome to the first of three books starring a brand-new group of modern-day McKettrick men. Readers who have embraced the irrepressible, larger-than-life McKettrick clan as their own won't want to miss the stories of Tate, Garrett and Austin—three Texas-bred brothers who meet their matches in the Remington sisters. When eldest brother Tate McKettrick sets his sights on his old high school sweetheart Libby Remington, the town of Blue River, Texas, will never be the same!

I also wanted to write today to tell you about a special group of people with whom I've become involved in the past couple years—the Humane Society of the United States (HSUS), specifically their Pets for Life program.

The Pets for Life program is one of the best ways to help your local shelter—it helps keep animals out of shelters in the first place. Something as basic as keeping a collar and tag on your pet all the time makes a big difference. If he gets out and gets lost, he can be returned home. Be a responsible pet owner, spay or neuter your pet and don't give up when things don't go perfectly. If your dog digs in the yard or your cat scratches the furniture, know that these are problems that can be addressed. You can find all the information about these— and many other common problems—at www.petsforlife.org. This campaign is focused on keeping pets and their people together for a lifetime.

As many of you know, my own household includes two dogs, two cats and six horses, so this is a cause that is near and dear to my heart. I hope you'll get involved along with me.

With love,

Paula Swe Miller

LINDA LAEL MILLER

McKETTRICKS OF TEXAS:
TATE

HQN™

ISBN-13: 978-1-61664-042-2

MCKETTRICKS OF TEXAS: TATE

Copyright © 2010 by Linda Lael Miller

This edition published by arrangement with Harlequin Books S.A.

® and TM are trademarks of the publisher. Trademarks indicated with ® are registered in the United States Patent and Trademark Office, the Canadian Trade Marks Office and in other countries.

Printed in U.S.A.

For Leslee Borger, my fellow cowgirl,
with love and appreciation.

McKETTRICKS OF TEXAS:
TATE

PROLOGUE

Silver Spur Ranch
Blue River, Texas

SPRING THUNDER EXPLODED overhead, fit to cleave the roof right down the middle and blow out every window on all three floors.

Tate McKettrick swore under his breath, while rain pelted the venerable walls like machine-gun fire.

Like as not, the creek would be over the road by now, and he'd have to travel overland to get to town. He was running late—again. And Cheryl, his ex-wife, would blister his ears with the usual accusations, for sure.

He didn't give a damn, she'd say, about their delicate twin daughters, because he'd wanted boys, as rough-and-tumble as he and his brothers had been. That was her favorite dig. She'd never know—because he wasn't about to let on— how that particular remark never failed to sear a few layers off his heart. He would literally have died for Audrey and Ava—the twins were the only redeeming features of a marriage that should never have taken place in the first place.

Since one good jab was never enough for Cheryl, she'd most likely go on to say that being late for their daughters' dance recital was his way of spiting *her,* their mother. He'd *used* his own children, she'd insist—he *knew* she hated it when he was late—yada, yada, yada.

Blah, blah, blah.

Tate didn't have to "use" the twins to get under Cheryl's hide—he'd done that in spades after the divorce by forcing her to live in Blue River, so they could share custody. Audrey and Ava alternated between their mother's place in town and the ranch, a week there, a week here, with the occasional scheduling variation. As soon as he picked them up on the prescribed days, Cheryl was off to some hot spot to hobnob with her fancy friends and all but melt her credit cards.

Tight-jawed with resignation, Tate plunked down on the edge of his bed and reached for the boots he'd polished before shedding his rain-soaked range clothes to take a hasty shower. Clad in stiff new jeans and the requisite long-sleeved white Western shirt, the cowboy version of a tux, he listened with half an ear to the rodeo announcer's voice, a laconic drone spilling from the speakers of the big flat-screen TV mounted on the wall above the fireplace.

He was reaching for the remote to shut it off when he caught his brother's name.

The hairs on Tate's nape bristled, and something coiled in the pit of his stomach, snakelike, fixing to spring.

"...Austin McKettrick up next, riding a bull named Buzzsaw..."

Tate's gaze—indeed, the whole of his consciousness— swung to the TV screen. Sure enough, there was his kid brother, in high-definition, living color, standing on the catwalk behind the chute, pacing a little, then shifting from one foot to the other, eager for his turn to ride.

The shot couldn't have lasted more than a second or two—another cowboy had just finished a ride and his score was about to be posted on the mega-screen high overhead—but it was long enough to send a chill down Tate's spine.

The other cowboy's score was good, the crowd cheered, and the camera swung back to Austin. He'd always loved cameras, the damn fool, and they'd always loved him right back.

The same went for women, kids, dogs and horses.

He crouched on the catwalk, Austin did, while down in the chute, the bull was ominously still, staring out between the rails, biding his time. The calm ones were always the worst, Tate reflected—Buzzsaw was a volcano, waiting to blow, saving all his whup-ass for the arena, where he'd have room to do what he'd been bred to do: wreak havoc.

Break bones, crush vital organs.

A former rodeo competitor himself, though his event had been bareback bronc riding, Tate knew this bull wasn't just mean; it was two-thousand pounds of cowboy misery, ready to bust loose.

Austin had to have picked up on all that and more. He'd begun his career as a mutton-buster when he was three, riding sheep for gold-stamped ribbons at the county fair, progressed to Little Britches Rodeo and stayed with it from then on. He'd taken several championships at the National High School Rodeo Finals and been a star during his college years, too.

It wasn't as if he didn't know bulls.

Austin looked more cocky than tense; in any dangerous situation, his mantra was "Bring it on."

Tate watched as his brother adjusted his hat again, lowered himself onto the bull's back, looped his hand under the leather rigging and secured it in a "suicide wrap," essentially tying himself to the animal. A moment later, he nodded to the gate men.

Tate stared, unable to look away. He felt an uncanny sensation like the one he'd experienced the night their mom and dad had been killed; he'd awakened, still thrashing to tear free of the last clammy tendrils of a nightmare, his flesh drenched in an icy sweat, the echo of the crash as real as if he'd witnessed the distant accident in person.

He'd known Jim and Sally McKettrick were both gone long before the call came—and he felt the same soul-numbing combination of shock and dread now.

A single, raspy word scraped past his throat. *"No."*

Of course, Austin couldn't hear him, wouldn't have paid any heed if he had.

The bull went eerily still, primal forces gathering within it like a storm, but as the chute gate swung open, the animal erupted from confinement like a rocket from a launchpad, headed skyward.

Buzzsaw dove and then spun, elemental violence unleashed.

Austin stayed with him, spurring with the heels of his boots, right hand high in the air, looking as cool as if he were idling in the old tire-swing that dangled over the deepest part of the swimming hole. Four long seconds passed before he even lost his hat.

Tate wanted to close his eyes, but the message still wasn't making it from his brain to the tiny muscles created for that purpose. He'd had differences with his youngest brother—and some of them were serious—but none of that mattered now.

The clock on the screen seemed to move in slow motion; eight seconds, as all cowboys know, can be an eternity. For Tate, the scene unfolded frame by frame, in a hollow, echoing void, as though taking place one dimension removed.

Finally, the bull made his move and arched above the ground like a trout springing from a lake and then rolling as if determined to turn his belly to the ceiling of that arena, and sent Austin hurtling to one side, but not clear.

The pickup men moved in, ready to cut Austin free, but that bull was a hurricane with hooves, spinning and kicking in all directions.

The bullfighters—referred to as clowns in the old days— were normally called on to distract a bull or a horse, lead it away from the cowboy so he'd have time to get to the fence and scramble over it, to safety.

Under these circumstances, there wasn't much anybody could do.

Austin bounced off one side of that bull and then the other, still bound to it, his body limp. Possibly lifeless.

Fear slashed at Tate's insides.

Finally, one of the pickup men got close enough to cut Austin free of the rigging, curve an arm around him before he fell, and wrench him off the bull. Austin didn't move as the pickup man rode away from Buzzsaw, while the bullfighters and several riders drove the animal out of the arena.

Tate's cell phone, tucked into the pocket of the sodden denim jacket he'd worn to work cattle on the range that day, jangled. He ignored its shrill insistence.

Paramedics were waiting to lower Austin onto a stretcher. The announcer murmured something, but Tate didn't hear what it was because of the blood pounding in his ears.

The TV cameras covered the place in dizzying sweeps. In the stands, the fans were on their feet, pale and worried, and most of the men took their hats off, held them to their chests, the way they did for the Stars and Stripes.

Or when a hearse rolled by.

Behind the chutes, other cowboys watched intently, a few lowering their heads, their lips moving in private prayer.

Tate stood stock-still in the middle of his bedroom floor, bile scalding the back of his throat. His heart had surged up into his windpipe and swollen there, beating hard, fit to choke him.

Both phones were ringing now—the cell and the extension on the table beside his bed.

He endured the tangle of sound, the way it scraped at his nerves, but made no move to answer.

Onscreen, the rodeo faded away, almost instantly replaced by a commercial for aftershave.

That broke Tate's paralysis; he turned, picked up his discarded jacket off the floor, ferreted through its several pockets for his briefly silent cell phone. It rang in his hand, and he flipped it open.

"Tate McKettrick," he said automatically.

"Holy Christ," his brother Garrett shot back, "I thought you'd never answer! Listen, Austin just tangled with a bull, and it looks to me like he's hurt bad—"

"I know," Tate ground out, trying in vain to recall what city Austin had been competing in that week. "I was watching."

"Meet me at the airstrip," Garrett ordered. "I have to make some calls. I'll be there as soon as I can."

"Garrett, the weather—"

"Screw the weather," Garrett snapped. Nothing scared him—except commitment to one woman. "If you're too chicken-shit to go up in a piss-ant rainstorm like this one, just say so right now and save me a trip to the Spur, okay? *I'm* going to find out where they're taking our kid brother and get there any way I have to, because, goddamn it, this might be goodbye. Do you *get* that, cowboy?"

"I get it," Tate said, after unlocking his jawbones. "I'll be waiting when you hit the tarmac, Top Gun."

Garrett, calling on a landline, had the advantage of hanging up with a crash. Tate retrieved his wallet from the dresser top and his battered leather bomber jacket from the walk-in closet, shrugging into it as he headed for the double doors separating the suite from the broad corridor beyond.

With generations of McKettricks adding wings to the house as the family fortune doubled and redoubled, the place was ridiculously large, over eighteen thousand square feet.

Tate descended one of the three main staircases trisecting the house, the heels of his dress boots making no sound on the hand-loomed runner, probably fashioned for some sultan before the first McKettrick ever set foot in the New World.

Hitting the marble-floored entryway, he cast a glance at the antique grandfather's clock—he hadn't worn a watch since his job with McKettrickCo had evaporated in the wake of the IPO of the century—and shook his head when he saw the time.

Four-thirty.

Audrey and Ava's dance recital had started half an hour ago.

Striding along a glassed-in gallery edging the Olympic-size pool, with its retractable roof and floating bar, he opened his cell phone again and speed-dialed Cheryl.

She didn't say "Hello." She said, "*Where the hell are you,* Tate? Audrey and Ava's big number is *next,* and they keep peeking around the curtain, hoping to see you in the audience and—"

"Austin's been hurt," Tate broke in, aching as he imagined his daughters in their sequins and tutus, watching for his arrival. "I can't make it tonight."

"But it's your week and I have plans…"

"Cheryl," Tate bit out, "did you hear what I said? Austin's hurt."

He could just see her, curling her lip, arching one perfectly plucked raven eyebrow.

"So help me God, Tate, if this is an excuse—"

"It's no excuse. Tell the kids there's been an emergency, and I'll call them as soon as I can. *Don't* mention Austin, though. I don't want them worrying."

"Austin is hurt?" For a lawyer, Cheryl could be pretty slow on the uptake at times. "What happened?"

Tate reached the kitchen, with its miles of glistening granite counters and multiple glass-fronted refrigerators. Cheryl's question speared him in a vital place, and not just because he wasn't sure he'd ever see Austin alive again.

Suppose it was too late to straighten things out?

What if, when he and Garrett flew back from wherever their crazy brother was, Austin was riding in the cargo hold, in a box?

Tate's eyes burned like acid as he jerked open the door leading to the ten-car garage.

"He drew a bad bull," he finally said, forcing the words out, as spiky-sharp as a rusty coil of barbed wire.

Cheryl drew in a breath. "Oh, my God," she whispered. "He isn't going to—to die?"

"I don't know," Tate said.

Austin's beat-up red truck, one of several vehicles with his name on the title, was parked in its usual place, next to the black Porsche Garrett drove when he was home. The sight gave Tate a pang as he jerked open the door of his mud-splattered extended-cab Silverado and climbed behind the wheel, then pushed the button to roll up the garage door behind him.

"Call when you know anything," Cheryl urged. "Anything at all."

Tate ground the keys in the ignition, and backed out into the rain with such speed that he nearly collided with one of the ranch work-trucks parked broadside behind him.

The elderly cowpuncher at the wheel got out of the way, pronto.

Tate didn't stop to explain.

"I'll call," he told Cheryl, cranking the steering wheel. He begrudged her that promise, but he couldn't reach his daughters except through his ex-wife.

Cheryl was crying. "Okay," she said. "Don't forget."

Tate shut the phone without saying goodbye.

At the airstrip, he waited forty-five agonizing minutes in his truck, watching torrents of rain wash down the windshield, remembering his kid brother at every stage of his life—the new baby he and Garrett had soon wanted to put up for adoption, the mutton-buster, the high school and college heartthrob.

The man Cheryl swore had seduced her one night in Vegas, when she was legally still Tate's wife.

When the jet, a former member of the McKettrickCo fleet, landed, he waited for it to come to a stop before shoving open the truck's door and making a run for the airplane.

Garrett stood in the open doorway, having lowered the steps with a hydraulic whir.

"He's in Houston," he said. "They're going to operate as soon as he's stable."

Tate pushed past him, dripping rainwater. "What's his condition?"

Garrett raised the steps again, shouldered the door shut and set the latch. "Critical," he said. "According to the surgeon I spoke to, his chances aren't too good."

Tate moved toward the cockpit, using the time his back was turned to Garrett to rub his burning eyes with a thumb and forefinger. "Let's go."

Minutes later, they were in the air, the plane bucking

stormy air currents as it fought for every foot of altitude. Lightning flashed, seeming to pass within inches of the wings, the nose, the tail.

Eventually, though, the skies cleared.

When they landed at a private field outside of Houston, an SUV Garrett had rented before leaving the capital waited on the hot, dry asphalt. The key was in the ignition; Garrett took the wheel, and they raced into the city.

They were all too familiar with the route to the best private hospital in Texas. Their parents had died there, a decade before, after an eighteen-wheeler jumped the median and crashed head-on into their car.

A nurse and two administrators met Tate and Garrett in the lobby, all unwilling to meet their eyes, let alone answer their questions.

When they reached the surgical unit, they found Austin lying on a gurney outside a state-of-the-art operating suite, surrounded by a sea of people clad in green scrubs.

Tate and Garrett pushed their way through, then stood on either side of their brother.

Austin's face was so swollen and discolored they wouldn't have recognized him if he hadn't crooked up one side of his mouth in a grin that could only have belonged to him.

"That was one bad-ass bull," he said.

"You're going to be all right," Garrett told Austin, his face grim.

"Hell, yes, I'm going to be all right," Austin croaked out. His eyes, sunken behind folds of purple flesh, arched to Tate. "Just in case, though, there's one thing I need you to know for sure, big brother," he added laboriously, his voice so low that Tate had to bend down to hear him. "I never slept with your wife."

CHAPTER ONE

Three months later

CHERYL'S RELATIVELY SMALL backyard was festooned with streamers and balloons and crowded with yelling kids. Portable tables sagged under custom-made cakes and piles of brightly wrapped presents, while two clowns and a slightly ratty Cinderella mingled with miniature guests, all of them sugar-jazzed. Austin's childhood pony, Bamboozle, trucked in from the Silver Spur especially for the birthday party, provided rides with saintlike equanimity.

Keeping one eye on the horse and the other on his daughters, six years old as of 7:52 that sunny June morning, Tate counted himself a lucky man, for all the rocky roads he'd traveled. Born almost two months before full term, the babies had weighed less than six pounds put together, and their survival had been by no means a sure thing. Although the twins were fraternal, they looked so much alike that strangers usually thought they were identical. Both had the striking blue eyes that ran in the McKettrick bloodline, and their long glossy hair was nearly black, like Cheryl's and his own. His girls were healthy now, thank God, but Tate still worried plenty about them, on general principle. They seemed so fragile to him, too thin, with their long, skinny legs, and Ava wore glasses and a hearing aid that was all but invisible.

Cheryl startled Tate out of his reflections by jabbing him in the ribs with a clipboard. Today, her waist-length hair was wound into a braided knot at the back of her neck. "Sign this," she ordered, sotto voce.

Tate had promised himself he'd be civil to his ex-wife, for the twins' sake. Looking down into Cheryl's green eyes—she'd been a beauty queen in her day—he wondered what he'd been drinking the night they met.

Gorgeous as Cheryl was, she flat-out wasn't his type, and she never had been.

He glanced at the paper affixed to the clipboard and frowned, then gave all the legalese a second look. It was basically a permission slip, allowing Audrey and Ava to participate in something called the Pixie Pageant, to be held around the time school started, out at the Blue River Country Club. Under the terms of their custody agreement, Cheryl needed his approval for any extracurricular activity the children took part in. It had cost him plenty to get her to sign off on that one.

"No," he said succinctly, tucking the clipboard under one arm, since Cheryl didn't look like she intended to take it back.

The former Mrs. McKettrick, once again using her maiden name, Darbrey, rolled her eyes, patted her sleek and elegant hair. "Oh, for God's sake," she complained, though he had to give her points for keeping her voice down. "It's just a harmless little pageant, to raise money for the new tennis court at the community center—"

Tate's mind flashed on the disturbing film clips he'd seen of kids dolled up in false eyelashes, blusher and lipstick, like Las Vegas showgirls, prancing around some stage. He leaned in, matching his tone to hers. "They're *six,* Cheryl," he reminded her. "Let them be little girls while they can."

His former wife folded her tanned, gym-toned arms. She

looked good in her expensive daffodil-yellow sundress, but the mean glint in her eyes spoiled the effect. "*I* was in pageants from the time I was five," she pointed out tersely, "and I turned out okay." Realizing too late that she'd opened an emotional pothole and then stepped right into it, she made a slight huffing sound.

"Debatable," Tate drawled, plastering a smile onto his mouth because some of the moms and nannies were looking in their direction, and they'd stirred up enough gossip as it was.

Cheryl flushed, toyed with one tasteful gold earring. "Bastard," she whispered, peevish. "Why do you have to be so damn pigheaded about things like this?"

He laughed. Hooked his thumbs through the belt loops of his jeans. Dug in his heels a little—both literally and figuratively. "If other people want to let their kids play Miss This-That-and-the-Other-Thing, that's their business. It's probably harmless fun, but *mine* aren't going to—not before they're old enough to make the choice on their own, anyhow. By that time, I hope Audrey and Ava will have more in their heads than makeup tips and the cosmetic uses of duct tape."

Eyes flashing, Cheryl looked as though she wanted to put out both hands and shove him backward into the koi pond— or jerk the clipboard from under his arm and bash him over the head with it. She did neither of those things—she didn't want a scene any more than he did, though her reasons were different. Tate cared about one thing and one thing only: that his daughters had a good time at their birthday party. Cheryl, on the other hand, knew a public dustup would make the rounds of the country club and the Junior League before sundown.

She had her image to consider.

Tate, by contrast, didn't give a rat's ass what anybody

thought—except for his daughters, that is, and a few close friends.

So they glared at each other, he and this woman he'd married years ago, squaring off like two gunfighters on a dusty street. And then Ava slipped between them.

"Don't fight, okay?" she pleaded anxiously, the hot Texas sunlight glinting on the smudged lenses of her glasses. "It's our *birthday,* remember?"

Tate felt his neck pulse with the singular heat of shame. So much for keeping the ongoing hostilities between Mommy and Daddy under wraps.

Cheryl smiled wickedly and rested a manicured hand on Ava's shoulder, left all but bare by the spaghetti strap holding up her dress—a miniature version of her mother's outfit. Audrey's getup was the same, except blue.

"Your daddy," Cheryl told the child sweetly, "doesn't want you and Audrey to compete in the Pixie Pageant. I was trying to change his mind."

Good luck with that, Tate thought, forcibly relaxing the muscles in his jaws. He tried for a smile, for Ava's sake, but the effort was a bust.

"That stuff is dumb anyway," Ava said.

Audrey appeared on the scene, as though magnetized by an opinion at variance with her own. "No, it *isn't,*" she protested, with her customary spirit. "Pageants are good for building self-confidence and making friends, and if you win, you get a banner and a trophy *and* a tiara."

"I see you've been coaching them to take the party line," Tate told Cheryl.

Cheryl's smile was dazzling. He'd spent a fortune on those pearly whites of hers. Through them, she said, "Shut up, Tate."

Ava, always sensitive to the changing moods of the parental unit, started to cry, making a soft, sniffly sound that tore at Tate's heart. "We're only going to be six *once*," she said. "And everybody's looking!"

"Thank heaven we're only going to be six once," Audrey interjected sagely, folding her arms Cheryl-style. "I'd rather be forty."

Tate bent his knees, scooped up Ava in the crook of one arm and tugged lightly at Audrey's long braid with his free hand. Ava buried her face in his shoulder, bumping her glasses askew. He felt tears and mucus moisten the fabric of his pale blue shirt.

"Forty?" she said, voice muffled. "Even *Daddy* isn't that old!"

"You're such a baby," Audrey replied.

"Enough," Tate told both children, but he was looking at Cheryl as he spoke. "When is this shindig supposed to be over?"

They'd opened presents, devoured everything but the cakes and competed for prizes a person would expect to see on a TV game show. What else was there to do?

"Why can't you just stop fighting?" Ava blurted.

"We're *not* fighting, darling," Cheryl pointed out quietly, before turning to sweep her watchful friends and the nannies up in a benign smile. "And stop carrying on, Ava. It isn't becoming—or ladylike."

"Can we go out to the ranch, Daddy?" Ava asked him plaintively, ignoring her mother's comment. "I like it better there, because nobody fights."

"Me, too," Tate agreed. It was his turn to take the kids, and he'd been looking forward to it since their last visit. Giving them back was always a wrench.

"Nobody fights at the ranch?" Audrey argued, sounding

way too bored and way too sophisticated for a six-year-old. Yeah, she was a prime candidate for the Pixie Pageant, all right, Tate thought bitterly—bring on the mascara and enough hairspray to rip a new hole in the ozone layer, and don't forget the feather boas and the fishnet stockings.

Audrey drew a breath and went right on talking. "I guess you don't remember the day Uncle Austin came home from the hospital after that bull hurt him so bad, before he started rehab in Dallas, and how he told Daddy and Uncle Garrett to stay out of his part of the house unless they wanted a belly full of buckshot."

Cheryl arched one eyebrow, triumphant. For all their land, cattle, oil shares and cold, hard cash, the McKettricks were just a bunch of Texas rednecks, as far as she was concerned. She'd grown up in a Park Avenue high-rise, a cherished only child, after all, her mother an heiress to a legendary but rapidly dwindling fortune, her father a famous novelist, of the literary variety.

But, please, nobody mention that dear old Mom snorted coke and would sleep with anything in pants, and Dad ran through the last of his wife's money and then his surprisingly modest earnings as the new Ernest Hemingway.

Cheryl had never gotten over the humiliation of having to wait tables and take out student loans to put herself through college and law school.

"I wonder what my attorney would say," Cheryl intoned, "if I told him the children are exposed to *guns,* out there on the wild and wooly Silver Spur."

While Tate couldn't argue that there weren't firearms on the ranch—between the snakes and all the other dangers inherent to the land, firepower might well prove to be a necessity at any time—it was a stretch to say the girls were "exposed" to them. Every weapon was locked up in one of several safes, and the combinations changed regularly.

"I wonder what *mine* would say," Tate retorted evenly, the fake smile aching on his face, "if he knew about your plans for this week."

"Stop," Ava begged.

Tate sighed, kissed his daughter smartly on the forehead, and set her on her feet again. "Sorry, sweetheart," he said. "Say goodbye and thanks to your friends. The party's over."

"They haven't even sung the song I taught them," Cheryl said.

Ava leaned against Tate's hip. "We're not good singers at all," she confided.

Somewhat to Tate's surprise, it was Audrey, the performer in the family, who turned on one sandaled heel, faced the assemblage and announced cheerfully, "You can all go home now—my dad says the party's over."

Cheryl winced.

The kids—and the pony—seemed relieved. So did the nannies, though the proper term, according to Cheryl, was *au pairs*. The mothers, many of whom Tate had known since kindergarten and dated in high school between all-too-frequent breakups with Libby Remington, the great love of his youth, if not his entire life, hid bitchy little smiles with varying degrees of success.

"The girls are a little tired," Cheryl explained, with convincing sincerity. "All this excitement—"

"Can we ride horses when we get to the ranch?" Audrey called, from halfway across the yard. "Can we swim in the pool?"

Tate made damn sure he didn't smile at this indication of how "tired" his daughters were, but it was hard.

Ava remained at his side, both arms clenched around his waist now.

"Their suitcases," Cheryl said tightly, "are in the hall."

"Let's load Bamboozle in the trailer," Tate told Ava, gently easing out of her embrace. "Then we'll get your stuff and head for the ranch."

Ava peeled herself away from Tate, walked over and took Bamboozle by the bridle strap, patiently waiting to lead the elderly animal to the trailer hitched to the back of Tate's truck. Audrey had disappeared into the house, on some mission all her own.

"Don't help," Cheryl snapped, out of one side of her mouth. "You've already done enough, Tate McKettrick."

"I live to delight you in every possible way, Cheryl."

Audrey poked her head out between the French doors standing a little ajar between the living room and the patio. "Can we stop at the Perk Up on the way out of town, Dad?" she wanted to know, as calmly as if the backyard weren't full of dismissed guests. "Get some of those orange smoothie things, like before?"

Tate grinned. "Sure," he told his daughter, even though the thought of stopping at Libby's coffee shop made the pit of his stomach tighten. He'd only gone in there the last time because he'd known Libby was out of town, and her sister, Julie, was running the show.

Which was ridiculous. They'd managed to avoid each other for years now, no mean trick in such a small town, but it was getting to be too damn much work.

"Just what they need—more sugar," Cheryl muttered, shaking her head as she walked away, her arms still crossed in front of her chest, only more tightly now.

Tate held his tongue. *He* hadn't been the one to serve

cake and ice cream and fruit punch by the wheelbarrow load all afternoon.

Cheryl kept walking.

Tate and Ava led the pony into the horse trailer, which, along with his truck, took up at least three parking spaces on the shady street in front of Cheryl's house. He'd bought the place for her as a part—a *small* part—of their divorce settlement.

"Boozle might get lonely riding in this big trailer all by himself," Ava fretted, standing beside the pony while he slurped up water from a bucket. "Maybe I should ride back here with him, so he'd have some company."

"Not a chance," Tate said affably, dumping a flake of hay into the feeder for the pony to munch on, going home. "Too dangerous."

Ava adjusted her glasses. "Audrey really wants to be in that Pixie Pageant," she said, her voice small. "She's going to nag you three ways from Sunday about it, too."

Tate bit back a grin. "I think I can handle a little nagging," he said lightly. "Let's go get your stuff and hit the road, Shortstop."

"I probably wouldn't win anyway," Ava mused wistfully, stopping her father cold.

"Win what?" Tate asked.

Ava giggled, but it was a strained sound, like she was forcing it. "The *Pixie Pageant,* Dad. Keep up, will you?"

Tate's throat went tight, but he managed a chuckle. "Sure, you'd win," he said. "And that's another reason I won't let you enter in the first place. Just think how bad all those other little girls would feel."

"Audrey could be Miss Pixie," Ava speculated thoughtfully, a small, light-rimmed shadow standing there in the horse trailer. "She can twirl a baton and everything. I keep on dropping mine."

"Audrey isn't entering," Tate said. Bamboozle was between them; he removed the pony's saddle and blanket, ran a hand along his sweaty back. "She'll just have to content herself with being Miss *McKettrick,* at least for the foreseeable future."

Ava mulled that over for a few moments, chewing her lower lip. "Do you think I'll be pretty when I grow up, Dad?"

Tate moved to the back of the trailer, jumped down, turned and held out his arms for Ava, even though she could have walked down the ramp. "No," he said, as she came within reach. "I think you'll be beautiful, like you are right now."

Ava felt featherlight as he swung her to the ground, and it gave him a pang. Was it his fault that the girls had been born too soon? Was there something he could have done to prevent all the struggles they'd faced just getting through infancy?

"You're only saying that because you're my dad."

"I'm saying it because it's true," Tate said.

Ava stepped back while he slid the ramp into place under the trailer, then shut and latched the doors. "Mommy says it's never too soon to think about becoming a woman," she ventured. "Things we do now could affect our whole, *entire* lives, you know."

Tate kept his back to the child, so she wouldn't see the fury in his face. He spoke in the most normal tone he could summon. "You'll only be a little girl for a few years," he answered carefully. "Just concentrate on that for now, okay? Because 'becoming a woman' will take care of itself."

Wasn't it only yesterday that the twins were newborns, making a peeping sound instead of squalling, like most babies, hooked up to tubes and wires, dwarfed by their incubators at the hospital in Houston? Now, suddenly, they were six. He'd be walking them down the aisle at their weddings before he knew what hit him, he thought bleakly.

He shoved one hand through his hair, longing to get back to the ranch and pull on battered jeans that had never known the heat of an iron. Shed the spiffy shirt, so fresh from the box that the starch in the fabric chafed his sign.

On the ranch, he could breathe, although he'd seriously considered moving out of the mansion, taking up residence in the old bunkhouse or a simple single-wide down by one of the bends in the creek.

Mothers and nannies streamed past, herding grouchy children toward various cars and minivans. A few of the women spoke to Tate, most of them cordial, while a few others wished Ava a happy birthday in subdued tones and ignored him completely.

Tate wasn't much for chatting, but he was friendly enough. When somebody spoke to him, he spoke back.

A scraping sound alerted him to Audrey, dragging her suitcase down the front walk on its wheels. He went to take the bag from her, stowed it in the front seat, on the passenger side, where his dog, Crockett, used to ride. Crockett had died of old age more than a year before, but Tate still forgot he wasn't around sometimes and stood with the truck door open, waiting to hoist his sidekick aboard.

"You got your bag packed?" he asked Ava, when she scrambled into the back seat, with Audrey. They both had those special safety rigs, booster chairs with straps and hooks.

"I've got plenty of clothes at the ranch," Ava responded, with a shake of her head. One of the pink barrettes holding her bangs out of her face had sprung loose, and her braid was coming undone. "Let's go before Mom makes us come back and sing."

Tate laughed, rounded the front of the truck and got behind the wheel.

"Beauty-Shop Betsey," Audrey scoffed. "What possessed Jeffrey's mom to buy us doll heads with curlers?" She'd been talking like a grown-up since she was two.

"Hey," Tate said, starting up the engine, waiting for the flock of departing vans and Volvos to thin out a little. God only knew when Blue River, official population 8,472, had last seen a traffic snarl like this. "If somebody goes to all the trouble of buying you a birthday present, you ought to appreciate it."

"Mom said we could exchange the stuff we don't want," Audrey informed him, with a touch of so-there in her tone. "Everybody included gift receipts."

Tate figured it was high time to change the subject. "How about those orange smoothies?" he asked.

TATE MCKETTRICK, LIBBY REMINGTON thought, watching as he drew his truck and horse trailer to a stop in front of her shop, got out and strode purposefully toward the door.

It bothered her that after all this time the sight of him still made her heart flutter and her stomach jump. Damn the man, with his dark, longish hair, ink-blue eyes, and that confident, rolling way he moved, as though he'd greased his hip sockets.

Although it was growing, with a population now of almost 9,000, Blue River wasn't exactly a metropolis, and that meant she and Tate ran into each other from time to time. Whenever they did, they'd nod and quickly head in separate directions, but they'd *never* sought each other out.

Poised to turn the "Open" sign to "Closed," Libby closed her eyes for a moment, hoping he was a mirage. A figment of her fevered imagination.

He wasn't, of course.

When she looked again, he was standing just on the other side of the glass door, peering through the loop in the *P* in *Perk Up,* grinning.

A McKettrick—a pedigree in that part of the country—Tate was used to getting what he wanted, including service on a Sunday afternoon, when the store closed early.

Libby sighed, turned the dead bolt, and opened the door.

"Two orange smoothies," he said, without preamble. "To go."

Libby looked past him, saw his twin daughters in the back seat of his fancy truck. An old grief rose up within her, one she'd worked hard to lay to rest. From the time she'd fallen for Tate, back in second grade, she'd planned on marrying him when they both grew up, been bone-certain *she'd* be the one to have his babies.

"Where's Crockett?" she asked, without intending to.

Sadness moved in Tate's impossibly blue eyes. "Had to have him put down a while back," he said. "He was pretty old, and then he got sick."

"I'm sorry," Libby said, because she was. For the dog.

"Thanks," he answered.

She stepped back to let Tate in, against her better judgment. "I'm fostering a couple of mixed breeds, because the shelter is full again. Want one—or, better yet, both?"

Tate shook his head. Light caught in his ebony hair, where the comb ridges still showed. "Just a couple of those smoothie things. Orange. Light on the sugar, if that's an option."

Libby stepped behind the counter, more because she wanted to put some kind of solid barrier between herself and Tate than to mix the drinks he'd requested. Her gaze strayed to the kids waiting in the truck again. They both looked like their father. "Will there be anything else?"

"No," Tate said, taking out his beat-up wallet. "How much?"

Libby told him the price of two orange smoothies, with tax, and he laid the money on the countertop. There were at least three drive-through restaurants on the outskirts of town; he'd pass them coming and going from the Silver Spur. So why had he stopped at her store, on Blue River's narrow main street, with a horse trailer hitched to his huge phallic symbol of a truck?

"You're sure you don't want something for yourself?" she asked lightly, and then wished she'd kept her mouth shut.

Tate's grin tilted to one side. He smelled of sun-dried laundry and aftershave and pure *man*. A look of mischief danced in his eyes.

When he spoke, though, he said, "It's their birthday," accompanied by a rise and fall of his powerful shoulders. His blue shirt was open at the throat, and she could see too much—and not quite enough—of his chest.

Libby whipped up the drinks, filling two biodegradable cups from a pitcher, attached the lids and set them next to the cash register. "Then maybe you'd like to give them a dog or two," she replied, with an ease she didn't feel. Being in such close proximity to Tate rattled her, but it probably didn't show. "Since it's their birthday."

"Their mother would have a fit," he said, reaching for the cups. His hands were strong, calloused from range work. Despite all that McKettrick money, he wasn't afraid to wade into a mudhole to free a stuck cow, set fence posts in the ground, buck bales or shovel out stalls.

It was one of the reasons the locals liked him so much, made them willing to overlook the oil wells, now capped, and the ridiculously big house and nearly a hundred thousand acres of prime grassland, complete with springs and creeks and even a small river.

He was one of them.

Of course, the *locals* hadn't been dumped because he'd gotten some other woman pregnant just a few months after he'd started law school.

No, that had happened to *her.*

She realized he was waiting for her to respond to his comment about his ex-wife. *Their mother would have a fit.*

Can't have that, Libby thought, tightening her lips.

"The ice is melting in those smoothies," she finally said. Translation: *Get out. It hurts to look at you. It hurts to remember how things were between us before you hooked up with somebody you didn't even love.*

Tate grinned again, though his eyes looked sad, and then he turned sideways, ready to leave. "Maybe we'll stop by your place and have a look at those dogs after all," he said. "Would tomorrow be good?"

He'd stayed with Cheryl-the-lawyer for less than a year after the twins were born. As soon as the babies began to thrive, he'd moved Cheryl and his infant daughters into the two-story colonial on Oak Street.

The gossip had burned like a brush fire for months.

"That would be fine," Libby said, back from her mental wanderings. Tate McKettrick might have broken her heart, but he'd loved his ancient, arthritic dog, Davy Crockett. And she needed to find homes for the pair of pups.

Hildie, her adopted black Lab, normally the soul of charity, was starting to resent the canine roommates, growling at them when they got too near her food dish, baring her teeth when they tried to join her on the special fluffy rug at the foot of Libby's bed at night. The newcomers, neither more than a year old, seemed baffled by this reception, wagging their tails uncertainly whenever they ran afoul of Hildie, then launching right back into trouble.

They would be very happy out there on the Silver Spur, with all that room to run, Libby thought.

A rush of hope made the backs of her eyes burn as she watched Tate move toward the door.

"Six?" she said.

Tate, shifting the cups around so he could open the door, looked back at her curiously, as though he'd already forgotten the conversation about the dogs, if not Libby herself.

"I close at six," Libby said, fanning herself with a plastic-coated price list even though the secondhand swamp cooler in the back was working fine, for once. She didn't want him thinking the heat in her face had anything to do with him, even though it did. "The shop," she clarified. "I close the shop at six tomorrow. You could stop by the house and see the dogs then."

Tate looked regretful for a moment, as though he'd already changed his mind about meeting the potential adoptees. But then he smiled in that way that made her blink. "Okay," he said. "See you a little after six tomorrow night, then."

Libby swallowed hard and then nodded.

He left.

She hurried to lock the door again, turned the "Closed" sign to the street, and stood there, watching Tate stride toward his truck, so broad-shouldered and strong and confident.

What was it like, Libby wondered, to live as though you owned the whole world?

On the off chance that Tate might glance in her direction again, once he'd finished handing the cups through the window of his truck to the girls, Libby quickly turned away.

She took the day's profits from the till—such as they were—and tucked the bills and checks into a bank deposit bag. She'd hide them in the usual place at home, and stop by First Cattleman's in the morning, during one of the increasingly long lulls in business.

The house she'd lived in all her life was just across the alley, and Hildie and the pups were in the backyard when she approached the gate, Hildie lying in the shade of the only tree on the property, the foster dogs playing tug-of-war with Libby's favorite blouse, which had either fallen or been pulled from the clothesline.

Seeing her, the pups dropped the blouse in the grass— the lawn was in need of mowing, as usual—and yipped in gleefully innocent greeting. Libby didn't have the heart to scold them, and they wouldn't have understood anyway.

With a sigh, she retrieved the blouse from the ground and stayed bent long enough to acknowledge each of the happy-eyed renegades with a pat on the head. "You," she said sweetly, "are very, *very* bad dogs."

They were ecstatic at the news. A matched set, they both had golden coats and floppy ears and big feet. While Hildie looked on, nonplussed, they barked with joy and took a frenzied run around the yard, knocking over the recycling bin in the process.

Hildie finally rose from her nest under the oak, stretched and ambled slowly toward her mistress.

Libby leaned to ruffle Hildie's ears and whisper, "Hang in there, sweet girl. With any luck at all, those two will be living the high life out on the Silver Spur by tomorrow night."

Hildie's gaze was liquid with adoration as she looked up at Libby, panting and swinging her plume of a tail.

"Suppertime," Libby announced, to all and sundry,

straightening again. She led the way to the back door, the three dogs trailing along behind her, single file, Hildie in the lead.

The blouse proved unsalvageable. Libby flinched a little, tossing it into the rag bag. The blue fabric had flattered her, accentuating the color of her eyes and giving her golden brown hair some sparkle.

Easy come, easy go, she thought philosophically, although, in truth, nothing in her life had *ever* been easy.

The litany unrolled in her head.

She'd paid $50 for that blouse, *on sale.*

The economy had taken a downturn and her business reflected that.

Marva was back, and she was more demanding every day.

And as if all that weren't enough, Libby had two dogs in dire need of good homes—she simply couldn't afford to keep them—and she'd already pitched the pair to practically every other suitable candidate in Blue River with no luck. Jimmy-Roy Holter was eager to take them, but he wanted to name them Killer and Ripper, *plus* he lived in a camper behind his mother's house, surrounded by junked cars, and had bred pit bulls to sell out of the back of his truck, along a busy stretch of highway, until an animal protection group in Austin had forced him to close down the operation.

Libby washed her hands at the sink, rubbed her work-chafed hands down the thighs of her blue jeans since she was out of paper towels and all the cloth ones were in the wash.

No, as far as placing the pups in a good home was concerned, Tate McKettrick was her only hope. She'd have to deal with him.

Damn her lousy-assed luck.

CHAPTER TWO

BY THE TIME they got to the ranch, Audrey and Ava were streaked pale orange from the smoothie spills and had developed dispositions too reminiscent of their mother's for Tate's comfort. The minute he brought the truck to a stop alongside the barn, they were out of their buckles and car seats and hitting the ground like storm troopers on a mission, pretty much set on pitching a catfight, right there in the dirt.

Tate stepped between them before the small fists started flying and loudly cleared his throat. The eldest of three brothers, he'd had some practice at keeping the peace—though he'd been an instigator now and again himself. "One punch," he warned, "*just one,* and nobody rides horseback or uses the pool for the whole time you're here."

"What about kicks?" Audrey demanded, knuckles resting on her nonexistent hips. "Is kicking allowed?"

Tate bit back a grin. "Kicks are as bad as punches," he said. "Equal punishment."

Both girls looked deflated—he guessed they had that McKettrick penchant for a good brawl. If their features and coloring hadn't told the story, he'd have known they were his just by their tempers.

"Let's put Bamboozle back in his stall and make sure the other horses are taken care of," Tate said, when neither of his daughters spoke. "Then you can shower—in separate parts of the house—and we'll hit the pool."

"I'd rather hit Ava," Audrey said.

Ava started for her sister, mad all over again, and once more, Tate interceded deftly. How many times had he hauled Garrett and Austin apart, in the same way, when *they* were kids?

"You couldn't take me anyhow," Audrey taunted Ava, and then she stuck out her tongue and the battle was on again. The girls skirted him and went for each other like a pair of starving cats after the same fat canary.

Tate felt as if he were trying to herd a swarm of bees back into a hive, and he might not have untangled the girls before they did each other some harm if Garrett hadn't sprinted out of the barn and come to his aid.

He got Audrey around the waist from behind and hoisted her off her feet, and Tate did the same with Ava. And both brothers got the hell kicked out of their knees, shins and thighs before the twin-fit finally subsided.

There was a grin in Garrett's eyes, which were the same shade of blue as Tate's and Audrey's and Ava's, as he looked at his elder brother over the top of his niece's head. "Well," he drawled, as the twins gasped in delight at his mere presence, "*this* is a fine how-do-you-do. And after I drove all the way from Austin to be here, too. Why, I have half a mind to send your birthday present right back to Neiman Marcus and pretend this is just any old day of the week, nothing special."

Simultaneously, Tate and Garrett set their separate charges back on their sandaled feet.

Audrey smoothed her crumpled sundress and her hair— females of all ages tended to preen when Garrett was around—and asked, with hard-won dignity, "What did you get us, Uncle Garrett?"

Last year, Tate remembered with a tightening along his jawline, it had been life-size porcelain dolls, custom-made by some artist in Austria, perfect replicas of the twins themselves. He was glad the things were at Cheryl's—they gave him the creeps, staring blankly into space. He'd have sworn he'd seen them breathe.

"Why don't you go around to the kitchen patio and find out?" Garrett suggested mysteriously. "Then you'll know whether it's worth behaving yourselves for or not."

Hostilities forgotten—for the time being anyway—the girls ran squealing for the wide sidewalk that encircled the gigantic house.

Whatever Garrett had bought for Audrey and Ava, it was sure to make Tate's offering—a croquet set from Wal-Mart—look puny and ill-thought-out by comparison.

Not that he put a lot of stock in comparison.

"I thought you were in the capital, fetching and carrying for the senator," Tate said, taking his brother's measure in a sidelong glance.

Garrett chuckled and slapped him—a little too hard—on one shoulder. "Sorry I missed the shindig in town," he said, ignoring the remark about his employer. "But I managed to get here, in spite of meetings, a press conference and at least one budding scandal neatly avoided. That's pretty good."

Tate sucked in a breath, let it out. Jabbed at the dirt with the heel of one boot. Garrett was a generous uncle and a good brother, for the most part, but he was living the wrong kind of life for a Texas McKettrick, and he didn't seem to know it. "I don't know what gets into those two," Tate said, shoving a hand through his hair. As far as he knew, he hadn't been in smoothie-range on the ride home, but he felt sticky all over just the same.

Whoops of delight echoed from the distant patio and Esperanza, the middle-aged housekeeper who had worked in that house since their parents' wedding day, could be heard chattering in happy Spanish.

"They'll be fine," Garrett said lightly. Easy for an uncle to say, not so simple for a father.

"What the hell did you get them this time?" Tate asked, starting in the direction of the hoopla. His mood was shifting again, souring a little. He kept thinking about that damn croquet set. "Thoroughbred racehorses?"

Garrett kept pace, grinning. He usually enjoyed Tate's discomfort—unless someone else was causing it. He was no fan of Cheryl's, that was for sure. "Now, why didn't I think of that?"

"Garrett," Tate warned, "I'm serious. Audrey and Ava are six years old. They have more toys than they could use in ten lifetimes, and I'm trying not to raise them like heiresses—"

"They *are* heiresses," Garrett pointed out, just as, a beat late, Tate had realized he would. "Over and above their trust funds."

"That doesn't mean they ought to be spoiled, Garrett."

"You're just too damn serious about everything," Garrett replied.

Just then, Ava ran to meet them, glasses sticky-lensed and askew, her grubby face flushed with excitement. "It's our very own *castle!*" she whooped. "Esperanza says some men brought it on a flatbed truck and it took them *all day* to put the pieces together!"

"Christ," Tate muttered.

"A crew will be here next week sometime, to dig the moat," Garrett told Ava. He might have been promising her a dress for one of her dolls, the way he made it sound.

"The *moat?*" Tate growled. "You're kidding, right?"

Garrett laughed. Would have given Tate another whack on the back if Tate hadn't sidestepped him in time. "What's a castle without a moat?"

Ava danced with excitement, as spindly legged as a spring deer. "There are *turrets,* Dad, and each one has a banner flying from the top. One says 'Audrey' and one says 'Ava'! There are stairs and rooms and there's even a plastic fireplace that lights up when you flip a hidden switch—"

Man, Tate thought grimly, that croquet set was going to be the clinker gift of the century. Damned if he was about to shop again, though, and he hadn't set foot in Neiman Marcus since he was sixteen, when his mother dragged him there to pick out a suit for the junior prom.

He'd endured that only because Libby Remington was his date, and he'd wanted to impress her.

Tate rustled up a grin for his daughter, but his swift glance at Garrett was about as friendly as a splash of battery acid. "A castle with turrets and flags and a prospective moat," he drawled. "Every kid in America ought to have one."

"You think *I* overdid it?" Garrett teased. "Austin had a line on a retired circus elephant—rehab is boring him out of his ever-lovin' mind, so he cruises the Internet on his laptop a lot—until I talked him out of it. Trust me, you could have done a lot worse than a *castle,* big brother."

Right up until he rounded the last corner of the house before the kitchen patio and the acre of lawn abutting it, Tate hoped the thing would turn out to be no bigger than your average dollhouse.

No such luck. It dwarfed the equipment shed where he kept the field tractor, a couple of horse trailers, several riding lawn mowers and four spare pickup trucks. Set on rock slabs, the castle itself was made of some resin-type material, resembling chiseled stone, and stood so tall that it blotted out part of the sky.

Audrey, wearing a pointed princess hat with glittered-on stars and moons and a tinsel tassel trailing from it, waved happily from an upper window.

Tate turned to Garrett, one eyebrow raised. "What? No drawbridge?"

"That would have been a little over the top," Garrett said modestly.

"Ya think?" Tate mocked.

Esperanza, beaming, flapped her apron, resembling a portly bird with only one wing as she inspected the monstrosity from all sides.

Tate waited until Princess Audrey had descended from the tower to fling herself at Garrett in a fit of gratitude—soon to be joined by Ava—before giving one wall a hard shove with the flat of his right hand.

The structure seemed sound, though he'd want to inspect every inch of it, inside and out, to make sure.

"Am I the only one who thinks this is ridiculous?" he asked. "An obscene display of conspicuous consumption?"

"The plastic is all recycled," Garrett avowed, all but reaching around to pat himself on the back.

Tate rolled his eyes and walked away, leaving Garrett and Esperanza and the girls to admire McKettrick Court and returning to the trailer to unload poor old Bamboozle. He settled the pony in his stall, gave him hay and a little grain, and moved to the corral fence to look out over the land, where the horses and cattle grazed in their separate pastures.

At least there was one consolation, he thought; Austin hadn't sent the elephant.

The sound of an arriving rig made him turn around, look

toward the driveway. It was a truck, pulling a gleaming trailer behind it.

A headache thrummed between Tate's temples. Maybe he'd been too quick to dismiss the pachyderm possibility.

Audrey and Ava, having heard the arrival, came bounding around the house, their shiny tassels trailing in the blue beginnings of twilight. Both of them were glitter-dappled from the pointed hats.

Tate and his daughters collided just as the driver was getting down out of the truck cab. A stocky older man, balding, the fella grinned and consulted his clipboard with a ceremonious flourish bordering on the theatrical.

"I'm looking for Miss Audrey and Miss Ava McKettrick," he announced. Tate almost expected him to unfurl a scroll or blow a long brass horn with a velvet flag hanging from it.

Tate was already heading for the back of the trailer, his headache getting steadily worse.

Somehow, despite his bulk, the driver beat him there, blocked him bodily from opening the door and taking a look inside.

By God, Tate thought, *if Austin had sent his kids an elephant...*

"If you wouldn't mind, Mr.—?" the driver said. His name, stitched on his khaki workshirt, was "George."

"McKettrick," Tate replied, through his teeth.

"The order specifically says I'm to deliver the contents of this trailer to the recipients and no one else."

Tate swore under his breath, stepped back and, with a sweeping motion of one arm, invited George to do the honors.

"Who placed this order," Tate asked, with exaggerated politeness, "if that information isn't privileged or anything?"

George lowered a ramp, then climbed it to fling up the trailer's rolling door.

No elephant appeared in the gap.

The suspense heightened—Audrey and Ava were huddled close to Tate on either side by then, fascinated—as George duly checked his clipboard.

"Says here, it was an A. McKettrick. Internet order. We don't get many of those, given the nature of the—er—items."

The twins were practically jumping up and down now, and Esperanza and Garrett had come up behind, hovering, to watch the latest drama unfold.

George disappeared into the shadowy depths, and a familiar clomping sound solved the mystery before two matching Palomino ponies materialized out of the darkness, shining like a pair of golden flames. Their manes and tails were cream-colored, brushed to a blinding shimmer, and each sported a bridle, a saddle and a bright pink bow the size of a basketball.

"Damn," Garrett muttered, "the bastard one-upped me."

"Yeah?" Tate replied, after pulling the girls back out of the way so George could unload the wonder horses. "Wait till you see what *I* got them."

LIBBY HAD EATEN SUPPER—salad and soup—watched the evening news, checked her e-mail, brought the newspaper in from its plastic box by the front gate and done two loads of laundry when the telephone rang.

Damn, she hoped it wasn't the manager at Poplar Bend, the town's one and only condominium complex, calling to complain that Marva was playing her CDs at top volume again, and refused to turn down the music.

In the six months since their mother had suddenly turned

up in Blue River in a chauffeur-driven limo and taken up residence in a prime unit at Poplar Bend, Libby and her two younger sisters, Julie and Paige, had gotten all sorts of negative feedback about Marva's behavior.

None of them knew precisely what to do about Marva.

Picking up the receiver, she almost blurted out what she was thinking—"It's not my week to watch her. Call Julie or Paige"—and by the time she had a proper "Hello" ready, Tate had already spoken.

No one else's voice affected her in the visceral way his did.

"I need those dogs," he said, almost furtively. "Tonight."

Libby blinked. "I beg your pardon."

"I need the dogs," Tate repeated. Then, after a long pause that probably cost him, he added, "Please?"

"Tate, what on earth—? Do you realize what time it is?" She squinted at the kitchen clock, but the room was dark and since she'd just been passing through with a basket of towels from the dryer, she hadn't bothered to flip on a light switch.

"Eight?" Tate said.

"Oh," Libby said, mildly embarrassed. The hours since she'd left the Perk Up had dragged so that she thought surely it must be at least eleven.

"You know I'll give them a good home," Tate went on. "The dogs, I mean."

Libby suppressed a sigh. The pups were curled up together on the hooked rug in the living room, sound asleep. Faced with the prospect of actually giving them up, she knew she was going to miss them—a lot.

"Yes," she agreed. "I know. You can pick them up anytime tomorrow. Just stop by the shop and I'll—"

"It has to be tonight, and—well—if you could deliver them—"

"Deliver them?"

"Look, it's a lot to ask, I know that," Tate said, "and I can't explain right now, and I can't leave, either, even though Garrett and Esperanza are both here, because it's the girls' birthday and everything."

"And you want to give them the dogs for a present after all?"

"Something like that. Lib, I know it's an imposition, but I'd really appreciate it if you could bring them out here right about now."

"But you haven't even seen them—"

"Dogs are dogs," Tate said. "They're all great. And I figure you wouldn't have suggested I adopt them if they weren't good around kids."

"It's normally not the best idea to give pets as gifts, Tate. Too much fuss and excitement isn't good for the animal or the child." What was she *saying?*

She'd been the one to suggest the adoption in the first place, and with good reason—the poor creatures needed the kind of home Tate could give them. With him, they would have the best of everything, and, more important, Tate was a dog person. He'd proved that with Crockett and a lot of other animals, too.

"We're not talking about dyed chicks and rabbits at Easter here, Lib," Tate replied. He was nearly whispering.

"What about kibble—and, well—things they'll need?"

"They can survive on ground sirloin until I can get to the store and pick up dog chow tomorrow," Tate reasoned. "I'm in a fix, Libby. I need your help."

The pups had risen from the hooked rug and stood shoulder to shoulder in the doorway now, ears perked, tails wagging. Her heart sank a little at the sight.

"Okay," Libby heard herself say. "We'll be there as soon as I can load them into my car and make the drive."

Tate let out a long breath. "Great," he said. "I owe you, big-time."

You can say that again, buster, Libby thought. *How about fixing me up with a new heart, since you broke the one I've got?*

The call ended.

"You're going to be McKettrick dogs now," Libby told the guys, with a sniffle in her voice. "Best of the best. You'll probably have your own bedrooms and separate nannies."

They wagged harder. It was impossible, of course, but Libby would have sworn they knew they were headed for a place where they could settle in and belong, for good.

"Heck," she added, on a roll, "you'll even get names."

More wagging.

Libby found her purse and, after considerably more effort, her car keys. Since she lived across the alley from her café and walked everywhere but to the supermarket, she tended to misplace them.

If her aging, primer-splotched Impala would start, they were on their way.

"Want to come along for the ride?" she asked Hildie, resting on a rug of her own, in front of the couch.

Hildie yawned, stretched and went back to sleep.

"Guess that's a 'no,'" Libby said.

The pups were always ready to go when they heard the car keys jingle, and she almost tripped over them twice crossing the kitchen to the back door.

After loading the adoptees into the back seat of the rust-mobile, parked in her tilting one-car garage on the alley, she slid behind the wheel, closed her eyes to offer a silent prayer that the engine would start, stuck the key into the ignition and turned it.

The Impala's motor caught with a huffy roar, the exhaust belching smoke.

Libby backed up slowly and drove with her headlights off until she'd passed Chief of Police Brent Brogan's house at the end of the block. The chief had already warned her once about emissions standards—she was clearly in violation of said standards—and she'd made an appointment at the auto shop to get the problem fixed, twice. The trouble was, she'd had to cancel both times, once because Marva was acting up and neither Julie nor Paige was anywhere to be found, and once because a water pipe at the shop had burst and she'd been forced to call in a plumber, thereby blowing the budget.

All she needed now was a ticket.

She caught a glimpse of the chief through his living-room window as she pulled onto the street. His back was to her, and it looked as though he were playing cards or a board game with his children.

Still, Libby didn't flip on her headlights until she reached the main street. Only when she'd passed the city limits did she give the Impala a shot of gas, and she kept glancing at the rearview mirror. Brent took his job seriously.

He was also one of Tate McKettrick's best friends. If by some chance he'd seen her sneaking out of the alley in a cloud of illegal exhaust fumes, she would simply explain that she was delivering these two dogs to the Silver Spur because Tate wanted them *tonight*.

She bit her lower lip. Tate had said he owed her big-time. Well, then, he could just get her out of trouble with Brent, if she got into any.

But Libby made it all the way out to the Silver Spur without incident, and Tate must have been watching for her, because he was standing in the big circular driveway, with its hotel-size fountain, when she pulled in.

The dogs went wild in the back seat, scrabbling at the doors and rear windows, yipping to be set free.

Tate's grin lit up the night.

He came to the car, opened the back door on the driver's side and greeted the pair with ear-rufflings and the promise of sirloin for breakfast.

The dogs leaped to the paving stones and carried on like a pair of groupies finding themselves backstage at a rock concert.

Frankly, Libby had expected a little more pathos when it came time to part, since she'd been caring for these rascals for over two months, but evidently, the reluctance was all on her side.

"Hey, Lib," Tate said, just when she'd figured he was planning to ignore her completely. "You saved my life. Want to come inside for some birthday cake?"

Lib. It wasn't the first time he'd called her by the old nickname, even recently. He'd used it over the phone earlier, conning her into bringing the dogs out to his ranch that very night. Hearing it now, though, in person instead of over a wire, caused a deep emotional ache in her, a sort of yearning, as though she'd missed the last train or bus or airplane of a lifetime, and would now live out her days wandering forsaken in some wilderness.

"I shouldn't," Libby said.

Tate crouched to give the dogs the attention they continued to clamor for, but his face was turned upward, toward Libby, who was still sitting in her wreck of a car. Lights from the enormous portico over the front doors played in his hair. "Why not?" he asked.

"It's late and Hildie's home alone."

"Hildie?"

"My dog," she said.

"Is she sick?"

Libby shook her head.

"Old?"

Again, a shake.

That deadly grin of his—it should have been registered somewhere, like an assault weapon—crooked up the corner of his mouth. "Will she eat the curtains in your absence? Order pizza and smoke cigars? Log onto the Internet and cruise X-rated Web sites?"

Libby laughed. "No," she said. Once, they'd been so close, she and Tate. She'd known his dog, Crockett, well enough to grieve almost as much over not seeing him anymore as she had over losing his master. It seemed odd, and somehow wrong, that Tate had never made Hildie's acquaintance. "She's a good dog. She'll behave."

"Then come in and have some birthday cake."

Libby looked up at the front of that great house, and she remembered stolen afternoons in Tate's bed, the summer after high school especially. Traveling further back in time, she recalled the night his parents came home early from a weekend trip and caught them swimming naked in the pool.

Mrs. McKettrick had calmly produced a bath sheet for Libby, bundled her into a pink terrycloth bathrobe, and driven her home with Libby, shivering, though the weather was hot and humid at the time.

Mr. McKettrick had ordered Tate to the study as she was leaving with Tate's mom. "We're going to have ourselves a *talk,* boy," the rancher had said.

So much had changed since then.

Tate's mom and dad were gone.

Her own father had long since died of cancer, after a lingering and painful decline.

Tate had married Cheryl, and they'd had twins together.

On the one hand, Libby really wanted to go inside and join the party.

On the other, she knew there would be too many other memories waiting to ambush her—mostly simple, ordinary ones, as it happened, like her and Tate doing their homework together, playing pool in the family room, watching movies and sharing bowls of popcorn. But it was the ordinary memories, she'd learned after losing her dad, that had the most power, the most poignancy.

With all her other problems, Libby figured she couldn't handle so much poignancy just then.

"Not this time," she said quietly, and shifted the Impala into Reverse.

"You need to get that exhaust fixed," Tate told her. The smile was gone; his expression was serious. Moments before, she'd been convinced he'd only invited her inside to be polite, wanted to repay her in some small way for bringing the dogs to him on such short notice. Now she wondered if it actually *mattered* to him, that she accept his invitation. Was it possible that he was disappointed by her refusal?

She nodded. "It's on the agenda. Good night, Tate."

He looked down at the dogs, still frolicking around him as eagerly as if he'd stuffed raw T-bone steaks into each of his jeans pockets. "What are their names?"

"They don't have any," Libby said. "I call them 'the dogs.'"

Tate chuckled. "That's creative," he replied. His body was half turned, as though the house and the people inside it were drawing him back, and she supposed they were. Garrett and Austin were both wild, in their different ways, but

Tate had been born to be a family man, like his father. "You're sure you won't come in?"

"I'm sure."

One of the big main doors opened, and the twins bounded out, dressed in identical pink cotton pajamas.

Libby's heart lurched at the sight of them, and she put the Impala back in Park.

"Puppies!" they cried in unison, rushing forward.

Libby sat watching as the pups and the little girls immediately bonded, knowing all the while that she had to go.

"Happy birthday," Tate told his daughters, with a tenderness Libby had never heard in his voice before. He glanced back at her, mouthed the word, "Thanks."

Libby's vision was blurred. She blinked rapidly and was about to suck it up, back out of that spectacular driveway and head on home, where she belonged, when suddenly one of the children, the one with glasses, ran to the side of her car and peered inside.

"Hi," she said. "We have a castle. Would you like to see it?"

Libby looked up at the front of the house. "Not tonight, sweetheart, but thank you."

"My name is Ava. You're Libby Remington, aren't you? You own the Perk Up Coffee Shop."

Although Libby couldn't recall actually meeting the girls, Blue River wasn't a big place, and practically everybody knew everybody else. "Yes, I'm Libby. I hope you're having a happy birthday."

"We *are*," the child said. "Uncle Garrett bought us our very own castle from Neiman-Marcus, and Uncle Austin sent us ponies. But *Dad* gave us what we *really* wanted—puppies!"

"Take these rascals inside and give them some water," Tate told his daughters. He lingered, while the "rascals" followed the twins into the house without so much as a backward glance at Libby.

Libby's throat tightened, partly because this was goodbye for her and the dogs, partly because of the little girls' obvious joy and partly for reasons she could not have identified to save her life.

"I actually bought them a croquet set," Tate confessed.

Libby frowned. In the old days, she and Julie and Paige had played a lot of backyard croquet with their dad, and she cherished the recollection. She'd been proud that when other daddies were on the golf course with their friends and business associates, hers had chosen to spend the time with her and her sisters. "What's wrong with that?"

He sighed, stood with his arms folded, his head tilted back. He'd always loved looking at the stars, said that was why he'd never be happy in a big city. "Nothing," he admitted. "But I kind of lost my head after the castle and the ponies were delivered. Call it male ego."

"You're not going to change your mind about the dogs, are you?" Libby asked, worried all over again.

Tate gripped the edge of her open window and bent to look in at her. His face was mere inches from hers, and for one terrible, wonderful, wildly confusing moment, she thought he was going to kiss her.

He didn't, though.

"I'm not going to change my mind, Lib," he said. "The mutts will have a home as long as I do."

"You wouldn't send them to town to live with your wife?"

"*Ex*-wife," Tate said. "No, Cheryl's not a dog person. Like the ponies, they'll live right here on the Silver Spur for the duration."

"Okay," Libby said, now almost desperate to be gone.

And oddly, *equally* desperate to stay.

Tate straightened, smiled down at her. Half turned again, toward the house. Toward his daughters and the dogs that were already loved and would soon be named, toward his brother Garrett and Esperanza, the housekeeper.

But then he turned back.

"I don't suppose you'd like to have dinner with me some night?" he asked, sounding as shy as he had that long-ago day when he'd asked her to the junior prom. "Soon?"

CHAPTER THREE

"I CAN'T PAY YOU," Libby warned, the next morning, when her sister Julie showed up at the shop, all set to bake scones and chocolate-chip cookies, her four-year-old son Calvin in tow. Clad in swim trunks and flip-flops, with a plastic ring around his waist, Libby's favorite—and *only*—nephew had clearly made up his mind to take advantage of the first body of water to present itself.

He adjusted his horn-rimmed glasses, with the chunk of none-too-clean tape holding the bridge together, and climbed onto one of three stools lining the short counter.

Libby ruffled his hair. "Hey, buddy," she said. "Want an orange smoothie?"

"No, thanks," Calvin replied glumly.

Julie, twenty-nine, with long, naturally auburn hair that fell to the middle of her back in spiral curls—also natural—and a figure that would do any exercise maven proud, wore jeans and a royal blue long-sleeved T-shirt. Thus her hazel eyes, which tended to reflect whatever color she was wearing that day, were the pure azure of a clear spring sky. She grinned at Libby and headed for the tiny kitchen in the back of the shop.

"You could take my week troubleshooting with Marva," she sang. "Instead of paying me wages, I mean."

"Not a chance," Libby said, but the refusal was rhetorical, and Julie knew that as well as she did. The three sisters rotated, week by week, taking responsibility for their mother, which meant visiting regularly, settling the problems Marva invariably caused with neighbors and hunting her down when she decided to take off on one of her hikes into the countryside and got lost. Marva was always up to something.

"Mom doesn't have anything better to do anyway," Calvin confided solemnly. He was precocious for his age, and he'd already been reading for a year. Julie, a high school English and drama teacher, was off for the summer, and her usual fill-in job at the insurance agency had fallen through for some unspecified reason. "You might as well let her make scones."

Libby chuckled and couldn't resist planting a smacking kiss on Calvin's cheek. "The community pool is closed for maintenance this week," she reminded him. "So what's with the trunks and the plastic inner tube?"

Calvin's eyes were a pale, crystalline blue, like those of his long-gone father, a man Julie had met while she was student teaching in Galveston, after college. As close as she and Julie were, Libby knew very little about Gordon Pruett, except that he'd owned a fishing boat and was a lot better at going away than coming back. He'd stayed around long enough to pass his unique eye color on to his son and name him Calvin, for his favorite uncle, but soon enough he'd felt compelled to move on.

Gordon didn't visit, but he wasn't completely worthless. He remembered birthdays, mailed his son a box of awkwardly wrapped presents every Christmas, and sent Julie a few hundred dollars in child support each month.

Most of the time, the checks even cleared the bank.

Calvin pushed his everyday glasses up his nose—he had better ones for important occasions. "I *know* the pool is closed for maintenance, Aunt Libby," he said, "but the kid next door to us—Justin?—well, his mom and dad bought him a swimming pool, the kind you blow up with a bicycle pump. His dad filled it with a garden hose this morning, but Justin's mom said we can't swim until the sun heats the water up. I just want to be ready."

Julie chuckled as she came out of the kitchen. She'd already managed to get flour all over the front of her fresh apron. "Hey, Mark Spitz," she said to her son, "how about going next door for a five-pound bag of sugar? Give you a nickel for your trouble."

Almsted's, probably one of the last surviving mom-and-pop grocery stores in that part of Texas, was something of a local institution, as much a museum as a place of business.

"You can't buy anything for a nickel," Calvin scoffed, but he climbed down from the stool and held out one palm, reporting for duty.

Libby gave him a few dollars from the till to pay for the sugar, and Calvin marched himself out onto the sidewalk, headed next door.

Julie immediately stationed herself at a side window, in order to keep an eye on him. No child had ever gone missing from Blue River, but a person couldn't be too careful.

"We've already *got* plenty of sugar," Libby said.

"I know," Julie answered, watching as her son went into Almsted's, with its peeling, green-painted wooden screen door. "I have something to tell you, and I don't want Calvin to hear."

Libby, busy getting ready for the Monday-morning latte rush, went still. "Is something wrong?"

"Gordon e-mailed me," Julie said, still keeping her careful vigil. "He's married and he and his wife pass through town often, on the way to visit his parents in Tulsa, and now Gordon and the little woman want to stop by sometime soon, and get acquainted with Calvin."

"That sounds harmless," Libby observed, though she felt a prickle of uneasiness at the news.

"I don't like it," Julie replied firmly. She smiled, which meant Calvin had reappeared, lugging the bag of sugar, and stepped back so he wouldn't see her. "What if Gordon decides to be an actual, step-up father, now that he's married?"

"Julie, he *is* Calvin's father—"

Julie made a throat-slashing motion with one hand, and Calvin struggled through the front door, might have been squashed by it if he hadn't been wearing the miniature inner tube with the goggle-eyed frog-head on the front.

"Here," he said, holding the bag out to his mother. "Where's my nickel?"

Julie paid up, casting a warning glance in Libby's direction as she did so. There was to be no more talk of Gordon Pruett's impending visit while Calvin was around.

"I'm bored," Calvin soon announced. "I want to go to playschool over at the community center."

"You should have thought of that when you insisted on wearing swimming trunks and the floaty thing with the frog-head," Julie responded lightly, heading back toward the kitchen with the unnecessary bag of sugar. "You're not dressed for playschool, kiddo."

"There's a dress code?" Libby asked. She generally took Calvin's side when there was a difference of opinion.

"No," Julie conceded brightly, "but I'd be willing to bet nobody else is wearing a bathing suit."

Two secretaries came in then, for their double nonfat

lattes, following by Jubal Tabor, a lineman for the power company. In his midforties, with a receding hairline and a needy personality, Jubal always ordered the Rocket, a high-caffeine concoction with ginseng and a lot of sugar. Said it got him through the morning.

"Expectin' a flood, kid?" he asked Calvin, who was back on his stool, shoulders hunched, frog-head slightly askew.

Calvin rolled his eyes.

Hiding a smile, Libby served the secretaries' drinks, took their money and thanked them.

Meanwhile, Julie made sure she stayed in the kitchen. Jubal asked her to the movies nearly every time their paths crossed, and even now he was standing on tiptoe trying to catch a glimpse of her while the espresso for his Rocket steamed out of the steel spigot.

"He's not so bad," Libby had said once, when Julie had sent Jubal away with another carefully worded rejection.

"Julie and Jubal?" her sister had said, her eyes green that day because she was wearing a mint-colored blouse. "Our names alone are reason enough to steer clear—we'd sound like second cousins to the Bobbsey twins. Besides, he's too old for me, he wears white socks and he always calls Calvin 'kid.'"

The admittedly comical ring of their names, Jubal's age and the white socks might have been overlooked, in Libby's opinion, but the gruff way he said "kid" whenever he spoke to Calvin bugged her, too. So she'd stopped reminding her sister that there was a shortage of marriageable men in Blue River.

"Scones aren't ready yet?" Jubal asked, casting a disapproving eye toward the virtually empty plastic bakery display case beside the cash register. "Out at Starbucks, they've *always* got scones."

Libby refrained from pointing out to Jubal that he never bought scones anyway, no matter how good the selection was, and set his drink on the counter. "You been cheating on me, Jubal?" she teased. "Buying your jet fuel from the competition?"

Jubal looked at her and blinked once, hard, as though he'd never seen her before. "You want to go to the movies with me tonight?" he asked.

Calvin made a rude sound, which Jubal either missed or pretended not to hear.

"I'm sorry," Libby said, with a note of kind regret in her voice. "I promised Tate McKettrick I'd have dinner with him."

Julie dropped something in the kitchen, causing a great clatter, and out of the corner of her eye, Libby saw Calvin watching her with renewed interest. Since he'd been born long after the breakup, he couldn't have registered the implications of his aunt's statement, but that well-known surname had a cachet all its own.

Even among four-year-olds, it seemed.

"Well," Jubal groused, "far be it from me to compete with a *McKettrick*."

Libby merely smiled. "Thanks for the business, Jubal," she told him. "You have yourself a good day, now."

Jubal paid up, took his Rocket and left.

The instant his utility van pulled away from the curb, Julie peeked out of the kitchen. "Did I hear you say you're going to dinner with Tate?" she asked.

Libby tried to act casual. "He asked me last night. I said maybe."

"That isn't what you told Mr. Tabor," Calvin piped up. "You lied."

"I didn't lie," Libby lied. First, she'd driven her car without the emissions repair, single-handedly destroying the environment, to hear her conscience tell it, and now *this*. She was setting a really bad example for her nephew.

"Yes, you did," Calvin insisted.

"Sometimes," Julie said carefully, resting a hand on Calvin's small, bare shoulder, "we say things that aren't *precisely* true so we don't hurt other people's feelings."

Calvin held his ground. "If it's not the truth, then it's a lie. That's what you always tell *me*, Mom."

Libby sighed. "If Tate asks me out again," she told Calvin, "I'll say yes. That way, I won't have fibbed to anybody."

"I can't believe you didn't say 'yes' in the first place," Julie marveled. "Elisabeth Remington, are you *crazy?*"

Libby cleared her throat, slanted a glance in Calvin's direction to remind her sister that the conversation would have to wait.

"Can I go to playschool if I put on clothes?" Calvin asked, looking so woeful that Julie mussed his hair and ducked out of her floury apron.

"Sure," she said. "Let's run home so you can change." She turned to Libby. "I put the first batch of scones in the oven a couple of minutes ago," she added. "When you hear the timer ding, take them out."

"Are you coming back?" Libby asked, as equally invested in a "no" as she was in a "yes." Once she and her sister were alone again, between customers, Julie would grill her about Tate. If Julie *didn't* return, the first batch of scones would sell out in a heartbeat, as always, and there wouldn't be any more for the rest of the day, because Libby always burned everything she baked, no matter how careful she was.

"Only if you promise to take my turn babysitting Marva

so I can—" Julie paused, cleared her throat "—leave town for a few days."

"We're going somewhere?" Calvin asked, immediately excited. On a teacher's salary, with the child support going into a college account, he and Julie didn't take vacations.

"Yes," Julie answered, passing Libby an arch look. "If your aunt Libby will agree to look after Gramma while we're gone, that is."

Calvin sagged with disappointment. "Nobody," he said, "wants to spend any more time with *Gramma* than they have to."

"Calvin Remington," Julie replied, without much sternness to her tone, "that was a terrible thing to say."

"You say it all the time."

"It's still terrible, all right?" Julie turned to Libby. "Deal or no deal?"

Agreeing would mean two weeks in a row on Marvawatch. But Libby needed those scones, if she didn't want all her customers heading for Starbucks. "Deal," she said, in dismal resignation.

Julie grinned. "Great. See you in twenty minutes."

"Crap," Libby muttered, when her sister and nephew had reached the sidewalk and she knew Calvin wouldn't hear.

Julie took half an hour to get back, not twenty minutes, and in the meantime there was a run on iced coffee, so Libby nearly missed the "ding" of the timer on the oven. She rescued the scones in the nick of time and sold the last one just as Julie waltzed in, all pleased with herself.

"You're going, aren't you?" she asked, as soon as the customer and the scone were gone. "If Tate asks you out to dinner again, you'll say 'yes,' not 'maybe'?"

"Maybe," Libby said, annoyed. "And thanks a heap for

sticking me with Marva for an extra week. I covered for you *last* month, remember, when you wanted to take your twelfth-grade drama class on that field trip to Dallas."

"They learned so much about Shakespeare," Julie said.

"And I came to understand the mysteries of matricide," Libby said, cleaning the spigots on the espresso machine with a paper towel. "Are you seriously planning to leave town so you can avoid Gordon and the new bride?"

"Yes," Julie answered. "According to his e-mail, he sold his boat, or it sank or both and it went for salvage—I forget. That means good old Gordon is thinking of settling down, and I don't want him asking for joint custody or something, just because he's got a wife now."

"I understand where you're coming from, Julie," Libby said, after taking a few moments to prepare, "but you won't be able to hide from Gordon forever—if he really wants to be part of Calvin's life, he'll find a way. And he has a right to at least *see* the little guy once in a while."

"Gordon Pruett is the most irresponsible man on the planet," Julie reminded Libby, her eyes suspiciously bright and her voice shaking a little. "I can't turn Calvin over to him every other weekend, or for whole summers or for holidays. For one thing, there's the asthma."

A silence fell between them.

Libby hadn't witnessed one of Calvin's asthma attacks recently, but when they happened, they were terrifying. Once, when he was still in diapers, he'd all but stopped breathing. Libby's youngest sister, Paige, an RN, had jumped up and made sure he wasn't choking, then grabbed him from his high chair at the Thanksgiving dinner table at a neighbor's house, yelled for someone to call 911 and rushed to the shower, where she'd thrust the by-then-blue baby under an icy spray, drenching herself in the process, holding him there until his lungs were shocked into action.

Libby could still hear his affronted, frightened shrieks, see him soaked and struggling to get to Julie, who bundled him in a towel and held him close, once he'd gotten his breath again, whispering to him, singing softly, desperate to calm him down.

Paige had calmly turned on the hot water spigot in the shower then, and filled the bathroom with steam, and Julie had sat on the lid of the toilet, rocking a whimpering Calvin in her arms until the paramedics arrived.

The toddler had spent nearly a week in the pediatric ward of a San Antonio hospital, Julie at his bedside around the clock, and it had taken Paige months to win back his trust. He was simply too little to understand that she'd saved his life.

Now, he used an inhaler and Julie kept oxygen on hand, in their small cottage two blocks from the high school. Paige, living across the street from them in an old mansion converted to apartments, was on call 24/7 in case Calvin needed emergency intubation. Given that she usually worked four ten-hour shifts at a private clinic fifty miles from Blue River and the fire department EMTs were all volunteers, with little formal training, Paige had tried to show both Julie and Libby how to insert an oxygen tube, using a borrowed dummy.

While Libby supposed she could do it if Calvin's life were hanging in the balance, she was far from confident. It was the same with Julie.

In frustration, Paige had finally recruited one of Blue River's EMTs, a former Marine medic named Dennis Evans, and instructed her sisters to call him if Calvin had a serious asthma attack while she was too far away to help.

Julie kept Dennis's number on the front of her refrigerator, seven bright red, six-inch plastic digits with magnets on the back.

So far, Calvin's medications kept his condition under control, but Libby could certainly understand Julie's vigilance. Whenever he went through a bad spell, Julie didn't sleep, and dark circles formed under her eyes.

"So," Julie said now, returning to the main part of the shop after another batch of scones had been baked, and another rush of business had whisked the goodies out the door before they'd even cooled, "let's talk about Tate."

"Let's not," Libby replied. She'd been a codependent fool to even *think* about accepting a date with him, considering that he'd probably begun the process of forgetting all about her as soon as she'd been forced to leave the university and come home to help look after her ailing father. She'd taken what courses she could at Blue River Junior College, which was really just a satellite of another school in San Antonio and had since closed due to lack of funding, but she'd only been marking time, and she knew it.

"You really loved him, Lib," Julie said gently, taking Calvin's stool at the counter and studying Libby with thoughtful eyes.

"That's the whole point. I loved Tate McKettrick. He, on the other hand, loved a good time." Libby sighed. She hated self-pity, and she was teetering on the precipice of it just then. She tried to smile and partly succeeded. "I guess it made sense that he'd be attracted to someone like Cheryl. She's an attorney, and she was raised the way Tate and his brothers were—with every possible advantage. I didn't even finish college. Tate and I don't have a whole lot in common, when you think about it."

Julie frowned, bracing her elbows on the countertop,

resting her chin in her palms. Her eyes took on a stormy, steel-blue color, edged in gray. "I really hope you're not saying you aren't good enough for Tate or anybody else, because I'm going to have to raise a fuss about it if you are."

Libby chuckled. "Julie Remington, making a scene," she joked. "Why, I can't even *imagine* such a thing."

Julie grinned, raised her beautiful hair off her neck with both hands to cool her neck, then let it fall again. "OK, so I might have been a bit of a drama queen in high school and college," she confessed. "You're just trying to distract me from the fact that I'm right. You think—you *actually think*—Tate threw you over for Cheryl because she fit into his world better than you would have."

Libby raised one eyebrow. "Isn't that what happened?"

"What *happened*," Julie argued, "is this—Cheryl seduced Tate. Oil wells and big Texas ranches can be aphrodisiacs, you know. Maybe she intended all along to get pregnant and live like a Ewing out there on the Silver Spur."

"Oh, come *on*," Libby retorted. "I might not admire the woman all that much, but it isn't fair to put all the blame on her, and you damn well know it, Jules. It isn't as if she used a date drug and had her way with Tate while he was unconscious. He could have stopped the whole thing if he'd wanted to—which he obviously didn't."

"That was a while ago, Lib," Julie said mildly, examining her manicure.

"All right, so he was young," Libby responded. "He was old enough to know better."

The front door of the shop swung open then, and Chief Brogan strolled in, sweating in his usually crisp tan uniform. He nodded to Julie, then swung his dark brown gaze to Libby.

"Do I smell scones?" he asked.

"Blueberry," Julie confirmed, smiling.

Brent Brogan, a fairly recent widower, was six feet tall with broad, powerful shoulders and a narrow waist. Tate had long ago dubbed him "Denzel," since he bore such a strong resemblance to the actor, back in Denzel Washington's younger years.

His gaze swung in Julie's direction, then back to Libby. "The usual," he said. "Please."

"Sure, Chief," Libby said, with nervous good cheer, and started the mocha with a triple shot of espresso he ordered every day at about the same time.

Brent approached the counter, braced his big hands against it, and watched Libby with unnerving thoroughness as she worked. "I would have sworn I saw that Impala of yours rolling down the alley last night," he said affably, "with the headlights out. Did you get the exhaust fixed yet?"

"That was my car you saw," Julie hastened to say.

It was a good thing Calvin wasn't around, because that was a whopper and he'd have been sure to point that out right away. Julie's car was a pink Cadillac that had been somebody's Mary Kay prize back in the mid-'80s. Even in a dark alley, it wouldn't be mistaken for an Impala, especially not by a trained observer like Brent Brogan.

Libby gave her sister a look. Sighed and rubbed her suddenly sweaty palms down her jean-covered thighs. "I had an appointment at the auto-repair shop," she told Brent, "but then a pipe blew in the kitchen and I had to call a plumber and, well, you know what plumbers cost."

Brent slanted a glance at Julie, who blushed that freckles-on-pink way only true redheads can, and once again turned his attention back to Libby. "So it *was* you?"

"Yes," Libby said, straightening her shoulders. "And if

you give me a ticket, I won't be able to afford to have the repairs done for *another* month."

The timer bell chimed.

Julie rushed to take the latest batch of scones out of the oven.

"I'm going to give you one more warning, Libby," Brent said quietly, raising an index finger. "Count it. *One.* If I catch you driving that environmental disaster again, without a sticker proving it meets the legal standards, I am so going to throw the book at you. Is—that—understood?"

Libby set his drink on the counter with a thump. "Yes, sir," she said tightly. *"That is understood."* She raised her chin a notch. "How am I supposed to get the car to the shop if I can't drive it?"

Brent smiled. "I'd make an exception in that case, I guess."

Libby made up her mind to put the repair charges on the credit card she'd just paid off, though it would set her back.

Julie looked toward the street, smiled and consulted an imaginary watch. "Well, will you look at that," she said. "It's time to pick Calvin up at playschool."

The pit of Libby's stomach jittered. She followed her sister's gaze and saw Tate walking toward the door, looking beyond good in worn jeans, scuffed boots and a white T-shirt that showed off his biceps and tanned forearms.

Scanning the street, she saw no sign of his truck, the sleek luxury car he sometimes drove or his twin daughters.

Libby felt as though she'd been forced, scrambling for balance, onto a drooping piano wire stretched across Niagara Falls. It was barely noon—Tate had suggested *dinner,* hadn't he, not lunch?

Either way, she reflected, trying to calm her nerves with common sense, she'd said "Maybe," not "Yes."

Tate reached the door, opened it and walked in. His grin

was as white as his shirt, and even from behind the register, Libby could see the comb ridges in his hair.

He greeted Brent with a half salute. "Denzel," he said.

Brent smiled. "Throw those blueberry scones into a bag for me," he said, though whether he was addressing Julia or Libby was unclear, because he was watching Tate. "I'd better buy them up before McKettrick beats me to the draw."

Tate was looking at Libby. His blue gaze smoldered that day, but she knew from experience that fire could turn to ice in a heartbeat.

"You had any more trouble with those rustlers?" Brent asked.

Libby ducked into the kitchen, nearly causing a sister-jam in the doorway because Julie had the same idea at the same time.

"Rustlers?" Libby asked, troubled.

"Not recently," Tate told his friend. Looking down into Libby's face, he added, "Rustling's a now-and-again kind of thing. Not as dangerous as it looks in the old movies."

Julie squirmed to get past Libby and leave to pick Calvin up at the community center.

"If you don't come straight back here," Libby warned her sister, momentarily distracted and keeping her voice low, "I'm only taking over with Marva for *half* of next week."

"Relax," Julie answered, turning back and grabbing a paper bag and tongs to fill the chief's scone order. "I'll bake all afternoon, and bring you a big batch of scones and dough-nuts in the morning. My oven is better than this one, and I really do have to fetch Calvin."

Libby blocked Julie's way out of the kitchen and leaned in close. "What am I supposed to do if Brent leaves and Tate is still here?" she demanded.

Julie raised both eyebrows. "*Talk* to the man? Maybe offer him coffee—or a quickie in the storeroom?" She grinned, full of mischief. "That's about the only thing I miss about Gordon Pruett. Stand-up sex with a thirty-three percent chance of getting caught."

Libby blushed, but then she had to laugh. "I am *not* offering Tate McKettrick stand-up sex in the storeroom!" she said.

"Now, that's a damn pity," Tate said.

Libby whirled around, saw him standing in the doorway leading into the main part of the shop, arms folded, grin wicked, one muscular shoulder braced against the framework. Color suffused Libby's face, so hot it hurt.

Julie fled, giggling, with the bag of scones in one hand, forcing Tate to step aside, though he resumed his damnably sexy stance as soon as she'd passed.

"Well," he remarked, after giving a philosophical sigh, "I stopped by to repeat my offer to buy you dinner, since the girls are over at the vet's with Ambrose and Buford and therefore temporarily occupied, but if you want to have sex in a storeroom or anyplace else, Lib, I'm game."

"Ambrose and Buford?" Libby asked numbly.

"The dogs," Tate explained, his eyes twinkling. "They're getting checkups—'wellness exams,' they call them now—and shots."

"Oh," Libby said, at a loss.

"Could we get back to the subject of sex?" Tate teased.

"No," she said, half laughing. "We most certainly can't."

He straightened, walked toward her, in that ambling, easy way he had, cupped her face in his hands. She loved the warmth of his touch, the restrained strength, the roughness of work-calloused flesh.

His were the hands of a rancher.

"Dinner?" he asked.

"Are you going to kiss me?" she countered.

He smiled. "Depends on your answer."

"If I say 'no,' what happens?"

"You wouldn't do a darn fool thing like that, now would you?" he asked, in a honeyed drawl. Although his body shifted, his hands remained where they were. "Turn down a free meal, and a tour of a plastic castle? Miss out on a perfectly good chance to see how Ambrose and Buford are adjusting to ranch life?"

He meant to "buy" dinner at his place, then. The knowledge was both a relief and a whole new reason to panic.

"Will Audrey and Ava be there?"

"Yes."

"Garrett?"

"No. Sorry. He had to get back to Austin."

"Pressing political business?"

Tate chuckled. "Probably a hot date," he said. "Plus, he's afraid I'm going to kill him in his sleep for giving my kids a goddamn castle for their sixth birthday."

"Hmm," Libby mused.

"Well?" Tate prompted.

"I have a question," Libby said.

"What's that?"

"Why now? Why ask me out now, Tate—after all this time?"

He looked thoughtful, and a few moments passed before he answered, his voice quiet. "I guess it took me this long to work up my courage." He swallowed hard, met her gaze in a deliberate way. "Nobody would blame you if you told me to go straight to hell, Libby. Not after what I did."

She took that in. Finally, she said, "Okay."

"Is that an okay-yes, or an okay-go-take-a-flying-leap?"

Libby had to smile. "I guess it's an okay-one-dinner-is-no-big-deal," she answered. "We *are* still talking about dinner, right?"

Tate chuckled. God, he smelled good, like fresh air and newly cut grass distilled to their essences. And she'd missed bantering with him like this. "Yes, we're still talking about dinner."

"Then, yes," Libby said, feeling dizzy. After all, she'd promised Calvin she'd undo her lie if she got the chance, and here it was.

"Right answer," Tate murmured, and then he kissed her.

The world, perhaps even the whole universe, rocked wildly and dissolved, leaving Libby drifting in the aftermath, not standing in her shabby little coffee-shop kitchen.

Tate deepened the kiss, used his tongue. Oh, he was an expert tongue man, all right. Another thing she'd forgotten—or *tried* to forget.

Libby moaned a little, swayed on her feet.

Tate drew back. His hands dropped from her cheeks to her shoulders, steadying her.

"Pick you up at six?" It was more a statement than a question, but Libby didn't care. She was taking a terrible risk, and she didn't care about that, either.

"Six," she confirmed. "What shall I wear?"

He grinned. "The twins are dining in shorts, tank tops and pointed princess hats with glitter and tassels," he said. "Feel free to skip the hat."

"Guess that leaves shorts and a tank top," she said. "Which means you should pick me up at six-thirty, because I'm going to need to shave my legs."

Mentally, Libby slapped a hand over her mouth. She'd

just given this hot man a mental picture of her running a razor along *hairy legs?*

"Here or at your place?" Tate asked, apparently unfazed by the visual.

"My place," Libby said. "I'd drive out on my own, but your friend the chief of police will arrest me if I so much as turn a wheel."

"Therein lies a tale," Tate said. "One I'd love to hear. Later."

"Later," Libby echoed, and then he was gone.

And she just stood there, long after he'd left her, the kiss still pulsing on her lips and rumbling through her like the seismic echoes of an earthquake.

CHAPTER FOUR

LIBBY CLOSED THE SHOP at five that day—no big sacrifice, since she'd only had one customer after lunch, a loan officer from First Cattleman's who'd left, disgruntled, without buying anything once he learned there were no more of Julie's scones to be had.

After cleaning up the various machines, stowing the day's modest take in her zippered deposit bag and finally locking up, she crossed the alley—trying not to hurry—and let a grateful Hildie out into the backyard.

The place seemed a little lonely without the formerly nameless dogs, but she'd see them that night, at Tate's. Given the way they'd thrown her under the proverbial bus when she'd dropped them off at the Silver Spur the night before, there was a good chance they'd ignore her completely.

"Now, you're being silly," she told herself, refreshing Hildie's water bowl at the sink, then rinsing out and refilling the food dish with kibble.

While Hildie gobbled down her meal, Libby showered, taking care to shave her legs, but instead of the prescribed shorts and tank top, she chose a pink sundress with spaghetti straps and smocking at the bodice. She painted her toenails to match, spritzed herself with cologne and dried her freshly shampooed, shoulder-length hair until it fluffed out around her face.

Libby owned exactly two cosmetic products—a tube of mascara and some lip gloss—and she applied both with a little more care than usual.

The phone rang at five minutes to six, and she was instantly certain that Tate had changed his mind and meant to rescind the invitation to have supper at the Silver Spur. The wave of disappointment that washed over her was out of all proportion to the situation.

But it wasn't Tate, as things turned out, calling with some lame excuse.

It was Gerbera Jackson, who cleaned for Marva three days a week, over at Poplar Bend.

"Libby? That you?"

"Hello, Gerbera," Libby responded.

"I know it isn't your week," Gerbera went on apologetically, "but I couldn't reach Miss Paige, or Miss Julia, either."

Gerbera, an old-fashioned black woman, well into her sixties, still adhered to the mercifully outdated convention of addressing her white counterparts as "Miss."

"That's okay," Libby said, hiding her disappointment. A problem with Marva meant the evening at the Silver Spur was history, the great event that never happened. "What's up?"

"Well, it's your mama, of course," Gerbera said sadly.

Who else? Libby thought uncharitably.

"I'm worried about her," the softhearted woman continued. "I recorded her stories for her, just like always, since her favorites are on while she's out taking those longs walks of hers, but Miss Marva, she doesn't want to look at them tonight. Told me not to bother putting a chicken potpie into the oven for her before I left, too. That's one of her favorites, you know."

Libby closed her eyes briefly, breathed deeply and slowly. Marva's "stories" were soap operas, and she hadn't missed an episode of *As the World Turns,* or so she claimed, since 1972, when, recovering from a twisted ankle, she'd gotten hooked.

"Not good," Libby admitted. When Marva didn't want to watch her soaps or eat chicken potpie, she was depressed. And when Marva was depressed, bad things happened.

"She hasn't been herself since they eighty-sixed her from the bingo hall for lighting up a cigarette," Gerbera added.

Just then, a rap sounded at the front door. Tate had arrived, probably looking cowboy-sexy, and now Libby was going to have to tell him she couldn't go to the Silver Spur for supper.

"I hate to bother you," Gerbera said, and she sounded like she meant it, but she also sounded relieved. If she had a fault, it was caring too much about the various ladies she cleaned and cooked for, whether they were crotchety or sweet-tempered. Until her nephew, Brent Brogan, had moved back to Blue River, with his children, after his wife's death, Gerbera had managed Poplar Bend full-time, living in an apartment there.

She spent more time with her family now, cooking and mending and helping out wherever she could. Brent claimed her chicken-and-dumplings alone had put ten pounds on him.

"No bother," Libby said, brightening her voice and stretching the kitchen phone cord far enough to see Tate standing on the other side of the front door. She gestured for him to come in. "She's my mother."

Some mother Marva had been, though. She'd left her husband and small, bewildered children years before, with a lot of noise and drama, and suddenly returned more than two decades later, after what she described as a personal epiphany, to install herself at Poplar Bend and demand regular visits from her daughters.

She had, for some reason, decided it was time to bond.

Better late than never—that seemed to be the theory.

Marva had money, that much was clear, and she was used to giving orders, but any attempt to discuss her long and largely silent absence brought some offhanded response like, "That was then and this is now."

For all Libby and her sisters knew, Marva could have been living on another planet or in a parallel dimension all those years.

Libby wanted to love Marva; she truly did. But it was hard, remembering how heartbroken their dad had been at his wife's defection—she'd run away with a man who rode a motorcycle and earned a sketchy living as a tattoo artist.

Clearly, the tattoo man had been out of the picture for a long time.

For their father's sake, Libby, Julie and Paige took turns visiting and handling problems Marva herself had created. They fetched and carried and ran errands, but Marva wasn't grateful for anything. *I am your mother,* she'd told Libby, in one of her cranky moments, *and I am entitled to your respect.*

Respect, Libby had retorted hotly, unable to hold her tongue, *is not a right. It's something you have to earn.*

Tate let himself in, at Libby's signal, and Hildie started playing up to him as though he were some kind of cowboy messiah.

"Thanks, Gerbera," Libby said, realizing she'd missed a chunk of the conversation. "I'll head over there right away and make sure she's okay."

Gerbera apologized again, said goodbye and hung up.

Libby replaced the receiver on the hook in the kitchen and went back to greet her breathtakingly handsome guest.

"Problem?" Tate asked mildly. He filled Libby's small

living room, made it feel crowded and, at the same time, utterly safe.

"My mother," Libby said. "I need to check on her."

"Okay," Tate replied. "Let's go check on her, then."

"You don't understand. It could take hours, if she's in one of her—moods."

Tate's shoulders moved in an easy shrug. "Only one way to find out," he said.

Libby couldn't let him throw away his evening just because her own was ruined. "You should just go home. Forget about supper." She swallowed. "About my joining you, I mean."

He was crouching by then, fussing over the adoring Hildie. She probably wanted to go home with him and be *his* dog. *Libby? That name seems vaguely familiar.*

"Nope," he said, straightening. "You and I and—what's this dog's name again?"

"Hildie," Libby answered, her throat tight.

"You and Hildie and I are having supper on the Silver Spur, just like we planned. I'll just call Esperanza and ask her to feed the girls early."

"But—"

Tate took in Libby's sundress, her strappy sandals, her semi-big hair. "You look better than fantastic," he said. Then he took Libby by the arm and squired her toward the front door, Hildie happily trotting alongside.

His truck was parked at the curb, and he hoisted Hildie into the back seat, then opened the passenger-side door for Libby. Helped her onto the running board, from which point she was able to come in for a landing on the leather seat with something at least *resembling* dignity.

"You don't have to do this," she said.

Tate didn't answer until he'd rounded the front of the truck and climbed behind the wheel. "I don't have to do anything but die and pay taxes," he replied, with a grin. "I'm here because I *want* to be here, Lib. No other reason."

Within five minutes, they were pulling into one of the parking lots at Poplar Bend, behind Building B. Marva lived off the central courtyard, and as they approached, she stepped out onto her small patio, smiling cheerfully. A glass of white wine in one hand, she wore white linen slacks and a matching shirt, tasteful sandals and earrings.

Libby stared at her.

"Well, *this* is a nice surprise," Marva said, her eyes gliding over Tate McKettrick briefly before shifting back to her daughter. "To what do I owe the pleasure?"

"Gerbera Jackson called me," Libby said, struggling to keep her tone even. "She was very concerned because you didn't want to watch your soap operas or eat supper."

Marva sighed charitably and shook her head. "I was just having a little blue spell, that's all," she said. She raised the wineglass, its contents shimmering in the late-afternoon light. "Care for a drink?"

Inwardly, Libby seethed. Gerbera was a sensible woman, and if she'd been concerned about Marva's behavior, then Marva had given her good reason for it.

Bottom line, Marva had decided she wanted a little attention. Instead of just saying so, she'd manipulated Gerbera into raising an unnecessary alarm.

"No, thanks," Tate said, nodding affably at Marva. "Is there anything you need, ma'am?"

Libby wanted to jab him with her elbow, but she couldn't, because Marva would see.

"Well," Marva said, almost purring, "there is that light

in the kitchen. It's been burned out for weeks and I'm afraid I'll break my neck if I get up on a ladder and try to replace the bulb."

Tate rolled up his sleeves. "Glad to help," he said.

Libby's smile felt fixed; she could only hope it *looked* more genuine than it felt, quivering on her mouth.

Tate replaced the bulb in Marva's kitchen.

"It's good to have a man around the house," Marva said.

Libby all but rolled her eyes. *You had one,* she thought. *You had Dad. And he wasn't exciting enough for you.*

"I guess Libby and I ought to get going," Tate told Marva. "Esperanza will be holding supper for us."

Marva patted his arm, giving Libby a sly wink, probably in reference to Tate's well-developed biceps. "You young people run along and have a nice evening," she said, setting aside her now-empty wineglass to wave them out of the condo. "It's nice to know you're dating, Libby," she added, her tone sunny. "You and your sisters need to have more fun."

Libby's cheeks burned.

Tate took her by the elbow, nodded a good evening to Marva, and they were out of the condo, headed down the walk.

When they reached the truck, Tate lifted Libby bodily into the cab, paused to reach back and pet Hildie reassuringly before sprinting around to the driver's-side door, climbing in and taking the wheel again.

As soon as he turned the key in the ignition, the air-conditioning kicked in, cooling Libby's flesh, if not her temper.

She leaned back in the seat, then closed her eyes. Stopping by Marva's place had been no big deal, as it turned out, and Tate certainly hadn't minded changing the lightbulb.

But of course, those things weren't at the heart of the problem, anyway, were they?

All this emotional churning was about Marva's leaving, so many years ago.

It was about her and Julie and Paige, not to mention their dad, missing her so much.

Marva had departed with a lot of fanfare. Now that she was back, she expected to be treated like any normal mother. Not.

"I guess your mom still gets under your hide," Tate commented quietly, once they were moving again.

Libby turned her head, looked at him. "Yes," she admitted. He knew the story—everyone around Blue River did. Several times, when they were younger, he'd held her while she cried over Marva.

Tate was thoughtful, and silent for a long time. "She's probably doing the best she can," he said, when they were past the town limits and rolling down the open road. "Like the rest of us."

Libby nodded. Marva's "best" wasn't all that good, as it happened, but she didn't want the subject of her mother to ruin the evening. She raised and lowered her shoulders, releasing tension, and focused on the scenery. "I guess so," she said.

The conversational lull that followed was peaceful, easy.

Hildie got things going again by suddenly popping her big head forward from the back seat and giving Tate an impromptu lick on the ear.

He laughed, and so did Libby.

"Do you ever think about getting another dog?" she asked, thinking of Crockett. That old hound had been Tate's constant companion. He'd even taken him to college with him.

"Got two," Tate reminded Libby, grinning.

"I mean, one of your own," Libby said.

Tate swallowed, shook his head. "I keep thinking I'll be

ready," he replied, keeping his gaze fixed on the winding road ahead. "But it hasn't happened yet. Crockett and I, we were pretty tight."

Libby watched him, took in his strong profile and the proud way he held his head up high. It was a McKettrick thing, that quiet dignity.

"Your folks were such nice people," she told Tate.

He smiled. "Yeah," he agreed. "They were."

They'd passed mile after mile of grassy rangeland by then, dotted with cattle and horses, all of it part of the Silver Spur. Once, there had been oil wells, too, pumping night and day for fifty years or better, though Tate's father had shut them down years before.

A few rusty relics remained, hulking and rounded at the top; in the fading, purplish light of early evening, they re-minded Libby of the dinosaurs that must have shaken the ground with their footsteps and dwarfed the primordial trees with their bulk.

"You're pretty far away," Tate said, as they turned in at the towering wrought-iron gates with the name *McKettrick* scrolled across them. Those gates had been standing open the night before; Libby, relieved not to have to stop, push the but-ton on the intercom and identify herself to someone inside, had breezed right in. "What are you thinking about, Lib?"

She smiled. "Oil derricks and dinosaurs," she replied.

Tate pushed a button on his visor, and the gates swung wide, then whispered closed again as soon as they passed through. Hildie, quiet for most of the ride, began to get rest-less, pacing from one end of the back seat to the other.

Once again, Libby dared hope her dog wasn't planning to move in with Tate and forget all about her, the way Ambrose and Buford apparently had.

"Derricks and dinosaurs," Tate reflected.

"You might say there's a crude connection," Libby said.

Tate groaned at the bad pun, but then he laughed.

When they reached the ranch house, he drove around back instead of parking under the portico or in the garage, and Libby gasped with pleasure when she caught sight of the castle.

It was enchanting. Even magical.

"Wow," she said.

Tate shut off the truck, cast a rueful glance over the ornate structure and got out to help Hildie out of the back seat.

Set free, Hildie ran in circles, as excited as a pup, and when Ambrose and Buford dashed out of the castle and raced toward her, all former grudges were forgotten. She wagtailed it over to meet them like they were long-lost friends.

The twins waved from separate windows in the castle, one at ground level and one in a turret.

"I've never seen anything like this," Libby said, shading her eyes from the presunset glare as she admired the oversized playhouse.

"Me, either," Tate said.

"Cometh thou in!" one of the little girls called from the tower.

Libby laughed. Tate shook his head and grinned.

Took Libby's hand just before he stooped to enter the castle, then pulled her in after him. The three dogs crowded in behind them, thick as thieves now that they weren't roommates anymore.

The inside was even more remarkable than the outside, with its fireplace and overhead beams and a stairway leading to the upper floor.

Libby wondered what Calvin would think of the place.

"It's so—big," she said slowly.

Ava nodded eagerly. "Dad says Audrey and I need to think about giving it to the community center, so other kids can play with it, too."

Libby glanced at Tate, saw that he was looking away.

"That's a very generous idea," she said, impressed.

"We haven't decided yet, though," Audrey put in, descending the stairs. "All Dad said was to *think* about it. He didn't say we actually had to *do* it."

Tate gestured toward the door. "I'm pretty sure supper is ready by now, ladies," he said. "Shall we?"

Audrey and Ava curtseyed grandly, spreading the sides of their cotton shorts like skirts.

"Yes, my lord," Ava said.

Tate laughed. *"Go,"* he said.

Both girls hurried out of the castle, the canine trio chasing after them, barking like dog-maniacs.

"'Yes, my lord'?" Libby teased, grinning, when the din subsided a little. "Now where would a pair of six-year-olds pick up an antiquated term like that?"

"Garrett probably taught them," Tate answered. "He likes to get under my skin any way he can."

Esperanza stood beside the patio table, laughing as she shooed the dogs out from underfoot and ordered the twins inside to wash their hands and faces.

Ambrose and Buford followed them, but Hildie paused, turned and scanned the yard, then trotted toward Libby with something like relief when she spotted her.

Touched, Libby bent to pat the dog's head.

Esperanza had outdone herself, preparing supper. There were tacos and enchiladas, seasoned rice and salad.

Libby enjoyed the food almost as much as the company,

and she was sorry when the meal ended and Esperanza herded the twins into the house for their baths.

Overhead, the first stars popped out like diamonds studding a length of dark blue velvet, and the moon, a mere sliver of transparent light, looked as though it had come to rest on the roof of the barn.

Libby was totally content in those moments, with Tate at her side and Hildie lying at her feet, probably enjoying the warmth of the paving stones.

When Tate squeezed her hand, Libby squeezed back.

And then they drew apart.

Libby stood and began to gather and stack the dishes.

Tate got to his feet and helped.

Libby had forgotten how big the kitchen was, and as they stepped inside, she did her best not to stare as she and Tate loaded one of several dishwashers and cleaned up. The pool was visible on the other side of a thick glass wall, a brilliant turquoise, and looking at it, Libby couldn't help remembering the skinny-dipping episode.

She smiled. They'd been so innocent then, she and Tate. So young.

And such passionate lovers.

Tate took her gently by the elbows and turned her to face him. Kissed her lightly on the forehead. "Thanks for saying 'yes' to tonight, Lib," he said. "It's good to have you back here."

Libby's throat tightened with sudden, searing emotion.

Tate cupped her chin his hand and tilted her face upward, looked into her eyes. "What?" he asked, very gently.

She shook her head.

He drew her close, held her tightly, his chin propped on the top of her head.

They were still standing there, minutes later, not a word

having passed between them, when Esperanza returned, the front of her dress soaked, her lustrous, gray-streaked hair coming down from its pins. Barking and the laughter of little girls sounded in the distance.

"The dogs," Esperanza told Tate breathlessly, "they are in the bathtub, with the children."

Tate sighed in benign exasperation, then stepped away from Libby. "I'll be back in a few minutes," he said. As he passed Esperanza, he laid a hand on her shoulder, squeezed.

"These children," Esperanza fretted. "I am too old—"

Libby hurried over to help the other woman into a chair at the table. Brought her a glass of water.

"Are you all right?"

Esperanza hid her face in her hands, and her shoulders began to shake.

It took Libby a moment to realize the woman was laughing, not crying.

Relieved, Libby laughed, too.

Tears of mirth gleamed on Esperanza's smooth brown cheeks, and she used the hem of her apron to wipe them away.

Then, crossing herself, she said, "It is just like the old days, when the boys were young. Always in trouble, the three of them."

Tate returned, pausing in the doorway to take in the scene. Like most men, he was probably wary of female emotion unleashed.

Libby took in every inch of him.

Tate McKettrick, all grown up, was *still* trouble.

The kind it was impossible to resist.

CHAPTER FIVE

LIBBY WAS UP EARLY the next morning, feeling rested even though she'd only had a few hours' sleep. After driving her home and walking her to her front door the night before, like the gentleman he could be but sometimes wasn't, Tate had kissed her again, and the effects of that tender, tentative touch of their mouths still tingled on her lips.

The sun was just peeking over the eastern horizon when she took Hildie for the first walk the poor dog had enjoyed since Ambrose and Buford had come to stay with them weeks before. It was good to get back into their old routine.

All up and down Libby's quiet, tree-lined street, lawn sprinklers turned, making that reassuring *chucka-chuck* sound, spraying diamonds over emerald-green grass. Hildie stopped for the occasional sniff at a fence post or a light pole or a patch of weeds—Julie, joint owner, along with Calvin, of a surprisingly active three-legged beagle named Harry, would have said the dog was reading her p-mail.

As Libby and Hildie passed Brent Brogan's house, a small split-level rancher with a flower-filled yard and a picket fence, Gerbera stepped out of the front door, bundled in a summery blue-print bathrobe, and hiked along the walk to get the newspaper.

Seeing Libby, Gerbera paused and grinned broadly.

"Land sakes," she said, "I thought you'd given up on walking that old dog. Never see you go by here anymore."

Libby paused, holding Hildie's leash loosely. "I was fostering two puppies," she explained, "and walking the three of them at once was too much. I did manage to get the little buggers housebroken, though."

Gerbera cocked a thumb toward the white-shingled house behind her. "I've been after that nephew of mine to go on down to the shelter and get his kids a pet. Give them some responsibility and get them to unplug those earphones and wires from their heads once in a while. But Brent always says it would be him or me that wound up looking after any cat or dog we took in, once the kids lost interest."

"Well, if you manage to change his mind," Libby said, always ready to promote adoption when she knew a good home was a sure thing, "the kennels are usually full."

Gerbera got the rolled-up newspaper out of its box and tucked it under her arm. "You want to come in and have coffee? Nobody around but me. Kenda and V.J. are still sleeping, like kids do in the summertime, and Brent's been gone most of the night—that's why I stayed over."

Ironically, since she owned the Perk Up and java was her stock-in-trade, Libby drank very little coffee. It made her way too hyper. "We've got a ways to go to finish our walk," she said, with a nod toward the Lab. "Hildie and I both need all the exercise we can get. Another time?"

Gerbera smiled. "Sure enough," she agreed, before launching into a good-natured report. "Your mama called me last night and fussed at me something fierce for getting you all worked up, but I could tell she was pleased to get a visit from you and a good-lookin' McKettrick man."

Libby might have been annoyed with someone else, but

Gerbera's intentions were always good. Hildie began to tug determinedly at the leash then, ready to go on, follow the route they always took, through several side streets, around the city park with its pretty gazebo-style bandstand, back home by way of the old movie house and the community center. "I think it was the good-lookin' McKettrick man that cheered her up, not me."

Something changed in Gerbera's face, something that went beyond the sparkle fading from her eyes and the way her mouth suddenly turned down a little at the corners. "Lordy," she said. "I swear, I get more forgetful every day!" She paused, drew in a breath. Her eyes were worried. "You don't *know,* do you? And how *would* you know?"

"Know what?" Libby asked, suddenly jittery, tightening her grip on Hildie's leash when the dog rounded the corner of the Brogans' fence ahead of her, pulling even harder now.

"Brent's been out there on the Silver Spur most of the night," Gerbera said slowly, "doing whatever he can to help. Libby, Pablo Ruiz is dead."

Libby gasped. Pablo was a friend, an institution in Blue River. He *couldn't* be dead. "What happened?" she managed to ask.

"There was an accident of some kind," Gerbera said, touching Libby's upper arm. "That's all I know."

An accident. Libby nodded, numbed by the news, thinking of Isabel, Pablo's wife, of Nico and Mercedes, their son and daughter, and the two nephews they'd brought to the United States, several years before, after Isabel's younger sister, Maria, had died of what turned out to be peritonitis.

Ricardo and Juan were teenagers now; honor students, well-mannered youths who stayed out of trouble; the kind of kids a community like Blue River was proud to call its own.

Nico, a close friend of Tate's, had once confided that when word of his aunt's death had reached them, he and Pablo had immediately set out for Mexico, expecting to find the boys living with neighbors in Maria's small village, or perhaps with their late father's family.

Instead, they'd been told that Ricardo and Juan had vanished, soon after Maria's death, and no one had seen them since.

There had been several more trips, Nico had said, each one a failure, before he and his father had finally tracked the children down to a nearby landfill. Both boys were filthy and half-starved, foraging for scraps of food, stealing and sleeping wherever they could find a safe place to lie down.

With a lot of help from Tate's cousin, Meg, a top executive with McKettrickCo at the time, Pablo had finally arranged for the boys to enter the country legally.

They had been almost feral in the beginning, those children, constantly afraid, stealing food, snarling and nipping when Pablo wrestled them into a tub and scrubbed them down on their first night in the United States. Eventually, Pablo and Isabel had won their trust, as well as their love.

What would happen to them now? What would happen to Isabel?

Libby's stomach did a slow, backward roll. "Oh, Gerbera," she whispered. "This is awful."

Gerbera nodded sadly. "I guess they look out for their own, though," she said. "Those McKettricks, I mean. And all the folks who work for them."

The reminder comforted Libby a little. It was true. Tate and his brothers would make sure Isabel and the boys lacked for nothing—that was the McKettrick way. And the long-term employees were like kin to each other.

Libby knew most of the dozen or so men who worked on the Spur year-round—everyone did. The married men lived with their wives and children in well-maintained trailers alongside one of the creeks, while the bachelors occupied a comfortable bunkhouse nearby. All of them got their mail and their groceries in Blue River, had their hair cut at the barber's or Valdeen's House of Beauty, came into the Perk Up on windy winter days for hot, strong coffee.

Gerbera shook her head, looking somber now. "I don't know what Isabel will do without that man. The kids, either. And now I wish I hadn't been the one to tell you, Libby. Brent specifically asked me not to 'broadcast' this until he was sure all the family had been informed."

Wanting to reassure her friend, Libby tried to smile. "Just about everybody in town owns a police scanner, so if Brent used his radio even once, the word's out." She spoke distractedly; half her mind had strayed to the Silver Spur; she couldn't help wondering how Tate and the children and Esperanza had taken the news. The other half was on Hildie, who was hunkered down and putting her full weight into the effort to drag her mistress back into motion.

"You'd better go on and I'd better get my old self ready for work," Gerbera said, noting the dog's antics with a sad smile.

Libby nodded, and she and Hildie were off again.

By the time they'd finished their walk almost an hour later, three different people had come to their front gates in bathrobes to ask if Libby had heard about Pablo Ruiz. They'd all gleaned the information from their police scanners, just as Libby had expected.

Nobody knew the exact cause; Chief Brogan had been closedmouthed about it, when he'd called in the coroner. All they'd been able to gather was that there had been an accident on the ranch, a fatal one.

Most likely, the chief had made calls he didn't want half the county listening in on, over his cell phone.

Back home, Libby took a hasty shower—her breakfast was half a banana, since she didn't have much of an appetite—dressed in jeans and a sleeveless cotton top, bound her hair back in the usual no-fuss ponytail, and skipped the mascara and lip gloss.

While Hildie napped in a patch of sunlight in the kitchen, Libby let herself out the back door, crossed the yard and the alley, unlocked the rear entrance to the Perk Up and nearly jumped out of her skin when Calvin leaped out at her from behind a box of pop-on cup lids and yelled, "Boo!"

The fight-or-flight response stopped Libby in her tracks, one hand pressed to her pounding heart.

Julie peeked out of the kitchen, wearing an apron and holding a mixing bowl in the curve of one arm and a batter-coated spoon in the other. "For Pete's sake, Calvin," she scolded merrily, "how many times have I told you that you shouldn't scare the elderly?"

"You are just *too* funny," Libby said, directing the terse remark to her sister and a warm smile to her nephew.

Calvin had left his swim trunks and frog-floater at home that day, and he looked very handsome in his miniature chinos and short-sleeved plaid shirt. He was even wearing his good glasses, the ones with no adhesive tape spanning the bridge.

"Something big going on at playschool today?" Libby asked, setting her purse on a high shelf and reaching for an apron.

Calvin nodded eagerly. "We're getting a castle!" he crowed. "With turrets and everything!"

So, Libby thought, Tate's girls *had* decided to donate their birthday present to the community center. That was quick.

"You're getting a castle today?" she asked Calvin, wondering if Tate had intended to give away the massive toy all along; perhaps called to make the arrangements almost as soon as it arrived on the Silver Spur.

Calvin swelled out his chest. "No," he said. "Justin's mom is best friends with my teacher, Mrs. Oakland, and she told Justin's mom that it would take time and sweat and a lot of heavy equipment to move the thing."

Having seen the castle, Libby agreed. "Then why are you so dressed up?" she asked.

Calvin gave a long-suffering sigh. In his oft-expressed opinion, adults could be remarkably obtuse at times. "Because we're going to have a meeting at recess and elect a king," he said, very slowly, so his elderly aunt could follow. "I'm on the committee."

Libby and Julie exchanged looks. Julie smiled and shrugged as if to say, "That's what you get for asking a dumb question," but her eyes—pale violet that day because her T-shirt was purple—were solemn. She raised her eyebrows.

"Yes," Libby told Julie, an expert at sister-telepathy, "I heard."

"Heard what?" Calvin wanted to know, following as Libby headed for the front of the shop to fire up the various gadgets and switch the "Closed" sign to "Open."

"That you're campaigning to be king," Libby hedged. "Do you have your speech ready? Buttons and bumper stickers to pass out to the voters?"

"If nobody else is going to point out that kings are not elected officials," Julie said, still stirring the batter, "I will."

Calvin looked worried. "Buttons and bumper stickers?" he repeated.

Libby's heart melted. She bent to kiss the top of her nephew's blond head. "I was just teasing, big guy," she said. "And your mom is right. To my knowledge, there is not now and never has been one single king of Texas."

Calvin beamed. "Then I could be the first one!" he cried, delighted. Since he wasn't even in kindergarten yet and was already serving on committees, Libby figured he might just pull it off.

She smiled again, went to unlock the cash register and see if she had enough change on hand for the day.

"Calvin," Julie said, pointing, "sit down at that table in the corner, please, and watch for customers. If you see one approaching, let us know."

Calvin obeyed readily, and he sat up so straight and looked so vigilant that a whole new wave of tenderness washed over Libby.

Julie immediately maneuvered her toward the kitchen, where they could talk with some semblance of privacy.

"Gordon followed up his e-mail with a phone call," she said, in a desperate whisper. "He's willing to take things slowly, but he *definitely* wants to get to know Calvin."

"Okay," Libby said. "What are you going to do?"

"Hide," Julie responded. "Calvin and Harry and I are going to hit the road. We'll be gone for as long as we have to—"

Libby held up both hands. "Julie! Are you *listening* to yourself? This is not something you can run away from. Besides, you have a house and a job and friends and—" she paused to clear her throat "—*family* in Blue River. Shouldn't you at least hear Gordon out?"

"Did Gordon hear *me* out when I told him I was expecting his baby?" Julie demanded, though she was careful to keep her voice down so Calvin wouldn't hear.

Libby knew there was no way to win this argument. Julie was just venting, anyway. "Did you hear about Pablo Ruiz?" Libby asked.

Julie's eyes widened. "No. What—?"

"He's dead, Jules. There was some kind of accident, yesterday or last night, on the Silver Spur—"

Julie gasped. "Not Pablo," she said, splaying the fingers of her right hand and pressing the palm to her heart.

Libby nodded sadly. "He was so proud of Mercedes," she whispered. Pablo and Isabel's only daughter would graduate from medical school in Boston in just a few weeks. She'd already been accepted into the internship program at Johns Hopkins: eventually, Mercedes wanted to become a surgeon.

Julie nodded, dashed at her wet eyes with the back of one floury hand, leaving white, sticky smudges on her cheek. "Do you remember how Pablo came and mowed our lawn every week, after Dad got too sick to leave the house?"

Libby did remember, of course, and she might have broken down and cried herself, if Calvin hadn't yelled, at that precise moment, "I see one! I see a customer!"

Pablo's smiling face lingered in Libby's mind. She'd tried to pay him once, for taking care of the yard, and he'd refused with a shake of his head and a quiet, heavily accented, "Friends help friends. Mr. Remington, he helped our Mercedes with her schoolwork. Nico, too, when he was applying for scholarships. It is a privilege to do what little I can. "

"The scones!" Julie blurted out, suddenly remembering that they were done, and rushed to pull a baking sheet from the oven.

Despite an almost overwhelming sense of loss, there was

work to be done. Libby straightened her shoulders and headed for the espresso machine again.

The customer Calvin had announced turned out to be Tate McKettrick, and he looked, as the old-timers liked to say, as if he'd been dragged backward through a knothole in the outhouse wall.

"I'm so sorry about Pablo," Libby said, wanting to go to him, take him in her arms, but uncertain of the reception she'd get if she did. The old sparks were definitely back, but she and Tate were older now and things were different. They had adult responsibilities—the shop for her, the children for Tate.

He was pale, he hadn't shaved—which only made him *more* attractive, in Libby's opinion—and his clothes, the same ones he'd worn the night before at supper, looked rumpled. What was he doing here, in the Perk Up, on the morning after he'd lost a dear friend and long-time employee?

He acknowledged her words of condolence with a nod. Shoved a hand through his hair. "It's either strong coffee," he said, "or a fifth of Jack Daniels. I figured the coffee would be a better choice."

"Sit down," Libby said, indicating the stools in front of the counter. "Where are the girls, Tate?"

He sat. Rested his forearms on the countertop. "With Esperanza. I haven't told them about Pablo yet—but of course they know something's going on…"

Calvin hurried over. "We're getting a *castle* at the community center, Mr. McKettrick," he announced exuberantly. "And I'm running for king."

"I heard about the castle," Tate said, with a wan smile. For a moment, his weary gaze connected with Libby's. "I didn't know there was going to be a special election, though."

"Only kids can vote," Calvin said importantly. "*Little*

kids, who go to playschool. The big ones don't even know we're going to elect a king."

"Ah," Tate said, "a coup. I'm impressed."

"What's a koo?" Calvin asked.

Tate sighed.

"Never mind, Calvin," Libby interceded gently. "Go back to your table and watch for customers."

"Why?" He pointed to Tate. "We've already *got* one."

Tate chuckled at that, but it was a raw, broken sound, and hearing it made the backs of Libby's eyes burn.

"Calvin," she said evenly, but with affection, "I *said* never mind."

"Jeez," Calvin protested, flinging his arms out from his sides and then letting them fall back with a slight slapping sound. "People talk to me like I'm a *baby* or something, and I'm *four years old.*"

"Go figure," Tate said, with appropriate sympathy.

Libby set a cup of black coffee in front of Tate.

Calvin stalked back to his post to keep watch, clearly disgusted and probably still wondering what a coup was.

"That kid," Tate remarked, after taking an appreciative sip of the coffee, "is way too smart. Is he really only four—or is he forty, and short for his age?"

The way Tate said "kid," reflected Libby, was a 180 from the way Jubal Tabor did. Why was that?

"Tell me about it," Julie interjected before Libby could respond, as she came out of the kitchen and set a plate of fresh scones in front of Tate, along with a little bowl of butter pats in foil wrapping. She'd wiped the flour smears from her face at some point, and even with the pallor of shock replacing the usual pink in her cheeks, she was radiantly lovely. "Eat these, McKettrick. You look like hell warmed over. Twice."

"You always had a way with words, Jules," he replied. But, his big hands shaking almost but not quite imperceptibly, he opened two pats of butter, sliced a steaming scone in two, and smeared it on. "And with cooking."

Libby was seized by a sudden, fiercely irrational jealousy, gone as quickly as it came, fortunately. No matter how many new recipes she tried, how many chef shows and demonstrations she watched on satellite TV, taking notes and doing her best to follow instructions, when it came to cooking, she was doomed to be below average.

She was, she supposed, painfully ordinary.

Julie was the gypsy sister, with many and varied talents, of which baking was only one. She could sing, dance and act. Her scones were already drawing in customers, and if she ever made her float-away biscuits, folks would break down the door to get at them. She was great with kids—*all* kids, from her students to Calvin.

On top of all that, Julie had the kind of looks that made men stop and stare, even when they'd known her all their lives.

Paige, the baby of the family, was the smart one, the cool, competent one. And she was just as beautiful as Julie, though in a different way.

Libby bit her lower lip. As for her—well—she was just the *oldest.*

She was passably pretty, but she couldn't carry a tune, let alone perform in professional theater companies, singing and dancing in shows people paid money to see— spectacular productions of *Cats* and *Phantom of the Opera* and *Kiss Me, Kate,* as Julie had done periodically, during her college years.

She didn't shine in a life-and-death emergency, like Paige.

And why was she even thinking thoughts like this, when

Pablo Ruiz, a man she'd liked and deeply respected, had just died—and long before his time, too?

"I don't see a single customer!" Calvin reported, his voice ringing across the shop.

"Keep looking," Julie counseled. "There's got to be one out there somewhere."

Libby was still watching Tate. Even wan and worn, with his dark beard growing in and his hair furrowed because he'd probably been raking his fingers through it all night, as all the ramifications of Pablo's death unfolded, he was a sight to stop her breath and make her heart skitter.

Here was *her* claim to fame, she thought gloomily.

She'd been dumped by Tate McKettrick.

For six months after the breakup, people had sent her cheery little cards and notes, most acting out of kindness, a few taking a passive-aggressive pleasure in her downfall. Her father had been diagnosed with pancreatic cancer by then—the dying by inches part would come later—but no one had mentioned her dad, in person or on paper. They'd written or said things like, "You'll find someone else when the time is right" and "It wasn't meant to be" and "What doesn't kill you makes you stronger."

Like hell. She'd been blindsided by Tate's betrayal. Fractured by it.

And here she was, letting him back in her life when she knew—*knew* what he could do to her.

While Libby was reconciling herself to reality, Julie collected her purse, jingled her car keys to attract Calvin's attention. "Time for playschool, buddy," she said. She squeezed Tate's shoulder as she passed him and promised Libby she'd be back in no time. If she needed scones for the midmorning rush—*if* she needed scones?—there were four dozen in the kitchen; Julie had baked them at home the night before, as promised.

As soon as Julie and Calvin had gone, Tate got off his stool, walked to the door, turned the "Open" sign to "Closed," and twisted the knob to engage the dead bolt.

Libby didn't utter a word of protest. She took the stool next to his, once he'd come back to the counter, and leaned his way a little so their upper arms just barely touched.

"Want to tell me what happened, cowboy?" she asked, very softly.

"Yeah," Tate said, pushing away his plate, now that he'd eaten the scones. He didn't meet her gaze, though. He just stared off into the void for a long time, saying nothing, though Libby saw his throat work a couple of times, while he struggled to control his emotions.

Libby simply waited.

"The dogs started raising hell, about half an hour after I went to bed," he told her, when he was ready. "They woke up Audrey and Ava, of course, since all four of them were bunking together. I went to see what was going on—I thought there was an intruder in the house or something, the way those mutts carried on. As soon as I opened the door to the girls' room, the pups shot past me, baying like bloodhounds picking up a strong scent. They ran down the stairs and straight to the kitchen—by the time I got there, they were hurling themselves at the back door like they'd bust it down to get out if they had to." He paused, drank the dregs of his coffee, but stopped Libby with a touch to her arm when she started to get up and go around the counter to get the pot and pour him a refill. After a long time, he continued. "Esperanza was awake by then, too, of course, and she kept the kids and the dogs inside while I went out to have a look around. I saw that the lights were on in the barn, and I'd turned them off after I checked on the horses an hour earlier, but I figured one of the ranch hands was out there, meaning to bunk in the hayloft. The younger ones do that sometimes, when they've had a fight with a wife or a girlfriend or gotten a little too drunk to go home."

He paused again then, swallowed hard, gazed bleak-eyed into that same invisible distance.

Once more, Libby bided her time. For Tate, not a talkative man, this wasn't just an accounting of what had taken place, it was a verbal epic, a virtual diatribe. Normally, he probably didn't say that much in half a day, never mind a few short minutes.

"I was pretty sure the dogs were just skittish because they're pups, and in a new place with new people," Tate went on presently. "They'd probably heard a rig drive in, I figured, and felt called upon to bark their damn fool heads off. I went outside, and I saw Pablo's company truck parked between the barn and that copse of oak trees."

Libby waited, seeing the scene Tate described as vividly as if she'd been there herself.

"It wasn't unusual for Pablo to turn up at the barn, even late at night—he didn't need much sleep and since he always had some project going on at his place, he stopped by often to borrow tools, equipment, things like that." Tate sighed. "I checked the barn, and Pablo wasn't inside, though all the horses were jumpy as hell, and, like I said, the lights were on. I headed for the truck, and I was nearly run down by a big paint stallion—that horse came out of nowhere.

"Pablo and I had talked about buying the stud if it went up for sale. We were going to turn him loose on the range, let him breed and see if any of the mares threw color—"

Libby touched Tate's arm, felt a shudder go through him. "Take your time," she said, very quietly.

"Pablo *had* bought that stallion," he went on, after swallowing a couple of times. "He picked him up from the buyer and brought him over, probably planning on leaving him in the holding pen until morning, when we could have the vet come and look the paint over before—"

Libby closed her eyes for a moment. By then, she'd guessed what was coming next.

Tate looked tormented. It seemed like a long time passed before he went on. "I found Pablo on the ground, behind the trailer, trampled to death."

Sorrow swelled in Libby's throat, aching there. Such accidents weren't uncommon, even among experienced men like Pablo Ruiz. Horses—especially stallions—were powerful animals, easily spooked and always unpredictable.

"I'm sorry, Tate," Libby said. "I'm so sorry."

He nodded, made a visible effort to center himself in the present moment.

The blue of his eyes deepened to the color of new denim and, very briefly, Libby pondered the mystery of why a loving God would give dark, thick lashes like that to a man instead of some deserving woman who would have appreciated them.

Like her, for instance.

Tate rose from the stool, stood so close to Libby that she could feel the heat of his skin, even through his clothes. She felt an irrational and almost overwhelming need to lead Tate to some private place, where the two of them could lie down, hold each other until things made sense again.

"How's Isabel?" Libby asked.

Tate had his truck keys out, but he hadn't moved toward the door. His concern for Pablo's widow was almost palpable. "She'll be all right in time, I guess," he said. "Esperanza checks on her every so often. Nico's been out of the country on business, but he'll be here as soon as he can."

Libby nodded.

Tate hesitated, then touched her face lightly with the backs of the fingers of his right hand. "Wish I could hold you," he said.

Talk about that old-time feelin'.

Libby choked up, and her eyes burned. "Probably not the best idea," she said, when she could manage the words. "You need to get some rest, and I have a business to run."

Tate dropped his hand to his side. "Yeah," he said. "I'd better get out of here. Esperanza's wonderful with the kids, but she can't say no to them. By now, they may have conscripted her and half the ranch hands to dig a moat around the castle."

Libby smiled slightly at the picture his words brought to mind, followed him to the door, and then outside, into the hot, dry sunshine beating down on the sidewalk and buckling the asphalt in the road.

"You'll call if you need anything?" she said, when Tate opened the door of his dusty truck to get behind the wheel.

He arched an eyebrow, and one corner of his mouth quirked upward, so briefly that Libby knew she might have imagined it. "You walked right into that one," he said. Then he leaned forward, kissed her briefly on the mouth, and got into his truck. "See you soon," he said.

See you soon.

"Come over and have supper with me tonight," she said, because she'd had to let go of Tate McKettrick one too many times in her life, and this time she couldn't. "Six o'clock," she hastened to add. "Bring the kids."

Idiot, Libby thought. *Why don't you just jump up onto the running board of that truck like some bimbo with hay in her hair and invite him to join you in an appearance on the* Jerry Springer *show?*

Maybe the episode could be called, "Women who chase after men who stomped on their hearts."

Tate flashed that legendary grin, the one folks claimed had been passed down through his family since the original patriarch, old Angus McKettrick, had broken his first heart back in the 1800s.

"Six o'clock," he confirmed. "We'll see about the kids."

Still ridiculously flustered, Libby finally registered that a number of her regular customers had gathered inside the Perk Up since she'd stepped outside with Tate, and they were peering out through the window as he drove away.

Embarrassed to be part of a spectacle, she hurried inside.

She could close up at five, she was thinking, hit the deli counter next door at Almsted's for cold chicken and potato salad and—whatever. She would improvise.

In the meantime, there were orders to fill.

What did kids like to eat? Libby wondered, her mind busy planning supper while her hands made lattes and frappes and iced mochas by rote. Hot dogs? Hamburgers?

The regulars had barely left when a tour bus full of senior citizens pulled up. They were on their way to San Antonio, Libby learned, to see the Alamo.

It was hectic, juggling all those orders, but Libby managed it, and stood waving in the doorway as the bus pulled away.

Long before Julie got back, sans King Calvin, the scones plus four bags of cookies hastily purchased at Almsted's were gone.

"What took you so long?" Libby asked, but she smiled a little as she waggled a handful of cash just plucked from the register.

"I had to walk Harry and put a load of towels in the washer," Julie answered, her eyes widening at the sight of all that loot. "What did you do, jimmy open an ATM?"

BONE-TIRED AND SICK to his soul, but looking forward to seeing Libby again just the same, Tate made a point of passing Brent's office on the way out of town.

Beth Anne Spales, the dispatcher/secretary the chief had inherited from a long succession of predecessors, stood in the small parking lot, watering droopy pink flowers in terracotta pots. She wore a floppy sun hat and gardening gloves, and waved when she recognized Tate's truck.

His mind tripped back to last night.

He'd called Brent as soon as he'd found Pablo's body, then he'd concentrated on rounding up the agitated stallion, shutting it up in the corral. The chief had arrived quickly, as had the county coroner, whose regular job was running the Blue River Funeral Home.

The task of telling Isabel what had happened to Pablo fell to Tate.

He'd driven over to the house by the creek, unsurprised to find lights burning in the windows, late as it was. Isabel would have waited up for Pablo; by then, she'd know something was wrong.

Except for telling Garrett and Austin about the car accident that had taken their parents' lives, and telling Libby that he'd gotten another woman pregnant and meant to marry her, relaying to Isabel the news that Pablo was dead was probably the hardest thing Tate had ever had to do. Tiny, quiet, dignified Isabel had *yowled* when he told her, like an animal caught in the steel teeth of a trap.

Now, in the bright light of a new day, Tate pulled up to the only stoplight in town, which happened to be red and would be for a while, since the timing device had quit working on New Year's Eve of 1999, thus convincing the nervous types that Y2K, with cataclysmic results, was indeed upon them. He rested his forehead against the steering wheel while he waited, breathing slowly and deeply.

He felt sick.

Someone honked a horn behind him, and Tate sat up straight, frowning when he saw that the light was still red. Glancing in the rearview mirror, he spotted Brent, driving the squad car.

"Pull over," Brent instructed, through that damn bullhorn of his.

Tate cursed under his breath and maneuvered the truck into the bank parking lot to his right. Buzzed down his window.

"I don't know what my crime was," he said, as Brent approached the driver's side door, "but it sure as hell wasn't speeding."

Brent flashed him the Denzel grin, though he looked even worse than Tate felt. "You shouldn't be on the road in the condition you're in," the chief said. "You're wiped."

"You shouldn't, either," Tate replied.

Brent sighed. Tucked his thumbs into that honking service belt of his. His badge looked dull in the bright light of day. Resting one foot on Tate's running board, he took off his sunglasses and squinted at his friend, looking worried. "You doin' okay, here, McKettrick?" he asked. "I know you were close to all the Ruizes, *especially* Pablo. You must be pretty broken up."

"I'll be all right," Tate said. *Eventually.*

"Isabel's in a big hurry to hold the funeral and move herself and those boys in with her sister, out in L.A.," Brent said. "Did she tell you that?"

"No," Tate answered. Thinking of the Ruiz house standing empty left him feeling as though he'd been punched in the gut. The place had been a second home to him and his brothers while they were growing up. Along with Nico, they'd fished and splashed in the cold water of the creek, stuffed themselves with apricots from Pablo's fruit trees, "camped out" in the Ruiz living room in sleeping bags. "No," he said again. "She didn't say anything about that. Seems like a pretty sudden decision."

Brent nodded. "It's her life," he said. "I just hope she's not being too hasty."

Tate agreed, and the two men parted ways.

Tate pondered Isabel's plans to move off the ranch as he drove toward home, navigating the familiar country roads by instinct. He nearly stopped off on the way to remind the woman that there was no hurry to clear out. He'd been planning on deeding the place over to Pablo anyhow, as soon as the old man retired.

In the end, though, Tate decided it was Isabel's own business if she wanted to live elsewhere. For all he knew, she'd hated living in the country all along, and here was her chance to live in a city.

When he pulled in next to the barn at home, Audrey and Ava and both dogs rushed him, were on him as soon as he stepped down out of the rig.

"Hey," he said.

"Can we ride our birthday ponies?" Audrey asked.

"Please?" Ava added.

Tate considered, decided a ride would be a good thing for everybody. He'd have to keep an eye on the pups, make sure they didn't try to weave back and forth between the horses' legs.

He'd planned on a few hours of shut-eye before going to supper at Libby's, but if they weren't out on the range too long, he and the kids, they could still make it.

"All right," he said, "saddle up."

The twins saddled their ponies with minimal help, having had lots of practice tacking up Bamboozle, while Tate threw a saddle on an old gelding named Bluejack.

Audrey and Ava were already outside, mounted on their matching "birthday" ponies, when Tate ducked his head to ride out through the barn door.

It was only then that he remembered the paint stallion, still in the holding pen at the back of the barn.

"Stay clear of the pen," he called to the girls. The steel fence surrounding the holding pen was twelve feet high, the poles set in concrete, and there wasn't more than six inches between the slats, though Ambrose or Buford might be able to dig their way under, he supposed. It didn't seem likely that they would.

Over the years, that pen had held bulls and many another stallion—some of them pretty determined critters. The steel surround had always held.

Still, *this* stallion was hell-born, a killer.

The huge animal tossed his head back and forth, snorted and pawed at the ground with his right front hoof. He looked ready to charge that fence, steel or no steel, concrete fittings or none.

A shudder ran down Tate's spine as he caught up to his daughters and rode on the side nearest the stallion.

"Is that the horse that stomped on Mr. Ruiz and crushed his heart?" Audrey asked, her blue eyes huge as she looked up at Tate. Her golden pony pranced fitfully beneath her, and no wonder—the poor little filly was a fifth the size of that stallion, if not less.

"That's the horse," Tate confirmed, his voice grating past his throat, fit to draw blood in the process. "Who told you Mr. Ruiz's heart was crushed?"

"I heard Esperanza telling somebody on the phone," Audrey said. "She didn't know I was listening."

"I see," Tate replied.

Ava looked back as they moved farther and farther from the pen and the pacing, whinnying stud, churning up clouds of dust.

"Why is he still on the Silver Spur," Ava asked reasonably, "if he hurt Mr. Ruiz?"

"Some of the ranch hands say he ought to be shot," Audrey observed worriedly. "Because he's a demon and won't ever be any different."

Tate knew, of course, about the talk going around the bunkhouse and the trailers along the creek, but he also knew Pablo wouldn't have wanted the horse destroyed. No, Pablo would have said the stud was wild and ought to be let out to run the range, siring foals and making a legend of himself.

The decision wasn't Tate's alone—the paint had killed a man, and the authorities would have a say in whether the animal lived or died. If the choice was his to make, Tate would have agreed with Pablo.

Some horses weren't meant to be tamed, just like some people.

"For now," Tate told his daughters solemnly, "here's all you need to know about that stud. Stay away from him, and keep your dogs away, too."

Ava looked back over one shoulder. "He doesn't look very happy," she said.

"I don't imagine he is," Tate agreed. "Do I have your word? You'll both stay as far from that stud as you can, no matter what?"

Both girls lifted their right hand, as though giving a oath.

"Unless we don't have any other choice, of course," Audrey said, after Tate had bent to open the wire-and-post gate so the three of them could ride through, headed for the range.

"Audrey," Tate said sternly, "I want your word—as a McKettrick."

Audrey rolled her eyes, then nodded.

Ava said, "You have my word."

Tate put the stallion from his mind then, rode with his girls and found that it cleared his head and his soul, just like always.

An hour later, back at the house, he dragged himself up to his bedroom, kicked off his boots and collapsed facedown on the bed, hoping to catch a little sleep before going back to town to have supper with Libby.

The twins joined him, and so did the dogs.

And just the same, he slept like a dead man.

CHAPTER SIX

DURING THE NEXT LULL, Libby locked up the shop for an hour and drove her car to the auto shop for the exhaust system repair, Julie following in her pink bomb to provide feminine moral support and a ride back.

Libby left the Impala with a mechanic and joined Julie in the Mary-Kay-mobile. She'd paid the cost in advance, using the profits from the coffee, scone and cookie sales she'd made to the people from the tour bus, but if the car needed extra work, especially something critical, she would have to use a credit card after all.

Julie reached over and patted her arm. "Don't worry," she said. "Gordon's check cleared this month. I can help you out if you need it."

"Thanks," Libby murmured, feeling like a charity case. "But doesn't that money go into Calvin's college account?"

"Most of the time," Julie said, checking all the mirrors before she backed out of her parking space. "It's no big deal, Lib. Pay me back when you can."

Relief coursed through Libby, but it didn't soothe all the places that ached. Things had seemed so wonderfully ordinary that morning when she'd taken Hildie out for her walk. Two kisses from Tate McKettrick the night before and she'd been walking on air.

The grass had been greener, the sky bluer.

Impossible things had begun to seem possible.

And then Gerbera had told her about Pablo Ruiz's death.

"Do you ever feel," she began, "as though no matter what you do, it's never going to be enough?"

Julie pulled right back into the parking space she'd just left, popped the elderly Cadillac into Park and shut off the engine. "Was that the voice of a depressed woman I just heard?" she asked. She spoke quietly, but at the same time she clearly meant to get a straight answer.

"I'm not exactly *depressed*," Libby said, thinking of Calvin getting out of playschool soon, and the shop closed for business and Hildie needing to be let out into the backyard for a little while. "*Overwhelmed* is more like it."

"Oh," Julie said. "Well, yeah, I know all about over-whelmed."

"I don't know how you do it," Libby said, with true admiration. "Raising Calvin alone, holding down a teaching job—"

"We all do what we have to," Julie replied when Libby fell silent, out of steam. "And I've wondered the same thing about you now and again, sister dear. You run the Perk Up by yourself most of the time, robbing Peter to pay Paul, and then there's Marva giving a grandstand performance every couple of weeks. Add on the way you always foster the overflow from the animal shelter and, hello, you make Wonder Woman look like an underachiever."

Libby blinked, surprised. "Wonder Woman?" she echoed, with an effort at a smile.

"You're too hard on yourself, Lib," Julie went on, after nodding once, with conviction. "No matter what comes at you, you just keep on trucking. I happen to admire that quality in a sister, or anybody else."

"Well," Libby responded, honestly puzzled, "what *else* can I do?"

Julie snapped her fingers. "See?" she said. "It doesn't even *occur* to you to quit. Do you think everybody's like that? My God, Lib, when Dad was sick, you were always there for him and for Paige and me, too. You were unstoppable, even after a body blow that would have dropped a lesser woman to her knees."

The body blow, of course, was Tate's defection to the Cheryl camp.

"That was pretty bad," Libby admitted, remembering. Bad? She'd lost fifteen pounds and a lot of sleep, developing dark circles under her eyes. She'd dated a string of losers, too, ready to settle for Mr. Wrong if only to spite Tate, because there was only one Mr. Right and he was taken.

Fortunately, Julie and Paige had intervened, threatening to lock her up in a closet, bound with duct tape, so she wouldn't be able to ruin her life before she came to her senses. For good measure, they'd planned to spoon Ben & Jerry's into her until she regained every pound she'd lost and ten besides.

Julie leaned far enough to tap lightly on Libby's temple with an index finger and ask, "What's really going on in there?"

Back when he was healthy, their dad had done that whenever one of his daughters got too introspective, or came down with a case of what he called "the sullens."

"Tate's coming to dinner tonight, at my place," Libby said. "And that pretty much cinches it: it's time to book a suite at the Home for Stupid Women and learn the secret handshake."

Julie erupted with laughter. "Forget it," she said. "The waiting list is probably way too long."

Libby laughed, too—as she wiped away tears with the heel of one palm. "Just my luck," she said, sniffling. She straightened her shoulders, raised her chin. "We'd better get going. Calvin will be through soon."

Julie started up the car again, and they were on their way. "There's one bright spot in all this," she told Libby.

"Oh, yeah? What would that be?"

"You'll get to have sex."

"Sex?"

"You know," Julie said, with a sly grin. "That fun, sweaty, noisy, slippery thing men and women do together, usually but not always in a bed?"

"Tonight isn't about sex, it's about *dinner,*" Libby said, turning red. "He's bringing the kids, the dogs and maybe even the housekeeper."

"You know damn well you're going to end up in bed with Tate McKettrick, sooner or later," Julie insisted. "And my money's on 'sooner.' Whenever the two of you are together, the air crackles."

"And you think I should just *go for it,* after all that happened?"

"That's exactly what I think. A lot of men aren't worth a second chance, but Jim and Sally McKettrick's boy? Definitely the one to bet on."

"The sisterly thing to say would be, 'Stay away from him. He hurt you once, and he'll hurt you again,'" Libby admonished.

"If that sister happened to be a cynic, maybe."

They reached the community center, and Julie parked the car. Calvin was on the playground, with a flock of other kids, engaged in a game of tag. Mrs. Oakland supervised, carrying a clipboard and wearing a whistle on a string around her neck.

"You're telling me you're not a cynic?" Libby countered. "You, the woman who's about to skip town to avoid a confrontation with her son's father?"

Julie sighed deeply, her hands tight on the steering wheel, watching Calvin with her heart in her eyes. "I'm not going anywhere," she said, very quietly. "Time to face the music." Then she turned to look at Libby. "And how was my plan 'cynical'?"

"Think about it," Libby said. "You didn't even consider the fact that Gordon might have turned over a new leaf, now that he's married and maybe even ready to settle down for real. You cared enough once to make a baby with him, but now you just assume he'll be nothing but trouble. If that isn't cynical, I don't know what is."

Julie smiled smugly. "Well, listen to you, Libby Remington," she said, as Calvin spotted them, spoke to Mrs. Oakland and, when the woman nodded her permission, ran toward the car. "Admitting it's possible for a man to *change.* Even one like, say, *Tate McKettrick.*"

"Shut up," Libby said.

"No possible way," Julie retorted. "And watch how you talk to me, or I won't help you cook a gourmet dinner that will have a certain dark-haired cowboy begging for your hand in marriage."

Libby's eyes widened. "You'd do that? *Prepare a gourmet dinner just to make me look good?*"

Calvin reached the car and lugged open the back door to scramble onto the seat.

"Of course I would," Julie said, before turning to smile at Calvin and ask him how his day went.

"I'm ahead in the polls!" he exulted.

"That's it," Julie answered. "No more *Meet the Press* for you, buddy."

Libby laughed. "Here he is now," she quipped, looking over her shoulder at Calvin, who was busy buckling himself into his car seat. "The man who would be king."

"WHAT WOULD YOU SAY to a partnership?" Libby asked Julie, later that afternoon, the two of them practically lost in the wilderness of pots, pans and bowls that was Libby's kitchen. Instead of reopening the shop, they'd raided Julie's cupboards and freezer for the makings of dinner, stopping at the supermarket for the few things she didn't already have.

"A partnership?" Julie echoed, dipping a spoon into a kettle of pesto sauce to do a taste test. "What kind of partnership?"

"At the Perk Up," Libby said, realizing too late what she was asking of her sister and wishing she hadn't brought the subject up at all. It wasn't as if the place were a runaway moneymaker—now that she had to compete with the famous franchise, she was operating in the red, for the most part.

Calvin's laugh, accompanied by a lot of happy barking from Hildie, came through the screen door.

"Never mind," Libby backpedaled, embarrassed. "It was just a thought."

"How about sharing that thought with me?" Julie inquired. She'd changed into shorts and a pink top while they were at her place, and her eyes were a silvery gray.

"It seems silly now."

"I can do silly," Julie grinned. "In fact, it's a way of life. Keeps me sane. Talk to me, Lib."

"I was just thinking—well, your scones are so popular, and you're not working at the insurance agency this summer, so…"

"Oh," Julie said, getting it. She puffed out her cheeks, the way she always did when something surprised her and she needed to stall for a few seconds so she could think.

"I told you it was silly."

"We could sell lots of other things besides scones," Julie mused, as if Libby hadn't spoken. "Soup and sandwiches and salads. Change the name of the place, serve high tea—"

"What's wrong with the Perk Up?" Libby interrupted, thrown off. She'd done a lot of brainstorming to come up with that moniker.

"Well," Julie said, with kind forbearance, "it's not very original, now, is it?"

Libby sagged a little, around the shoulders. "I guess not," she admitted. Then, "Wait a second. You're actually considering my offer?"

"Of course I'd go back to teaching in the fall," Julie said. "That will mean cutting back to part-time here, doing the baking at night and on weekends. But, yes. I think the idea has merit."

"You do?"

Julie grinned, glanced at the stove clock. Wiped her hands on her apron before taking it off. "Yep," she said. "Calvin and I are out of here. My, how time flies when you're making pesto."

"You're going to *leave?*"

Julie widened her eyes and mugged a little. "Uh, *yeah,*" she said. "The salad is in the refrigerator. There are hot dogs, in case the kids don't like pasta. You do know how to heat hot dogs, don't you?" After Libby tossed her a look, she went on, undaunted. "All you have to do is boil the noodles and zap the pesto in the microwave and *voilà!* Pasta à la Julie."

"Stay," Libby pleaded.

Julie ignored her, walking to the back door and whistling through her teeth. "Yo, Calvin!" she called. "Time to boogie!"

"Julie—"

Julie turned, her arms folded. "You can do this, Lib," she said firmly. "Go change your clothes. And—hey—why don't you go wild and wear some lip gloss?"

AROUND FIVE O'CLOCK, showered, semi-rested and shaved, Tate studied his reflection in his bathroom mirror. "What the hell are you doing, McKettrick?" he asked himself, resting his hands on the countertop and leaning in.

There was no time to come up with an answer—a light rap sounded at his door. "Are you decent?" Audrey called, from the other side.

Tate chuckled. Was he decent? Well, that depended on who you asked.

He adjusted the collar of his cotton shirt. He'd almost gone with a suit, one of the tailored numbers left over from his days with McKettrickCo, but in the end, he'd opted for his usual jeans and plain shirt. He didn't want to seem too eager, and besides, he'd be going to a good friend's funeral in a couple of days. One suit in a week was plenty.

"Who wants to know?" he teased.

"Audrey McKettrick, that's who!" his daughter yelled in reply.

"*And* Ava McKettrick!" cried the other daughter, not to be outdone.

"Come in," he said.

The door flew open and the twins and their dogs crowded through the gap.

"Uncle Garrett is on his way," Audrey reported.

"Uncle Austin, too," Ava added.

"I know," Tate answered, steering the pair and their faithful animal companions into the larger space that was his room. He sat down on the side of the bed to pull on his boots.

"Are they coming because they want to go to Mr. Ruiz's funeral?" Audrey asked.

"Yes," Tate said simply. He'd called them both, late the night before, to tell them what had happened. Pablo had been like a member of the family, and he'd really stepped up when their folks were killed. For a while, he'd functioned as a sort of surrogate father, and Isabel had mothered them as much as they'd allow.

Ava hiked herself up to perch on the bed beside him, and Audrey took the other side. "It's sad when somebody dies," Ava said solemnly.

"Yeah," Tate agreed. "It's real sad." Since the twins hadn't been born yet when their McKettrick grandparents passed away, he wondered what, if anything, they knew about death.

"Our goldfish died," Audrey confided. "Mom flushed them."

"Things like that happen," Tate said.

"They don't flush *people,* do they?" Ava asked, clearly concerned. "When they die, I mean?"

Tate wrapped an arm around both his girls, held them close for a moment. "No," he said gently. "They don't flush people."

"People are too *big* to flush, ninny," Audrey told her sister, leaning around Tate to look at Ava.

"No name calling," Tate ordered. Then he noticed that the girls were still in their playclothes. "Better clean up your acts," he said, "if you want to go to Libby's with me."

"Esperanza is cooking," Ava told him. "She says Mrs. Ruiz will need to have lots of food on hand, with so many people coming to visit."

"I imagine that's so," Tate said. "But what does it have to do with supper at Libby's?"

"We want to stay here and help Esperanza," Audrey replied.

"She keeps crying," Ava added. "I bet she's used a *million* tissues today."

"*Plus,*" Audrey said, "Uncle Garrett and Uncle Austin will be here."

"Right," Tate acknowledged, giving the pair another simultaneous squeeze and clearing his throat before standing up. "It's possible, you know, that Esperanza might want to be alone for a while. And your uncles probably won't show up for hours yet."

"Esperanza needs us," Ava insisted, her eyes huge with a sorrow she felt but didn't understand, even though Tate had explained as best he could.

"We'll see," Tate said.

When they'd all trooped down to the kitchen, he saw that Esperanza was indeed cooking—with a vengeance. Fresh vegetables and stacks of her homemade tortillas, among other things, all but covered the center island, and lard smoked in a skillet on the stove.

Esperanza sniffled once, approached and straightened his shirt collar. "You look much better," she said.

He grinned. "Thanks," he replied, well aware of the girls crowding in behind him. "How about you, Esperanza? Are you doing all right?"

"When I am busy," she responded, "then I am also all right."

He nodded; he understood that particular tactic well.

"The girls," the housekeeper said. "You will let them stay?"

Tate raised one eyebrow. "If that's what you really want, sure."

Esperanza nodded. "It *is* what I really want," she confirmed.

Tate believed her. "All this food is for the Ruizes?" he asked, indicating the mountains of produce and other edibles. "They won't have room for all this—their house is pretty small."

Esperanza smiled moistly. "Isabel and her children will have much company," she said, "and anyway, Garrett and Austin are coming. They are always hungry when they've been away from home."

He leaned a little, placed a kiss on the top of Esperanza's head. "I won't be late," he said. As he passed the stove, he pushed the skillet back off the flames.

Ambrose and Buford would have gone along for the ride— they got hair all over the legs of his jeans letting him know they were more than willing—but he decided to leave them at home, since the girls were staying behind with Esperanza.

Before heading for the garage, he raided Esperanza's flower garden for a handful of pink daisies and a few sprigs of that white stuff florists always added to bouquets.

Instead of driving the truck, as he almost always did, he took his green Jaguar—the thing had been sitting in the garage for months, gathering dust. Maybe he'd blow out the carburetor on the last straight stretch before town.

And maybe not.

Brent Brogan—aka Denzel—was an equal-opportunity lawman. Best friends or not, he wouldn't hesitate to pull Tate over and write him a whopping ticket if he caught him speeding.

Especially in a Jag.

Tate thought of his daughters, and how they'd grow up with one parent—Cheryl—if he got killed being stupid on the empty road.

He stayed within the speed limit, all the way to Libby's place.

The flowers were starting to wilt, lying there on the passenger seat; he picked them up carefully, wishing he'd taken the time to stick them in a fruit jar full of water or something.

You're stalling, McKettrick, he told himself, sitting there in his too-fancy car in front of Libby's *not*-so-fancy house.

Libby appeared on the porch, wearing another sundress, this one pale yellow. The light was just right, and he could see through the fabric. She'd be embarrassed if she knew, so he wouldn't tell her. Anyhow, he enjoyed the view.

"Where are Esperanza and the girls?" she called, taking a few steps forward and shielding her eyes from the sun with one hand.

"They're busy tonight," Tate answered. "I like your dress." *And what's under it.*

"Are those flowers?" she asked, and then blushed.

"I believe so," Tate joked, checking out the yard as he came through the gate. He didn't give a rat's ass about the overgrown lawn, but if he kept staring at Libby the way he had been, she might realize her dress was transparent and put on something else, thus ruining his whole night. "When was the last time somebody mowed the grass?"

"I keep meaning to get to it—"

Tate climbed the steps, bent his head to kiss her lightly on the mouth and handed over the flowers. "The lawn looks fine, and so do you," he murmured.

She laid a hand on his chest. "The neighbors might be watching," she whispered.

"Well, if they have that much free time," Tate replied, "one of them should have mowed your lawn by now."

Libby took his hand, pulled him inside.

"I'll just put these flowers in a vase and warm up the pesto sauce," she said, walking away.

His gaze fell to her delectable backside and got riveted there.

His groin tightened, and he wished he'd worn a hat so he'd have something to hold in front of his crotch until his hard-on went down.

Better yet, he thought, he could peel that see-through dress off over Libby's head, lay her down on a bed or ease her up against a wall and lick every golden inch of her and put the hard-on where it belonged.

This is not helping, said the voice of reason.

But Tate was well beyond reason by then.

And furthermore, he wasn't hungry. Not for pesto sauce, anyhow.

Light poured through the kitchen window as Libby stood at the sink, filling a vase from the faucet for the flowers. She might as well have been stark naked.

Hildie, her dog, gave him a sleepy look from the hooked rug in front of the refrigerator and then sighed and closed her eyes to get some more shut-eye.

Tate stepped behind a high-backed chair and pulled it in front of him. He just got harder, though, when Libby turned, smiling, and approached to set the flowers in the center of the table.

Her smile lost a little of its sparkle. She ducked her head a little, to look up into his face. "Is something wrong?"

Lots of things were wrong.

There was a damn plastic castle in his yard, and it might be weeks before he could get it moved to the community center.

Cheryl would be back in a few days, full of fresh poison, and she'd make a point of whisking Audrey and Ava back to town ASAP, because she knew it twisted his insides into a knot when they left the Silver Spur.

And Pablo Ruiz was dead.

He lowered his gaze, not trusting himself to speak, not wanting Libby to see what was in his eyes.

She rounded the table, pushed the chair aside, and put her arms around him.

Her eyes widened when she felt his erection, and fetching pink color bloomed in her cheeks. "Yikes," she said.

Tate chuckled. "'Yikes'?"

"I'd forgotten how—big you get. When you're—when— oh, God, why do I even *try* to talk?" Her face was on fire now.

So was his body.

He placed his hands on either side of her waist. "It's okay, Lib," he said, grinning in spite of all the sadness and hopeless need inside him. "We're both adults, here. And *big* isn't a word most men are offended by—not in that context, anyway."

Libby was wearing her hair down that night, instead of in a ponytail, and she swept it back off her shoulders—a gesture so inherently feminine that Tate's condition immediately got worse.

Or better.

Her eyes misted over. "What are we doing?" she asked, in a near whisper.

"Getting ready to make love?" Tate suggested hopefully.

"It scares me."

"Making love?"

"No," she said, slipping her arms around his neck and giving a little sigh as she let herself lean against him. "How much I want it. How much I want you."

He put his hands to her cheeks, eased her head back for the kiss he planned to give her. "Far be it from me," he murmured, as their breaths mingled, "to deny a lady what she wants."

Libby made a little moaning sound then, part need and part frustration, as he read it, and pulled back out of his arms before he could kiss her.

"Julie's wrong," she said, near tears. "I *am* stupid."

"Never," Tate said, and he meant it. Libby had every reason not to trust him, with her body or anything else, but she was one of the smartest and most resourceful people he knew. "I'm the stupid one, Lib. I had a chance to wake up every morning until the day I die with you beside me, and I blew it. If it's any comfort to you, I'll never stop regretting that."

He turned then, fully intending to leave her house and her life and stay gone.

"Wait," she said, just as he reached the doorway that lead into the living room.

Tate stopped, but he didn't turn around.

Libby didn't speak again for so long that he thought she might have sneaked out the back door, leaving him standing there in the doorway like the fool he was.

"Tate." The way she said his name—it caught at his heart, and a few other vital organs, too. When they were together before, that tone had meant only one thing: that she wanted him.

He made himself turn back to her, even though every shred of good sense he possessed advised against it.

Libby was standing a few feet away, holding out one hand.

Confused, Tate just stood there, drinking in the sight of her and wishing he could thank whoever it was who'd skimped on the cloth for that dress. It might as well have been made of yellow cellophane.

She seemed shy, unaware of how beautiful she was. And very uncertain.

Tate felt as though he'd been underwater too long, and blood thundered in his ears. He was a man poised on the precipice of something big, something life-changing, and as much as he wanted Libby Remington, he was scared. They'd had great sex as kids. But they weren't kids anymore.

What if it was too soon?

What if it was too late?

What if it wasn't as good as before?

Good God, what if it was *better?*

Tate knew these renegade thoughts made no real sense, but he couldn't seem to rein them in.

Libby smiled, almost sadly. "Is something wrong, Tate?"

His boot soles might have been nailed to the floor, he stood so still.

Finally, he shook his head. Libby was the hometown-sweetheart type, the kind of woman a man was proud to take home to the folks, but she'd been a passionate lover, too.

He took a step toward her, closed his hand around hers. Pulled her against him, so that their torsos collided. And he kissed her. Gently at first, then, slowly and carefully, he turned up the heat.

Libby trembled—he knew she was torn between pulling away and giving herself to him then and there—and put her arms around his neck again.

Tate kissed her harder, cupped her perfect little rear end in his hands—he'd have sworn under oath that she was naked under that dress—and hoisted her up a little, her cue to wrap her legs around him.

She did.

Tate moaned, tore his mouth from hers, breathless. "Where?" he rasped.

"Right here, if you don't hurry," Libby replied, with a

little laugh, a nervous mingling of desire and reticence, kissing him again.

Too preoccupied to see where he was going, Tate pushed open three different doors before he finally found her bedroom. Walking wasn't that easy, with a woman wound around him and their mouths welded together, but it was a challenge he meant to meet.

"Stop," Libby said with obvious reluctance, just as he was about to lower her sideways onto the bed, push the dress up around her waist and do what came naturally. "Tate, *stop*. Please."

He stopped.

She unclenched her legs and stood on her feet again, her face flushed, her conflict naked in her eyes.

"It's too soon," she told him miserably. "What if the time isn't right and we're not ready?"

Tate McKettrick was a Texas boy, raised right. If Libby didn't want to make love, that would be a disappointment, but of course he wasn't going to force the issue. Waiting would be hard, but Libby was worth it.

Anyhow, he hadn't brought condoms, and she probably wasn't on the pill. They'd been apart for a long time, and a lot had happened in between then and now.

Libby raised her hands to his face, and just that was almost his undoing. "Time," she said. "We need a little time first, that's all."

"How *much* time?" Tate rasped.

She laughed softly, but her eyes—her beautiful, expressive eyes—were awash in tears. "Enough to make sure we're not making a mistake," she said. "There's a lot to think about."

With a sigh, he sat down on the edge of Libby's bed, took

her hand and pulled her onto his lap. Putting his arms around her, he rested his forehead against her right ear. "Did you wear that dress to torture me?" he asked, partly sighing the words, and partly grinding them out. His breath was still fast and shallow.

"What?" Was that surprise he heard in her tone, or mischief?

"Come on, Lib," Tate said. "I've seen toilet paper with more substance than that dress."

She laughed. *"Toilet paper?* Well, that's romantic, McKettrick."

He raised his eyes then, looked into hers, and the realization hit him like a whisky barrel rolling downhill.

God help him, *he loved her.*

She sobered a little, still content, it appeared, to sit on his lap in a dress made out of spun nothing and stitched together with a short length of zilch. "You okay, cowboy?" she asked quietly.

"No," he said, because lying to Libby Remington had always been impossible, and that was still so. "Not really."

Libby ran the pad of one thumb over his mouth, lightly. "When was the last time somebody held you just because you needed holding, Tate McKettrick?" she asked.

The question made his throat cinch up tight and his eyes sting. Even if he'd had the voice to answer, he wouldn't have known what to say.

She slipped off his lap to sit beside him on the mattress, kicked away her sandals and then scooted to the middle, to lie down. And she waited, without a word.

Tate hesitated, but the pull of her was too strong. He took off his boots and stretched out beside her, confused by all the things she made him feel.

Libby had made it clear that she wasn't ready to make

love, yet she took him in her arms and rested her forehead against his chest.

He was lost in the softness of her body, the scent of her hair and the silken feel of her skin, the solace she seemed to radiate from somewhere in the core of her being.

I love you, he wanted to say.

But it was too soon for that, too.

So he simply lay there and let Libby hold him. Just because.

CHAPTER SEVEN

THE SHIFT HAPPENED between one heartbeat and the next.

Lying there on her bed, facing Tate, Libby felt her heart soar and then plummet, as though she were riding some cosmic roller coaster. She'd loved this man since he was a boy and she was a little girl, barely older than Audrey and Ava were now.

Over the years, that love had changed, always finding its level. Like a river, it had sometimes overflowed its banks, and she'd been swept away by its force. After Cheryl arrived on the scene, it had gone underground, leaving only cracks and debris on the surface.

Now, the river was rising rapidly, springing up from some elemental and seemingly inexhaustible source of devotion, not only within Libby, but *beyond* her, bubbling and churning, swirling into violent eddies. This time, there would be no stopping it, no changing its course, no stemming the tide.

It would be what it was, and what it was becoming, and that was that.

Powerless before the enormity of it, Libby wept in stricken silence.

Tate must have felt her tears through his shirt, because he turned her gently onto her back, so he could look down into her face.

"What?" he asked, breathing the word, rather than saying it.

Libby shook her head. Even if she hadn't been afraid to tell him what she was feeling, she wouldn't have known how to put it into words. It was as though she'd died, and then been resurrected as a different woman, with a new soul.

Tate kissed her cheekbones, her eyelids. "Lib," he persisted, his voice husky. "What is it?"

A sob tore itself from her throat, raw and hurting, and, shaking her head again, she tried to roll onto her other side, turn her back to him. But he didn't allow it.

The former Libby, practical and wary, emotionally bruised and battered, had stopped him from making love to her for a lot of very good reasons.

The new one wanted him with an incomprehensible ferocity, an instinctual craving that would not be refused, delayed or modified.

Libby took Tate's hand, brought it to her mouth, and flicked at his palm with the tip of her tongue.

He made a low sound in his throat, but he never closed his eyes. He consumed her with them, drew her into that boundless blue, where all but her most primitive instincts faded away.

She moved his hand again, this time to cup her right breast, crooned when he used the side of one thumb to caress her nipple through the gossamer cloth of her dress and the thin silk bra beneath. Her back arched, of its own accord, and her heart thrummed so loudly that the sound of it seemed to fill the room, push at the walls.

Libby knew, in those moments, only one word—his name.

It came out of her, that name, on a long, low groan, and she struggled to get free of the dress, would have ripped it away as though it were burning, if Tate hadn't pulled the garment up and then off over her head.

She felt her bra go next, her bare breasts spilling free.

Tate closed his mouth over one aching nipple, then the other, and at the same time slipped his hand inside her panties to part her, tease her with gentle plucking motions of his fingers.

Libby cried out, flailing and whimpering, desperate to be naked, to be utterly vulnerable to him in every way. When the panties were gone, first dragged down over her thighs and knees and ankles so she could kick free of them, he parted her legs and, with the heel of his palm, made slow circles at her center until she was wet with the need of him.

To his credit, Tate tried to reason with her, his voice low and ragged, reminding her that only minutes before, she'd wanted to wait, take things slowly. But he couldn't have known about the river flowing within her, flowing *through* her from some other world, with all the force of an ocean surging behind it.

At some point, he must have realized there would be no turning back, because he knelt astraddle of her thighs, pulling his shirt out of his jeans, working the buttons, tossing the shirt aside.

When he leaned over to kiss her, Libby ran her hands over his chest, his shoulders, up and down his arms and his sides, frantic to touch him, to chart the once-familiar terrain of his body.

The kiss was devastating, a thorough taking in its own right, and Libby struggled to breathe when Tate broke away from her, nibbled his way down the length of her neck, suckled at one breast and then the other.

And still Libby spoke a language composed of a single word.

"Tate." She reveled in the sound of it. "Tate."

He moved down then, slid his hands under her, squeezing, hoisting her high off the bed. When he nuzzled through and took her into his mouth, she instantly splintered, shouting now, riding a ghost horse made of fire.

The long climax convulsed her, time and again, drove the breath from her lungs and melted her very bones, leaving her limp in its aftermath. She couldn't see or hear or speak— she could only feel.

And Tate wasn't through with her.

He draped her legs over his shoulders, squeezing her buttocks slightly as he continued to use his mouth on her, now nibbling, now sucking, now flicking at her with his tongue.

The next release was cataclysmic; and it, too, went on and on, something eternal.

Transported, Libby gave one continuous, straining moan as her body buckled and seized, rose and fell, quivered and went still.

Tate was relentless, feasting on her, summoning up every sensation she was capable of feeling.

She flung her head from side to side, pleaded and threatened and coaxed, all by uttering his name alone.

He sucked on her until she'd given him everything, and then he demanded even more.

Aware of him viscerally, in every fiber and cell, though he might have been an invisible lover for all she could see through the haze of near-desperate satisfaction that had settled over her after that last orgasm, she knew when he moved to take off his jeans.

She moaned and parted her legs for him when he covered her again, an act that took all the strength she had left.

"Libby," she heard him say, through the blissful void, "if

you want me to stop, say so now, because once I'm inside you, I'm not going to pull out until it's over."

She managed only the slightest demur, still floating in a warm sea of sweet ambrosia. She wanted him inside her, deep, deep inside her, but not because she expected another climax. She'd come so many times, with so much intensity, that she was soft and moist and peaceful inside.

Until he took her in earnest, that is.

With the first powerful thrust, he opened a whole new well of need, a blazing lake of fire. Libby's eyes flew open, and she gasped in wanting and alarm.

He drove into her, nearly withdrew, drove again.

Libby went wild beneath him, digging her heels into the bed to thrust herself upward to meet him, stroke for stroke, clawing at his back and his shoulders and any part of him she could get hold of, calling to him, raging at him in her one-word litany.

They shattered simultaneously, Tate holding her high and driving into her with short, rapid thrusts. Through a storm of dazzling light, as her own body convulsed in helpless ecstasy, she saw him throw back his head, as majestic and powerful as a stallion claiming a mare. She saw the muscles straining in his neck and chest and felt the warmth of his seed spilling into her.

When it was over, he collapsed beside her with a hoarse exclamation, still spanning her with one arm and one leg.

Libby drifted, seemingly outside her body, and it was a long time before she settled back into herself. The landing was soft, featherlight—at first. But as her scattered wits began to find their way home, flapping their wings and roosting in her heart and her brain and the pit of her stomach, her very spirit began to ache.

What had she done?

What if she was pregnant?

What if she wasn't?

Tears gathered inside her, filled her, but she could not shed them, even though she yearned for the relief crying would bring.

Tate held her, brushing her forehead with his lips, murmuring to her that everything would be all right. She'd see, he promised. *Everything would be all right.*

For him, it would be. After all, he was a man.

He would get up, shower, get dressed and go back to his regular life—to his beautiful children and his sprawling ranch and all the rest of it.

The lovemaking hadn't changed him; he knew who he was, who he had always been and always would be: Tate McKettrick.

Libby, on the other hand, had been permanently altered by the experience they'd just shared, and she was going to have to get to know herself all over again.

The task seemed so daunting, so huge, so *impossible,* that she didn't know where to start.

She slept, awakened, slept again.

When she woke up the next time, Tate was gone.

His absence blew cold and bitter through her soul, like a winter wind.

Except for the aftershocks still rocking her sated body at regular intervals, she might have dreamed the whole thing.

Now came reality.

AUSTIN AND GARRETT WERE sitting at the kitchen table when Tate got home that night, a little after midnight.

Seeing his brothers, he immediately tucked in his shirt, something he'd forgotten to do before he left Libby's house.

He felt heat rise in his neck and pulse along his jawline as Austin gave him that familiar, knowing once-over.

"Been with a woman," Austin said to Garrett. Except that he was thinner, and his brownish hair was in even worse need of barbering than usual, Austin resembled his old, pre-Buzzsaw self.

Physically, Tate knew, Austin had largely recovered.

But something deeper had been injured that day in the rodeo arena, and the jury was still out on whether or not he would come back from that.

"Yep," Garrett agreed sagely, shoving a hand through his dark blond hair. His fancy white politician's shirt was open to the middle of his chest, and, like Austin, he was nursing a glass of whiskey. Scotch on the rocks, unless Tate missed his guess. "He's definitely been with a woman."

Tate chose to skip the Scotch and have coffee instead. Since Esperanza had long since scrubbed out the pot and set it for the morning, he brewed a cup of instant, using the special spigot on the sink. "You can both shut up," he grumbled, "any old time now."

With all he'd felt making love to Libby Remington again, there was a lot of mental and emotional sorting to do. Dealing with his brothers was something he would have preferred to avoid, at least until morning.

Austin laughed, and something in the tone of that laugh brought home a previously unconsidered reality to Tate. His kid brother probably hadn't been in rehab all that long; more likely, he'd been shacked up someplace with a woman.

Maybe several.

"At least he didn't give *my* present to the twins to the community center," Austin told Garrett, more than slightly smug. No matter how much Tate protested, they both spoiled their only nieces extravagantly. Cheryl allowed it, but it galled Tate.

He didn't want Audrey and Ava growing up thinking they were entitled to everything they wanted.

Garrett scowled. "It's a perfectly good castle," he said, and belched unceremoniously.

Tate wondered how long the both of them had been swilling Scotch and swapping lies. "Maybe," he growled, "you two could stop talking about me as though I'm not even here."

"Would that be fun?" Austin asked Garrett. In Austin's world, everything had to be fun. He was the Western version of Peter Pan; Tate had long since given up the hope that his kid brother would ever grow up. He had more money than sense, and his looks—fatal to women—worked against him, in Tate's opinion.

Austin was used to coasting. Everything came too easily to him, and the effect on his character was less than impressive.

"No," Garrett said, after due and bleary consideration. "It would not be fun."

Tate took a jar of freeze-dried coffee from the cupboard and set it on the counter with more force than the enterprise really called for. "Some things never change," he said. "You're both as dumb as you ever were."

"Well, *he's* in a mood," Garrett remarked, and, after belching again, poured himself another double shot.

"God," Tate said, stirring coffee crystals into hot water and then approaching the table, "I hope you never get elected president. Two-and-a-quarter-plus centuries down the swirler. Everything Washington, Lincoln and FDR accomplished, gone."

Garrett belched again. "Now that was just plain low," he said.

"Downright mean-spirited," Austin agreed.

"You're both sloshed," Tate accused.

"Of course we're sloshed," Garrett said, his eyes suddenly haunted. "Pablo is dead. Jesus, stomped to death by a horse."

Austin looked away, but not before Tate saw that his eyes were wet. Ever quick to compose himself, Austin soon met Tate's gaze. "You found him?"

Tate nodded.

"Christ," Austin commiserated, shoving the bottle in Tate's direction. "Here. Put some of that in your chamomile tea, or whatever it is you're drinking."

"Austin?" Tate said quietly.

"Yeah?"

"Fuck off."

"So who's the woman?" Austin asked, typically unfazed. It had taken a murderous bull named Buzzsaw to get to him.

"Not Cheryl, I hope," Garrett said.

"Watch it," Tate warned, before lowering his voice to add, "She might be a bitch, but she's also the mother of my children."

"Her one redeeming virtue," Austin said.

Tate studied his youngest sibling carefully. Previously, he would have dodged a conversation with his brothers, but suddenly he was in another mode entirely. "Were you telling the truth, outside the operating room the day you were hurt, when you said you never slept with Cheryl? Because she claims it happened."

Austin raised his glass, already nearly empty again, in a mocking salute. "Nobody lies when they know they might be facing their Maker," he said. He downed what remained of his Scotch. Sputtered a little. His McKettrick-blue eyes were both looking in the same direction, but not for long if he kept drinking like that. "Besides, Tate, you're *my brother.* Much as I'd like to punch your lights out most of the time, I wouldn't do *that* even if the opportunity came my way—which, regrettably, it did."

An uncomfortable silence ensued.

More Scotch was poured.

"I'm not letting *that one* drop," Tate said.

Austin sighed, glanced in Garrett's direction.

Evidently, no help was forthcoming from the future president of the United States, who was already three sheets to the wind. If he ever made it to the White House, the tabloids would have no trouble at all digging up dirt on him.

Resigned and even a little regretful, Austin said, "I was in Vegas, for the finals. Cheryl showed up, told the desk clerk at the hotel that we were married. She must have shown him ID—her last name was McKettrick at the time, remember. Anyhow, when I got back to my room, after the ride and the buckle ceremony at South Point, Cheryl was waiting."

Tate and Garrett were both watching him, Tate with tight-jawed annoyance, Garrett with pity.

"And?" Tate prompted.

"And she was naked," Austin admitted.

"Good God," Garrett told his younger brother, "you *are* stupid, admitting a thing like that. Are you *trying* to get those perfect white teeth knocked out of your head?"

Austin flushed. "She was naked," he insisted.

"So you said," Tate observed.

"And crying," Austin added.

"Boo-hoo," Garrett said.

"God help America," Tate said, "if *you* ever get your name on the ballot."

"The press would make hash out of him," Austin remarked to Tate, cocking a thumb at Garrett, "before he ever got the nomination."

Garrett scowled, but said nothing. He could have bullshitted a lot of people, but his brothers weren't among them. They knew him too well.

"Cheryl was naked and crying in your hotel room *and*—?" Tate prompted, glaring at Austin.

"And," Austin said, with drunken dignity, "she said you didn't even ask for a divorce, you just told her you were filing for one. Did I mention she was in my bed?"

There had been more to Tate's decision to end the marriage, of course, but Cheryl, indignant that he'd refused to overlook her one-night stand with a prominent judge in Dallas and go on as if nothing had happened, wouldn't have included that part of the story.

Nor did Austin and Garrett need to know it.

"No," Tate said evenly. "You skipped that part, but you did say she was naked, so I guess it figures."

"She was in his bed," Garrett said, with portent. Where the hell had he been for the last minute or so?

"Thank you, Mr. President," Tate said. "And shut the fuck up, will you?"

"Listen to him," Garrett remarked to Austin. "I think I'll establish a national committee on casual profanity. Too many people swear. We need to get to the bottom of this, nip it in the bud, cut it off at the pass—"

"One more word," Tate told Garrett, "and I'm stuffing that whiskey bottle down your throat."

Garrett belched again.

Tate turned back to Austin. "Cheryl was in your bed," he reminded him.

"She was?" Austin said.

Tate reached across the table and got his kid brother by the shirt collar. "She was," Tate agreed. "And the next thing you did was—?"

Austin grinned. "Well, first, I wished you weren't my brother, and her husband, because mega-bitch that she is, Cheryl is one hot woman. I didn't ask her what she was after, because that was pretty obvious. She wanted to pay you back for divorcing her, in spades. I told her she needed therapy, and then I picked up my gear, walked out and slept on the couch in my buddy Steve Miller's suite."

"The buckle guy?" Garrett asked, evidently determined to be part of the conversation, even though he'd long since lost track of it.

"Yeah," Tate said tightly, "the *buckle guy.*"

Miller, a representative of the company responsible for designing and constructing the fancy silver belt buckles winning cowboys were awarded at various rodeos around the country, was familiar to all three of them.

"I think I'll go to bed now," Garrett announced.

"Hell of an idea," Tate agreed. "That will save me the trouble of kicking your ass."

Garrett got out of his chair and stumbled in the general direction of his part of the house. The place was Texas-big, which meant they each had their own private wing, and it was not only possible but common for them to live for months under the same roof and still keep pretty much to themselves.

"He's drunk," Austin confided drunkenly.

"Ya think?" Tate asked.

Suddenly, Austin was sober. His blue eyes were clear. "I didn't sleep with Cheryl," he said.

Tate gave a great sigh. "I believe you," he said. And it was true.

"Hallelujah," Austin said, with some bitterness.

"It wouldn't hurt you to hit the sack, either," Tate told him. "You're going to have one bitch of a hangover tomorrow, if there's any justice in this world."

Austin laughed. "Lucky for me there isn't," he said, and poured himself more Scotch. "You were with Libby Remington tonight, weren't you?"

"Officially none of your damn business," Tate proclaimed.

"Might as well admit it. Somebody turned you inside out tonight, big brother, and I'm betting it was Libby."

"Okay." Tate sighed, his energy flagging now that he and Austin had settled the Cheryl incident. "It was Libby."

Austin grinned. "You're a couple again? That's good."

Tate's jaw clamped, and he had to take a second or so to unstick the hinges. "It's not that simple," he said.

"Because—?"

"Because I sold her out," Tate rasped. Basically, he thought, he was no better than Cheryl. He hadn't been married to Libby when he'd gone swimming in the romantic equivalent of a shark tank, letting things go way too far with the wrong woman, but they'd had an understanding. She'd trusted him completely, and he'd betrayed that trust.

He'd wounded her on a deep level, and he wasn't naive enough to think that had changed, just because Libby had wanted sex. Libby had always enjoyed sex, and unless he missed his guess, she'd been doing without for quite a while.

On the other hand, maybe that was just wishful thinking.

She was a beautiful, desirable woman, and he wasn't the first—or the last—man to notice.

"Sounds to me," Austin observed dryly, after taking a few moments to mull over Tate's grudging admission that he had indeed been with Libby that night, "like all must be forgiven. Lib's nobody's fool—none of the Remington women are. If she took you into her bed, big brother, she's willing to forget the past, and that's a rare thing, especially for a woman."

The summer after he'd graduated from high school, Tate recalled, Austin had dated Libby's youngest sister, Paige. For a while there, things had been hot and heavy, if any part of the rumors flying around town had been true, but in the end, Paige had had the good sense to throw Austin over when she'd enrolled in nursing school that September and he'd gone right on risking his neck at the rodeo.

"At what point," Tate rasped, irritated, "did I say that Libby and I went to bed together?"

Austin chuckled. The sound, like the expression in his eyes and the set of his shoulders, was different somehow. His little brother had changed in ways Tate couldn't quite put his finger on.

"You didn't need to say it," Austin replied. "Your shirt was still half out of your pants when you came through the door a little while ago, your hair's furrowed from her fingers, and I'd bet money you've got a few claw marks under your clothes, too." He paused, obviously savoring Tate's silent but furious reaction to his blunt observations. "Even without all that, I'd know by the look in your eyes."

"You're wasted on rodeo," Tate all but growled. "You ought to be with the CIA or something."

Austin smiled. "Is all this going somewhere?" he asked. "You and Libby, I mean?"

Tate sighed. "Damn if I know," he said. "It could have been just one of those things."

"Or not," Austin said.

"While we're reading each other's minds," Tate ventured, "I see by my crystal ball that you haven't been in rehab most of these long months, as you led the rest of us to believe. Who is she and how serious is it?"

Austin wore a muted version of his old devil's grin while he decided whether he wanted to answer or not. "She's a waitress in San Antonio," he revealed, after considerable pause, "and it's over."

"You still think about Paige Remington every once in a while?" Tate knew he was pushing his luck, but that was a McKettrick family tradition, so long established that it was probably hereditary by now.

Austin looked away. "Yeah, sometimes," he admitted, and Tate thought they were getting somewhere, for a moment or two. As if. "When that happens, I wear garlic around my neck and nail the doors and windows shut at night."

Tate decided to let the subject drop. Shoved a hand through his hair, pushed back his chair. "Guess I'll look in on the kids and then turn in for the night. You'd better do the same, because with Pablo's funeral coming up in a few days and people coming from half a dozen states to pay their respects, things are bound to get wild around here."

Austin nodded, stood up, ready to head for his wing of the house. "What about the stud, Tate? Why's he still on the place, after he trampled Pablo like that?"

Tate thought of his little girls, asleep upstairs, and wouldn't let himself imagine the things that could happen if the devil-stallion ever got out of that pen. "The state vet took blood samples. He'll decide whether the stallion ought to be put down or not when the paperwork comes back."

Austin huffed out a breath. "You know what Dad would have done," he said. "Taken a rifle out there and dropped that horse in his tracks with a single bullet to the brain."

"Granddad, maybe," Tate answered, shaking his head. "But not Dad. What happened to Pablo was an *accident,* Austin. Something spooked the stud, just as Pablo went to lead him down the ramp from the trailer and through the corral gate. Anyhow, you know Pablo wouldn't want him destroyed."

Austin reflected a few moments. "You know I hate to see any animal put down if there's a choice, Tate," he said, his eyes clear as he met his brother's gaze, "but sometimes it has to be done."

"I know that," Tate said, though maybe he sounded a little peevish.

Austin's grin flashed; mercurial changes were a way of life with him. "I could ride that paint," he said. "Settle him down a little."

"The hell you will," Tate snapped, because grin or no grin, he knew the chances were 80 percent or better that his brother wasn't kidding. "Buzzsaw damn near killed you, and now you want to give that crazy stud a shot at breaking your neck?"

"Good ole Buzzsaw," Austin replied. "If it's the last thing I ever do, I'll ride that son-of-a-bitch to the buzzer. I'll trail him from rodeo to rodeo if I have to, but I'll draw him and I'll ride him."

Tate went cold, through and through. "You can't be serious," he marveled. "You get on that bull again, and it *will* be the last thing you ever do."

"It's the principle of the thing," Austin said.

"Like hell it is," Tate argued, with more heat than he thought he had in him after all those go-rounds with Libby. "It's your dumb-ass McKettrick pride. You're a world champion, several times over, so there's nothing more to prove. Every cowboy gets thrown sooner or later, and Buzzsaw isn't the first bull to pitch you into the dirt, so why not let well enough alone?"

"There *is* something to prove," Austin countered quietly. "To myself."

Tate shook his head. "What? That you're certifiable?"

Austin looked Tate directly in the eyes. "I've never been scared of anything much in my life," he said. "But I'm scared of that bull. And that's something I can't live with, Tate. You know what Dad always said—if you get thrown from a horse, you'd better get right back on, because if you don't, the chances are good you never will."

Tate's gut clenched. He was the eldest; he'd always been the protector. Austin had just announced that he planned to commit suicide, and short of using some kind of unlawful imprisonment, Tate wouldn't be able to stop him.

Still, he couldn't let it drop. "Dad was talking about cow ponies, Austin," he reasoned, "not devil-bulls with blood in their eye."

Austin shrugged one shoulder. "Buzzsaw will be in the finals in Vegas this December, and so will I. There's got to be a showdown. And I'll draw him for my ride, because it's meant to be that way."

"Unless you don't enter," Tate said, chilled. "And you're a damn fool if you do."

"I've been called a lot worse," Austin answered. And then he turned and walked away from Tate, on his way to the stairs leading to his private living space on the second floor.

For a long time, Tate just stood there, his jawline tight, his fists bunched at his sides. At the moment, unlawful imprisonment looked like a viable option.

Then he shut out the lights and went upstairs.

Audrey and Ava were asleep in their beds, with one dog each curled up at their feet.

Quietly, he approached, straightening Audrey's covers and then Ava's, kissing each of them lightly on the forehead, so they wouldn't wake up.

Cheryl would be back in a few days, he thought, trying to resign himself to giving up his daughters again. Renewed by her time away from Blue River, she'd have rearmed herself, come up with new arguments for why the twins ought to compete in the Pixie Pageant. She'd work hard to wear him down; she probably knew the effort was destined for failure, but that would only inspire her to get sneaky.

And Cheryl was real good at sneaky.

Audrey stirred in the midst of some dream, gave a soft sigh.

Her mother's daughter, she'd been working on him over the past few days, angling for his permission to enter the pageant, just as Ava had warned that she would. *Was* he just being bull-headed, refusing to sign, as Cheryl said?

Little-girl pageants offended him—he hated the costumes and the emphasis on looks—but surely they weren't *all* bad. Otherwise-sensible people—he did not include Cheryl in that category—allowed their kids to participate. Seemed to view it as a confidence builder, like playing on a soccer team or something.

Sure, there were few winners and a lot of losers, but that was life, wasn't it?

On top of all that, this particular shindig was local, not a stopover on the pageant circuit. They were holding it at the

Blue River Country Club, a place as familiar to him as the post office or the feed store.

Maybe he'd been wrong, made the decision too quickly.

Audrey opened her eyes just then, smiled up at him. "Hi, Daddy," she said sleepily.

"Hello, sweetheart," he said, his voice coming out hoarse. This fathering business, he reflected, was not for cowards. You made one hard decision and there was another one coming along right behind it.

"Did you have fun at Libby's house?" his daughter asked, stretching.

Ava, in the next bed, slept on, dead to the world.

"Sure did," Tate told her.

"Esperanza cried all night," Audrey confided, worried. "I don't think she's ever going to stop."

Tate's throat tightened, aching right along with his heart. He could only shield his daughters from the hard realities, like death, for so long. "She'll probably do that for a while," he said quietly, leaning to kiss her forehead again. "But things will get better in time, you'll see."

Audrey nodded, yawned and closed her eyes. "'Night," she murmured.

Tate made as little noise as he could, leaving the room and closing the door behind him, assailed by the knowledge that while things *would* eventually get better, they might just get a whole lot worse first.

CHAPTER EIGHT

WHEN SATURDAY AFTERNOON rolled around, every business in town was closed for Pablo's funeral. Esperanza, Tate and both his brothers were among the first to arrive at the small Catholic church that would soon be bulging with mourners from every walk of life.

Since Cheryl had arrived home that morning, a day early and in a weirdly tractable state of mind, Tate had reluctantly allowed her to take the kids back to her place ahead of time. An open-casket funeral was no place for a couple of six-year-olds; they wouldn't understand about Pablo lying there in a box, still and waxy in the suit he'd bought to wear to his daughter's graduation from medical school.

A furious ache grabbed at Tate's heart as he walked slowly up the center aisle to pay his respects before the service got started. He and his brothers, along with one of Pablo's nephews and two of Isabel's, would be the pallbearers when it was time to carry the coffin outside to the hearse parked squarely in front of the churchyard gate.

There would be no graveside ceremony. Pablo had long ago arranged to be cremated, and despite church regulations he'd left written instructions with Isabel that he wanted his ashes spread on the Silver Spur, where he'd lived and worked and raised his children. When she'd shared that request with Tate, he'd called to make the arrangements.

Up close, Pablo fulfilled all the funereal clichés. He looked natural, as though he were merely sleeping, and his expression was strangely peaceful, but when Tate touched his friend's hand, he felt a chill so cold it burned like dry ice.

"We'll look after Isabel, Pablo," Tate said, in a ragged whisper. "We'll see that she and the kids have everything they need."

A hand landed on Tate's right shoulder, and he was startled, since he hadn't heard anyone approaching. He turned to see Brent standing behind him, Denzel-handsome in a freshly pressed uniform.

"This isn't your fault, old buddy," Brent said. His intuition was a force to be reckoned with; sometimes it seemed to Tate that his friend could read minds.

"If only I hadn't told Pablo I'd buy that stud if it went up for sale," Tate answered. Isabel had just arrived, a small, veiled figure, surrounded by sons and daughters and sisters and cousins and solicitous friends. "I should have been out there to help unload that horse. Would have been, if Pablo had just called to let me know he was bringing him in."

Brent dropped his hand to his side. "I've got some regrets myself," he said. "Sooner or later, you've got to let go of the if-onlys, Tate, because you'll go crazy if you don't."

Tate nodded; he was familiar with his friend's regrets, most of which centered around his young wife, who'd been shot in a scuffle on the concourse of an outdoor mall. He left Brent beside the casket and made his way to the front pew, where the Ruizes were settling in. Nico, the eldest son, lithe and dark and intense as a matador, put out his hand in greeting. Back when they were all kids, Nico had spent a lot of time at the main ranch house with Tate and his brothers, but over the years, they'd drifted apart.

"Thanks for being here, Tate," Nico said, swallowing hard to control his emotions.

Tate would have traveled from any part of the planet to say goodbye to Pablo Ruiz, and Nico knew that. Saying thanks was just a formality.

Tate nodded, too choked up to speak.

Isabel, already seated, her face nearly invisible behind the layers of black netting comprising her veil, put out her frail hands to Tate, and he squeezed them with his own, felt her trembling. He nodded to Mercedes, who was weeping silently, and the younger boys, Juan and Ricardo. They were still in high school, Tate knew, and the luminous sorrow in their nearly black eyes tore at him.

How well he remembered the ache of that bleak and fathomless loss of a parent—he still felt it sometimes, when he was riding alone on the range, along trails he'd traveled so many times with his dad, or when he saw women around his mother's age, dressed up for church or some luncheon out at the country club. Sally McKettrick had dearly loved any occasion that gave her an excuse to wear a splashy hat, a pastel suit and high heels.

Some change in the atmosphere made Tate scan the pews as he left the Ruizes, intending to take his place alongside Esperanza and his brothers and brace himself to get through all that was to come.

His gaze settled on Libby—he hadn't seen her since the night they'd skipped supper to make love—and even in those grim circumstances, she warmed something inside him. Her dress was navy blue and her hair swept away from her face, caught up in back with some kind of clip. Julie stood next to her, clad in dramatic black, and Paige was there, too, wearing a dark brown pantsuit, her short cap of glossy black hair catching colored light from the stained-glass windows.

Tate took a step toward the three sisters, his attention focused solely on Libby, but the aisle was already crowded, and he couldn't get through.

"Tate," he heard Esperanza whisper. "Here we are."

He looked to his right, saw the housekeeper sitting in a nearby pew, between Garrett and Austin, who appeared to be supporting her with the pressure of their shoulders. Garrett studied the Remington women as they found places and sat down, but Austin stared straight ahead, with determined disinterest, toward the altar and Pablo's gleaming casket.

Just before Tate joined the others in their pew, Libby's gaze found and connected with his. Nothing in her expression changed—he might have been a total stranger instead of the man who had so recently shared her bed—but an invisible cord seemed to stretch between them, drawing taut and then snapping back on Tate with an impact that made him blink.

He took a seat next to his family.

Other mourners crowded into the church, and it got so warm, even with the laboring air-conditioning system, that people began to sweat. The organist took her place and sonorous music joined with the oppressive heat, creating a humid stew of sound.

Tate longed to loosen his tie, but out of respect for Pablo and the Ruiz kin, he refrained.

Altar boys appeared, carrying lighted candles, followed by Father Rodriguez, a slight, trundling man who moved like one carrying an enormous weight on his narrow shoulders.

A pregnant woman toward the front fainted, and there was a brief flurry while she was revived with smelling salts and led out of the sanctuary by a side door. Esperanza, who had been weeping for days, sat dry-eyed now, all cried out except for the occasional sniffle. Although she had liked Pablo, as had everyone else for miles around, Tate knew the bulk of her grief was reserved for Isabel, left a widow with two children still at home.

Esperanza had lost a husband, too, before she left Mexico as a relatively young woman, but if she had kids of her own, she had never mentioned them to Tate. A woman of benevolent and unflagging faith, she believed both her own lost love and Pablo Ruiz were safe in heaven, and that those forced to go on alone were the ones to be pitied.

Although Tate wasn't sure there was such a place as heaven, he hoped so. Hoped his folks and Pablo and Crockett, his old dog, were all together somewhere, in some bright and painless place where there were horses to ride and plenty of green grass for their grazing.

Father Rodriguez conducted Mass in solemn Latin—no doubt Pablo, an old-fashioned Catholic, had wanted it that way—and then various people took their turns going up front to say a few words about Pablo. Tate was among them, as were Garrett and Austin. He was never able to remember, after that day, exactly what he'd said—only that he'd gotten through the brief speech without losing his composure.

It had been a close one, though.

After him, Libby rose, made her way to the microphone, and told the sweltering congregation, her voice trembling, how Pablo had come to the Remington house faithfully, every single week after her father got sick, how he'd mowed the lawn and weeded and raked the flower beds and fixed whatever needed repair, from the rain gutters to the washing machine. She honestly didn't know, she said, what they would have done without him.

The story stung Tate in some deep and tender place, one he'd never explored.

The townspeople had rallied to help the Remingtons in every possible way. Had *he* done anything?

His gut roiled with the guilt he'd never been able to shake.

Oh, yeah. He'd done something, all right. Far from home, overwhelmed by the demands of law school and, most of all, missing Libby, he'd gotten drunk at a party and wound up in bed with Cheryl. Gotten her pregnant, for good measure.

Tate lowered his head.

Garrett, sitting beside him, nudged him back to the here-and-now with a motion of one elbow.

Having completed her short eulogy, Libby returned to her pew and sat down, and someone else got up to speak.

The service ended after two full hours, and Tate, Garrett and Austin joined Pablo and Isabel's nephews up front.

The coffin's bright brass handles gleamed. The lid was lowered, and one of the Ruiz women cried out then, a piercing, anguished sound—and the organist began the recessional.

Red, yellow and blue light from the stained-glass windows played over the mounds of white flowers draped across the top of the casket as the six men carried it down the aisle, toward the dazzle of afternoon sunshine at the open doors.

The casket, surprisingly light, was loaded carefully into the back of the hearse. People streamed out of the church, milled in the yard and on the sidewalk, talking in quiet voices, some of them wiping their eyes with wadded handkerchiefs, others hugging, consoling each other. Some smiled through their tears, perhaps remembering how Pablo had loved to tell stupid jokes, or share the produce from his garden, or drop off a pan of Isabel's fine enchiladas when they were sick or out of a job or mourning the loss of a loved one.

Isabel, Nico and Mercedes and the boys accepted hugs and handshakes and exhortations to call if they needed anything at all, and looked profoundly relieved when the funeral director steered them toward a waiting limousine. They were settled quickly inside, and then gone.

Tate looked around for Libby, the way a man might look for water when his throat was parched, found her standing under an oak tree, dappled in sun and shadow, Paige and Julie close by as always. They spoke quietly to friends, and though they bore little resemblance to each other, Tate knew it would have been clear even to a stranger that they were related. Something indefinable bound them together, made them a unit.

The heat was oppressive, but somehow, Libby looked cool as a mountain spring in that dark blue dress. Once in a while, her gaze strayed to Tate, only to bounce away again when their eyes met.

By tacit agreement—because that was the way things were done in places like Blue River, Texas—folks waited and foot-shuffled and fanned themselves with their simply printed programs, giving Isabel and her brood plenty of time to get home and get settled before they began stopping by with the ritual salads and spiral-cut hams and bakery goods. Personal condolences would be offered and graciously received, along with sympathy cards containing checks of varying size.

However much Isabel and the others might have preferred to be alone with each other and their memories of Pablo, the gathering at the modest house beside the winding creek was as important as the funeral. There would be a guestbook, and sooner or later, when she'd emerged from the haze of bereavement, Isabel would examine it, page by page, taking in the names of all those who'd cared.

With the throng still clogging the path between himself and Libby, Tate saw no way to get to her without shouldering his way through. So he shook hands with neighboring ranchers, kissed the cheeks of his mother's friends, and waited.

Finally, when he'd decided that enough time had passed, Father Rodriguez got into his dusty compact car to drive out to the Ruiz house, with Esperanza to keep him company on the way.

Maybe, Tate thought, he'd get a chance to talk to Libby over postfuneral coffee and a paper plate heaped with food he didn't want. On the other hand, she might have written their encounter off as a lapse of judgment and decided to steer clear from there on out.

Nobody would have blamed her for that, least of all Tate himself.

JULIE TOOK THE WHEEL of the pink Cadillac, while Libby claimed the passenger seat and Paige slipped into the back.

"For God's sake," Paige said distractedly, "turn on the air-conditioning. It's hot as hell's kitchen in here."

Julie complied, casting a brief glance in Libby's direction.

An understanding passed between them, no words necessary.

Paige, as upset over Pablo Ruiz's death as any of them, had spent most of the service trying not to look at Austin McKettrick and failing visibly.

Libby rolled down her window and fluttered the church bulletin under her chin. "Austin looks good," she commented, keeping her voice light, "for somebody who tangled with a bull not all that long ago."

"He's an idiot," Paige said, with a dismissive tone that didn't fool either of her sisters. They well remembered that, although Paige had been the one to end things with Austin, she'd grieved for months afterward.

Libby and Julie exchanged glances again, but Julie had to navigate the after-funeral traffic, so she quickly turned her attention back to the road.

"If only all idiots were that good-looking," Julie contributed. "How many guys have a whole calendar devoted just to pictures of them?"

"Shallow," Paige retorted, though she owned the calendar in question. "A Year of Austin," it was titled—she kept it pinned to the laundry room wall at her place, even though it was out of date, open to July and the image of her favorite cowboy riding a wild bull and wearing a stars-and-stripes shirt. "Austin McKettrick is *shallow*. And he'll never grow up."

"He looks pretty grown up to me," Libby observed, with a slight smile.

Julie made an eloquent little sound, part growl and part purr.

"Shut up," Paige said, peevish. "Do we have to go out to the Ruizes' place? It will be jammed, and it's so hot. I'd rather go back to your house and keep Calvin and the dog company."

"Of *course* we have to go to the Ruizes'," Julie answered, in her big-sister voice, waving to people walking along the sidewalk. "How would it look if we didn't at least stop by? And it isn't as if Calvin and Harry are home alone. Mrs. Erskine is looking after them until we get back."

Paige sighed. She could be dramatic at times—especially when she knew she might come face-to-face with the man she'd dumped before starting nursing school. "I can't believe Pablo is gone," she said. "I just saw him at the post office a few days ago. He told me some silly knock-knock joke."

The caravan of cars and pickup trucks wound out of Blue

River into the countryside; Libby imagined how it would look from high overhead—like a big metal snake.

She shifted in the seat, rolled her window back up when the AC finally kicked in. A sort of delicious unease stirred in her as she recalled making love with Tate—she both dreaded and anticipated seeing him again, up close and personal. Which meant she had no business remarking on Paige's reluctant fascination with Austin at the funeral.

"Why do things like this happen?" Libby asked, knowing there was no real answer.

"Good question," Julie said, with a little shudder. "What an awful way to die."

A silence fell, and a replay of their dad's lingering death flashed in Libby's mind. He'd been heavily sedated, in no physical pain to speak of, at least toward the end, but he'd suffered just the same, she'd seen that in his eyes. A proud man enduring the indignities of a failing body.

Her own eyes burned, though they were dry, and her throat tightened until it ached. Julie, who always seemed to know what she was thinking, reached over to pat her arm.

It wasn't far to the part of the Silver Spur where Pablo and Isabel had made their home for so many years, but the ride seemed interminable that day. Dust boiled up off the winding country roads, sometimes rendering the vehicles ahead all but invisible.

No more was said about Pablo's death, or about unfortunate romantic attachments to certain men. Of the three of them, Julie was the only one unscathed by the legendary McKettrick charm, though, of course, she had demons of her own.

Gordon Pruett, Calvin's biological father, for instance.

Julie and Libby talked about the pros and cons of going into business together, turning the Perk Up into a café, but the conversation was dispirited, stopping and starting at odd times, when one or the other of them remembered why they were driving to the Silver Spur.

They were neither the first nor the last to arrive—there were cars and trucks everywhere, parked at strange angles at the edges of the Ruizes' expansive lawn. Julie found a place for the Cadillac, wedged it in and thrust out a sigh of resignation.

"Here goes," she said, shutting off the engine and shoving open her door.

The engine went through the usual sequence of clicks and clatters as it wound down.

Libby unsnapped her seat belt and climbed out, too, teetering a little because the ground was uneven and she wasn't accustomed to wearing high heels—she owned exactly one pair, relics of her high school prom—but Paige didn't move at all.

Bending her knees slightly, Libby rapped on the car window.

"I'm coming," Paige called testily, but she remained still.

The yard was crowded with people, most of them helping themselves to bottles of water jutting from metal tubs full of ice or food set out on long, portable tables tended by ladies from Isabel and Pablo's church.

Libby followed her sister's gaze and spotted Austin at the center of things, shaggy-haired but clean-shaven, and spruced up in a suit he probably wore as seldom as possible.

"Come on, Paige," she urged, growing impatient. She wanted to get on with it, so she could go home, peel off her sweaty clothes and the pantyhose that were chafing the insides of her thighs and take a long, cool shower, and the only way to get there was *through* the next stage of the ordeal. "Austin isn't going to bite you."

"That," Julie remarked, just loudly enough for Paige to hear her through the car window, "might be the problem."

Paige's pale, perfect complexion pulsed with pink. She thrust open the door and got out, glaring at Julie, who was characteristically unfazed. She linked arms with Paige, Libby taking the other side, and the three of them forged ahead.

They found Isabel first, and offered their condolences.

They signed the guestbook, and then joined the crowd on the lawn, accepting plates brimming with food they would only nibble at.

They would *circulate,* like the well-mannered Texas women they were, and make their escape at the customary signal from Libby. She was and always had been constitutionally incapable of standing in green grass without taking off her shoes; when she slipped them back on, everyone would say their farewells and converge on the car.

Libby couldn't have missed Tate, even if she'd tried. He towered over almost everyone else gathered in the Ruiz yard, his hair blue-black in the afternoon sunshine. Aware that he was making his way toward her, pausing to speak to this one and that one, Libby surrendered to the inevitable and waited, her shoes dangling by their narrow straps from her left index finger, her plate sagging in her right hand.

"Pretty good turnout," he said, when he reached her. Tate had never been good at small talk.

"Yes," Libby agreed simply, not inclined to make things easy for him.

Color flared up in his neck and under his jawline, then subsided. "About what happened—"

Libby raised both eyebrows, pretending confusion. As if she hadn't practically dragged the man to bed and then carried on like a she-wolf in heat while he did all the right things to her.

"Dammit, Libby," he muttered, onto the game, "knock off the deer-in-the-headlights routine. This is hard enough."

The phrase *hard enough* made an inappropriate giggle bubble into the back of her throat. She barely swallowed it in time.

"I assume," she said, with false ease, "you're referring to our having sex?"

"Will you keep your voice down?" Tate said, on a rush of breath.

"If I remember correctly," she continued, in an exaggerated whisper, having already made certain no one was close enough to overhear, "we *did* have sex."

"I'm not denying that," Tate snapped.

"Why bring it up?" Libby asked mildly, knowing full well why he'd mentioned the tryst. He wanted to make sure she understood that the encounter had been meaningless, a fling. She mustn't expect anything more.

"Because," Tate said, leaning in close, his forehead nearly touching hers, "things have changed."

The statement took Libby by surprise, and when she widened her eyes and raised her brows this time, she wasn't pretending. "Changed?" she echoed stupidly.

Tate took her by the elbow, the one on the left, with the shoes dangling from the corresponding finger, and hustled her away from the gathering to stand in the small orchard, under one of Pablo's cherished apricot trees. She looked around, spotted Julie arguing quietly with Garrett, and Paige and Austin standing with their backs to each other, not a dozen feet apart, both of them stiff-spined.

Clearly, neither of her sisters would ride to her rescue.

"Tate, what…?"

"Stop it," Tate rasped. "*Something happened,* Libby, and I'm not going to pretend it didn't."

Another giggle, this one hysterical, tried to escape Libby, but she dropped her shoes and put her hand over her mouth to keep it in.

Tate let out his breath, and his broad shoulders sagged a little under the fine fabric of the tailored suit he was sweltering in. Once again, Libby imagined a cold shower, but this time Tate joined her in the fantasy, and the resulting surge of heat nearly melted her knees.

"I want another chance with you," he said, stunning her so thoroughly that he might as well have aimed a Taser gun at her and pulled the trigger. Shoving a hand through his hair, he sighed again. "I know I don't deserve it," he went on. "But I'm asking for another shot."

The plate fell from Libby's hand, potato salad and cold chicken and something made with green gelatin and sliced bananas plopping at their feet. Both of them ignored it.

"*What?*" Libby sputtered, amazed.

An expression of proud misery moved in Tate's strong face, was gone again in an instant. "A simple 'no' would do," he said. Maybe the misery had gone, but the famous McKettrick pride was still there.

"You—you mean, it wasn't—well—just one of those things?" Libby managed.

"'Just one of those things'?" His tone was almost scathing. "Maybe you have that kind of sex all the time, Lib, but *I don't.*"

This round, the giggle got past all her defenses. It was a shaky sound, a little raspy. "You think I have sex all the time?" she asked, only too aware that she was prattling and completely unable to help herself. Whenever sex and Tate

McKettrick occupied the same conversation, or even the same thought, her IQ seemed to plummet. Incensed by this sudden realization, she raised both hands, palms out, and shoved them hard into Tate's chest. *"You think I have sex all the time?"*

Through the haze surrounding her, Libby sensed that heads were turning.

She caught a glimpse of Julie hurrying in their direction. Paige was probably on the way, too.

"Dammit, Libby," Tate almost barked, "this is a *wake.*"

Libby shoved him again, and then again. Enjoyed a brief mental movie in which he tumbled backward and landed on his fine McKettrick ass under Pablo's apricot trees.

Tate proved immovable, though, since he was so much bigger than she was. Just as Julie reached them, he grasped Libby's wrists to stay the blows.

"Look," he ground out, "that didn't come out right. I meant—"

Libby felt dazed, literally beside herself. Her heart pounded, and she was sure she was hyperventilating.

Julie stooped to snatch up Libby's shoes. "Time to go," she chimed.

Slowly, Tate released his hold on Libby. "I'm sorry," he said.

Libby stared at him, nearly blinded by tears. Didn't resist when Julie tugged her away, keeping to the edge of the crowd.

Paige caught up, double-stepping.

"What just happened here?" Julie asked moderately, when they were all in the car.

Before, the blast of cool hair from the vents on Julie's dashboard had been a blessed relief; now, it made Libby hug herself and shiver. Her lower lip wobbled, and she couldn't bring herself to look at her sister.

"I'm not sure," Libby said brokenly, but only after Julie had put the Cadillac into Reverse, stepped on the gas and negotiated a series of complicated maneuvers, involving a lot of backing up, inching forward and backing up again. "Things just—got out of hand."

"I'll say," Paige commented, from the back seat.

Fresh mortification washed over Libby. "Please tell me we weren't yelling."

"You weren't yelling," Julie said.

"Really? Or are you just saying that?"

Julie chuckled. "Honey, neither of you *had* to yell. The air crackled like it does before a good ole Texas lightning storm. From the looks of things, the two of you were either going to kill each other or make a baby on the spot."

Libby slid down in the seat, horrified. "Oh, my God," she moaned.

"McKettrick men," Paige offered calmly, "can turn a sane woman crazy."

Tate's words came back to Libby. *This is a wake.*

"Isabel will never forgive me," she said.

"Isabel," Julie soothed, in her practical way, "was inside the house by the time hostilities broke out, lying down with a cold cloth over her eyes. And don't look now, but sparks flying between you and the McKettricks' number one son aren't exactly breaking news around these parts."

Libby's embarrassment was now total. How would she face people after making such a scene? What had come over her?

She tried to retrace the conversation in her mind, to pinpoint exactly where she'd stepped on a land mine, but it was all a nonsensical jumble of he said/she said.

Except that Tate had basically accused her of being promiscuous.

Hadn't he?

"This is it," Libby decided aloud, as they bumped over the rutted dirt road leading back toward the highway. "I'm leaving town forever. I'll change my name, dye my hair—"

Paige unhooked her seat belt and poked her head between the front seats. "Don't be silly," she said. "Everybody makes a complete and utter fool of themselves now and then."

"Gee," Libby nearly snarled, "*that* was a comforting thing to say."

"If it's any consolation," Paige pressed on, undaunted, "Tate looked as if he wished the ground would open up and swallow him."

"It isn't," Libby replied.

"Let's not bicker," Julie interjected.

"We're *not* bickering," Paige bickered. "I was merely stating a fact. Playing the fool once in a while is only human."

"Paige?" Julie said sweetly.

"What?"

"Shut the hell up."

Paige sagged backward, fastened her seat belt back with a metallic snap, grumbling something under her breath.

"*You* never made a fool of yourself," Libby accused her youngest sister, her gaze colliding with Paige's in the rear-view mirror. "Miss Perfect."

Paige rolled her eyes. "You've got a short memory," she shot back. "I tried to run Austin McKettrick over with a golf cart once, if you'll recall."

"Chased him right down Main Street," Julie reminisced fondly. "Good thing he was so quick on his feet."

"Shut up," Paige said.

"That was my line," Julie answered.

Libby began to laugh. Like the giggles she'd battled earlier, this laughter was more a release of tension than amusement Still, it *had* been funny, watching Austin sprint down the white line, sometimes backward, laughing at Paige as she swerved behind him at lawn-mower speed.

Austin had finally taken refuge on the courthouse steps, gasping for breath, and Paige had plainly intended to drive right up after him. Fortunately, she'd commandeered a golf cart instead of an army tank—the front wheels bumped hard against the bottom stair and then the engine died. *Un*fortunately, she'd nearly been arrested and would probably have gone to jail for attempted assault if Austin hadn't refused to press charges.

"Okay," Libby admitted, turning to look back at Paige, "there was that one lapse. But I've never seen you lose your temper, before or since, which makes me wonder if you're an alien or something."

"Some of us," Julie remarked loftily, "have sense enough not to get involved with a McKettrick in the first place."

"Oh, for Pete's sake." Paige scoffed. "I saw you shaking your finger beneath Garrett's nose back there. If he wanted to get under your skin, he could—it's a gift. They all have it."

"Please," Julie said, gliding up to a Stop sign pocked with bulletholes, a common sight in that part of Texas, and signaling a left turn before swinging that big pink boat out onto the asphalt to head for town. "Me and *Garrett McKettrick?* The man is a *politician.* You know what I think of *that* species."

"He's also good-looking in the extreme," Libby pointed out.

"Not to mention McKettrick-rich," Paige added.

"He's a player," Julie went on. "God knows how many women he's stringing along."

Again, Libby's gaze connected with Paige's in the rearview mirror.

"Uh-oh," Paige said.

"I don't care about looks," Julie insisted. "*Or* money. Garrett McKettrick is definitely not my type."

"What *is* your type?" Libby asked, glad to be talking about something besides the debacle with Tate, back there in the Ruizes' orchard.

"I don't have one," Julie said. "I've resigned myself to being single. In fact, I *like* being single. Calvin and I are doing just fine on our own, thank you very much. The last thing we need is a man complicating our lives."

"What about sex?" Paige asked. "Don't you miss that?"

Libby began to feel overheated again. Why did *sex* have to come up in every conversation? She went months without thinking about the subject at all—much—and now it seemed to be in her face every time she turned around. What was up with that?

"You don't have to be married," Julie reminded her sisters, "to enjoy sex."

"No," Paige agreed, "but a *man* helps."

Libby's face flamed as her flesh prickled with remembered sensations: Tate's mouth on her neck, on the insides of her elbows and the backs of her knees, on her—well, *everywhere.*

"Don't tell me you're using a vibrator," Paige said, like it was a crime or something. "You're still young, Julie. You need a man."

Julie's neck was bright red. "Who said anything about a vibrator?" she snapped. "And how do you know I'm not having a wild, passionate affair? I do have *some* secrets from you two, after all."

"No, you don't," Paige replied smugly. "If you were seeing someone, I'd know it, and so would everybody else in Blue River."

Here it comes. Libby bit down on her lower lip, closed her eyes.

But Paige was on a roll. "That's the problem with small towns," she went on mercilessly. "When somebody goes to bed with somebody else—" here, she paused for effect "—word gets around in no time. Take Libby and Tate, for instance."

Libby winced.

"Libby," Julie said, sounding intrigued, as well as shocked, *"you didn't."*

"Oh, yes, she did," Paige trilled, the triumphant little sister avenging a multitude of childhood slights.

Libby covered her face with both hands and groaned.

"Is this true?" Julie asked slowly.

Libby would gladly have violated a lifetime of principles just then and lied like a pro, but she knew both her sisters would see right through it. They knew each other too well.

"Yes," she said, after a very long time. "Yes, I slept with Tate McKettrick. Are you satisfied?"

"No," Julie said succinctly. "But I'll bet *you* were."

CHAPTER NINE

As FAR AS TATE was concerned, the house was just too damn big.

He knew Garrett and Austin were around, but they were keeping to themselves, and with the kids back at Cheryl's place and Esperanza helping with the clean-up over at the Ruizes', Tate might as well have been alone on the planet.

Except, of course, for Ambrose and Buford.

Most likely missing the twins, the pups had found his best work boots next to the back door and systematically chewed them to pieces.

With a pang, he thought of Crockett. As a pup, his old dog had had a penchant for chewing boots, too. And Charlie, one of Crockett's many predecessors, had reduced a custom-made pair, Tate's dad's pride and joy, to shreds.

Tate recalled how scared he'd been. Another kid's father had shot a dog for a far lesser crime, and even though Jim McKettrick, a strict but fair father, had never raised a hand to any of his sons or their mother, Tate had been sure his beloved dog was facing immediate execution.

Eight years old at the time, he'd left home with Charlie, the two of them headed overland in the general direction of Oklahoma, going by the compass he'd gotten for Christmas. He was lugging the dog's plastic food bowl and a rolled-

up sleeping bag and not much else, with no specific destination in mind.

His dad caught up to them on horseback about an hour
into the journey, probably tipped off by one of the ranch
hands. On a busy spread like the Silver Spur, it was hard for
a kid to get away with much of anything since somebody
was always watching, ready to run off at the mouth at the
first opportunity.

"Where you headed?" Jim had asked, almost casually,
pulling his well-worn hat down low over his eyes and shifting easily in the saddle. His big chestnut gelding snorted,
peeved at being reined in when he'd rather be punching
cattle.

Tears had welled up in Tate's eyes; all those years later,
he could feel the burn of them, a sort of dry, scalding sensation. "Me and Charlie figured we ought to leave," he'd
answered, dropping his head for a moment before meeting
Jim's steady gaze. "Charlie went and chewed up your good
boots—the ones Mom had made for your birthday, with our
brand and the Alamo and the flag of the Republic on them."

Jim had taken off his hat then, run the sleeve of his sweat-
stained chambray shirt across his face and leaned forward a
little, resting one forearm on the saddle horn. "I see," he'd
said quietly, before putting the hat back on. "And you reckoned that lighting out on your own was the best course of
action?"

Tate had swallowed hard. Now, he was going to be in
trouble for running away, he guessed, on top of Charlie
taking a bullet in the head out behind the barn. Having no
answer at hand, he'd simply looked up at his father and
waited forlornly for the collapse of the known universe.

Jim had sighed, swung one leg over the gelding's neck,

and jumped to the ground. Approaching Tate and the dog, he'd crouched to ruffle Charlie's mismatched ears, one a grayish-brown, one white. A stray who'd shown up at the ranch one day with his ribs showing and his multicolored coat full of burrs, Charlie wasn't much to look at, but except for boot-chewing, he pretty much behaved himself.

"Look at me, boy," Jim had said, his voice gentle.

Tate had met his father's fierce blue gaze. "You gonna shoot Charlie, Dad?" he'd asked.

"Now why in the devil would I do a thing like that?"

"That's what Ryan Williams's dad did when their dog wrecked the new carpet."

"Well, son," Jim had drawled reasonably, still sitting on his haunches, "I'm not Ryan Williams's dad, now am I? I'm yours."

Tate's heartbeat had quickened, and he'd almost flung himself into his father's arms before he remembered that he was eight years old and too big for that kind of stuff. "I guess I'm still in trouble, though?"

Jim had looked away, probably to hide a grin. "I guess you are," he'd answered presently. "Running away from home is a dangerous thing to do, Tate. Your mother is half frantic, calling all over the countryside looking for you."

"How about Charlie? Is he in any trouble?"

Jim had chuckled then. Stood up tall, with the sun behind him. "Charlie's in the clear. Dogs chew things up sometimes, because they don't know any better. You, on the other hand, don't have that excuse. You *do* know better. You're going to have to do extra chores for a month, and you can forget that school field trip to Six Flags next week, because you won't be going along."

Tate had merely nodded, too relieved that Charlie was

going to be all right to care about staying behind when everybody else in the whole school went to Six Flags. He knew he'd care plenty when the time came, though.

His dad had laid a hand on his right shoulder. "Let's go on home now," he said, "before your mother calls in the FBI."

Tate had ridden back to the ranch house in front of Jim, clutching the dog bowl and the sleeping bag, Charlie trotting cheerfully alongside the horse.

Back in the present, Tate crouched the way his father had done that day. Ruffled one dog's ears, then the other's. "You're a pair to draw to," he said. "And this'll teach me to leave my boots by the back door when I come in from the range."

After that, he took the mutts outside.

They headed straight for the castle, sniffing the ground, probably trying to track Audrey and Ava.

Tate missed his daughters sorely as he watched their dogs searching for them. Even when he was a kid, broken homes were common, but he and his brothers had grown up under one roof, with parents who loved them and each other, and until the split with Cheryl, the concept had been foreign to him.

Now, he was all too familiar with it.

The dogs returned to him, tails wagging, taking their failure to scare up the twins in their stride. He wished he could accept the kids' absence as philosophically as the pups had.

When Garrett's black sports car zoomed backward out of the garage, Tate was so startled that he almost left his hide in a pool on the ground and stepped out of it like a pair of dirty jeans.

Seeing him, accurately reading the glower taking shape on his face like clouds gathering to dump a ground-pocking rain, Garrett winced. Rolled down his window.

"Sorry," he told Tate, with a sheepish grin.

Maybe if it hadn't been for Pablo's funeral and the way he'd blown things with Libby in the orchard and the kids being gone from home again, Tate would have held his temper. As things stood, though, his brother's careless mistake pushed him one step over the line.

Rounding the ridiculously expensive car, he slammed both fists down onto the shiny hood and glowered hard at Garrett through the bug-specked windshield.

"Hey!" Garrett protested, shoving open the driver's side door and piling out, face flushed, eyes flashing. "What the *hell*—"

Tate advanced on Garrett, seething. Gripped him by the front of his white dress shirt and hurled him back against the car. "Did you even glance in your rearview mirror before you shot out of that garage like a goddamm bullet?" he yelled. "What if one of the kids had been behind you, or one of these dogs?"

Garrett paled at the mention of possibilities he obviously hadn't considered.

Tate let his hands fall to his sides, stepped back out of his brother's space.

A few awkward beats of silence passed.

"You all right?" Garrett asked at last, his voice hoarse.

Tate looked away, didn't answer because anything he said would only make bad matters worse.

"Tate?" Garrett pressed, never one to leave well enough alone.

Tate met Garrett's gaze, held it steadily, still holding his tongue.

"Look," Garrett said, "I'll be more careful after this. It's been one hell of a day for all of us, and I guess I just wasn't thinking."

"You think this was a bad day?" Tate said, after grinding

his back molars together for a second or so. "That wouldn't begin to cover it if you'd killed somebody just now."

Garrett surveyed him. "I said I was sorry, Tate," he replied evenly. "I said I wouldn't make the same mistake a second time. What more do you want—a strip of my ornery McKettrick hide?"

"I'll have a lot more than a *strip* of your hide if you ever do a damn fool thing like that again."

Garrett sighed and straightened his shoulders, and Tate could almost see the politician in him coming to the fore. Trouble was, Garrett *wasn't* a politician, he was a rancher, though it looked like he was going to be the last one to figure that out. "Can we start over, here? Before we wind up rolling around in the dirt the way we did when we were kids?"

Tate thrust out a breath. Allowed himself a semblance of a smile at the memory of all those barnyard brawls. Their mother had broken up more than one by spraying her three sons with a garden hose. Their dad's method had been more direct: he'd simply waded into the middle of the fray, got them by the scruff and sent them tumbling in three different directions.

"Okay," he said. "Let's start over."

Garrett grinned. Then he got into his car, drove it into the garage and backed out again, covering about an inch per hour.

Watching Tate, he raised both eyebrows as if to say, *Satisfied?*

"Where were you headed in such a hurry, anyhow?" Tate asked.

"The senator," Garrett said, the grin gone, "is having an emergency."

"The senator," Tate replied, "is *always* having an emergency. What is it now? Did the press catch him naked in a hot tub with three bimbos again?"

"That," Garrett replied, stiff with indignation, "is not what happened."

"Right," Tate scoffed. It was a wonder to him how Garrett's famously incompetent boss and so-called mentor kept getting reelected to the U.S. Senate.

"You know what you are, Tate?" Garrett countered, scowling. "You're a sore loser. You voted for the opposition, they lost by a landslide and now you're raking up muck. I'm surprised at you."

Tate gripped the edge of the open window and stooped a little to look directly into his brother's face. "Pull your head out of your ass, Garrett," he said. "*The senator,* as you so augustly refer to him, is a crook—and that's his *best* quality. When are you going to stop cleaning up his messes and set about making some kind of life for yourself?"

"A life like yours?" Garrett retorted, his eyes fairly crackling with blue fire. "Playing the gentleman cowboy while a bunch of ranch hands do the real work? Don't kid yourself, Tate. You might be all grown up on the outside, but inside, you're still the rich kid from the biggest ranch in four counties, feeling like you ought to apologize to folks who have to earn a living. When the kids are with Cheryl, you just mark time until they come back. Maybe that looks like a life to you, but I'd call it something else."

Physically, Tate didn't move. On the inside, though, he pulled back, stunned by Garrett's words—and the sickening knowledge that they were at least partly true.

"Oh, hell," Garrett said, sounding pained. "I didn't mean that—"

"Sure you did," Tate broke in gruffly. "And maybe I had it coming."

Garrett started to open the car door, waited pointedly until

Tate got out of the way. "It wasn't your fault, what happened to Pablo," he said calmly, once he was on his feet again.

"Wasn't it?" Tate countered bitterly. "Pablo wasn't a young man. He shouldn't have been transporting that stallion on his own. *I'm* the one who thought it would be a good idea to breed ourselves some spotted ponies."

"And Pablo should have called you beforehand, let you know what was going on. You could have helped unload the horse, or arranged for someone else to make the delivery." Garrett paused, probably following the obvious mental trail, and frowned. "You might have been killed yourself, Tate."

Tate didn't reply. He was too busy imagining his girls with one parent—Cheryl. She'd have them in boarding school by puberty at the latest, and spend the bulk of her time trying to figure out how to get into their trust funds.

Garrett started to get back into the car. "I'd better get back to the capital," he said. "The senator has been under a lot of stress lately."

A sour taste filled Tate's mouth at the mention of the politician his brother revered so much, and he spat.

Garrett reddened. "His enemies are trying to discredit him," he said hotly. "The press dogs his every step and his older brother is dying of prostate cancer. Maybe you could cut the senator just a *little* slack."

"I'm sorry about his brother," Tate allowed. By his reckoning, the senator's other problems were his own doing.

Garrett glared. "The senator," he said, "is a truly great man."

Tate shook his head, resisted the need to spit again. "You've definitely got a blind spot where Morgan Cox is concerned, Garrett, whether you'll admit as much or not. What has to happen before you *get* it? You're climbing the ladder to success, all right, but it's up against the wrong wall."

"What you need," Garrett retorted furiously, after maybe thirty seconds of internal struggle, "is a woman. Maybe you'd have a better temperament than a grizzly with a bad toothache if you got laid. Why don't you go find yourself a lady again, and bang her, and get the burrs out from under your hide?"

Tate folded his arms. "I really hope," he said, "that that wasn't a reference to Libby Remington. Because if it was, I'm going to have to kick your ass from here to Houston and back."

A grin crooked up one corner of Garrett's mouth. The man, Tate reflected, was tired of living, egging him on like that. "Wait a second," Garrett said. "That little set-to the two of you had in the Ruizes' orchard this afternoon—"

"That was nothing," Tate said flatly, and without a hope in hell that Garrett would believe him.

"Damn," his brother went on, in the tone of the man enjoying a sudden revelation, "you could do a lot worse than Libby Remington. Come to think of it, you *did* do a lot worse than Libby Remington. Did I mention that I ran into Cheryl at a party in Austin the weekend before the twins' birthday?"

"No," Tate said. "Maybe you didn't mention it because you know I don't give a rat's ass what Cheryl does, as long as she takes good care of my kids when they're with her."

Garrett snapped his fingers. "Maybe that was it," he said, clearly delighted to be nettling Tate.

"In about another second," Tate replied, "I'm going to wipe up the ground with you, little brother."

Garrett removed his cuff links, rolled up his sleeves. "Bring it on," he said.

That was when the spray struck them, ice cold and shining like liquid crystal in the last light of a long, difficult day.

Both of them roared in surprised protest and whirled

around to find Austin standing a few yards away, holding the garden hose and grinning like an idiot with a winning lottery ticket in his pocket.

"Peace, brothers," he said, and drenched them completely with another pass of the hose.

Water shot through the open window of Garrett's car and made a sound like fire on the fancy leather seats, then sluiced down the inside of the windshield.

Tate laughed out loud, but Garrett bellowed with rage and advanced on Austin, dripping wet, ready to fight.

Tate went after their kid brother, too, but for a different reason.

Water fights were something of a McKettrick tradition, and it had been way too long since the last one.

JULIE SEEMED A LITTLE TROUBLED when she and Paige dropped Libby off in the alley behind the house they'd all grown up in.

"Are you sure you won't come home with us for supper?" she asked. "My special spaghetti casserole has been simmering in the slow cooker all day and Calvin would love to see you."

Libby, standing by her back gate with the straps of her high heels in one hand and her clutch purse tucked under the opposite arm, shook her head and smiled. "I'd love to see Calvin," she said sincerely, "but Hildie needs a walk, and I plan on getting to bed early tonight. The sooner I fall asleep, the sooner this day will be over."

Paige, out of the back seat and about to climb in up front, rose onto her tiptoes to peer at Libby over the roof of the car. "No hard feelings, Lib?" she asked hopefully.

Libby shook her head again. "No hard feelings," she replied.

"I could bring over some spaghetti casserole," Julie fretted. "Leave it on the porch if you and Hildie are still out walking when I get here—"

Libby cut her off. "Julie," she said, *"I'm fine."*

Paige got into the passenger seat and shut the door.

Libby waved. *"Goodbye."*

Still, Julie waited until Libby had fished her keys out of her bag, unlocked the back door and stepped inside to greet an overjoyed Hildie.

Behind her, Libby hear the Cadillac drive off.

After receiving a royal welcome from her favorite canine, Libby opened the door again, and Hildie trundled out into the yard. By the time the dog returned, Libby had washed out and filled the usual bowls with kibble and water.

While Hildie ate and drank, Libby exchanged her dress for tan cotton shorts and a T-shirt. The hateful pantyhose went into the bathroom trash can, and she flung the shoes to the back of her closet. Short socks and a pair of sneakers completed the ensemble.

The walk was pleasant, restoring Libby a little, and by the time she and Hildie got home, she was getting hungry. Wishing she hadn't been quite so quick to turn down Julie's offer to drop off some of her famous spaghetti casserole, Libby was taking a mental inventory of the contents of her refrigerator as she stepped through the front gate, and didn't immediately notice the figure huddled on the porch steps.

Hildie gave a half-hearted little bark—she wasn't much of a guard dog—and Libby stopped in her tracks, fighting an urge to pretend she had the wrong house, turn around and flee.

"Marva?" she asked, instead.

Her mother wore a black and gold, zebra-striped caftan from her extensive collection of leisure garments, along with plenty of makeup. "It's about time you got home," Marva accused, making a petulant face. "I don't have a house key anymore, you know."

Libby considered the distance between the condominium complex and her place, and frowned. Marva often took long walks, but never without her prized athletic shoes, and tonight she was wearing metallic-gold flats with pointed toes. "How did you get here?" Libby asked.

Marva jutted out her chin, still angling for a welcome, evidently. "I took a cab," she said. "It's not as if I could count on any of my *children* for a ride, after all."

Libby remembered to latch the gate, leaned down to unhook Hildie's leash. There was precisely one taxi in Blue River, and it was often up on blocks in the high weeds behind Chudley Wilkes's trailer-house, though he'd been known to fire it up when someone called, wanting a ride someplace and willing to pay the fare.

"Are you hungry?" Libby asked, sitting down beside her mother on the step. Up close, she could see that Marva's red lipstick had gone on crooked and was mostly chewed off. "I could make scrambled eggs—"

"The cabdriver was a hayseed," Marva went on, as though Libby hadn't spoken at all. "He claims he's related to John Wilkes Booth, on his mother's side. Booth's mother, not his."

"Chudley likes to spin a yarn, all right," Libby said. "Not many people call for a taxi in a town this size, so he has a lot of time to study the family tree. Over time, he's grafted on a few branches."

"Aren't you going to ask me in?" Marva asked. "I came all this way, and you just leave me sitting on the front porch like some beggar."

Libby figured there no use pointing out that she'd just offered to whip up some scrambled eggs and hadn't planned to serve them on the front porch. "Of course you can come in," she said, rising.

All this time, Hildie had been standing on the walk, head tilted to one side, studying Marva as though she had sprouted out of the ground only moments before.

"Whose dog is that?" Marva fussed, though she'd made Hildie's acquaintance at least once before. "I don't like dogs. It will have to stay outside." She made a go-away motion with the backs of her hands. "Scat! Go home."

"Hildie is my dog," Libby said carefully, a sick feeling congealing in the bottom of her stomach. "She *lives* here."

"Shoo," Marva said, paying no attention to Libby. Most of her conversations were one-sided; she did all the talking and none of the listening. "Go away."

Hildie hesitated, then backed up a few steps, confused.

"Mother," Libby said, annoyed, as well as alarmed, "*don't*. Please. You're scaring her."

But Marva had turned her head to stare at Libby. "Did you just call me 'Mother'?"

Libby wasn't sure how to answer. Years ago, before she'd packed a suitcase and left, Marva had hated being addressed by that term, or any of its more affectionate variations.

"It doesn't matter," she finally said. "Let's go in and I'll start the scrambled eggs." Then, more firmly, she called her dog. "Come on, Hildie."

Hildie hesitated, uncertain, then lumbered toward Libby, full of trust.

"I won't be in the same house with that horrible creature," Marva warned.

"Then you'll have to eat your supper out here," Libby

replied, very quietly, "because Hildie is coming inside with me." *And, furthermore, she is not a "horrible creature."*

Marva began to cry, sniffling at first, then wailing. "You hate me! I'm all alone in the world!"

The truth was, Libby didn't hate Marva—she'd shut that part of herself down a long, long time ago—but she couldn't have said she loved her, either.

"Come inside," Libby urged gently. "I'll brew some tea. Would you like a nice cup of tea?"

Marva stepped over the threshold, stood in the small, modestly furnished living room, looking around. She didn't seem to notice when Hildie slunk in behind her and took refuge behind the couch.

"I lived here once," Marva said, as though she'd just recalled the fact.

"Yes," Libby confirmed, at once suspicious and sympathetic. "You lived here once."

And then you left. Even though Paige and Julie and I begged you not to go.

"Where did he die?" Marva asked. Her mascara had run, and her hair was starting to droop around her face, but the expression in her eyes was lucid. "Show me where he died."

Libby moved to stand where her father's rented hospital bed had been, during the last months of his life. "Here," she said. "Right here."

I was holding his hand. Paige and Julie were here, too. And the last word he said was your name.

"On the living-room floor?"

"In a hospital bed."

"Well, I'm not surprised. The man had no imagination."

Libby struggled to hold on to her temper. She'd lost it once already today, and she wasn't about to let it go again.

Moments before, she'd considered the possibility that Marva was genuinely ill. Now, she suspected she was being played, manipulated—again. "Dying doesn't require much imagination," she remarked, with no inflection whatsoever. "A lot of courage, perhaps."

Dad raised us, provided for us, sacrificed for us. He loved us and we knew it. That's more than you ever did.

"Courage!" Marva huffed. "Will Remington was a small-town schoolteacher, content to plod along, living in this rattrap of a house and calling it home. Driving a secondhand car and buying day-old bread and clipping coupons out of the Wednesday paper. How much courage does that take?"

"A lot, I think," Libby said calmly. *He washed our hair. He told us bedtime stories and listened to our prayers before we went to sleep. Maybe it took some courage to hear his children asking God to send their mother home, night after night. Maybe, damn you, it took courage just to keep getting up in the morning.*

Marva whirled on her. "You do, do you?" she challenged hotly. "You think your father was such a hero? Well, let me tell you something, missy—Will was dead his whole life. *I'm* the one who did all the living!"

Hildie peered around the end of the couch and growled pitiably.

Libby left the room, trembling, and came as far as the inside doorway with her car keys in one hand. She jangled them at her mother. "It's time for you to go," she said.

Marva frowned. "What about the scrambled eggs?"

"I'm fresh out," Libby replied. "Of eggs, I mean."

"But I'm hungry!"

"Then we'll get you a hamburger on the way over. Let's go."

"This is a fine how-do-you-do," Marva ranted. "I come

to visit my own daughter, in my own home, and I get the bum's rush!"

"This isn't your home," Libby said. *And I wish to God I wasn't your daughter.* "Things have changed. You moved out years ago."

Hildie whimpered. She wasn't used to stress.

"Please," Marva pleaded, with such pathos that, yet again, Libby wasn't sure if the woman was mentally ill or had simply changed her tactics. "Let me stay here. Just for tonight."

"Let's go," Libby said, hardening her heart a little against the inevitable guilt. What if Marva actually was sick? What if she was having a breakdown or something?

"I'm your mother," Marva reminded her.

Yes, God help me. You are. But I don't have to love you. I don't even have to like *you.*

"And I'm lonely," Marva persisted, when Libby didn't speak. "None of you girls are willing to make room in your lives for me."

Libby closed her eyes. *Don't go there*, she warned herself.

"Suppose I die? You'll be sorry you treated me this way when I die."

A year after you left, I started telling people you were dead. They all knew better, because they remembered you. They remembered the scandal. But they pretended to believe me, just to be kind.

"Dad loved you so much," Libby blurted out. Or was it the little girl she'd once been, not the woman she was, doing the talking? "He never stopped believing you'd come back."

"I couldn't take you with me," Marva said, true to form. Libby might not have spoken at all. "You were practically babies, the three of you. And we lived like gypsies, Lance and me." She paused, and a dreamy expression crossed her face, all the more disturbing because of her smeared makeup. "Like gypsies," she repeated softly.

Lance. Libby had never known Marva's lover's name.

Not that it mattered now.

She bit her lower lip, tried to think what to say or do, to get through to Marva, and jumped when a light knock sounded at the front door.

Hildie retreated behind the couch.

"Libby?" Paige let herself in, a small, lidded dish in her hands. "I brought you some of Julie's casserole—she insisted—" Seeing Marva, Paige's brown eyes widened. "Oh," she said.

"Yeah, oh," Libby confirmed. She could have hugged her little sister, she was so glad to see her. As a nurse, Paige would know if Marva needed medical help. "She's acting strangely," she added, gesturing toward their mother.

"Don't talk about me as though I weren't even here," Marva huffed.

The lid on Julie's dish rattled a little as Paige set it aside on the small table beside the door.

"I love casserole," Marva said, smiling happily.

Paige marched right over, confident as a prison matron taking charge of a new arrival, grasped their mother firmly by the arm and hustled her toward the door. "Some other time, maybe," she said cheerfully, casting a reassuring look at Libby. "Right now, Marva, you and I are going to take a little spin in my car."

"Thank you," Libby mouthed.

"You owe me," Paige said.

And just like that, the latest Marva episode was over.

For now, anyway.

Libby locked the front door, leaving the casserole dish right where it was, and turned to Hildie.

It took fifteen minutes to persuade the poor dog to come out from behind the couch.

THE WATER FIGHT TURNED out to be a dandy—even the dogs got involved. When it was over, Tate and Garrett and Austin all sat in the kitchen in their wet clothes, drinking beer and talking about the old days.

It was generally agreed that when it came to dousing people with a hose, their mother was still the all-around champ. She'd had an advantage, of course—raised Southern, none of them would have considered wresting the thing out of her hands and soaking her in retribution, the way they would have done with each other.

Sober and a little chilled, Tate was about to head upstairs to take a hot shower and hit the sack, the dogs set to follow on his heels, when his cell phone rang.

He picked it up off the table, checked the digital panel to see who was calling and flipped it open. "Cheryl? Are the kids all right?"

"Yes," Cheryl said. "They're fine. Sound asleep."

Tate glanced at the clock; it was after eleven. "And you're calling me at this hour because—?"

"Don't be mean," she purred.

Good God. Was she *drunk?* What if the house caught fire, or one of the kids got sick?

"Cheryl, are you all right?"

Austin scraped back his chair and rose from the kitchen table, shaking his head. Garrett gave Tate a pitying look and headed for his own part of the house. Evidently, he'd forgotten the senator's "emergency," whatever it was.

"No," Cheryl burst out, sobbing all of the sudden. It still amazed Tate, the way she could change emotional gears so quickly. "I'm *not* all right. I'm divorced. I'm an attractive, educated woman, in the prime of my life, stuck in Blue River, Texas, for the next twelve years—"

"Have you been drinking?"

"Would you care if I had been?"

"Hell, yes, I'd care," Tate snapped. "You're alone with my children."

"I'm perfectly sober, and they're *my* children, too."

Tate drew in a long, deep breath, released it slowly. This was no time to needle her. "Yes," he said, in what he hoped was a reassuring tone of voice. "They're your children, too."

Cheryl was quiet for a few moments, so quiet that Tate began to wonder if she'd hung up. "We could try again, Tate," she said tremulously. "You and me. We could try again, make it work this time."

Tate closed his eyes. If she wasn't drunk, she must have snorted something. The subject of reconciliation had come up before, usually after she and some boyfriend had had a falling-out and gone their separate ways.

"No, Cheryl," he said, when he figured he could trust himself to speak. "You don't really want that, and neither do I."

"Because of Libby Remington," she said, with a trace of bitterness. "That's why you won't try to save our marriage. Did you think I wouldn't hear about you and Libby, Tate?"

Save their marriage? They'd been divorced for five years.

"We're not going to talk about Libby," Tate replied, silently commending himself for not reminding her that this marriage she wanted to save had long since died an acrimonious—and permanent—death. "Not tonight, anyway."

"I hate this town." Three-sixties were common with Cheryl when she was upset. There was no telling where she'd try to take the conversation next.

"The solution is simple, Cheryl," Tate reasoned. "Let Audrey and Ava live with me. You'd be free to do whatever you wanted, then. You could live anyplace, practice law again."

"You'd like that, wouldn't you?" The question, though softly put, was a loaded one, and Tate proceeded accordingly.

He was already on his feet, heedless of his damp clothes, rummaging for his truck keys. Austin lingered, leaning against one of the counters, sipping reheated coffee and not even bothering to pretend he wasn't eavesdropping. The dogs waited patiently to go upstairs, wagging their tails.

"I'll take care of the mutts," Austin said, between swallows of coffee.

Cheryl's rant continued, rising in volume and making less and less sense.

Tate nodded his thanks to his brother and stepped into the garage.

"Are you *listening,* Tate McKettrick?" Cheryl demanded.

"I'm listening," Tate said, climbing into his truck and pushing the button to open the garage door behind him. It rolled up silently, an electronic wonder. "Keep talking."

She started crying again. "It would have been so perfect!"

"What would have been perfect?" Tate asked, backing out into the moonlit Texas night, stars splattered from one horizon to the other.

"Our life together," Cheryl said, after a small, choked sob.

"How do you figure that?" There was a limit to Tate's ability to play games, and he'd almost reached it.

"We could have had it all, if only—"

Tate frowned, turning the truck around, pointing it toward town. "If only what?"

"If only you hadn't been in love with Libby Remington the whole time," Cheryl said. "She came between us, from the very beginning. You never got over her."

"That's crazy, Cheryl," he said, racing down the driveway to the main road.

She went off on another tangent, something about her lonely childhood, and how money didn't buy happiness, and she'd *always* wanted a real family of her own.

You could have fooled me, Tate thought.

But he listened, and when she ran down, he got her talking again.

Long minutes later, he braked in front of Cheryl's house, bolted from the truck, leaving the door open and the engine running, and strode to the front door.

"Let me in," he said, into his cell phone.

"Let you in? Where are you?"

Tate shoved his free hand through his hair and let out his breath. "On your porch," he said. "Open the damn door, Cheryl. *Now.*"

CHAPTER TEN

CHERYL SWUNG her front door open slowly, and Tate, just snapping his cell phone shut on their disturbing conversation, which had spanned the distance between the ranch and her house in town, was stunned. He'd expected to find his ex-wife an emotional train wreck, given the way she'd whined and fussed. Instead, her skin glowed with what looked like arousal, her makeup was perfect, her dark hair wound neatly into a single, glossy braid reaching nearly to her waist. And in her eyes, Tate saw a guarded glint of triumph.

"Come in," she said, her voice throaty and all Texased-up with heat and honey, a neat trick since she didn't have a drop of Southern blood in her.

And the keyword was *trick*.

Tate stood stiffly on the doormat. If he allowed his gaze to drop, even slightly, he knew he'd get the full impact of what she was wearing—a sexy nightgown that revealed a lot more than it covered up and barely breezed past her thighs. She held a glass of white wine in one hand.

"Want some?" she asked, ever the mistress of the double entendre, and took a sip.

"This was a *setup?*" The question was rhetorical, of course, and the situation wasn't all that surprising, but Tate seethed with indignation just the same. She'd cast her line into the water using the kids as the bait—something she often accused *him* of doing—knowing he'd have no choice but to take the hook.

In that moment, Tate's dislike for his former wife deepened to outright contempt.

Cheryl retreated a step, an oddly graceful move, almost dancelike, and then he couldn't help taking her in. He waited for a visceral response—though mad as a cornered rattler, he was as well-supplied with testosterone as any other man—and was a little surprised when it didn't come.

"A setup?" Cheryl replied softly, her lower lip jutting out in a pout. "I wouldn't exactly put it *that* way."

Tate swayed slightly on his feet, caught in a swift, spinning backwash of fury, averted his eyes and shoved a hand through his hair. "I need to see the kids," he said, on a long, raspy breath. "Then I'm leaving."

Even without looking directly at Cheryl, he knew when her face crumbled. He also knew the reaction didn't stem from the heartbreak of unrequited love. Cheryl had never loved him, any more than he'd loved her. They'd simply collided, at an unfortunate intersection of their two lives, both of them distracted by unrelated concerns, and two innocent and very precious children had been the result.

She stepped back again, gesturing with her left hand, still holding the wine, slopping some onto the spotless white carpet as she did so. "They're asleep. They won't even know you're here," she said wearily. "But suit yourself. You always do."

Tate turned sideways to pass her, headed straight for the stairs. The words *You always do* lodged between his shoulder blades like a knife, but he shook them off out of habit. All he wanted to do right then was gather his girls up, one in each arm, and carry them out of there, take them *home,* where they belonged. Audrey and Ava were McKettricks—they needed to grow up on the land.

Cheryl, however dysfunctional, was neither drunk nor high. Pissed off as he was, Tate had realized that the moment she'd opened the door. Under the terms of their custody agreement, this was Cheryl's week with the twins, and he couldn't rightly intervene.

At the same time, he wasn't about to leave that house without making sure Audrey and Ava were okay. If there were consequences, so be it.

He was halfway up the staircase when his daughters appeared at the top, barefoot and sleepy-eyed, wearing their matching pink pajamas, the ones with the teddy bears printed on the fabric. They huddled close to each other, their small shoulders touching.

Even as babies, they'd done that. They'd only begun to thrive, in fact, when some perceptive pediatric nurse had cornered their doctor and persuaded him to let them share an incubator.

Tate's heart did a slow, backward tumble at the memory.

The idea had made sense to him then, and it made sense to him now. Audrey and Ava had been together in Cheryl's womb, aware of each other on some level, possibly since conception. Born too early, each had still needed the proximity of the other.

"What's wrong, Daddy?" asked Audrey, always quick to read his expression and generally the first to speak her mind.

Tate turned his head to look back over one shoulder at Cheryl. By some devious magic, she'd donned a rumpled robe made of that bumpy cloth—he could never remember what it was called—pale lavender and worn thin in places. She was projecting Mommy vibes so effectively that, for one moment, he thought he must have imagined the sexy night-gown she'd had on when she'd answered the door, the glass of wine in her hand.

"Want some?"

It was the gotcha look in Cheryl's green eyes that convinced Tate he was still sane, though that probably wasn't the reaction she'd been going for. This whole thing was some kind of game to her; she got a weird satisfaction out of jacking him around, and when she felt thwarted, the next attempt was bound to be a real son-of-a-bitch.

"Daddy?" Ava prompted, clasping Audrey's hand tightly now, leaning into her sister a little more. "Is everything okay?"

Tate put Cheryl out of his mind, focused all his attention on his children. *We have to stop this,* he thought. *Somehow, Cheryl and I have got to call a truce.*

"Everything's fine," he said, with a lightness he hoped was convincing. "I was in town, so I came by to tuck you in and say good-night, that's all."

Both girls looked relieved.

"Did you bring Ambrose and Buford?" Audrey asked.

Tate shook his head. "No, sweetie," he answered. "They were headed off to bunk in with your uncle Austin when I left the house."

Behind him, Cheryl cleared her throat, an eloquent little sound. Tate made no attempt to decode it.

"I'd be happy to tuck both of you in," she told her daughters, her tone sunny. "Unless you'd really rather have your daddy kiss you good-night than me."

Tate closed his eyes, sickened. *Unless you'd really rather have your daddy kiss you goodnight than me.* With Cheryl, everything was a contest, a case of either/or—even the love of their children.

"Why can't you *both* kiss us good-night?" Ava asked, her voice fragile.

Tate gazed up at his daughters, full of love and despair and tremendous guilt. They were tearing these children apart, he and Cheryl, and whether he wanted to believe it or not, he was equally responsible.

It had to stop—no matter what.

"One at a time, though," Audrey said. "Because you always fight when you're in the same room."

God in heaven, Tate thought.

"Daddy first," Ava said.

"Certainly," Cheryl chimed, and Tate knew by her voice that she'd turned away. "Why consider *my* feelings? I'm only your mother."

"Cheryl," Tate ground out, not daring to face his ex-wife. "Don't. *Please,* don't."

Cheryl said nothing, but he could feel her bristling somewhere behind him, a little off to the side, a porcupine about to throw quills in every direction.

By deliberate effort, Tate unfroze his muscles and climbed the stairs, forcing a smile. Reaching the top, he herded the little girls, now giggling, in the direction of the large, pink and frilly room they shared.

He tucked them back into their matching canopy beds.

He kissed their foreheads.

He told them he loved them.

And he waited, perched on the cushioned seat set beneath the bay windows overlooking the street, until, at long last, they slept.

Tate dreaded going downstairs again, because it might mean another run-in with Cheryl. He wasn't sure how much self-restraint he had left, and while he'd never struck a woman in his life and didn't intend to start now, words could be used as effectively as fists, and the ones crowding the back of his throat in those moments were as hard and cold as steel.

Fortunately, there was no sign of Cheryl, although as soon as he'd stepped over the threshold onto the porch, he heard the dead bolt engage behind him with a resolute thump. She must have been lurking just inside the living room.

He started down the walk, wasn't even half surprised when Brent Brogan's cruiser pulled in behind his truck. While he'd been saying good-night to Audrey and Ava, waiting for them to drift off into peaceful, little-girl dreams, Cheryl had been summoning the police.

Another segment in the continuing drama.

Suppressing a sigh, Tate opened the gate in the picket fence and stepped through it, onto the sidewalk. "Evenin'," he said, with a half salute, when Brent rolled down his driver's side window to look him up and down. "Slow night, Chief?"

Brogan shook his head. "Not according to the former Mrs. McKettrick," he said, with a nod toward the house. "What are you doing here, Tate? It's pretty late, in case you haven't figured that out already."

Tate stayed where he was, shoved his thumbs into the waistband of his jeans, which were still a little damp from the water fight with Garrett and Austin, hours before. He found that strangely comforting. "She called you," he said flatly.

"She called me," Brent confirmed. "Cheryl said she felt threatened."

Tate gave a raspy chuckle. Thrust the splayed fingers of his right hand through his hair. "Did she? Well, Denzel, that's bullshit and you know it. About forty-five minutes ago, she called *me,* too, and I'd have sworn she was either high or drunk, going by the things she said and the way she sounded. I got here as fast as I could, because, as you may recall, my *kids* live here when they're not on the ranch."

Brent shut off the cruiser's engine, pushed open the door, got out to stand facing Tate there beside the quiet street. He was wearing civilian clothes, instead of his uniform, which meant he was off duty. "I've got to knock on that door, see Ms. Darbrey with my own eyes, and hear her say she's all right," he said. And when Tate started to speak, Brogan held up a hand to silence him. "It's procedure. She's a citizen, she called in a complaint, and whatever my personal opinion of the lady might be, it's my job to follow through. "

Tate understood, though it rubbed him a little raw in places that, even for professional reasons, Brent couldn't take him at his word. After all, they'd been buddies since second grade, when his friend's dad, Jock Brogan, had come to work on the Silver Spur as a wrangler and all-around handyman, glad to have a steady paycheck and a trailer to live in. Jock's seven-year-old son had arrived by bus a week later, right on time for the first day of school, sweating in the suit and bow tie he'd worn to his mother's funeral a month before, as it turned out, and scared shitless.

It had taken some time, but eventually Brent, a city boy, had loosened up a little, gotten used to ranch life, and asked Tate to teach him "something about horses." Within a couple of months, the new kid was riding like a Comanche warrior, keeping up with Tate and Garrett, Austin and Nico Ruiz as easily as if he'd been born in the saddle. Being in the same class at school, and with a lot of common interests, Tate and Brent had formed a special bond.

They'd competed in junior rodeos together.

Played on the same baseball and basketball teams in their teens.

On the day they graduated from high school, Brent announced that he was joining the Air Force instead of going on to the university with Tate, the way they'd always planned. Jock Brogan had scrimped and done without and worked overtime to save enough to cover the better part of his son's college expenses, Brent said, and he wasn't going to take a dime of that money. He'd always wanted to be a cop, he'd reminded Tate, and the military was willing to provide all the training he needed and pay him wages in the bargain.

He could be an asset to his dad from then on, instead of a liability.

Standing there in the night, waiting for Brent to satisfy himself that Cheryl was still in one piece, the words Garrett had thrown in his face earlier that night came back to Tate.

—inside, you're still the rich kid from the biggest ranch in four counties, feeling like you ought to apologize to folks who have to earn a living—

Tate tipped his head back, looked up at the blanket of stars spilling lavishly across the Texas sky. *Was* he "still that rich kid," always wishing he could make up somehow for having more, just by virtue of being born a McKettrick, than so many other people did?

People like Brent Brogan.

People like Libby.

Did he want a second chance with her because what she made him feel was real love—or was he just feeling guilty because she'd had a tough road from early childhood on, while he'd coasted blithely through life until a truck crossed the median one night and crashed into his parents' car, leaving both of them fatally injured?

Brent returned, slapped him companionably on the back.

"Uh-oh," he joked. "You're looking introspective. And that's almost *always* a bad sign, old buddy."

Tate sighed. Managed a grin. He did have a tendency to think too damn much, there was no denying that.

"Did you find my ex-wife tied up in a closet? Swathed in duct tape?" he asked.

Brent grinned. "No."

"Damn the luck," Tate said.

"Let's get a cup of coffee," Brent suggested.

"Look, it's been one hell of a day and—" Tate began, but the protest fell away, half-finished. There was no reason to hurry home—the kids weren't there, and Austin, while not the most dependable person on earth, could be trusted to take care of two sleeping dogs.

"Don't I *know* it's been one hell of a day," Brent agreed wearily. "I was at the funeral, remember, and the wake, too. Had a long talk with Nico, in fact, once the leftovers had been stuffed into Isabel's fridge and most everybody else had gone home. Follow me to my place, and I'll brew up some java and tell you about it."

"If I don't get some sleep," Tate said, with a shake of his head, "I won't be good for much of anything tomorrow, so I'll pass on the java this time."

"All right," Brent replied, opening the door of the cruiser, keyring in hand. When he hesitated, Tate knew his friend had more to say. "I spoke to Isabel Ruiz," Brogan went on. "She's going to L.A., all right, moving in with her sister."

The decision seemed hasty, but in the final analysis, it wasn't his business what Isabel did. So Tate merely nodded, opened the door of his truck and climbed in. It hurt to imagine that sturdy but humble house, buzzing with life and laughter for as long as he could remember, standing empty, with just the whisper of the creek or a passing wind to break the silence.

Pablo was gone for good; that was something he had to come to terms with in much the same way he'd had to accept the loss of his mom and dad. Things changed, that was the one thing a man could count on, and folks came and went, and you never knew when the last thing you'd said to them, or failed to say, might really be the last chance you were ever going to get, one way or the other.

On the lonely drive back to the ranch, through a sultry summer night, Tate missed his old dog even more than usual. It would have been a fine thing to have Crockett riding shotgun, as he'd done before, a sympathetic listener with his ears perked up and his eyes warm with canine devotion.

Had Crockett been there, Tate would have told him how worried he was about Audrey and Ava, and the way they were growing up, bouncing back and forth between two different houses. He'd have said what a hard thing it was knowing Pablo had died so senselessly, hard, too, wondering if he could have prevented what happened somehow, and if his friend had suffered or had had time to be afraid before the end came.

He might even have said that he loved Libby, not in the fevered, grasping way of a boy, as he had before, but hard and strong and steady, in the way of a man, but he'd rather do without her for the rest of his days than risk hurting her again.

Tate might have said a lot of things to Crockett that night, but all that actually came out of his mouth was a quiet, "I sure do miss you, old dog."

BY THE NEXT DAY, Libby was entirely recovered from her mother's unexpected visit the night before, and *mostly* over making such an idiot of herself out at the Ruizes' place after Pablo's funeral.

She rarely did anything impulsive—she couldn't afford the luxury—but that bright summer morning, after she and Hildie had taken their walk, Libby decided not to open the Perk Up for business at the usual time.

Today, she just felt like playing hooky.

So she scribbled a message on a piece of yellow-lined paper, crossed the alley and let herself into the shop by the back way, passed through the kitchen into the main area and taped the sign to the glass in the front door.

CLOSED FOR REPAIRS, the notice read. BACK BY NOON. PROBABLY.

The "repairs" Libby needed to make weren't the kind that required wrenches and screwdrivers, and while she fully intended to be serving coffee and smoothies and scones, if Julie had baked any, by midday, she wasn't sure that would happen. That was why she'd added the "probably"—to give herself an out if the need should arise.

Back home, Libby switched her shorts and tank top for her best jeans and a sleeveless blue cotton blouse, then put on a pair of comfortable sandals. Brushed her hair, leaving it loose instead of binding it back in the usual ponytail, and applied some lip gloss.

Hildie, munching kibble in the kitchen when her mistress jingled the car keys in invitation, looked up, cocked both ears as she considered her options and promptly went back to eating her breakfast.

Libby smiled at that. "I'll be back soon," she promised, stroking the dog's broad back with one hand before heading out the door.

Standing on the back porch, she looked around her yard

and wished she hadn't let the shrubs and flower beds get so out of hand. She'd never been much of a gardener, mostly because she'd never had the time, but now she felt a new and strangely keen longing to get her hands dirty, to weed and water and plant things just to watch them grow.

First, of course, she'd have to prepare the ground, and that would be a big job, one that might take weeks. By the time she'd finished, folks around Blue River would probably be fertilizing and tilling their garden plots under, to lie fallow until spring, when the nursery section down at the feed store would be awash in starter plants and brightly colored seed packets.

Before getting into her car and backing it into the alley, she looked under dusty tarps in the detached garage until she found her dad's old push-mower. The blades were probably dull; maybe later, she'd heft the ancient apparatus into the trunk of the Impala and take it out to Chudley Wilkes for sharpening. When he wasn't running his one-taxi empire, Chudley fixed things.

Just *thinking* about mowing the lawn empowered Libby a little, though she supposed she'd be whistling a different tune once she'd made a few swipes through the high grass. As kids, she and Julie and Paige had taken turns doing yard chores, and she remembered the blisters, the muscle aches and all the rest.

They'd begged their dad to invest in a gas-powered mower, but he'd said hard work and exercise were good for the character. Of course, he hadn't been able to afford fancy equipment, especially with three young daughters to raise.

With a pang, Libby paused to pat the dusty handle. Indeed, hard work and exercise *were* good for the character—and she'd get a sense of accomplishment, the incomparable scent of fresh-cut grass and a tighter backside out of the deal.

Chudley's place was in the opposite direction from where she was headed, and stopping there would delay the opening of her coffee shop by at least an hour, but Libby popped open the Impala's trunk and hoisted the mower inside anyway. It was heavier than it looked, that machine, and the handles stuck out, so the trunk wouldn't close again.

She'd just have to alter her plans slightly, Libby concluded, after standing there in the alley biting her lower lip for a few moments. She'd drop the mower off at Chudley's first, then go on about her business. If Wilkes happened to be going through one of his ambitious phases—these were famously rare—the machine might be ready to cut grass later in the day.

Libby got behind the wheel, cranked up the engine and jostled off down the alley, wincing every time she hit a bump, causing the lid of the trunk to slam down on the shaft of the mower.

The Wilkes's home, two trailers welded together sometime in the fifties and surrounded by what seemed like acres of rusted-out cars, treadless tires and miscellaneous parts of God-knew-what, had been an eyesore for so long that folks around Blue River had long since stopped getting up petitions to force Chudley and his wife, Minnie, to clean the place up.

Libby pulled into the gravel driveway and waited a few moments before pushing open her car door, since Chudley had been known to keep mean guard dogs and once, reportedly, even an ostrich that might have killed the UPS man if Minnie hadn't rushed outside and driven it off with a broom handle.

Outsiders might have scoffed at that tale, thinking the odds were in the big bird's favor. Anybody who thought that had never met Minnie Wilkes.

She stepped out onto the sagging porch, wiping her hands on a faded apron and squinting, probably trying to place the green Impala. Six feet tall, with shoulders like a linebacker's, Minnie was a formidable sight, even pushing eighty, as she must have been.

Libby got out of the car. Smiled and waved. "It's me, Mrs. Wilkes," she called. "Libby Remington."

A blinding smile broke across Minnie's face. In her youth, the story went, she'd been quite a looker. Nobody'd ever been able to work out what caused her to throw in her lot with a little banty-rooster like Chudley. "Will's girl? Well, now, you've turned out just fine, haven't you? You still smitten with Jim and Sally McKettrick's oldest boy?"

Libby felt a little pinch inside her heart. Was *smitten* the word? "I see him around town," she said, approaching the gate, with its rusted hinges and weathered wooden latch, then hesitating. "Is that ostrich still around?"

Minnie's laugh boomed out over the seemingly endless expanse of junk. "Now there's a yarn that got right out of hand," she said, still standing on the porch. "Started out with one cussed old rooster, too stringy for the stewpot. Stubby—that was the rooster—went after the UPS man, right enough. But by the time that driver got through spreadin' the story around Blue River and half the county, I'll be darned if poor old Stub wasn't seven feet tall and a whole different kind of bird."

Libby smiled, started to open the gate.

Minnie stopped her. "You just stay right there, honey. We got another rooster pecking around here somewheres, and he might come at you, spurs out and screechin' like a banshee, if he don't happen to like your looks or somethin'."

Libby shaded her eyes and waited for her heartbeat to

slow down, so her words wouldn't come out sounding shaky. "I was hoping Chudley could sharpen my lawn-mower blades," she said.

"He'll do it," Minnie said, with a decisive nod. "He's out on a taxi run just now, takin' Mrs. Beale home from the supermarket—she bought more than she could carry in that little pushcart of hers again—but he ought to be back soon. *One Life to Live* is fixin' to come on any minute now, and Chud never misses it."

Libby went around to the back of the car to unload the mower. Minnie, who had a light step for such a big woman, appeared beside her, elbowed her aside and lifted the all-metal machine from the trunk as easily as if it were a child's toy, made of plastic.

"I'd invite you in for a neighborly chat," Minnie said, holding the mower off the ground with one hand, the way she might have held a rake or a hoe. "But Miss Priss had her kittens on the couch yesterday, and she ain't ready to move them just yet. What with Chudley's magazines and such, there's no other place to sit."

Libby smiled. "Thank you just the same," she said. "But I'd have had to say 'no' anyway, because I've got so much to do today."

Minnie, bless her, looked relieved. She was known as much for her pride as for her bad housekeeping, and Libby had always liked her. Wouldn't have hurt her feelings or embarrassed her for anything.

"I'll see that Chudley brings this here piece of machinery by your place later on," Minnie said. "Good as new."

Libby opened the car door, reached for her purse.

"Keep your money," Minnie huffed, already trundling back through the gate, taking the mower along with her. "I meant to send over one of my sugar pies when your daddy was sick, and I never got around to it. Always felt bad about that—Will Remington was a fine man—but if it ain't one thing around here, it's another. Anyhow, Chudley will fix this mower right and proper, and I'll feel a sight better about not buildin' that sugar pie."

Libby's eyes burned. She knew the Wilkeses could have used even the small amount of money Chudley probably charged for sharpening the blades of a push lawn mower, but she wouldn't have discounted Minnie's belated but heartfelt condolence gift on any account. It would have been kinder to slap the woman across the face.

"Thank you, Mrs. Wilkes," she said.

Minnie plunked the mower down next to the porch steps, which dipped visibly under her considerable weight. Her thick hair, dyed an unlikely shade of auburn and bobby-pinned into a messy knot on top of her head, bobbed a little when she spoke, as it might tumble down around her shoulders. "You're a woman grown now," she said, with firm good grace. "Old enough to call me Minnie, if it suits you."

"Minnie," Libby repeated. It *did* make her feel more like a mature adult, addressing an older woman of slight acquaintance by her given name.

By the time she added a "Goodbye" Minnie had already disappeared back inside the conjoined trailers. After all these years, the seam still showed, a brownish, welded ribbon wrapping the structure like a gift and stopping directly above the front door.

Libby got back into her car, backed slowly into the turn-around and pointed the Impala back down the driveway toward the county road.

There, she stopped and looked both ways. On the left was

an old porcelain toilet, red flowers—possibly geraniums—billowing from the bowl, riotous with well-being.

She smiled.

And to think people considered this place a blight upon the landscape.

CHAPTER ELEVEN

A WEEK HAD PASSED since Pablo Ruiz's funeral, and during that time, Tate McKettrick hadn't called once. Maybe, Libby thought, watching as a rare and badly needed rain pelted the road out in front of the Perk Up, her dad had been right, in years past, when he used to moralize that there wasn't much point in buying the cow when you could get the milk for free.

Libby sighed. A few days ago, she'd bitten the bullet and called Doc Pollack to ask for a prescription for birth control pills, which she'd filled at Wal-Mart, her cheeks burning with mortification. She knew every single person in Blue River, and they knew her, and it was just her luck that Ellie Newton, her high school nemesis, happened to be clerking in the pharmacy that day.

A brief scenario unfolded on the screen of Libby's mind, in which Ellie switched on a microphone and announced to the whole store that, in case they hadn't heard, Libby Remington was catting around with Tate McKettrick again. And after he'd made a fool of her in front of the whole county, too, throwing her over for that fancy woman he'd met in Austin.

Yes, folks, the imaginary version of Ellie Newton proclaimed in triumph, she had the proof right here, a little packet of pills.

While none of that *actually* happened, Libby would have sworn she'd seen just the tiniest spark of smug judgment in Ellie's eyes as she rang up the purchase.

Ellie's husband, Joe, worked on the Silver Spur as a ranch hand, Libby reflected; alone in the Perk Up with all the chores caught up, she had way too much time for introspection. Suppose Ellie had driven straight out there to the nice single-wide trailer she and Joe shared and told Joe that Libby was on birth control pills? *Further* suppose, Libby thought, gnawing on her lower lip, that Joe, hearing this news, went straight to his boss, none other than Tate McKettrick, and told *him?*

Tate would think she was hot to trot, jumping right on the pill when they'd been to bed exactly once.

And maybe she *was* hot to trot. With Tate, anyway.

Libby pressed the fingertips of both hands to her temples. What was the big deal here? This wasn't 1872. Consenting adults *had sex,* preferably responsible sex, all the time. And it wasn't as if she planned to keep the pills a secret from Tate—she just wanted to be the one to tell him, that was all.

It didn't help that business was slow.

A lot of Libby's regular customers had gone on vacation—good Lord, did they travel in a *herd,* or something? Every year, it seemed they all left at once.

No tour buses passing through town en route to the Alamo or Six Flags or some art or music fest in Austin stopped at Libby's place.

Even her sisters weren't around much—Paige was working double shifts at the clinic, and Julie had been helping out at Calvin's playschool, since the venerable Mrs. Oakland was recovering from an impacted wisdom tooth.

The McKettrick twins' castle was due to be delivered soon—volunteer fathers had dug and poured a cement foundation for it, along with a well for a very shallow fishpond nearby. Unless Mrs. Oakland's swelling went down soon, Julie would be in charge of the dedication ceremony.

All by her lonesome in the Perk Up, Libby wished the place had a jukebox, so she could have dropped some coins into the slot and played a sad song.

Instead, she checked the clock—4:37 p.m.—and made an executive decision; she'd close up early. Go home and let Hildie out for a run in the backyard.

Chudley had returned her lawn mower, sharpened and rust-free and ready to go, the day before. If the rain let up soon enough, she'd cut the grass.

If it didn't, she'd clean out some of the flower beds. Maybe it was too late in the season to plant, but just pulling the weeds would be an improvement.

After locking up, Libby crossed the alley and let herself into her yard through the back gate. The dust-scented rain had slackened to a drizzle, and a cool breeze dissipated some of the humidity.

While Hildie was outside, Libby changed into shorts, a sleeveless sweatshirt and flip-flops. She poured kibble in the dog's empty bowl, refilled her water dish and pushed open the screen door.

Hildie crunched happily away while Libby went outside, set her hands on her hips, and looked up at the gray sky. Texas had been in the grip of a drought for more than a decade, so any kind of precipitation was welcome, but her spirits dipped a little lower just the same.

The only sure remedy for the blues, at least in Libby's experience, was physical work—if it brought out a sweat and left her with achy muscles, so much the better. She hauled the mower out of the garage, considered the fact that it was made almost entirely of steel and put it back.

Work therapy was one thing. *Shock* therapy, courtesy of a lightning bolt, was another.

Hildie, finished with her supper, then scratched politely at the screen door from the inside.

Libby smiled, mounted the porch steps and let the dog out.

She was on her knees, pulling up weeds, when Hildie, lying under her favorite tree, out of the misty rain, rose to her haunches and gave an uncertain woof, more greeting than challenge.

Something tickled Libby's nose, so she ran a gloved hand across her face before turning around, expecting to see Julie, or Paige or even Marva.

But it was Tate who stood watching her, a slight smile curving his mouth upward at one side. "Hey," he said.

Libby swallowed. *If I filled a prescription for birth control pills, it's my own business,* she thought. "Hey," she replied, feeling stupid.

Tate hadn't *mentioned* her prescription, had he? Most likely, Ellie hadn't told Joe and therefore Joe couldn't have told Tate. Ellie had been a mean gossip in high school, it was true, but that was years ago and besides, she'd found religion—and Joe—since then.

"I tried to call," he said, when the silence stretched. "But you didn't pick up."

Libby hadn't thought to check her voice mail when she came home from the Perk Up—she didn't get that many calls. Paige and Julie usually just stopped by when they wanted to talk to her.

"What can I do for you?" she asked, her face heated.

Tate, wearing comfortable jeans, a T-shirt and old boots, crossed the grass and crouched beside her. "Well," he drawled, "you can *relax*, for a start."

Libby fought an insane urge to weep, and that used up any energy she might have employed in talking. Anyway, she was too afraid she'd say something even stupider than *What can I do for you?*

Gently, Tate used the backs of his fingers to wipe a smudge of dirt from Libby's cheek. "I've missed you, Lib," he said. "A lot."

She swallowed.

One of his powerful shoulders moved in a partial shrug. That ghost-of-a-grin touched down on his mouth again, and she noticed that his eyelashes were spiky from the moisture in the air. "The last time we were together," he reminded her, "things didn't go all that well."

Libby stood up, telling herself it was because her knees were starting to cramp, and dusted her hands off against the damp fabric of her shorts.

Tate stood, too. His dark hair curled a little in the light rain.

It was all Libby could do not to bury her fingers in that hair. The thought made her flesh tingle, all over.

She raised her chin a notch, remembering the minor spectacle the two of them had made, out there in Pablo's orchard after the funeral.

"I'll apologize if you will," she said.

Tate laughed. "Deal," he said. Then he sobered, and the blue of his eyes seemed to intensify. "I'm sorry."

Libby's breath caught, just looking into those eyes. "Me, too."

If black holes were that color, she thought, the entire universe would have been sucked into oblivion long ago.

"Maybe I could make it up to you with dinner," Tate said.

Libby blinked, pulled herself back from the blue precipice. Looked down at her muddy shorts and T-shirt. "I'd have
to change clothes first," she heard some foolish woman say.

Tate grinned. "I was thinking of steaks at my place," he
told her. The grin rose to dance, mischievous, in his eyes.
"We suspended the dress code years ago. In fact, we never
really had one, unless you count Mom's stubborn refusal to
allow barn boots any farther than the back porch."

"I can't go like this," Libby said, still serious. "I'm all
muddy and—and sweaty."

Tate chuckled. "All right," he said, "if you're going to insist, may I suggest that yellow dress? The one you wore the
other night?"

Libby's cheeks burned again. Right. The yellow dress
he'd said he could see through—the one she'd been so eager
to get out of, after making such a big, damn deal about how
it was too soon to make love.

And now she had a packet of birth control pills in her
medicine cabinet.

Libby pretended she hadn't heard his suggestion and
started for the house.

He chuckled.

Hildie, the traitor, hung back so she could walk with Tate.

While Tate waited in the kitchen with the dog, Libby
headed for the bathroom. A glance at herself in the mirror
over the sink made her shake her head.

A streak of good Texas garden dirt ran the length of her
right cheek, and her hair, caught up in the customary ponytail, would frizz like crazy when she turned it loose.

She started the shower running, adjusting the faucets until
she got just the right temperature—tepid, with the merest

hint of a chill. She used a lot of conditioner after shampooing, hoping her hair wouldn't do its fright-wig thing.

Finished with her shower in record time, Libby dried off, pulled on her faded pink cotton robe, and collected clean jeans, fresh underwear, and a long-sleeved black and white T-shirt from her room.

Although she felt strangely rushed, she took the time to blow-dry her hair and even applied some mascara, though she skipped the lip gloss.

Just because she had birth control pills in her medicine cabinet didn't mean she wanted to go sending "Seduce me" messages to Tate McKettrick by making her mouth all shiny and inviting.

Of course, if Tate hadn't been in the picture, she wouldn't have called Doc Pollack and then endured Ellie Newton's studied indifference to get the prescription in the first place.

Gripping the edges of the sink, Libby looked at her steam-blurred image in the mirror.

"You're *asking* for trouble, Libby Remington," she told herself.

Then she opened the bathroom door and stepped into the hallway.

Mustn't keep trouble waiting.

TATE LOADED HILDIE INTO the back seat of his truck, but although he'd opened the front passenger-side door for Libby, he stood back instead of helping her aboard, just so he could watch that sweet little ass in action, under the perfectly fitted jeans, as she made the climb.

Hot damn. A silent groan reverberated through him.

"Are the girls at the ranch?" Libby asked, once she was settled and he was behind the wheel. Hildie leaned between the seats and licked Tate's right ear just as he turned the key in the ignition.

He laughed, not at the question but at the dog, and immediately drew a confused glance from Libby.

"No," he said, as Hildie rested her muzzle on his shoulder and gave a contented little sigh. If only *all* females were so docile. "Audrey and Ava are in New York with their mother for a couple of days. Cheryl's folks moved into an assisted-living place in Connecticut a few months back, and she's putting their apartment on the market."

Libby offered no comment, only a nod. She shifted uncomfortably in the seat—and Tate figured she'd probably been counting on having the kids around as a sort of buffer.

Esperanza, Garrett and Austin were all at the main house, as it happened, but Tate wasn't taking Libby to the mansion. Where they were going, it would be just the two of them—and the old dog drooling on his shirt as he drove toward the outskirts of town.

"Are we going to talk?" Tate asked, when they'd traveled several miles in silence.

She smiled softly. "Do we need to?"

Damn. He wanted to pull over to the side of the road, right then and there, take Libby Remington into his arms and kiss her senseless.

"Probably," he said hoarsely.

"About—?"

"Things," Tate said, thrown by the scent of her, the warmth of her, the softness he could sense from three feet away, no touching necessary. Highly desirable, but not necessary.

"Things like—?"

"Like where we're headed, you and I," Tate said.

Libby's smile was faint and a little saucy. "I assumed,

since you're behind the wheel, that you had our destination all figured out."

"That isn't what I mean," Tate said, mildly irritated, "and you know it."

"Where are we going, Tate?" Libby asked, with exaggerated patience, of the smart-ass variety. There was an undercurrent of excitement there, too, unless he missed his guess.

"On one level," Tate replied, "I'd say we're on our way to a soft spot in some tall grass." Out of the corner of his eye, he saw her blush, and took some satisfaction in that. "On another level—the long-range one—everything depends on you, Libby."

Libby turned in her seat, her eyes flashing a little. He could see her nipples jutting against the inside of her blouse, so he figured she was up for the proposed tumble in the grass.

All right by him.

"Now, why would everything depend on me?" she asked, her eyes wide.

Tate didn't give her an answer until he'd brought the truck to a stop at the edge of the yard that had been Pablo and Isabel's for so long.

"You're the one with all the forgiving to do, Lib," he said, gripping the steering wheel and staring straight ahead through the windshield. The lumber and other building supplies he'd been buying and hauling out from town all week waited, moist from the drizzling rain.

Libby turned slightly in the seat, gently eased Hildie back, off his shoulder. "Tate McKettrick," she said, "look at me."

He did. A big lump rose in his throat. He wanted her physically, but there was so much more to it than that.

"If you're talking about that fling with Cheryl," Libby told him, "I forgave you for that a long time ago."

Tate raised his hand to her cheek, brushed it lightly with the backs of his knuckles. "Maybe you believe that," he said, "but I'm not sure I do."

Her eyes widened again, and patches of pale pink pulsed in her cheeks, then faded. "If you could go back in time," she asked, after several long moments, "what would you change, Tate? Can you even imagine a world without your children in it?"

Tate unhooked Libby's seat belt, laid his hands on either side of her face so she wouldn't look away before she heard him out. "No," he said gruffly, "but if I had the kind of power we're talking about here, *you and I* would have conceived the twins. They'd be ours, together."

She turned her head, and her lips moved, light as the flick of a moth's wings, against his palm.

Fire shot up Tate's arm, set his heart ablaze, spread to his groin and hit a flash point. He barely contained the groan that rose from somewhere in the very center of his being.

Libby met his gaze again. Held it. "Do you know what would have made it impossible to forgive you, Tate? If you'd denied those little girls, or bought your way out of the situation somehow—a lot of men in your position would have done that—but you took all the fallout. You did right by your children, and I'm pretty sure you *tried* to do right by Cheryl—"

In the back, Hildie whimpered, wanting out.

Tate shut off the engine, but made no move to get out of the truck and lower Hildie to the ground. "What about *you,* Lib?" he asked miserably. "I sure as hell didn't do right by you, now did I?"

She reached across, touched his arm. "I'm a big girl now," she said. "I'm over it."

"Over it enough to trust me?"

She thought for a moment, then nodded. "Until you give me reason not to," she said.

Hildie began to carry on in earnest.

Tate got out of the truck, opened the back door and two-armed the chubby old dog out of the vehicle and onto the ground.

Libby got out, too, and stood at the edge of the Ruizes' lawn, looking toward the house. Tate watched as she shook her head in response to some private thought.

"I guess you heard," he ventured, after a while, "that Isabel decided to take the boys and go live with her sister." He was distracted, still thinking about how she'd said she'd trust him until he gave her a reason to stop.

Libby Remington was an amazing woman.

Libby turned her head to look at him again, nodded. "She didn't waste much time getting out of here," she observed, and there was a deliberately noncommittal note in her voice that diverted some of Tate's attention from the riot she'd caused in his senses.

He hooked his thumbs into the waistband of his jeans and tilted his head to one side. Hildie squatted a few feet away, then came back to stand between him and Libby, tail wagging, tongue lolling, eyes hopeful that a good time would be had by all, dogs included.

"I told Isabel she was welcome to stay here on the Spur for as long as she wanted," Tate said quietly, "but she decided to leave right away. Nico said she saw Pablo everywhere she looked, and that was too painful."

Libby considered that, nodded. Hildie went off, found a short, crooked stick in the grass, brought it to Libby, and dropped it at her feet.

With a smile, Libby bent, picked up the stick and tossed it a little way.

Hildie trundled awkwardly after it. Brought it back.

"Why the impromptu dinner invitation, Tate?" Libby asked mildly. "And what's with all the lumber and shingles and bags of cement?"

Tate bent, picked up Hildie's stick, and threw it a little farther than Libby had. While the dog searched through the wild grass that grew beyond the edge of the lawn, Tate held out a hand to Libby.

"Come on," he said. "I'll explain while I show you around."

Libby hesitated, then took his hand. Hildie had found the stick, clasping it between her teeth, but she seemed to be done playing fetch for the time being.

Tate took care not to crush Libby's fingers as he led her up the front steps and into the house. The sexual charge that had arced between them on the drive out of town had gone underground, though Tate knew it would reassert itself sooner rather than later.

He watched Libby as she looked around, waited for the dog to waddle in, then quietly shut the door.

Over the few days since Isabel and Pablo's relatively few possessions had been loaded into a rented truck and hauled away, Tate had removed the old flooring and knocked out several walls. Sheets of drywall waited to be nailed in place once the new framing was in.

Libby's expression was curious and a little pensive when she looked at him. "I still don't understand," she said. "All this—?"

Tate put a hand to the small of her back and steered her toward the kitchen. It was the only room in the house he hadn't torn apart—yet.

"I'm planning on living here, Libby," he said, and his heart beat a little faster, because her reaction to that news was vitally important to him. "Maybe not for good—but for a while."

"Why?" she asked reasonably, folding her arms. The last light of day flowed in through the window behind her, and to Tate, she looked almost luminous, like a figure in stained glass.

"I'm not sure I can explain," he answered, reaching out to flip a switch so the single bulb dangling from the middle of the ceiling illuminated the kitchen. "I want to see what it's like to live in a regular-size house. Drive to a job every day. Actually work for a living."

Libby smiled faintly at that. She *did* live in a "regular-size house," and she certainly made her own way in the world. "I wouldn't know about commuting," she quipped, "but working for a living is overrated, in my opinion."

Tate shoved a hand through his hair, more nervous than he'd expected to be. He'd planned this evening carefully, right down to the steaks marinating in the refrigerator and the coals heating in the portable barbecue grill out back and the good red wine tucked away in one of the cupboards. It had made so much sense during those night hours spent prying up carpeting and stripping walls to the insulation and framework.

Libby came to him, laid her palms to his chest.

The gesture was probably meant to be comforting, but she might as well have hit him with a couple of defibulator paddles, given the effect her touch had on him.

"Tate?" Libby urged.

He sighed. He'd meant to ask Libby to move in with him, come and live in that modest house by the bend in the creek as soon as the remodeling was done; but now he realized what a half-assed, harebrained idea it was. Libby wasn't ready for that kind of constant intimacy, and he wasn't, either.

The twins barely knew Libby, and of course the reverse was true, as well. He would make any sacrifice for his children, but he couldn't expect Libby to feel the same way.

"Give me a minute," he finally said, his voice hoarse, "to pull my foot out of my mouth."

She moved closer, frowning, then slipped her arms loosely around his waist. "What are you talking about?" she asked.

A reasonable question, Tate thought. "I wish I knew," he said.

Libby rested her head against his chest for a few moments, as though she were listening to his heartbeat, and the smell of her hair made him feel light-headed—it was as though all the oxygen had suddenly been sucked out of the room.

Finally, she looked up at him, and her eyes were at once tender and curious. "You're serious about living here, aren't you?" she asked.

Tate nodded. Maybe she'd hate the idea—that would be a problem for sure. And maybe she wouldn't give a damn—which would be even worse.

"And for some reason," Libby went on, "my opinion matters to you."

"Yes," he ground out. "For some reason, it does."

"Why?" Libby seemed completely, honestly puzzled.

"Because—" Again, Tate's neck burned. "Well, because it *would* matter to some women—they'd think I was crazy, moving out of a place like the ranch house, into this one…"

Libby brought her chin up a notch and set her hands on her hips. "Would it matter to you, if I thought you were crazy?"

"No," he answered, after some thought. "If you *didn't* think that, I'd figure you hadn't been paying much attention."

She laughed, stood on tiptoe to kiss the cleft in his chin. Then she looked around. "Alone at last," she said. "Do you want me as much as I want you, Tate?"

"Yeah," he replied, "and I've got the hard-on to prove it."

"So I've noticed," Libby crooned, grinding into him again. This time, there was no mistaking things—the move was deliberate.

"You might want to watch it," Tate warned, his hands making their own way to where they wanted to be—cupping Libby's ass and lifting her closer so he could do a little grinding of his own. "This time, I'm prepared. I have condoms."

Libby moaned, her eyes half-closed, her head back. A fetching wash of pink played over her cheekbones.

When Libby was fifteen and Tate was seventeen, he'd taken her virginity in the back seat of his dad's car, and she'd looked just the way she did now—flushed, eager, unafraid.

"I'm prepared, too," she said, so softly that Tate barely heard her.

His knees weak, Tate dropped into one of the four folding chairs he'd bought to go with the card table, his temporary dining suite. Standing Libby between his knees, he unsnapped her jeans, undid the zipper, pulled them down, waited for her to protest.

She didn't.

In fact, she kicked off her shoes and shed her jeans, right there in the kitchen. She was wearing ice-blue panties, trimmed in lace.

He nipped at her through the moist crotch, and she groaned, entwining her fingers in his hair.

"What do you mean, you're prepared?" he murmured, hooking his thumbs under the elastic waistband.

"I'm—I'm on the p-pill—" she gasped.

Had the table been sturdier, Tate would have laid Libby down on it and eaten her thoroughly, but he knew the thing wouldn't support even her slight weight. So he lowered her panties and plied her with gentle motions of his fingers until she was good and wet. Then he opened his jeans and eased her down slowly, onto his shaft, giving her a little at a time.

She wanted to ride him, and hard—that was evident in the way she moved, or tried to move.

Tate grasped her hips and stopped her. "Easy," he murmured. "Slow and easy, Lib."

She made a strangled sound, her eyes sultry, but she let him set the pace. Let him strip off her lightweight T-shirt and open her bra, so her perfect breasts were there for the taking.

Tate enjoyed them at his leisure until Libby made another sound—this one exasperated—and drew him into a kiss so hot that he nearly lost control and came right then and there.

"Do it," she gasped, when the kiss finally ended, "damn you, Tate McKettrick, *do it!*"

He chuckled, a raspy sound, and took her in earnest then, raising and lowering her, fast and then faster, deep and then deeper.

The release was cataclysmic, blinding Tate, rending a long, hoarse shout from him, like that of a dying man. Through it, he heard Libby, calling his name over and over again.

And then they were both still.

Slowly, the world reassembled itself around them.

"*Damn,* woman," Tate growled. "That was good."

Libby giggled. "Yeah," she said, moving to disengage herself. "Is there a working shower in this place?"

Tate stopped her from rising off him by tightening his grasp on her hips. He was getting hard again, and she was in for another ride.

"No," he said, raising her and then lowering her again, until she'd taken all of him, until she gasped. "No shower."

"Tate—"

He bent his head, tongued her right nipple until she groaned and arched her back, offering him full access. "Ummm?" he asked, his mouth full of her then.

"I—oh, God—I'm already coming—I—"

Tate slid his hands up, supporting her with his palms so she could lean back, give herself up to the orgasm.

He watched, fighting his own release, as Libby arched away from him, golden-fleshed, nipples hard and moist from his mouth, her hair falling free, her beautiful body buckling and seizing with pleasure.

When she cried out his name, and a long, sweet shudder of full surrender went through her, Tate couldn't hold back anymore. He let himself go, with a raspy shout, and she rocked on him until he'd given her everything he had to give.

"I'm not sure I can survive a whole lot of that," she admitted, a long time later, when they'd helped each other, bumbling and fumbling, back into at least some of their clothes.

"We need to spend more time together," Tate said. "Get in some practice."

Libby sighed contentedly. "And we'd—*practice* a lot?"

Tate grinned. "Maybe not on the kitchen floor, though. I was sort of planning on buying a bed, but, yeah, there would be a lot of rowdy sex."

Libby made a comical move that might have meant her underpants were wedged in where they shouldn't be. "I like rowdy sex," she said.

He laughed. Padded over to the fridge for the steaks. "So I've noticed," he responded.

Suddenly, she looked sad, and some of the glow was

gone. "What if sex is all we have together, Tate? All we've *ever* really had."

Tate, halfway to the back door with the package of steaks in one hand by then, turned to look at her. "Then I'd say we were pretty damn lucky," he responded. "But there's more, and you know it."

"Not that I'm angling to get married," she blurted out. Then she blushed miserably and groaned. "But nobody said anything about marriage, did they?"

"You're not ready for that," Tate told her, setting the meat on the counter and going back to stand facing her, "and neither am I. I've got things to prove to you, Libby."

She blinked. "Like what?"

"Well, first of all, you need to be sure you can trust me. For a lifetime."

"What if I told you I trust you now?" Another pause. "Although you're perfectly right—we're not ready to get married. I hope I didn't seem—well—*pushy.*"

He grinned. "Never that," he said.

The steaks turned out perfectly.

They went on to the main ranch house and took a shower together in his en suite bathroom and made love again.

They slept, arms and legs entangled after hours of love-making, in his bed.

He should have known it had all been too easy.

CHAPTER TWELVE

A PHONE SHRILLED in the night, jarring Libby, in lurching stages, out of a rest so profound that no shred or tatter of a dream could have reached her. She opened her eyes, blinking, to utter darkness, and knew only that she wasn't in her own bed—the mattress, the bedding, the angles were all wrong.

"Tate McKettrick," Tate said, his voice gravelly with sleep and the beginnings of alarm.

Libby sat up, drawing her knees to her chest and wrapping her arms around her shins.

"Calm down, Cheryl," Tate went on. "I can't understand you—"

Libby closed her eyes a nanosecond before she heard the click of a lamp switch. Light flared against her lids, a fiery orange-red. She looked at Tate, blinking.

He sat up. "Take a breath," he said, shifting the phone from his right ear to his left, so he could close his fingers around Libby's hand and squeeze once. He threw back the covers, got out of bed, began pulling opening drawers, dressing—jeans, a T-shirt, socks and boots.

"Okay," he said. "Okay."

Libby's heart thrummed. A call at that hour—3:17 a.m. by the digital clock on Tate's night table—could not be good.

Tate was listening again; the glance he tossed in Libby's direction bounced away without connecting.

For the briefest moment, she felt dismissed, invisible.

"Put her on, Cheryl," Tate said. A long pause. "Cheryl? I said *put Ava on the phone.*"

Libby scrambled off the bed, nearly fell because she was so entangled in the top sheet. Her clothes were on the far side of the room, and she tripped twice, hurrying to get to them.

"Yes, Ava," Tate said, "it's Dad. What's the problem, Shortstop? I thought you were excited about visiting New York."

Libby could hear the timbre of the child's voice, if not the words. Ava was practically hysterical.

She forgot about getting into her clothes and went back to the bed, carefully managing the train of bedsheet in the process, plunking down on the end of the mattress and watching Tate as he paced, listening, nodding.

"You'll be home in a few days, honey," he told his daughter gently, when there was a break in the conversation.

Tate sat down beside Libby, slipped his arm around her waist.

She felt a little less like an outsider.

"Ava?" Tate waited. "I love you. I'll be right here when you get back. You can ride your ponies, and we'll go fishing in the creek—"

More hysteria on the other end of the line.

Tate sighed, and his shoulders sagged a little. "Let me talk to your mother."

Again, Libby wanted to flee. She didn't know exactly what she was hearing, but she was sure she shouldn't be hearing it.

Tate's entire bearing seemed to change when his ex-wife came back on the phone. "Yes," he said. "Yes—sometime tomorrow. I'll let you know. And, Cheryl? Don't call in twenty minutes and say you've changed your mind. We're not going to pretend this didn't happen."

Libby lowered her head, waited.

Finally, Tate snapped his phone shut.

For a long time, he just sat there beside Libby, looking down at the floor.

Libby shifted, ran a hand down his back. "Anything I can do to help, cowboy?" she asked quietly. She didn't want to interfere, but she couldn't just sit there, either.

"I have to head for New York," he said. "First thing in the morning."

Libby nodded. Waited. If Tate wanted to explain, he would. If he didn't, that was okay, too.

Tate shoved a hand through his hair. His eyes were bluer than usual, and bleak, even as he tried to smile. "This is what my life is like, Lib," he said, very quietly. "I have an ex-wife and two kids and executive control over a ranch the size of some counties. There's always some kind of crisis, and a lot of them seem to happen in the middle of the night."

Libby drew the sheet more closely around her. "Audrey and Ava—they're okay?"

Tate held her against his side, rested his chin on top of her head. She felt his nod. "I didn't get the whole story," he said, "but the gist of it seems to be that getting her parents' apartment ready to put on the market is more work than Cheryl expected it to be, and the girls aren't making it any easier because they're fussy and homesick. Apparently, Ava had a pretty bad dream tonight—Cheryl showed the twins around the school she went to and asked them how they'd like to go there when they start first grade in the fall, and that must have freaked Ava out." He paused, sighed. "According to our divorce agreement, neither Cheryl nor I can reside anywhere but Blue River, Texas, without forfeiting custody to the other—but knowing my ex-wife, I'd say she figures I might give ground if I thought the girls really wanted to grow up somewhere else."

"Cheryl wants to live in New York?"

"Who knows?" Tate asked, letting go of Libby, standing. "I've never been able to figure out what Cheryl wants. I'm not sure *she* knows, actually."

Libby watched as he took a leather carry-on bag from the enormous closet, threw in a change of clothes and some shaving gear. "So you're going to bring the twins back home?"

He turned, looked at her. "Yeah," he said. Sadness moved in his eyes. "Ava wants to be in Blue River, anyway. I'm not so sure about Audrey. She might choose to stay on and come back with Cheryl, after the apartment's ready to be sold."

Libby stood, still draped in the top sheet, and crossed the room to pick up her clothes. While she didn't know Tate's daughters very well, she *had* figured out that Audrey was the bolder of the two. Ava, with her glasses and hearing aid, while just as bright as her sister, was shy.

"Lib—would you like to come along? To New York, I mean?"

Libby hadn't expected that question. She'd just assumed Tate would want to travel fast and light—get to the city, collect his children, bring them back to Texas.

Excuses rushed through her mind. She had the Perk Up to run, there was Hildie to consider—and what about mowing the lawn and cleaning out the flower beds?

What she actually *said* was, "It could be pretty confusing for the twins—my just showing up like that." She dressed slowly, not looking at Tate. "They're not used to seeing us together, after all."

Tate sighed. "Point taken," he said. "But if we're going to keep seeing each other, they need to start getting used to our being together, Lib."

She was wearing all her clothes by then, but she still felt naked, stripped to the soul. "Maybe it's a little soon to spring that on them," she ventured. "Our spending time together, I mean."

He left off packing then, crossed the room, took her gently by the shoulders. "When I've finished the house," he said, "I plan on asking you to come and live with me. You might as well know that." Curving his fingers under her chin, he lifted her face so he could look directly into her eyes. "As for sex—I'll be granting no quarter, Libby. Whether we're sharing a house and a bed or not, I promise you, I'll seduce you every chance I get, any way I can, any-*place* I can."

Libby blushed so hard it hurt. Tate knew what she liked, in and out of bed. He knew all the right words to say, all the secret, special places where she loved to be caressed, nibbled, teased.

But, then, Libby knew a few things herself.

Two could play that game.

"You'd better be real quick to make the first move, cowboy," she said, unfastening his jeans, pushing her hand inside, loving the way he groaned, the way he swelled when she closed her fingers around him. "Or you might just find *yourself* being seduced."

Tate swallowed hard. "Libby—"

"No quarter, Tate," she said, working him, enjoying the

way he responded. "No prisoners. If I want you, I'll have you. On the spot."

A powerful shudder moved through him, even as he gave a strangled laugh, perhaps at her audacity.

"In fact," Libby murmured, "I'm pretty sure I want you right now."

"*Libby—*"

"Right—here—"

He moaned aloud as Libby proceeded to prove her point.

TATE CAUGHT AN EARLY flight out of Austin, and the landing at LaGuardia went without a hitch. Since he'd only brought a carry-on—he didn't plan on staying even overnight—he didn't have to wait with the crowds around the luggage carousels.

The cab line was long, as usual, but it moved quickly.

The drive into the city passed almost unnoticed—Tate's mind was back in Texas, for most of the ride, with Libby.

When the taxi stopped in front of Cheryl's parents' building, though, he made the necessary mental shift—time to think about the business at hand.

He paid the cabdriver and turned, bracing himself.

The doorman stood under a green-and-white awning, eyeing him warily.

"My name's Tate McKettrick," Tate said. "I'm here to see Ms. Darbrey."

The older man smiled fondly at the mention of Cheryl. "I'll buzz her," he said, stepping inside and pressing one of a series of brass buttons gleaming on a panel behind his desk.

Tate waited outside, taking in the sounds and sights of a great city just gearing up for a new day. He was a rancher—body, mind and spirit—but he liked New York, liked the energy and buzz of the place.

The doorman returned, holding the door open. "Go right up, Mr. McKettrick," he said. "Apartment 17B."

Tate merely nodded and, gripping the handle of his carry-on, passed the doorman and headed for the elevator.

Outside 17B, minutes later, Tate stopped to prepare himself for whatever he might have to deal with. Since he'd been announced, there wasn't much point in knocking or ringing the doorbell.

On the other side of the door, a sequence of sliding chains and turning bolts began. Then the door opened, and Ava, still wearing pajamas, launched herself into his arms.

Audrey was there, too, but she stood back a little way, and Tate felt dread pinch his heart as he studied her small face.

He kissed Ava's cheek as he closed the door, gathered Audrey against his side.

Cheryl appeared in the arched doorway leading into the gracious living room, with its gas fireplace, built-in bookcases, and high, ornately molded ceilings. She looked coolly elegant in white slacks—the tails of her red silk shirt were tied at her midriff, revealing a flat, tanned stomach, and her hair was plaited into a single braid.

"Come in," she said. "Breakfast is almost ready."

"Are we going home today?" Ava wanted to know. "Are we going back to Texas?"

Cheryl's face tightened a little, but her smile remained in place. Nobody would have guessed, to look at her, that she'd called Tate in the middle of the night complaining that the twins in general and Ava in particular were about to drive her out onto the nearest ledge.

"We're going home today," Tate confirmed quietly, setting Ava on her feet.

Then, to Cheryl, he said, "Is there coffee?"

She nodded. "You haven't shaved," she remarked, and her cat-green eyes narrowed a little. Wheels were turning behind that alabaster-smooth forehead. "Late night, maybe?"

"I was in a hurry," he said, galled that he'd explained even that much.

They were in the living room now, and he looked around. No moving boxes, he noted. No clutter, either. Gone were her father's teetering stacks of reference books, notes and file folders bulging with clippings.

Cheryl's parents had fallen on hard times—mostly of their own making—long before she and Tate were married, but they *had* managed to hold on to the apartment, mainly by mortgaging it repeatedly.

By the time the twins were born, the place had gone into foreclosure and Cheryl was making noises about bringing Mom and Dad to live with her and Tate, in Blue River.

Tate, unable to get cell reception, had promptly called his lawyer from a hospital pay phone and instructed him to buy the Park Avenue place outright and put the deed in Cheryl's name.

Her folks had gone on living there until just a few months ago, when she'd finally made the decision to move them into an assisted-living place. He was picking up the tab for that, too, since they couldn't afford it on their own.

"I want to go home today," Ava said firmly.

Audrey made a face. "You're such a baby."

"Hush," Tate said.

In the kitchen, which was as spacious as the living room and also showed no evidence that anybody had been packing for a move, Cheryl set out four mismatched antique plates on the round table. The piece, Tate decided, was probably supposed to look antique and French—"distressed," his ex-wife termed it—meaning it had been falsely aged with things like sandpaper and rusty bicycle chain, swung hard.

He could identify.

In a classic *you-big-dumb-cowboy* moment, Tate realized that Cheryl had never had any intention of selling the apartment. She'd probably spent the girls' weeks with him right here, getting settled. Making new friends, or reconnecting with old ones, circulating her résumé.

"Mommy got a job offer," Audrey said, confirming his thoughts.

"Audrey Rose," Cheryl said, "*hush.* I wanted to tell your daddy about that myself."

Tate's blood seemed to buzz in his veins; the feeling was a combination of pissed off and thank God. Calmly, he washed his hands at the kitchen sink, sat down in the chair his ex-wife indicated. Although his glance sliced to Cheryl, he held his tongue and kept his face expressionless.

Avoiding his gaze, Cheryl served him hot, strong coffee, while the girls had orange juice. Bagels and smoked salmon, cream cheese and capers followed, and fresh strawberries finished off the meal.

"Go and get dressed, both of you," Cheryl told the kids when they'd obviously eaten all they intended to, for the time being at least.

They balked a little, especially Ava, who seemed reluctant to let Tate out of her sight for fear he'd vanish, but the pair finally hurried off to put on their clothes.

"It's a long commute between here and Blue River," Tate commented quietly.

Cheryl sighed, and her cup rattled in its saucer when she reached for it. "I could be there every other weekend," she said, avoiding his gaze. When she finally looked at him, though, he saw a different woman behind those green eyes, a woman he'd probably never known in the first place.

"The job—it's a good one, Tate."

"I'm happy for you," he said, without sarcasm.

"Don't ruin this for me," she whispered. *"Please."*

"I'm not out to ruin anything for you, Cheryl," Tate told her reasonably, and in all truth. "But we have a custody agreement, and I'm not willing to change it."

Tears brimmed in Cheryl's eyes. "Ava wants to live with you, on the Silver Spur. I thought Audrey could—"

Tate leaned forward in his chair, careful to keep his voice down. "You thought Audrey could *what?*" he asked.

"Stay here, with me," Cheryl said. "Just during the week. Tate, Audrey loves New York, just like I do. It would be so good for her—"

"You want to split them up?"

Cheryl's shoulders moved in a semblance of a shrug, but there was nothing nonchalant in her expression. She looked miserable. "I know it's not an ideal situation," she said. Then she bit down on her lower lip, and when she spoke again, her voice had dropped to a desperate whisper. "I can't stay in Blue River until our daughters are eighteen, Tate. I just can't. I'll lose my mind if I try!"

Tate felt sorry for Cheryl in that moment—she was a beautiful woman, with a law degree and a lot of ambition. She wasn't cut out for the kind of life she'd been living in Blue River; she needed a career. She needed the throb and hurry of a city around her, subway trains rumbling under her feet, traffic lights changing, horns honking 24/7.

"I understand that," he said, and he did. "But, as I said, we have an agreement, Cheryl. It would be wrong—*worse* than wrong—to separate the twins, have them grow up apart."

Cheryl put her hands over her face and began to cry.

Tate loved Libby Remington—the time he'd just spent with her had left him more convinced of that than ever—but as bitter as his and Cheryl's marriage and divorce had been, he didn't like seeing her hurting the way she was.

"I'm going home later today," he told his ex-wife quietly, even gently, "and I'm taking Audrey and Ava with me. If you really want to practice law again though, here in New York or anywhere else, you ought to do it."

She lowered her hands. Her eyes were wet, puffy and a little red around edges. "Do you mean that?"

In the near distance, Tate heard his daughters approaching, engaged in some little-girl exchange that was part giggle and part squabble.

"Yes," he said. "I mean it."

"You wouldn't hold it against me—think I was a bad mother—if I stayed here?"

Born and raised in the country, among old-fashioned folks, a mother willingly living apart from her children was a foreign thing to Tate. Times were changing, though—maybe not for the better—and Cheryl had worked hard to earn that law degree. Barely gotten to use it.

"I think," he replied carefully, "that what you do with your life is your own business."

Audrey and Ava burst into the kitchen, wearing jeans and short-sleeved cotton blouses with little red and white checks.

"All packed to go back to Blue River?" Tate asked.

Ava nodded.

Audrey looked less certain. That gave him a pang.

"I need to talk to your mom alone for a few more minutes," he said. "Ava, maybe you could help your sister get her things together."

Audrey glanced at Cheryl, then turned and followed Ava out of the room again.

Cheryl shifted in her chair, cupped her hands around her coffee mug, as though to warm them. "I know I was supposed to sell this apartment, Tate, but—"

"Let's worry about that later," Tate said, when her words fell away. "This is a big decision, Cheryl. It might be the right one, and it might be one you'll come to regret someday. Possibly, it's both those things, life being what it is."

She swallowed, nodded. "What will you tell them?" she asked, her voice small. "When you take Audrey and Ava back to Texas, what will you tell them?" She glanced anxiously at the doorway, then her gaze swung back to Tate's face and clung. "It isn't that I don't love the kids."

"I know you love them," Tate said gruffly, and he *did* know. Like most people, Cheryl was probably doing the best she could. The insight made him feel incredibly sad. "I won't try to convince them otherwise, I promise."

"Thank you, Tate."

He pushed back his chair, meaning to stand, but Cheryl stayed him by touching his arm.

"Have another cup of coffee," she said. "There's no big rush, is there?"

Tate sighed. He liked New York well enough, but the walls of that apartment seemed to be creeping in on him, an inch or two at a time. "How are your folks doing at the assisted-living place?" he asked, while Cheryl hurried to the counter for the coffeepot.

Cheryl looked sad as she refilled his cup, then her own. It felt strange, her pouring coffee for him. "Not so well," she said, setting the pot on the table and sinking into a chair. "Every time I call or visit, they beg to come back here.

When begging doesn't work, they start accusing me of things, like *stealing* their home out from under them—"

Tate guessed it was a tough row to hoe, having aging parents, but from his point of view, it sure beat not having any at all. "That might pass, once they get used to the new place," he said. "And if it doesn't, well, you know they don't really mean any of those things."

Cheryl sniffled, nodded.

A silence descended on that kitchen. They'd never had much to say to each other, unless they were talking about the girls.

Half an hour later, Tate was in a cab with both his daughters, headed for LaGuardia. Ava fairly bounced on the seat, she was so happy to be going home, but Audrey was—subdued, he guessed he'd call it.

"You like the Big Apple, Shortstop?" he asked her, squeezing her small hand.

She looked up at him, nodded. "Mommy was going to let me audition for TV commercials," she said wistfully. "And take singing and dancing lessons, too."

"I see," Tate said seriously, because to his daughter, these *were* serious matters.

"She thought you might let us live in New York with her for a while," Audrey added. "So you'd have more time to get reacquainted with Libby."

An acid sting shot through Tate's stomach. "I do like spending time with Libby," he confirmed evenly. "But I'd miss you way too much if you lived here."

Audrey's remarkably blue eyes widened slightly. "Then you still want us around? Wouldn't we be underfoot?"

Tate turned in Audrey's direction, tightened his arm around Ava's shoulders at the same time. "Of course I want you around," he said. "And you can get underfoot all you want."

Audrey smiled. "Okay," she said, and with a little sigh, she rested the side of her head against his chest.

"She still wants to be in the Pixie Pageant," Ava said righteously, folding her arms. "You don't even know when you're being *played,* Dad."

Tate hugged Ava closer. "I'm smarter than I look," he told her, and kissed the top of her head. Then he squeezed Audrey again. "Is that true, monkey? You really want to take on this Pixie thing?"

Audrey nodded. "I just want to *try,* Daddy. I'll be okay if I don't win."

Sometimes the maturity of a six-year-old could take a man by surprise.

"Tell you what," Tate said, when he'd mulled the insight over for a few moments. "When we get home, I'll look into this pageant deal and see if it's something we can both live with. Sound fair to you?"

The little girl beamed. "Sounds fair to me," she said, putting up her right hand for Tate's high-five.

ONCE THEY'D CHECKED IN, gone through security and boarded a plane bound for Austin, where Tate's truck would be waiting in the airport parking garage, the twins, seated side by side across the aisle from him, flipped the pages of the catalogs and airline magazines like a pair of vertically challenged adults.

They were only six.

And they would be grown women long before he was ready for that to happen.

The girls each had a suitcase, so they had to wait in

baggage claim for a while, but soon enough they were in the truck and on their way to the ranch.

Ambrose and Buford were waiting when they arrived, barking their fool heads off and jumping as if they'd swallowed a bucket of those Mexican beans, but they stayed well clear of the truck—which meant that, between the two of them, they might have a lick of sense.

There was a big, blank spot in the yard where that ridiculous castle had stood, but if Audrey and Ava noticed at all, they didn't react. They were too glad to see the pups again.

The feeling was certainly mutual.

Tate grinned and shook his head as he watched his daughters, in their expensive playclothes, kneeling in the grass to accept canine adoration in the form of face-licking and happy yips and impromptu wrestling matches on the ground.

Esperanza came out onto the patio, wearing yet another apron from her vast collection, waving.

Audrey and Ava and the dogs scrambled toward her, all but tumbling over each other, and as he watched, Tate's throat thickened and his eyes burned.

He belonged on that land, and so did his children.

After all, they were McKettricks.

CHAPTER THIRTEEN

LIBBY WAS MOWING her lawn, sweat-soaked and bug-bitten, even after the streetlights had come on, determined to finish the job come hell or high water. Hildie sat on the front porch, head tilted to one side, ears perked, watching her mistress with pitying curiosity.

A light rain began, a mist at first, then a sprinkle, cooling Libby's overheated flesh and at the same time causing her to grit her teeth. *Here's the high water,* she thought, *so hell can't be far behind.*

She stopped at the edge of the flower bed below the front porch, turned the mower grimly in the opposite direction, and saw Tate McKettrick pull up to the curb in his big truck.

The rain made his dark hair curl at the ends and dampened his white shirt.

At once embarrassed to be caught looking like the proverbial drowned rat and delighted to see Tate, no matter what, Libby froze.

Tate opened the gate, came through, shut it again.

Hildie gave a welcoming woof and started down the porch steps, but Libby neither moved nor spoke. The rain came in fat droplets now, spiking her eyelashes and blurring her vision.

Tate bent to ruffle Hildie's ears in greeting, then straightened to face Libby. He pried the handle of the push-mower from her fingers and leaned in to land a kiss on her right temple.

Damn, but he smelled good.

"Hey," he said.

Libby waited, her heart pounding, full of both delicious relief because he'd come back from New York and potential misery because he might have brought his ex-wife home with him.

Nobody knew it better than Libby did: This man would do *anything* for his kids, including marry a woman he'd never claimed to love. He'd done that once already, and she had no doubt whatsoever that he'd do it again, if he thought it was best for Audrey and Ava.

Tate smoothed Libby's soggy bangs back off her forehead, his touch light and, at the same time, electric. "You do realize," he began, in that easy and oh-so-familiar drawl of his, "that lightning could strike at any time?"

Libby stared up at him, baffled. As far as she was concerned, lightning had *already* struck, way back in second grade, when she'd suddenly looked at Tate McKettrick, that pesky ranch kid with all the freckles and the lock of dark hair forever falling into his blue eyes, in a startling new—and *old*—way. Barely seven at the time, Libby wouldn't have been able to articulate the feeling then, except to say it was like remembering—without the actual memories.

Heck, she wasn't sure she could articulate it *now,* and she was all grown up. Love? Lust? Some combination of the two?

Who knew?

All grown up into a pesky ranch *man,* sans the freckles but still with an impish glint in his too-blue-to-be-legal eyes, Tate chuckled and steered Libby up the porch steps, Hildie following.

Libby stood just out of the rain, watching as Tate went back down the steps, easily hoisted the heavy push-mower off the ground, carried it onto the porch and set it in a corner, where it would stay dry.

She finally found her voice. "Did you bring the twins home?"

Tate nodded, opened the screen door, laid his hand on the small of her back and gently pushed her into the lighted living room.

"They're sound asleep in their own beds, and Esperanza is looking after them," he said, his eyes traveling the length of her, from her sturdy hiking boots to her jean shorts to the blouse with the tie front. He frowned as he closed the door behind him. "What's with the all-weather yardwork?" he asked. "You didn't hear the thunder? See the flashes of lightning? On top of all that, it's *dark.*"

Libby had been jumpy all day—and some of the night, too. She'd been so busy over the last five years, looking after her dad, starting the Perk Up, and now helping out with Marva, too. Her life had been hectic, yes, but now it seemed things happened at warp speed; one moment, she was in bed with Tate, the next, she was trying to mow the lawn in the rain.

"I guess I just have too much energy," she said. *I'm going crazy, and it's your fault. For so long I could pretend you didn't exist, that we didn't have a history. Now I can't pretend anymore, because you won't let me.*

Tate folded his arms, and she saw a muscle bunch in his jaw, then relax again. "You need to warm up, Lib; your lips are blue and your teeth are chattering a little. Take a hot shower, and while you're doing that, I'll warm up some milk for you."

Warm milk? Not what she would have expected from a confirmed cowboy like Tate. And she got the clear impression that he wasn't planning to strip out of his own rain-dampened clothes and join her in the shower, either.

This was both a disappointment and a relief.

Libby swallowed, just to keep from sighing. She hated warm milk unless it was liberally disguised with chocolate.

"Okay," she said, and her voice sounded tinny in her ears, as though she were one of those old-fashioned talking dolls, and someone had just pulled the string in her belly.

Resigned, she headed for the bathroom.

Fifteen minutes later, Libby joined Tate in the kitchen; by then she was wearing cotton pajamas, her unsexiest robe, and furry slippers from the back of her closet. As hot and muggy as that Texas night was, she felt oddly chilled.

Tate sat at the table, ruminating as he sipped instant coffee from a mug, but he rose to his feet when he spotted Libby, the chair scraping back behind him as he stood. "Sit down," he said.

His serious tone, on top of all that thinking, worried Libby. *Had* Tate and Cheryl reconnected somehow, while he was in New York, as she had secretly feared they would? Decided to give their marriage another try, if only for the children's sake?

"Why are you here?" she asked, crumpling a little on the inside.

Tate drew back a chair for her, waited in silence until she sat. Then he poured hot milk for her, added a dollop of brandy from a dusty bottle stored on the shelf above the broom closet, brought it to the table.

"We need to talk," he said.

Libby's heart began to thrum. *Here it comes,* she thought,

*the part where he says he still has feelings for Cheryl, or the
kids need him 24/7 or we're just plain moving too fast and
need to take a breather...*

"Okay," she replied hoarsely, glad he couldn't see her
hands knotted together in her lap because the tabletop was
in the way. Then she squared her shoulders, raised her chin,
looked him right in the eye, and waited.

"Drink the milk," Tate said. "It has to be hot to work."

Libby unknotted her hands, picked up the cup, took a sip.

It wasn't half bad—but it wasn't half *good,* either.

She made a face.

Tate grinned, reached across to smooth away her milk
mustache with the pad of one thumb.

Libby set the cup down, felt some of the tension drain
from her muscles.

Tate's expression changed; he leaned slightly forward, his
dark brows lowered but not quite coming together. "What
do you know about this Pixie thing?" he asked gravely.

Libby blinked, mystified. And almost dizzy with relief,
because he hadn't said he and Cheryl were getting back
together.

"'Pixie thing'?" she echoed.

Was he asking if she believed in fairies, little people?

Tate looked deep into her eyes and a grin broke over his
face. "Sorry," he said. "I guess I should have laid a little
groundwork before I threw that question at you. I'm talking
about the Pixie Pageant. It's some kind of shindig they're
holding at the country club, for charity. Like a beauty contest, but for little girls."

"Oh," Libby said, vaguely remembering a piece she'd
skimmed in the *Blue River Clarion,* the town's weekly newspaper, "*that* Pixie Pageant."

Tate's jaw tightened. "Audrey is real set on signing up for the thing," he said.

Libby smiled. "What about Ava?"

"Ava thinks it's silly and wants no part of it. I happen to agree. But, like I said, Audrey is determined."

"A determined McKettrick," Libby mused, grinning. "Just *imagine* it."

Tate gave a wan grin at that, relaxed a little. "I've been dead set against this—Audrey joining up with this Pixie outfit, I mean—from the first. There are so many ways she could get hurt—"

Libby chuckled, took another sip of the milk-brandy mixture, and set her cup down. "As opposed to some *safe* activity, like rodeo?" she teased. Tate, Garrett and Austin had all been involved in the sport from earliest childhood.

Tate sighed, shoved a hand through his hair, leaving moist ridges where his fingers passed. "I get your point," he said, and sighed again. A pause followed, long and somehow comfortable. Tate finally ended it with, "What do you think I should do? Let Audrey sign up for this thing, or stand my ground?"

"I think," Libby said carefully, "that this is a conversation you should probably have with Cheryl, not me."

"I know what Cheryl thinks. I want to know what you think, Libby."

Her heart beat a little faster. She drew a fast, deep breath and huffed it out. "Why?" she asked.

"I need an unbiased opinion."

"Did you ask Esperanza?"

"Yes, as a matter of fact," Tate answered. "I did. And she's biased."

"For or against?"

"For," Tate admitted. "She thinks the whole thing is harmless and if Audrey gives it a try, she'll lose interest. Get it out of her system."

"Makes sense," Libby said, still careful. This was dangerous ground; Cheryl was the twins' mother, Esperanza had been the family housekeeper forever. But *she,* Libby, was what to them? Their father's girlfriend?

Not even that.

She was someone he slept with when they weren't around.

"Come on, Lib," Tate urged.

"What makes you so sure *I'm* unbiased?" Libby asked, more than a little hurt, now that she thought about it. The term merely meant "impartial," she knew that, but it sounded so indifferent in this context—she might have been someone stopped by a survey taker, on the way out of a supermarket, for heaven's sake. *Did she prefer laundry detergent with or without bleach?*

Tears scalded her eyes.

"I'm overreacting," she said. "I'm sorry."

Tate looked as though he wanted to touch her, rise from his chair and pull her into his arms, or tug her onto his lap.

But he did none of those things.

He cleared his throat. Looked away from Libby, then looked back. "Tell me something," he said.

Something tensed in the pit of Libby's stomach. "What?"

"If we get together, you and I," Tate ventured quietly, "you'll be around the kids a lot. Does that bother you?"

"*Bother* me?"

"If they hadn't been conceived—"

Adrenaline stung through Libby's system. "You're *not* suggesting that I blame *those precious children* for *our* breakup?"

"It would bother some women," Tate said, sounding a little defensive and a lot relieved.

"I'm not one of those women," Libby told him, her voice tight. While it was true that she didn't know Audrey and Ava very well, she had always loved them, albeit from afar, because they were Tate's.

"Good," Tate said. "Now, how about giving me an opinion on the Pixie Pageant?"

She laughed. "You never give up, do you?"

"Never," he answered, but he wasn't laughing, or even smiling.

Libby was quiet for a while, thinking. Finally, she said, "Okay, here's my opinion—you should check the pageant out, talk to the people putting it on, find out exactly what's involved. If it's something you can live with, let Audrey compete if she still wants to."

Tate sighed. "What if I miss something?" he asked.

Libby smiled uncertainly. "Miss something?"

"I'm a man, Lib. I don't know squat about this Pixie thing. They'll probably need tutus and stuff—"

Libby pictured Tate shopping for tutus and put a hand over her mouth to keep from laughing. Then, seeing that he was truly concerned, she sobered. "Can't Cheryl take care of that kind of thing?"

"Cheryl," Tate said, "is staying in New York for the time being. Right now, she plans on coming back here every other weekend, to be with the kids, but I don't suppose that will last long."

Libby stared at him. "Cheryl is staying in New York," she repeated stupidly.

"I didn't mention that before?"

"You didn't mention that before."

"Oh." Tate pushed back his chair, stood. "Well, she is. Will you help me, Lib? With the Pixie Pageant, I mean?"

Libby stood up, went to him, rested against his chest. "Yes," she said. "I'll help you."

He grinned down at her, sunshine bursting through a bank of dark clouds. "Do you have any idea how sexy you look in those pajamas and that worn-out bathrobe?"

Libby made the time-out sign, straightening the fingers of her left hand and pressing them into the palm of her right.

"What?" Tate asked, sounding innocent, though the twinkle in his eyes was anything *but* innocent.

"No sex," Libby was surprised to hear herself say. "Not tonight, anyway. I'm still recovering from last time."

"Recovering?" Tate asked, pretending to be hurt. The twinkle remained, though.

"Yes, *recovering,*" Libby said, blushing. "It's not just sex when we're together, Tate. Not for me."

He raised a questioning eyebrow, looked intrigued.

Ran his hands down her back and cupped her bottom.

"Lib?" Tate prompted, when she didn't say anything else.

She caught her breath, found her voice, lost it again.

Sex wasn't just sex to Libby, not with Tate McKettrick. But how the hell was she supposed to explain that, without coming right out and saying that she still loved him? That, like a fool, she'd never *stopped* loving him, even while he was another woman's husband?

Even after his and Cheryl's divorce, Libby had been careful to stay away from Tate. She managed pretty well, too, until the day of the twins' birthday, when he'd walked into the Perk Up and the earth had shifted on its axis.

No, for Libby, sex with this one man was cosmic. It was a personal apocalypse, followed by the formation of new universes.

The one thing it would never be was *just sex.*

Libby didn't even have names for the things she felt when she and Tate were joined physically, and for hours or even days afterward.

"It's getting late," she said, avoiding Tate's eyes because she knew she'd get sucked into them like an unwary planetoid passing too near to a black hole if she let him catch her gaze just at that moment. "Maybe you should go."

He held her close again. She breathed in the scent of him, knew she would be powerless if he made the slightest move to seduce her.

"You're okay?" he asked, his voice hoarse, his breath moving through her hair like the faintest breeze. He propped his chin on top of her head, a sigh moving through his chest.

"I'm okay," she confirmed.

He moved back, curved a finger under her chin, and lifted. "Lib?"

She looked up at him.

Don't kiss me.

I'll die if you don't kiss me.

God help me, I've lost my mind.

"Everything's going to be okay," he told her.

She nodded. Tears threatened again, but she managed to hold them back.

He kissed her forehead.

And then he drew back, no longer holding her.

He bent to ruffle Hildie's ears in farewell.

Then he left.

Libby poured the remains of her milk—now cold—down the sink. She listened to Tate's retreating footsteps, fighting the urge to run after him, call him back, beg him to spend the night. She heard the front door open, close again. Then, distantly, the sound of his truck starting up.

Only then did she walk through the living room to lock up.

She switched off the lamps, went back to the kitchen, let Hildie out into the yard one last time.

Once the dog was inside again, Libby retreated to the bathroom, where she brushed her teeth and shed the robe, hanging it from the peg on the back of the door.

"What a pathetic life I lead," she said, looking at the robe, limp from so many washings, the once-vibrant color faded, the seams coming open in places.

Hildie, standing beside her, gave a concerned whimper, turned and padded into Libby's room.

The two of them settled down for the night, Libby expecting to toss and turn all night, sleepless, burning for the touch of Tate's lips and hands, the warm strength of his arms around her, the sound of his heart beating as she lay with her head on his chest.

Instead, sweet oblivion ambushed her.

She awakened to one of those washed-clean mornings that so often follow a rainstorm, sunlight streaming through her bedroom window.

DAWN HADN'T BROKEN WHEN Tate got out of bed, but a pinkish-apricot light rimmed the hills to the east. He hauled on jeans, a T-shirt, socks and boots. He'd shower and change and have breakfast later, when the range work was done.

He looked in on his girls in their room, found them sleeping soundly, each with a plump yellow dog curled up at her feet. His heart swelled at the sight, but he was afraid to let himself get too happy.

Things were still delicate with Libby.

And Cheryl could change her mind about New York, the apartment, all of it, at any time—come back to the house in

Blue River and start up the whole split-custody merry-go-round all over again.

The thought made his stomach burn.

Quietly, Tate closed the door to his daughters' room and made his way along the hallway, toward the back stairs leading down into the kitchen.

The aroma of brewing coffee rose to meet him halfway.

He smiled.

Esperanza was up, then. Maybe he'd have to reconsider his decision not to take time for breakfast, since she might not let him out of the house until he'd eaten something.

Tate paused when he stepped into the brightly lit kitchen.

Garrett stood at the stove, wearing jeans, boots and a long-sleeved work shirt, frying eggs. "Mornin'," he said affably.

Tate blinked, figuring he was seeing things.

Even when he was on the ranch, which wasn't all that often, Garrett never got up before sunrise, and he sure as *hell* never cooked.

"You're dead and I'm seeing your ghost," Tate said, only half kidding.

Garrett chuckled. There was something rueful in his eyes, something Tate knew he wouldn't share. "Nope," he replied. "It's me, Garrett McKettrick. Live and in person."

Tate fetched a mug from one of the cupboards, filled it from the still-chortling coffeemaker on the counter, watched his younger brother warily as he sipped. "What are you doing here?"

"I live here," Garrett said. "Remember?"

"Vaguely," Tate replied. "To be more specific, what are you doing *in the kitchen, at this hour, cooking,* for God's sake?"

"I'm hungry," Garrett answered quietly. "And if you

never went to bed in the first place, it doesn't count as getting up early, does it?"

"Oh," Tate said. His brain was still cranking up, unsticking itself from sleep.

"Have some eggs," Garrett said, looking Tate over, noting his get-up. "Planning on playing cowboy today?"

Tate felt his neck and the underside of his jaw turn hot, recalling Garrett's earlier jibe about feeling guilty over the money and the land, making a show of working for a living. He took a plate from the long, slatted shelf and shoveled a couple of eggs—"cackleberries," their grandfather had called them—onto it.

They both sat down at the big table in the center of that massive room, and Tate took his time responding to Garrett.

"Yeah," he finally ground out. "I'm planning on 'playing cowboy' today." He let his gaze roll over Garrett's old shirt once, making his point. "Where did you get that rag? From wherever Esperanza stashes the cleaning supplies?"

Garrett chuckled, glancing down at his clothes. "Found them in the back of my closet," he said. "On the floor."

"Okay," Tate said, "I'll bite. What's with the getup?"

Garrett sighed. Possibly practicing his political skills, he didn't exactly answer the question. "The lights were on in the bunkhouse and all the trailers along the creek when I came home a little while ago," he explained, before a brief shadow of sadness fell over his face. He needed a shave, Tate noticed, and there were dark circles under his eyes. "Except the Ruizes', of course. That was dark."

Tate dealt with his own flash of sorrow in silence. He knew Garrett had more to say, so he just waited for him to go on.

"I knew the men were up and around, getting ready for a long day herding cattle or riding fence lines," Garrett eventually continued. "I decided to put on the gear, saddle up and see if I still have it in me—a day of real work."

Tate felt a surge of something—respect, pride? Brotherly love?

He didn't explore the emotion. "These eggs aren't half bad," he said.

"Well," Garrett answered, "don't get used to it. I don't cook, as a general rule."

Tate chuckled, though it was a dry, raspy sound, pushed back from the table, carried his plate to the sink, rinsed it and set it in the dishwasher. Leaned against the counter and folded his arms, watching as Garrett finished his meal and stood.

"Everything all right?" Tate asked, very quietly.

"Everything's *fine,* big brother," Garrett replied. He was lying, of course. From the time he was knee-high to a garden gnome, Garrett hadn't been able to lie and look Tate in the eye at the same time.

Now, he looked everywhere *but* into Tate's face.

"Let's go," Tate said, after a few moments, making for the door.

Just then, Austin came down his personal stairway, clad in work clothes himself, though his shirt was only half-buttoned and crooked at that, and he had a pretty bad case of bed-head. Wearing one boot and carrying the other, he hopped around at the bottom of the steps until he got into the second boot.

"Is there any grub left?" he asked.

"You're too late," Garrett told him.

"Shit," Austin said, finger-combing his hair. "Story of my life."

"Cry me a river," Tate said, with a grin and a roll of his eyes, pulling open the back door.

The predawn breeze felt like the kiss of heaven as it touched him.

He thought about Libby, sleeping warm and soft and deliciously curvy in her bed in town. Since about the last thing he needed right then was a hard-on, he shifted his mind to the day ahead, and the plans he'd made for it.

He strode toward the barn, Garrett and Austin arguing affably behind him, glanced back once to see Austin tucking his shirt into his jeans, none too neatly. It was like the old days, when they were boys, and their dad roused them out of their beds at the crack to do chores, not only in the summer but year-round. The Silver Spur was their ranch, too, Jim McKettrick had often said, and they had to learn how to look after it.

So they fed horses and herded cattle from one pasture to another.

They shoveled out stalls and drove tractors and milked cows and fed chickens.

The chickens and the dairy cows were long gone now, like the big vegetable garden. The quarter-acre plot had been his mother's province; she and Esperanza had spent hours out there, weeding and watering, hoeing and raking. Tate and his brothers had done their share, too, though usually under duress, grumbling that fussing with a lot of tomatoes and green beans and sweet corn was women's work.

"You eat, don't you?" Sally McKettrick had challenged, more than once, shaking a finger under one of their noses. "You eat, you *weed,* bucko. That's the way the *real world* works."

Reaching the barn door, Tate smiled to himself, albeit sadly. Most of the bounty from that garden had gone to the ranch hands and their families and to the little food bank in town. And what he wouldn't give to be sweating under a summer sun again, with his mom just a few rows over, working like a field hand and enjoying every minute of it.

He switched on the overhead lights.

The good, earthy scents of horse and grass-hay and manure stirred as the animals moved in their stalls, nickering and shifting, snorting as they awakened.

Tending the horses wasn't new to Tate—he'd taken the job over from a couple of the ranch hands when he and Cheryl split and she moved into the house in town—though he rarely got to the barn this early in the day.

The work went quickly, divided between the three of them.

Austin turned his childhood mount, Bamboozle, out with the other, larger horses, since the little gelding was used to them and they were used to him, but Audrey's and Ava's golden ponies had to be kept in a special corral, for their own safety.

In the meantime, Tate saddled Stranger, the aging gelding, a strawberry roan, that had belonged to his father. Garrett chose Windwalker, a long-legged bay, while Austin tacked up a sorrel called Ambush.

In his heyday, Ambush had been a rodeo bronc, and he could still buck like the devil when he took the notion.

Austin, being Austin, probably hoped today was the day.

Tate grinned at the thought, shook his head.

His little brother was stone crazy, but you had to love him. Most of the time.

The paint stallion kicked and squealed in his holding pen, scenting the other horses, wanting to be turned loose.

"What are you planning on doing with that stud?" Garrett asked, as the three of them rode away from the barn, toward the range.

"Brent said we might have to put him down," Tate answered. He hated the idea, knew Pablo would have hated it, too, but there had been a death—and that meant the authorities had a say in the matter.

"And you're just going to go along with whatever he says?" Austin wanted to know.

Tate bristled. "The law's the law," he said. "I'd rather not shoot that horse, but I might not have a choice."

"You could just let him go," Garrett suggested. "Say he got out on his own somehow."

"And lie to Brent?" Tate asked. "Not only the chief of police, but my best friend?"

Garrett went quiet.

Austin didn't seem to have anything more to say, either.

So they rode on, the purple range slowly greening up ahead of them.

The herd bawled and raised dust in the dawn as cowboys converged from all directions, some coming from the bunkhouse, which had its own rustic but sturdy stables, and from the various trailers along the creek. Some of the men were on horseback, while others drove pickups with the Silver Spur brand painted on the doors.

Tate and his brothers fell in with the others as easily as if they had never been away from the work, driving cattle between different sections of land to conserve the sweet grass, rippling like waves under a rising wind.

Resting the roan, Stranger, at the creek's edge, Tate nodded as Harley Bates rode up alongside him. Harley had ridden for the McKettrick brand almost as long as Pablo had, though Tate didn't know him as well. Married when he signed on, Bates lived in one of the coveted trailers, although his wife had long since boarded a bus out of town, never to be seen again.

"It ain't the same without ole Pablo," Harley said, resettling his hat, which, like the rest of his gear, had seen better days.

"No," Tate agreed.

Bates shifted in his saddle, and the odor of unwashed flesh wafted Tate's way. "I see you've been fixing up that house by the bend in the creek."

A beat passed before Tate figured out what the man was talking about. He nodded again. "So I have," he said.

"Guess it'll go to the new foreman," Bates speculated. All the men were probably wondering who would replace Pablo Ruiz, and they'd either put Bates up to finding out, or he'd come up with the idea on his own, maybe hoping for a raise in pay and more spacious quarters than the one-bedroom single-wide he banked in now.

"Yep," Tate answered, standing in the stirrups to stretch his legs a little before turning to meet the other man's gaze. "You're looking at the new foreman," he said. "For the time being, anyway. I'll be moving into the Ruiz place myself, as soon as the renovations are finished."

Whatever Harley Bates had expected to hear, it wasn't that. His small eyes popped a little, and his jaws worked as though he were chewing on a mouthful of gristle. "*You're* the new foreman?"

Tate nodded. He couldn't blame the other man for being surprised, even skeptical. After all, the foreman did real work, especially on a spread the size of the Silver Spur. Although Tate could ride and brand and drive post holes with the best of them, he couldn't claim that he'd filled his dad's boots.

And that was why he'd decided to take on the job. If he was going to run the Silver Spur, he had to get serious about it. He had to learn all there was to know about every aspect of running the ranch.

Although it stung, he knew Garrett had been at least partly right, accusing him of playing at being a rancher.

Bates took off his hat, slammed it once against his thigh, and slapped it on again with such force that it bent the tops of his ears.

Tate suppressed a sigh. "Tell the men there'll be a meeting tonight," he said. "Six o'clock, at the new place."

"You mean, the Ruiz place?" Bates all but snarled.

"I mean, the new place," Tate answered evenly. "Six o'clock. I'll provide the chicken and the beer."

Bates scowled, nodded once, wheeled his horse around and rode away.

CHAPTER FOURTEEN

TATE APPEARED at the Perk Up at four-thirty that afternoon, with his daughters and their dogs, though Buford and Ambrose waited in the truck.

Julie stayed in the kitchen, but Calvin stood at Libby's side, watching as Audrey and Ava bounced into the shop. They were wearing jean shorts and matching cotton blouses, blue and white checked.

"It was nice of you to give us your castle," Calvin said, very solemnly. "Thanks." Although he had yet to be elected king, he apparently considered himself a spokesperson for the community.

And by *us,* of course, Calvin meant the town of Blue River—the wonder toy was now installed on the lawn at the community center, and according to Julie, so many kids wanted to play in and around the thing that parents had been recruited to supervise. A few people even wanted to sell tickets.

Audrey and Ava looked at each other, then up at Tate, then at Calvin.

"You're welcome," Ava said, with great formality. She was definitely the more serious twin, Libby noted, though no less confident than her sister.

"Daddy made us do it," Audrey added forthrightly. "But we still have our ponies."

"You have *ponies?*" Calvin said, with wonder in his voice. Then, again, as though such a thing were almost beyond the outer reaches of credibility, *"You have ponies?"*

Audrey nodded at him. "Three, if you count Uncle Austin's. His horse is Bamboozle, but we call him Boozle for short, and he's really old, and we haven't named our ponies yet—they're twins, like we are, or at least they *look* like twins. They're not, really, but they're the same age and the same color and—" She paused, though not for very long, to haul in a breath. "Are you a friend of Libby's?"

Tate and Libby exchanged amused glances.

"She's my aunt," Calvin replied, with a note of pride that warmed Libby's heart.

Audrey smiled at him. "Maybe you can come out to our place sometime, and ride Boozle. He's old, like I said. Uncle Austin got him when he was ten. Uncle Austin was ten, I mean, not the pony."

"How come you weren't at our birthday party?" Ava asked. "We know you from daycare at the community center. Your name is Calvin."

Calvin was unfazed. "I don't think I was invited," he said reasonably.

"Oh," Ava said.

"How old are you?" Audrey wanted to know.

"Four," Calvin admitted, squaring his little shoulders.

"Well, that's probably why," Ava said matter-of-factly. "You're practically a baby."

"I am *not* a baby!" Calvin asserted indignantly.

Libby rested a hand on his shoulder.

"You talk like a grown-up," Audrey allowed, and after surveying Calvin thoughtfully for a moment or so, she graciously conferred her approval. "He's right, Ava. He's not a baby."

"Guess not," Ava agreed, with the barest hint of reluctance.

Calvin was clearly mollified. Grinning toothily and adjusting his glasses yet again with the poke of one slightly grubby finger, he said, "It was probably a real girly party, anyhow. Lots of pink stuff."

Tate chuckled, subtly steering the girls toward the stools at the short counter. Libby had noticed, and appreciated, the way he'd paid careful attention to the exchange between the three children but hadn't intervened.

"Of course it was girly," Ava said, looking back at Calvin over one shoulder. "We're *girls.*"

"Orange smoothies all around?" Libby piped up, figuring it was time to change the subject.

"Yes, please," Ava said, speaking like a miniature adult.

"Please," Audrey echoed, scrambling up onto a stool.

"Me, too, Aunt Libby," Calvin chirped, getting into the spirit of the thing. "But I want strawberry, please."

Julie stuck her head out of the kitchen. Nothing wrong with her hearing, Libby thought, with an inward smile. It was probably a mother thing.

"No way, José," Julie told Calvin. "You'll spoil your supper."

"It's not even five o'clock yet," Calvin complained.

"Grandma's coming over for meat loaf," Julie reminded him, "and she likes to eat early, so she can get back to her condo in time to watch her TV shows. We're picking her up in a little while, and we have to run a few errands first."

Calvin sighed his weight-of-the-world sigh. It rarely worked with Julie, and this instance was no exception, but with Calvin, hope sprang eternal.

"You'd be welcome to come out to the Silver Spur sometime soon and ride Bamboozle," Tate told the little boy quietly, his gaze shifting to Julie's face. "If it's all right with your mom, that is."

Julie smiled. She liked Calvin to have new experiences, and riding horses on the McKettrick ranch certainly qualified. As kids, Julie, Paige and Libby had been to lots of parties on the Silver Spur, but those days seemed long ago and far away.

In fact, Libby hadn't been on a horse since before she and Tate broke up over Cheryl.

"That would be nice," Julie told Tate. "Thank you."

He nodded. He looked ridiculously good in his dark blue T-shirt and battered jeans, and the shadow of a beard growing in only added to the testosterone-rich effect. "My pleasure," he drawled.

The timbre of his voice found a place inside Libby and tingled there.

She shook off the sensation and finished brewing up the orange smoothies, setting them in front of Audrey and Ava and smiling.

"There you go," she said.

They smiled back at her.

Several moments of silence passed.

"Audrey needs a tutu," Ava announced, without preamble, after poking a straw into her smoothie and slurping some up. She rolled her lovely blue eyes at Libby and giggled. "She's pixilated."

Tate took the third stool, next to the cash register. Rested his muscular forearms on the countertop and intertwined his fingers loosely. He had an easy way about him, as if it were no trouble to wait around.

Not every man was that patient, Libby thought.

"Pixilated?" she asked, to get her mind off Tate's patience and his muscular forearms and his five-o'clock shadow.

She was only partly successful.

"Ava's talking about the Pixie Pageant," Tate said easily.

Libby liked the way he could just sit there, not needing to fiddle with something to keep his fingers busy. There was a great *quietness* in Tate McKettrick, a safety and serenity that reached beyond the boundaries of his skin, big enough to take in his daughters, the old dog, Crockett, his family and the whole of the Silver Spur Ranch.

And maybe her, too.

Libby met his eyes, an effort because she felt shaken now, as though something profound had just happened between her and Tate. Which was silly, because the situation couldn't have been more ordinary, nor could the conversation.

"I guess things checked out okay, then? The Pixie Pageant is a go?"

Tate nodded, looking beleaguered but mildly amused. *Females,* his manner seemed to say: *Sometimes there's no figuring them out.*

"Yeah," he said. "It checked out, and it's a go. A lot depends on your definition of *okay,* though."

She smiled, resisting an impulse to pat Tate's shoulder, and poured him a cup of coffee. "On the house," she said.

Libby realized she'd lost track of her sister and her nephew, shifted her focus.

"Julie?"

Julie, it turned out, was ready to leave; she'd gathered her belongings and her son and was standing almost at Libby's elbow, a knowing and slightly bemused smile resting prettily on her mouth.

Of course Libby knew what was going through her

sister's mind; Julie and Paige could stop worrying about their big sister if Libby and Tate got back together.

"See you tomorrow?" Libby asked, wishing Julie would stay just a little longer.

"Sure," Julie replied hastily, barely looking back. "Tomorrow."

"Bring scones," Libby called after her.

Julie laughed, gave a comical half salute and left the shop. The bell jingled over the door, and Calvin looked back, one hand smudging the glass, his eyes full of yearning.

The sight gave Libby a pang. She knew the feeling: on the outside, looking in. It grieved her to see the knowledge in Calvin—he was so young, and she loved him so much.

"We just came from the country club," Tate told Libby, when Julie and Calvin had left, and she'd snapped out of the ache over her nephew's little-boy loneliness. He watched with an expression of mystified fondness as his daughters giggled over their drinks. "The pageant is a one-day thing. As far as I can tell, it's no big deal."

"You have to have a talent to win," Ava interjected.

Audrey elbowed her. "I *have* a talent," she said.

"Oh, yeah?" Ava countered. "*What* talent?"

"That's enough," Tate said, though he seemed as still and as calm as ever. "Both of you."

"I *do too* have a talent," Audrey insisted, as though he hadn't spoken. What were these two going to be like as *teenagers?* "I can sing. Mom says so."

Tate tried again. "Girls," he said.

"If you call that singing," Ava said, with a little shrug and a flip of her ebony hair. "I think you sound awful. Anyhow, you know how Mom is about this pageant thing. Her eyes get all funny when she talks about it."

Although the reference to Cheryl made her mildly un-comfortable, Tate's expression made Libby want to smile. But since that might have undermined his parental authority, she didn't.

For all his calm, he was obviously at a loss, too. What to do?

The answer, Libby could have told him, was nothing at all. This was simply the way sisters related—twins or not. She and Paige and Julie still bickered, but it didn't mean they didn't love each other. There was nothing Libby wouldn't have done for Paige and Julie, and she knew the reverse was true, as well.

Libby opened her mouth to make a stab at explaining, re-alized she didn't have the words, and closed it again.

"One more word," Tate told the children, "and nobody rides horseback, swims in the pool, goes to the library or plays a video game for a whole month."

Two sets of cornflower blue eyes widened.

"Okay," Ava breathed, looking and sounding put-upon. She adjusted her glasses, though not by shoving them up-ward at the bridge of her nose, the way Calvin did.

"That's a word," Audrey pointed out triumphantly. "*Okay* is a word!"

"You just said a *whole bunch* of words!" Ava cried.

"Let's go pick up the fried chicken and beer," Tate said, shoving off his stool to stand, and the girls scrambled off their stools, too, orange smoothies in hand.

He paid for the drinks.

"Daddy's having a cowboy meeting at the house where Mr. and Mrs. Ruiz used to live," Ava said to Libby, her tone and expression serious. "He's going to tell them where the bear shit in the buckwheat."

Tate flushed, the color throbbing in his neck and then pulsing briefly above his jawline and darkening his ears a little. *"Ava."*

"That's what you told Uncle Austin," the little girl retorted. "I *heard* you."

"Esperanza's going to take care of us while Daddy's at the cowboy meeting," Audrey explained, rapid-fire. "Because cowboys cuss and we shouldn't be around to hear things like that. So we get to have tacos for supper and make popcorn and spend the whole night in Esperanza's suite and watch as many movies as we want to, even if it's a hundred!"

"Wow," Libby said, very seriously, widening her eyes a little for emphasis, "a hundred movies?"

"More like one movie, a hundred times," Tate said dryly.

Libby laughed.

Ava spoke up again. "I don't see why it takes a whole meeting just to tell people where a bear—"

Tate cupped a hand around the child's mouth. "Maybe I could stop by your place later, so we could talk about the tutu and stuff?" he said, his eyes practically pleading with Libby to agree.

The image of Tate McKettrick shopping for a tutu was beyond funny. She could hold back another burst of laughter, but not the twinkle she knew was sparkling in her eyes as she enjoyed the mind-picture.

"What time does the buckwheat meeting get over?" Libby asked sweetly, resting her hands on her hips and heartily enjoying Tate's obvious discomfort. At the same time, it touched her heart, the way he cared so much about being a good father, getting things right.

Even to the extent of shopping for tutus, when it came to that.

Her throat ached. Her dad had been the same way.

She missed him so much.

"Eight o'clock, maybe," Tate said, looking hopeful. "Is that too late?"

"Not for me," Libby answered, "but *you* look a little tired, cowboy."

He flashed her a grin, maybe to prove he wasn't all *that* tired.

The twins were at the shop door by then, still squabbling.

Tate bent his head, spoke quietly into Libby's ear. "I'll save you some chicken and beer," he said. "Meet me at the new place later, and bring the dog if you want to."

"Maybe," Libby said firmly, unsettled now. "Last time—"

The patented McKettrick grin came again, even more dazzling than before. "Yes," Tate said. "I remember."

Libby was wavering, and she didn't want him to know that.

She all but pushed Tate to the door, and that made the girls laugh.

"Later?" he asked. His voice was a sexy rumble.

"Don't count on it," Libby said, but she was rattled and planning on showing up at his place for sure and they both knew it.

Tate smiled and left, shepherding his daughters across the street, hoisting them into the back seat of the truck, assisting with buckles and belts affixed to safety seats while gently fending off a pair of overjoyed pups.

Libby watched, resting her forehead against the glass in the front door of the Perk Up.

When she sensed that Tate was about to turn in her direction, she pulled back quickly and turned the "Open" sign to "Closed."

She locked the door.

Shut down all the machines and cleaned them.

Tucked the day's profits into a deposit bag, and the bag into her purse. Although the Perk Up had been doing a lot better financially since Julie had started baking scones and other goodies, Libby had been giving most of the money to her sister.

Which meant she was still just breaking even, most days.

At home, she let Hildie out into the backyard, as usual, and went back inside when she heard the phone ringing.

"Have you seen Marva?" Julie blurted anxiously.

"No," Libby said. "Isn't she at the condo?"

"No, she's not at the condo!" Julie almost screamed. "Libby, she stole my car!"

Libby sagged against the counter. "Oh, my God, Julie, Calvin wasn't—?"

"Calvin wasn't in the car, thank heaven," Julie answered, only moderately less hysterical than before.

Libby echoed that sentiment, letting out her breath, then asked, "Have you called Chief Brogan?"

Julie was beside herself. "Are you kidding? Call the cops on my own mother? Libby, I can't do that!"

"Calm down," Libby said firmly. "Julie, *calm down*. Take a slow, deep breath."

"But my car—my mother—oh, my *God*—"

"I'll be right over," Libby said. "If I see Marva along the way, I'll do my best to flag her down."

The words were disturbingly prophetic, as it turned out.

Libby had no more than uttered them when she heard an odd noise, looked through the window over the sink, and saw Julie's pink Cadillac speeding down the alley, bouncing over the ruts, tailpipe dragging and throwing off blue and orange sparks.

It all happened quickly, and yet Libby took in the scene in vivid and minute detail.

Marva was at the wheel, the windows rolled down. She was smoking a long brown cigarette jutting from a holder and singing along with the Grateful Dead at the top of her lungs.

"I don't believe this!" Libby gasped into the phone, one hand pressed to her heart. "I just saw her go by!"

"Try to catch her," Julie pleaded. "Go! Now!"

"Oh, right," Libby said, feeling pretty frantic herself, now. "Maybe I could sprint to the corner and just leap onto the hood and pound on the windshield with my fists. Julie, I know you're upset, but will you get real?"

"Libby, you've got to *do* something!"

"I'll go after her, but she's driving so fast the wheels are barely touching the ground. Get here as quickly as you can, and call Paige, too."

"Get *where* as quickly as I can?"

"To wherever I am, of course." With that, Libby hung up with a bang, raced out the back door and down the steps, passing Hildie, who had settled herself comfortably in her favorite shady spot under the big tree.

"Stay!" Libby told the dog.

Hildie hadn't shown any signs of moving so much as a muscle, but a person couldn't be too careful.

"Marva!" Libby yelled, running for the alley.

Dust roiled, but there was no sign of the Caddie.

"Marva," Libby repeated, this time as a plea.

She was about to go back inside the house, since she'd forgotten the keys to the Impala and it wouldn't be much use giving chase on foot when she heard the crash.

It was deafening, so loud it seemed to shake the earth and the fillings in Libby's teeth.

Glass tinkled.

A horn tooted and then honked steadily, a long, terrifying drone.

A cloud of dust billowed far above the roof of Libby's shop, and except for the horn everything was silent, for one quivering moment.

And then the roof of the Perk Up collapsed.

Libby stood staring, unable to move.

A siren blared somewhere.

"Oh, no," Libby whispered. *"Oh, no."*

Running full out, Libby dashed through the narrow space between Almsted's Grocery and her coffee shop. More dust and plaster showered down on her.

The horn continued to blow.

Libby finally reached the sidewalk, and there was the pink Cadillac—or part of it, at least—taillights still shining bright red, half buried under the rubble of the Perk Up.

A crowd, probably driven from Almsted's by prudence, clustered on the sidewalk.

Brent had already arrived; his cruiser was parked at the curb, lights flashing dizzily, siren shrieking fit to wake all the corpses in the Blue River Cemetery. Along with several passersby and members of the volunteer fire department, the chief dug frantically through fallen timbers and old drywall and shards of glass with his bare hands.

Where she got the strength, Libby did not know. But somehow she pushed through until she was shoulder to shoulder with Brent, and dug hard.

The roof of the car appeared, and the driver's-side window. Unbroken, thank God. The windshield had held, too.

"Marva?" Libby whispered.

Marva turned and looked at her dreamily, both hands still resting on the steering wheel. Except for a small cut above her right eyebrow, she seemed to be all right, but there was no way of knowing that until she'd been examined by a doctor, of course.

Marva rolled down the car window. "Oops," she said.

"Is she drunk?" Chief Brogan demanded of Libby. He was sweating, like everybody except Marva, who looked cool as could be.

"I doubt it," Libby said, as wave after wave of residual shock washed over her. She had to grip the edge of the open window to steady herself. "Are you all right, Marva?" she asked, in someone else's voice.

Marva nodded. "I'm fine," she said calmly.

The Perk Up was a complete shambles, but Marva was alive and, it appeared, unhurt. For the moment, nothing else really mattered.

It would be a short moment.

"I forgot how to stop," Marva said, amazed. "I can't believe I forgot how to stop."

"Does anything hurt anywhere?" Brent asked.

Marva shook her head. Her gaze meandered slowly from Libby's face to Brent's. "Am I under arrest?" she asked. "I'm stone sober, you know. And I didn't actually *steal* this car, either. It belongs to my daughter, and I'm sure Julie will vouch for everything I say."

Libby, dizzy, put a hand to her own forehead.

"Let's not worry about the legal implications right this minute, ma'am," Brent answered, very politely. "For now, we're just going to concentrate on making sure you're all right."

"I demand a lawyer," Marva said.

"You don't need a lawyer," Libby said.

"She might," Brent countered, in a whisper.

"Winston," Marva said, tilting her head back and closing her eyes, "will kill me."

"Winston?" Libby asked, puzzled.

"My husband," Marva answered, without opening her eyes. "Winston Alexander Vandergant the Third."

Libby blinked. "Your—?"

"Husband." Marva sighed.

"Would you mind spelling that?" Brent asked, taking a little notebook from his shirt pocket and clicking a pen with his thumb.

Marva calmly spelled out the entire name.

Brent wrote it down.

"You have a husband?" Libby echoed.

"Call him," Marva told Brent. "He'll straighten out this whole situation. Winston is just a whiz when it comes to problem solving."

Brent merely nodded.

Two EMTs politely elbowed Libby and Brent aside so they could remove Marva from the car.

Libby was standing on the sidewalk when Paige roared up to the curb in her subcompact car, Julie in the passenger seat.

By then, the paramedics had put a neck brace on Marva and placed her carefully on a stretcher. She was loaded into the ambulance; according to protocol, she would be examined at the Blue River Clinic, and if her injuries were serious, transported from there to a trauma center.

Julie, standing on the littered sidewalk, assessed Marva, the collapsed roof of the Perk Up and her nearly buried car. *"What happened?"*

"I think that's obvious," Paige said dryly, but she ran over and climbed into the ambulance just as the doors were about to be closed, scrambling inside to take Marva's hand. The vehicle raced away.

Libby ran home, retrieved the keys to her Impala from the kitchen, backed the car out of the garage, and stopped for a still-stunned Julie in front of what was left of the Perk Up.

They headed for the clinic.

"Where's Calvin?" Libby asked, as she navigated the familiar streets. By then, her brain was clearing; she was starting to think in practical terms again.

"With Marva's neighbor, Mrs. Kingston," Julie answered.

Libby nodded, reassured. Mrs. Kingston, unlike their mother, was quite sane. A responsible human being.

"She could have killed herself," Julie fretted. "Marva, I mean."

"Right," Libby agreed tensely. "And a lot of other people, too."

Her mind raced. Julie's Cadillac might be salvageable, but the Perk Up was a total loss. What was she going to do now? How was she going to earn a living?

She'd barely been getting by as it was.

Ashamed of worrying about herself when Marva might be lapsing into a coma in the back of the ambulance at that very moment—she doubted it, but anything was possible— Libby blinked a couple of times and bit down hard on her lower lip. "Julie, how did Marva manage to swipe your car?"

Julie closed her eyes tightly, hugged herself. "I left the keys in the ignition. I was talking to that nice Mrs. Kingston, Marva's neighbor—she has the loveliest climbing roses and I wanted to know how often she pruned and fertilized because I'm thinking of putting in a garden next spring myself and—"

Libby broke into the nervous flow of her sister's conversation. "Do you know how lucky we are that Calvin wasn't in the car? Or behind it, or *in front* of it—"

"Do *you* have to remind me of what *could* have happened?" Julie snapped. "It seems to me that what *did* happen is bad enough!"

"I'm sorry," Libby said, to keep the peace.

Julie reached over, squeezed her hand. "Me, too," she said. "I shouldn't have snapped at you."

Less than a minute later, they reached the clinic, a small brick building on the eastern edge of town. Thanks to the generous support of the McKettricks and other oil-and-cattle-rich families in that part of Texas, the facility was well-staffed, with four different doctors working in rotation, several nurses, a full office staff and assorted technicians.

The equipment was state-of-the-art, and there were two spacious four-bed wards for overnight patients.

Paige was waiting in the parking lot looking fidgety, when Libby and Julie wheeled in.

The three of them hurried past the parked ambulance, its rear door still standing open. Brent's cruiser stood beside it, empty.

The receptionist explained that Dr. Burt was examining Marva, and they might as well sit down because it would be a while.

Paige led the way into the small waiting room, plunked some coins into a vending machine, and watched as a cup dropped down a chute and began to fill with steaming coffee.

"She has a husband," Libby said, apropos of nothing. "Marva, I mean."

"*A husband?*" her sisters chorused.

"Winston Alexander Vandergort the Third, or something like that."

"Who?" Julie asked.

"That's all I know," Libby insisted, defensive.

Julie began to pace. "A husband," she muttered.

"Do you both have insurance?" Paige asked, ever practical, her gaze traveling between Libby and Julie.

"Yes," Julie said. "But that Cadillac was a classic. Irreplaceable."

"So was my business," Libby said. "Irreplaceable, I mean."

"Let's not panic here," Paige said.

"That's easy for you to say," Libby said.

"Yeah," Julie agreed.

"Everything will work out," Paige insisted.

Again, easy for *her* to say. She had a good job, with benefits, and she definitely didn't live from paycheck to paycheck, either. *Her* car hadn't been wrecked. *Her* coffee shop hadn't been reduced to a pile of broken boards and bits of plaster.

"We'll *manage,*" Paige said, putting one arm around Libby's shoulders and one around Julie's and squeezing. "I promise."

"We?" Libby challenged.

"We," Paige confirmed. "I have savings. I can help—"

"I won't take your money," Libby said.

"Neither will I," Julie agreed.

Brent came out of one of the exam rooms and approached them.

"Well," he said, "we won't be charging your mother with driving under the influence, anyway. Which is not to say her sanity isn't in question."

"But is she going to be all right?" Julie asked anxiously, staring up at Brent.

"She seems to be," Brent replied patiently. "The doctor

wants to run a CT scan and take some x-rays. Could be a long wait."

Julie glanced down at her watch. "Calvin is probably worried," she said, pale with anxiety.

"Let's pick him up and bring him here," Paige suggested. She looked up at Brent. "Would you mind giving us a ride back to my car, Chief? I left it at the Perk Up to ride in the ambulance with Marva."

"Sure thing," Brent replied, cocking a thumb toward the cruiser. "Hop in."

Julie nodded, then shook her head. Gave a despairing little giggle at her own contradictory response. "I mean, I don't have a car seat now—"

"I do," Paige reminded Julie. She'd purchased the seat at a garage sale two summers before, because she and Calvin spent a lot of time together when her schedule clicked with Julie's. "I'm beginning to think you're in worse shape than Marva is. Are you all right?"

"My car is buried under tons of rubble," Julie answered, almost snappishly. "Why wouldn't I be all right?"

They both climbed into the back seat of Brent's cruiser, still bickering.

Yep, Libby thought sadly, Julie's car was under tons of rubble. And that rubble had once been her business. Her livelihood.

Not that it had ever been all that lively.

Paige got out of the cruiser, came back to Libby and brought her cell phone out of her purse, handing it over. "Just in case," she explained.

Libby stared down at the device. It was a moment before she remembered Brent was still there.

Looking up at him, she calmly asked for Tate's cell number.

Brent gave it to her, and Libby nodded her thanks and keyed in the digits as she walked around the corner of the clinic to stand in the side parking lot, out of earshot.

She watched as the cruiser pulled out onto the highway, then looked up, surprised to see that the moon was already visible, even though the sun hadn't fully set. The sky blazed crimson and lavender and apricot.

He answered after two rings. "Tate McKettrick," he said, a puzzled note in his voice.

Of course, Libby realized, Paige's number would have come up in the caller ID panel, since she was calling on her sister's phone.

Libby leaned back against the brick face of the Blue River Clinic, suddenly exhausted. "It's me," she said. "Libby."

"Lib? Are you all right?"

She had to swallow a throatful of tears before answering. "I'm okay," she said, and then it all came tumbling out, in a crazy rush. "But Marva—my mother—drove my sister's Cadillac through the front of the Perk Up, so we're all down here at the clinic so I can't make it to your place for leftover chicken and beer—and I don't suppose it even matters that much but I—"

"Libby," Tate said, firmly but with kindness. "Honey, take a breath."

Honey.

Libby fell silent. Honey. What an ordinary, beautiful word.

"Was anybody hurt?" Tate asked. His voice was level.

Libby's chest ached and her eyes burned and she still didn't trust herself to stand up straight, even though the bricks comprising the clinic's outer wall were digging right through her blouse into the flesh of her back. "Marva's being examined right now," she said.

"I'll be there as soon as I can," Tate said.

"Tate, no, I—I'm fine, really."

"I'm on my way."

"But—"

He hung up.

Slowly, Libby closed Paige's phone.

She hadn't expected Tate to drop everything and come to her—had she? If not, why had she called him in the first place, going to the trouble to borrow a phone and ask Brent Brogan for the number?

Damn. She didn't want to wind up like Marva, needy and manipulative.

Doing numbers on people.

Her eyes stung.

The automatic doors swung open, and one of the nurses stepped out, looked around. Seeing Libby, the woman smiled.

She was fortyish, and Libby remembered her vaguely from the Perk Up. Yes. Double mocha with extra espresso and chocolate shavings.

"Your mother would like to see you," she said. "And maybe a doctor should have a look at those scratches on your hands."

Libby nodded, then shook her head. "I'm okay," she said. "I just need to wash up." Dropping Paige's phone into her purse, she followed the nurse into the clinic, through the lobby and back to one of the exam rooms.

Going straight to the sink, Libby washed her hands, saw that the scratches weren't deep.

Marva was alone, lying on a gurney. She wore a hospital gown, and a plain white blanket covered her legs.

She was so still that, for one terrible moment, Libby thought her mother was dead.

"Marva?"

Marva turned her head, smiled. Stretched out a hand to Libby.

"I don't know what came over me," Marva confided, her voice croaky and miserable. "Suddenly, I just *had* to drive again, and there was Julie's car—"

"Shh," Libby said. "We can talk about it later, when we're sure you're all right."

Tears filled Marva's eyes, rolled over her temples into her mussed-up hair. "I'm sorry, Libby," she said. "I'm so sorry."

Libby just stood there, with no idea how to respond, willing herself not to cry.

Marva gazed up at her, squeezed her hand once, and let go.

There was, it seemed, nothing more to say.

CHAPTER FIFTEEN

TATE MUST HAVE HAD the pedal to the metal all the way in from the ranch, because he was waiting in the lobby when Libby left Marva's exam room. Just seeing him was like a deep draught of cold well water after a long spell of thirst.

Libby walked into his arms. He embraced her loosely, and she rested her forehead against the hard wall of his chest.

"She's sorry," Libby told him, her voice muffled. "My mother is *sorry.*"

Tate rocked her slightly, from side to side. "It's okay, Lib," he murmured. "Everything will be okay."

Why did people keep *saying* that? Everything would be okay for Paige, with her top-notch nursing skills and high-paying job. Everything would be okay for Julie, too, because she had Calvin and a career she loved. And everything would *certainly* be okay for Tate and all the other McKettricks, if only because they *were* McKettricks.

Libby loved her sisters and was proud of their accomplishments.

But she was tired of false reassurances.

Her shop was gone.

She had virtually no savings.

And jobs weren't exactly plentiful in Blue River.

There had been lower points in her life, of course—when

Marva left, so long ago, when her dad died, when, with no warning at all, she'd lost Tate.

The pain of that most recent and totally unexpected loss seared through her, as fresh as if it had just happened. Libby knotted her fists and pushed pack from Tate.

He paled slightly, under his rancher's tan. "I drove by the shop on my way here," he told her, his voice gravelly. "Libby, I can help—"

"Stop," Libby said. Realizing her hands were still bunched against Tate's chest—she could feel the strong, steady *thud-thud-thud* of his heart—she splayed her fingers for a moment, drawing in the substance of him like a breath of the soul. And then she let both hands fall to her sides. "Don't say what I think you're about to say, Tate. I can't take money from you."

Julie and Paige had returned, along with Calvin; Libby was aware of them, on the periphery of the haze that seemed to surround her and Tate.

"Libby," he said. "Listen to me. Please."

She shook her head. Stepped back a little farther.

Both Paige and Julie had worked their way through college with the aid of scholarships and loans. They'd made something of themselves.

Paige saved lives.

Julie shaped young minds.

What had *she* done? Started a doomed coffee shop—one that had barely brought in survival wages even in the best of times—right there in the old hometown.

She'd loved one man her whole life—Tate McKettrick—and he'd betrayed her. While she'd forgiven Tate, she knew she'd never forgive *herself* if the same thing happened all over again.

Tate's hands still rested lightly on her shoulders.

He couldn't have known what she was thinking—that maybe it was time for her to leave Blue River, leave Texas. Go someplace entirely new, where she might be able to get some perspective. Come up with some goals.

No, he couldn't have known, but he looked as though he did.

The truth? Libby Remington had had only one goal, one dream, ever, and it was hopelessly old-fashioned. Politically incorrect to the nth degree.

All Libby had ever wanted was to marry Tate, love him and be loved in return, to bear and raise his children. To get old with him, and have flocks of grandbabies.

It would all be easier, she supposed, if Tate weren't rich— if he really were just a foreman on a big ranch, a hired hand with a steady paycheck, a simple three-bedroom house beside a creek and a good truck to drive. Instead, he was a multi-*multi*-millionaire, with his choice of beautiful women—supermodels, movie stars and professional women of all sorts. Doctors. Lawyers. Indian chiefs.

What did he want with her?

Sex?

Their lovemaking had been transcendental for Libby, but Tate was a man—to him, sex was sex. He probably took it where he could get it—and God knew, she had no compunction about giving it to him.

"Is Marva all right?" Julie asked, hovering a few feet away and wringing her hands.

Libby saw herself and Tate through Julie's eyes, standing almost toe-to-toe, as though he'd been comforting her in the aftermath of bad news.

"We haven't heard anything yet, Jules," Libby said, hugging her sister.

Julie hugged her back, sniffled.

Libby's eyes roamed, stopped on her nephew. Calvin was on the other side of the lobby, admiring the colorful fish in the clinic's fish tank. Paige stood beside the little boy, but she was watching her sisters and Tate, not the bright, flashing population of the large saltwater tank.

"Look, Aunt Paige," Calvin crowed, pointing a chubby finger at one of the fish and almost certainly leaving a smudge on the glass. "That one is transparent—I can see his guts!" He bent closer, and even though his back was to Libby, she knew when he adjusted his glasses. "And *that* one has a red line inside it, like a thermometer."

The mood lightened a little.

Julie stepped back out of Libby's embrace, and her gaze moved between Libby and Tate. She smiled slightly, turned and joined Calvin next to the fish tank.

Paige approached Libby. "May I have my cell phone back, please?" she asked. "It might be a long night, and I think the time has come to order pizza."

"Pizza!" Calvin whooped, overjoyed.

In spite of the stress and frustration and a host of other emotions, Libby laughed. She dug through her purse, found Paige's phone and handed it to her sister.

"Just tell me what kind of pizza you want," Tate said. "I'll go pick it up."

Calvin materialized immediately. It was almost as if he'd teleported himself from the fish tank across the lobby to where they stood. "Are you going to the Pizza Shack, Mr. McKettrick? Can I go with you? Where are your kids? Do you have any boys, or just girls?"

Tate crouched, so he could look Calvin straight in the eye. "Your mom and your aunts are kind of worried right now," he said seriously. "I think they need a man around, so maybe you ought to stay here."

Calvin's glasses had wriggled down his freckled nose, and he replaced them with the usual thrust of his right index finger. He threw his shoulders back a little, and raised his chin. "They're all pretty good at taking care of themselves," he told Tate. "And you didn't answer my other questions."

Tate's mouth quirked up at one corner. "My daughters— Audrey and Ava—are at home. And, no, I don't have any boys." As he stood up again, he caught Libby's gaze. "Yet," he added quietly.

She felt the usual achy heat, and rose above it as best she could.

The man was an addiction, and she was thoroughly hooked.

Ready to leave town to get away from him one moment, charmed out of her socks the next.

As if getting charmed out of her *socks* was any part of the problem.

"I have the regulation car seats in my truck," Tate told Julie. "And we wouldn't be gone long."

"*Please,* Mom," Calvin pleaded. "I need a male role model. I spend way too much time around women. Mrs. Oakland said so."

Julie flushed to her ears. "Mrs. Oakland said that, did she?"

"Maybe it was Justin's mom," Calvin faltered.

"You're sure he wouldn't be any trouble?" Julie asked Tate.

"I'm sure," Tate said. This time, he didn't look at Libby. She might have vaporized, for all the notice he seemed to take of her.

"I'll call in the order," Paige put in, cell phone in hand. "The usual?" she asked her sisters.

Libby merely nodded, wanting Tate McKettrick out of

her space so she could think straight, but Julie, the thoughtful one, had the good manners to ask if he'd prefer something other than thick-crust Hawaiian with extra cheese.

He said he'd already eaten.

"Do I get to go or not, Mom?" Calvin demanded.

"Go," Julie relented, and though she was smiling, Libby glimpsed pain in her sister's eyes.

Calvin let out a yippee that made the receptionist look up from her desk behind the glass window and smile.

The little boy fairly skipped out of the clinic, but he stayed close to Tate, as if to prove to anyone concerned that he meant to behave himself and follow all the rules.

Paige finished placing the pizza order, closed her phone, and dropped it into her purse. "You really ought to grab that one," she said, nodding in Tate's direction and simultaneously elbowing Libby lightly in the ribs. "He's obviously a good father."

Before Libby had to reply, Dr. Burt Renton appeared, a weary smile creasing his familiar face. The physician, a widower with no children, had been born and raised in Blue River, and returned home as soon as his training was finished to open an office on Main Street. After thirty years in practice, he'd tried to retire, but all that idleness, as he called it, "wasn't good for my character." He'd been working part time at the clinic since it had opened for business nearly a decade before.

Julie, Paige and Libby all hurried toward him, stood in a tight little semicircle at the edge of his personal space, waiting.

"I ran a CT scan, the usual blood tests and took x-rays," Dr. Burt told them kindly. "Your mother is shaken up, but with a few days of rest and some pampering, she'll be fine. "

Libby backed up a step. Maybe it was the word *pampering*.

Julie and Paige looked at her curiously.

Julie was the first to get the message. Her face softened, and Libby could have hugged her for the understanding in her eyes.

"Marva can stay with Calvin and me," Julie volunteered.

Guilt nudged Libby back into the half circle of sisters. She was the firstborn, and, as such, she had certain responsibilities. Marva was, for all her shortcomings, *her* mother, too.

She opened her mouth to say she'd look after Marva for as long as necessary, but the words wouldn't come out.

"I'd like Marva to stay here overnight," Dr. Burt was saying, "just to be on the safe side. That way, the nurses can keep an eye on her."

"Tell them to hide their car keys," Paige quipped, but she was watching Libby, still curious, maybe even a little worried.

Dr. Burt chuckled at that, but his eyes were solemn. "She feels very bad about that. Says she doesn't know what came over her."

In her mind, Libby saw her mother's tear-filled eyes again, heard her voice.

I'm so sorry.

"No one was hurt," Julie said. "That's the important thing."

"You can look in on Marva if you'd like. She's been sedated, though, so she'll probably drift off to sleep pretty soon." Dr. Burt pointed toward the corridor on the right, where the two large in-patient rooms were. "She has Unit B all to herself."

Julie and Paige started for the corridor immediately.

Libby remained where she was.

"I saw her earlier," she said when Dr. Burt glanced at her.

A few minutes later, Tate and Calvin returned with several huge pizza boxes and, with Libby's help, arranged the feast on the low-slung coffee table in the small waiting room. Calvin had scored a stack of paper napkins six inches high.

The child's face was luminous with delight. "Tate said we could get cold drinks out of the vending machine here," he said importantly. "And I get to ride horses on the Silver Spur whenever I want and go fishing in the creek as long as my mom approves and there's at least one grown-up with me."

"Wow," Libby said softly, ruffling her nephew's sweaty hair.

Over the pile of pizza boxes, her gaze connected with Tate's. "That's a lot of food," she said.

Calvin jumped right in with an answer. "Tate said the people who work here might want to eat, too," he said, before helping himself to a slice, breaking off a long strand of cheese with a karate chop.

Tate grinned, watching him.

"Tate used to have a dog named Crockett," Calvin went on, with his mouth partially full. "Crockett rode with him everywhere—they were buddies."

Libby's throat tightened. "Crockett was a good dog," she said, remembering.

She heard Julie and Paige approaching the waiting room, talking in low, hurried voices.

Tate didn't look at Libby; his gaze had turned toward the doorway, and he stood as her sisters entered.

"I *thought* I smelled pizza!" Julie said, leaning down to give her son a quick squeeze.

"Do you think Grandma would like some?" Calvin asked. His face was smeared with tomato sauce by then, and what was probably a piece of pineapple had gotten stuck in his hair.

"She's asleep," Paige told her nephew brightly.

Julie and Paige used a bottle of hand sanitizer from Julie's purse, helped themselves to napkins and pizza, and began to eat.

Tate didn't touch the food, and neither did Libby, until Paige finally plopped a slice onto a napkin and forced it into her hands.

Tate got up and left the room to let the staff know there was pizza aplenty and they were welcome to join the party. The invitation brought a fairly steady stream of hungry people in scrubs, but Tate didn't come back.

Having eaten all she could get down—a little less than half of the portion Paige had given her—Libby excused herself and left the waiting room.

She could see Tate through the plate glass door at the front of the clinic, talking on his cell phone. His expression was serious, he was pacing and he kept thrusting a hand through his hair.

Libby hurried away, headed for the restroom, not wanting him to see her and think she'd been looking for him. Even though that was exactly what she'd been doing.

Once she'd washed her hands, stinging mildly now, from the scratches she'd gotten digging Marva out, splashed her face with cold water and grinned humorlessly into the mirror, to make sure there was no pizza detritus stuck between her teeth, she straightened her spine and marched back to the lobby.

Now that Marva had been examined and was resting comfortably, according to Dr. Burt, there was no point in sticking around. She'd go home, attend to the ever-patient Hildie, and then she'd switch on the TV set and stare mindlessly at the screen until she couldn't keep her eyes open anymore.

She could start thinking about the rest of her life tomorrow—or the day after that.

Or she could just pack a bag, gas up the Impala, load Hildie and her kibble and bowls into the back seat and strike out for parts unknown.

Yes, sir, she could go out there and *accomplish something.*

What that something would be, she had no idea.

Which was why she didn't want to think just yet.

"I guess I'll go on home now," she announced to her sisters and nephew and a couple of x-ray technicians, from the doorway of the waiting room. "Hildie will be waiting for me."

"Sure," Julie said uncertainly, leaning a little, to look past Libby. "Did Tate leave? I didn't get a chance to repay him for the pizza, or even say thank you."

Libby shrugged one shoulder. "He was outside a little while ago," she answered as casually as she could. "Talking to someone on his cell phone. Maybe something came up out at the ranch."

"Marva will be at our place after she's released," Julie told Libby. "In case you want to stop by and see her or anything."

Libby merely nodded, promising nothing.

She wanted to get away from the clinic.

She wanted this day to be over.

She waved a farewell to her family and the x-ray guys, turned and ran directly into Tate.

He steadied her by gripping her upper arms. If he hadn't, she would have fallen.

Libby pulled free, went around him.

He followed her through the automatic door and outside without speaking, or touching her.

It was dark and sultry, and the sky was splattered from horizon to horizon with enormous stars. Like the sunset earlier, the sight made Libby's breath catch.

Texas.

It was fine and dandy to think about starting over someplace far away.

But could she *really* call anywhere else "home"? Would she even be able to breathe properly outside the Lone Star State?

"Come home with me, Libby," Tate said, somehow steering her away from her car and toward his truck without laying a hand on her.

"Tate, I have a dog to feed and walk, and you have children—"

"We'll pick Hildie up on our way out of town. Along with your toothbrush and whatever else you figure you need to get you through till morning." He cleared his throat. "The twins are okay. They're with Esperanza."

Libby stopped, looked up at him. "Look, I know I agreed to come out to the Ruiz—to *your* place for chicken and beer, but—" She spread her arms wide, let her hands slap against her sides.

A slight and damnably sexy grin tugged at his mouth, was gone again. "But?" he prompted, his right hand resting lightly on the small of her back, ready to turn her gently, the way he'd turn a mare if she started off in the wrong direction.

"But what?" she challenged.

Tate chuckled. "I was waiting for an excuse. And you're going to have to do better than that poor old dog. She'd love a road trip to anywhere, and you know it."

She should have told him right then.

Speaking of road trips…she could have said, *I'm thinking of leaving Blue River for a while. You might say I have to find myself. No, that's too corny. Nobody worries about finding themselves anymore. Which just goes to show how out of touch I am, when it comes to the world outside central Texas.*

Libby choked up again. "Tate, what do you *want?*"

"Not what you think I want," he told her, opening the

driver's-side door of the Impala so she could get in. "Not *just* that, anyhow."

Libby didn't know which was making her crazier, the conversation she was carrying on with Tate, or the one in her own head. "Good night," she said. "And thank you for the pizza."

She reached into her purse, closed her fingers around her keys, took a couple of stabs at the ignition before she managed to start the engine.

"You're not getting rid of me that easily," Tate said affably, before closing her door and turning to walk away.

Libby watched him climb into his truck, blinked when his headlights came on, bright. He dimmed them, but she was still dazzled.

Almost a minute passed before Libby could see well enough to drive. Tate drove to the parking lot exit, but waited until she pulled in behind him.

She followed *him* to *her* house.

What was wrong with this picture?

Libby parked in the garage, off the alley, careful not to look toward the late, great Perk Up Coffee Shop. Wondered if Julie's car had been pulled from the rubble yet, and whether or not the vehicle could be salvaged.

Tate parked in front of the house.

By the time Libby had unlocked the back door and nearly been run over as Hildie shot from the house like a popcorn kernel from hot oil, Tate was there and ready to follow her up the porch steps and into the kitchen.

"You know," Libby said to Tate, leaving the door open for Hildie but wishing she could slam it for the sake of emphasis, "some people would consider this stalking. Your walking in here like this, I mean."

"If you want me to leave," Tate replied reasonably, "all

you have to do is ask." He opened her refrigerator, scanned
the contents, sighed with what might have been resignation,
helped himself to a soda, popped the top and raised the can
briefly, as though toasting her.

Libby opened her mouth, closed it again.

Tate drank deeply of the soda, swallowed audibly. At
least he didn't belch.

"That Calvin," he said, "is one cute kid. And a fair hand
to have along on a pizza run."

Libby couldn't help softening, thinking of her nephew
and how glad he'd been to spend some time in Tate's company. "He's so smart, it's scary," she said.

Hildie, having completed her tour of the yard, scratched
at the screen door. Libby opened it to let her in, filled her
kibble dish and freshened her water.

"Calvin wants to get to know his dad," Tate said.

The statement fell between them like a flaming meteor.

Libby stood utterly still. Even though she'd encouraged
Julie to work out some kind of visitation agreement with
Gordon Pruett, she understood her sister's reluctance. Gor-
don might be a good man—or he might be a jerk.

Julie would be taking a big chance by letting Gordon into
her life and Calvin's, but if he chose to force the issue legally,
she wouldn't have a choice

"Calvin said that?" Libby nearly whispered, after a heartbeat or two.

Tate nodded. "Is this a problem?"

"It could be," Libby said simply. She wasn't comfortable
discussing Julie's private business, and Tate seemed to know
that, didn't press.

Libby shut and locked the back door. Hildie stood looking back and forth between Tate and her mistress instead of curling up on her dog bed, as she normally would have done.

"You have to promise we won't have sex," Libby blurted out. Tate was like some big, hard, human magnet, standing there in her kitchen. She felt the pull of him in every cell in her body—any second now, she'd go *splat,* like a bug on a windshield.

Tate indulged in a rather obvious struggle to hold back a grin, and one of his eyebrows rose into an ironic arch. "Forever?" he asked. "Or just for tonight?"

"Just for tonight," Libby said. "Forever seems unreasonable."

He chuckled. "Forever," he said, "is downright *impossible.* But I won't make love to you tonight, Lib. I promise you that much." He paused. "Not even if you tear my clothes off in an insane fit of unbridled desire."

"Don't hold your breath waiting for *that* to happen, cowboy," she said, with a lofty sniff.

Please God, don't let me tear off his clothes in an insane fit of unbridled desire.

"If I have to promise," Tate said, "so do you."

"Oh, for Pete's sake," Libby said. "All right."

With that, she went into her bathroom and got her hairbrush and her packet of birth control pills. There was no need to take pajamas along, because she intended to sleep in her clothes.

If she slept at all.

They went to the main ranch house, instead of Tate's "new" place by the creek, and except for a single light burning under the portico, the massive structure was completely dark.

Libby panicked a little. "Tate, Audrey and Ava—"

"It's a big house," Tate said. "And besides, we're not going to have sex anyway, so I don't see the problem."

"I don't want to confuse them," Libby said.

"Neither do I," Tate answered, and another grin twitched at his mouth.

"You don't think it will be confusing when they wake up tomorrow morning and I'm in their house?"

"I think they need to get used to seeing you around," Tate said quietly.

Libby didn't dare go there. It was late, she'd been through a lot that day, and if she wasn't careful, she might say something she'd regret.

For the rest of eternity.

Tate pulled up to one of the garage doors, pushed a button on his visor, and drove in.

Once he'd parked and shut off the truck, he turned to Libby.

She looked neither left nor right. She *certainly* wasn't going to look in Tate's direction.

"Lib," Tate said, pulling the keys from the ignition, "don't look so worried. All I want to do is take care of you."

All I want to do is take care of you.

Libby could barely remember what it was like to be "taken care of" by anyone. Before her dad had gotten sick— long before—she'd felt safe, as though somebody always had her back.

But since then? Not so much.

She straightened her spine, found she still couldn't look directly at Tate.

He opened the door, rounded the truck, set Hildie gently on the cement floor, opened Libby's door and unbuckled her seat belt.

"Come on," he said.

He took her by the hand, led her through the darkened house, up the stairs, into his room. Hildie followed.

There, Tate stripped Libby bare, pulled one of his T-shirts over her head, and tucked her under the covers of his bed.

Then he lay down on top of those same covers, pulled her into his arms, and held her, his embrace strong and sure, until she slept.

CHAPTER SIXTEEN

LIBBY AWOKE WITH A START, sunlight burning through her lids.

She opened her eyes, found herself almost nose to nose with one of the twins—Ava, she realized. The child was wearing glasses.

"Good morning," Ava said, grinning.

Oh, dear God. She was in Tate McKettrick's bed—*with* Tate McKettrick.

And here was his six-year-old daughter.

Libby blinked, glanced wildly around, having no idea what to say or do, and saw that Tate was still sleeping. He was wearing all his clothes, boots included, and lying on top of the covers, though one leg and one arm sprawled across Libby's body.

"Good morning," Libby whispered back to Ava, embarrassed but trying hard to behave in a normal way.

Whatever that might be, in these circumstances.

Tate stretched, his powerful body lengthening as he rolled away from her. He yawned lustily and opened his eyes.

"Hey," he said to Ava, resting a hand on Libby's shoulder, as if to console or reassure her. Or maybe because he knew she wanted to bolt.

"Hey, Daddy," Ava replied, still showing no overt signs of trauma at finding a woman in bed with her father. "Esperanza said to tell you breakfast is ready and Uncle Austin already fed the horses and did the chores and stuff."

Tate groaned, but it was a comfortable sound, good-natured. "So much for setting a good example as the new foreman," he said.

"That's all you're worried about?" Libby whispered.

He grinned down at her. "If you don't make a big deal out of this," he said casually, and there was a subtle singsong note to his tone, "nobody else will, either."

He was right, of course.

The child didn't seem curious, let alone traumatized, but making a fuss might change the easy flow of things.

New concerns assailed Libby. She put a hand over her mouth. How could the man wake up with *good breath?* He had—but she probably hadn't.

"Go and tell Esperanza we'll be right down," Tate told Ava. His voice was easy, as if he and Libby shared a bed *every* night. "Take Hildie with you—I imagine she'd like to go outside and then have a little of Ambrose and Buford's dog food."

Ava nodded importantly. "Come on, Hildie," she said, with cheerful authority. "Let's go."

Hildie got up, gave Libby one questioning glance, and then followed the little girl out of the master bedroom.

Libby tried to get out of bed the moment the door closed behind Ava and Hildie, but Tate pressed her back down with one hand splayed in the middle of her stomach and deliberately kissed her on the mouth.

Thoroughly.

Libby finally turned her face away, even though she'd liked the kiss.

"If you don't let me up," she said, "you're going to be sorry."

Tate chuckled at that—the threat was clearly an empty one—but he let Libby get up.

She found her way to the bathroom, which was roughly the size of her kitchen and living room combined, used the facilities, and rummaged through cupboards and drawers under the long marble countertop until she found a new toothbrush, still in its package.

She was standing at one of the antique brass sinks, scrubbing her teeth, when Tate ambled in, calm as you please, shedding clothes as he walked. The long mirror over the counter reflected his every move in exquisite detail.

He was completely, wickedly, *deliciously* naked by the time he reached the shower. In all that time, he hadn't so much as glanced in Libby's direction.

She, on the other hand, couldn't help staring.

From behind the glass door of the room-size shower, Tate grinned at her.

Libby tore her gaze away, flushing to the roots of her hair.

Stomped out of the bathroom and searched until she found her clothes, neatly folded and stacked on the seat of a sumptuous leather chair facing the cold fireplace.

Libby hauled them on, with the exception of her underpants; she wadded those into a ball and stuffed them into her purse.

Libby probably would have sneaked out of the house, sprinted down to the main road and *hitchhiked* into town, except that she couldn't abandon Hildie, not even knowing the dog was perfectly safe.

Besides, Ava had already seen her. In bed with Tate.

By now, the little girl had surely told her twin and Esperanza—and that was the *optimistic* count. Ava had mentioned Austin, saying he'd done the barn chores, so he might have heard, as well. And if Garrett happened to be around, he probably knew, too.

Dressed, but having no real idea what to do next, Libby plunked down on the edge of the bed. At least Tate had kept his word.

He'd slept on top of the covers, in all his clothes.

She'd been underneath them the whole night, clad in one of his T-shirts.

They hadn't made love. Libby figured she should have been happier about that than she was.

Because the shower was still running, indicating that she could expect a few more moments of privacy before Tate returned, she pressed the T-shirt to her face, drew in his scent. It seemed to seep into her cells and settle there, that lusciously distinctive smell, destined to remain a part of her forever, like her DNA.

Damn.

Just yesterday, at the clinic, despite a lot of misgivings, Libby had basically made up her mind to leave Blue River, start over somewhere else, make something of herself.

Like what? she wondered now.

Nothing occurred to her.

The sound of running water fell away into silence.

A minute or so later, Tate strolled out of the bathroom, barefoot, wearing button-front jeans and not much else. His hair was wet, though he'd towel-dried it and, from the looks of the ridges, he'd run his fingers through several times.

Could it be that he was as nervous as she was?

Surely not.

He crooked a grin at Libby. "Hungry?" he asked.

"I just want to go home," Libby said, blushing. Looking down at the floor.

What would she do at home?

Dig more weeds?

Cut more grass?

Get down on her knees on the sidewalk in front of her erstwhile shop and paw through the rubble looking for—what? A stray dream? A few tattered hopes?

"No problem," Tate said, his voice was quiet and so gentle that it made her want to cry. "If you want to go home, I'll take you there."

Libby didn't know what to say after that. Since Tate hadn't given her an argument, as she'd expected, she was stuck for a response.

The house in town was home—her dad had died there. She and her sisters had grown up under that roof, within those walls—but Julie and Paige had moved on.

She'd gotten stuck, somehow.

Tate disappeared into the massive walk-in closet, returning with one arm thrust into the sleeve of a light blue shirt, the other about to go in. His muscular chest was fully visible, lightly sprinkled with dark hair and tanned by occasional exposure to the sun.

He tossed Libby a pair of jeans and a yellow ruffled blouse; both garments were vaguely familiar.

Libby caught them, a funny little skitter dancing in her heart, let them rest in her lap, her head lowered. "Are these Cheryl's things?" she asked, thick-throated.

"No," Tate said gently. "They're yours."

Libby's gaze shot to his face. Her throat tightened even more, and her cheeks blazed. *Of course,* Tate wouldn't give her his ex-wife's clothes to wear. What had she been thinking?

"You left them here once, a long time ago, when my folks were away," he reminded her, a grin resting on his mouth and twinkling in his eyes. He probably knew what was going through her mind, or pretty close to it, anyhow. "Esperanza was visiting her cousin, and Garrett and Austin were both gone, too, on the rodeo circuit. We spent the whole weekend pretending we were married—remember?"

Libby felt a bittersweet pang of mingled nostalgia and sorrow. Back then, marrying Tate McKettrick had seemed like a sure thing. They'd nearly eloped several times in their late teens and Libby sometimes wished they'd gone through with the plan.

Sometimes, and only until she came to her senses.

She and Tate had been so young. She'd had to drop out of college and come back to Blue River to take care of her dad after he got sick. Tate might have given up school, too, and eventually come to resent Libby and the demands she made on his time.

And Audrey and Ava wouldn't have been born.

Inconceivable.

The silence seemed to have weight.

"You don't really think I can still get into these jeans," Libby joked, to break the spell.

Tate laughed. "Can I stay and watch you try?"

Libby giggled, waved him away. "Get out," she said.

He smiled, buttoning his shirt to the middle of his breast-bone. "I was headed downstairs for coffee anyhow," he said. "Bring you some?"

She shook her head, stroking the yellow blouse. She'd loved the thing, saved her allowance and babysitting money to buy it. Felt so sexy with all those sun-colored ruffles floating around her. "No thanks," she said. "Maybe some tea?"

"You got it," Tate said.

With that, he left the huge room, closing the double doors behind him.

LIBBY HASTENED INTO THE bathroom, shut the door and wriggled into the jeans. They were a little tight, but they zipped up, and the blouse looked as good as it ever had.

Libby's raised spirits drooped a bit, though, as she considered the prospect of going downstairs and facing Esperanza and the twins.

She made up the bed, which was barely mussed, a stall tactic for sure.

Tate returned just as she was fluffing the pillows. Sipping from one cup, he carried a second. "The coast is clear," he said. "Audrey and Ava are out in the barn, with all three dogs and the ponies. Esperanza is with them, supervising."

Libby accepted the fragrant tea with a nod of thanks, took a sip, and felt better instantly. "Have they come up with names yet?" she asked. "For the horses, I mean."

"I don't think so." Tate grinned, touching Libby's hair lightly. His voice was low and throaty and he smelled so...clean. "It's a big decision."

"Maybe you could drive Hildie and me home, while they're busy?"

Not that she wanted to go.

Tate sighed. "Lib, they already know you're here."

She lowered her head, breathing in the steam rising off her tea.

Tate curved a finger under her chin and looked into her eyes. "Relax," he said. "We talked about this. Audrey and Ava need to get used to seeing you around."

"*You* talked about it," Libby said. "*I* didn't venture an

opinion. Tate, they're children. And I'm not their mother. Letting them 'get used' to changes and their finding me in their father's bed first thing in the morning are not the same thing."

"You don't believe in total immersion?" Tate teased.

"Don't be a smart-ass," Libby countered.

"Sorry," he responded, after a long sip from his coffee. "I probably can't deliver on that one—not long term, anyhow."

"Be serious," she whispered angrily. "We're talking about your *children,* here."

Tate leaned in, touched his forehead to hers. "I'm aware of that," he whispered back, with exaggeration. "Lighten up a little, Libby. It's not as if Ava came in here and found us swinging naked from the curtain rods and yelling, 'Yahoo.' Yes, you were in my bed, but I was on top of the covers, wearing all my clothes." He backed up a little. Waggled his eyebrows. "Which, by the way, was a noble sacrifice on my part, and if ever there was a fine opportunity for a quickie, it's right now."

Libby laughed, in spite of herself. Gave him an affectionate push with her free hand, carefully balancing her tea in the other. "You really are impossible," she said.

"You'd forgotten that? That I'm impossible?" Tate asked. "I'm hurt."

"I should go home now."

"Why?"

"You know why."

"No, Libby. I don't know why. It's not as if you have to open the shop."

Her shoulders dropped a little. Of course she hadn't forgotten what Marva had done to the Perk Up, but she *had* managed to keep the full reality at a bearable distance.

Until now.

"Thanks," she said, terse now. It was a defense, not against Tate, but against a part of herself—the hoochy-mama part, born to boogie. She turned away, cup in hand, headed for the door.

Tate caught hold of her arm. "Let's take a breath here, Lib," he said. "Stay and have some breakfast. I'll saddle up some horses and we'll ride. I've already called the clinic, and your mother is doing fine. She wants to stay another day, in fact. Sounds to me like she's enjoying the attention."

"You talked to my mother?"

"No," Tate said. "To one of the nurses. I called her when I was downstairs."

Libby let out her breath, and Tate set his coffee aside, and her tea, and took a light hold on her shoulders.

"How long has it been since you've been on the back of a horse?" Tate asked, his chin resting on top of her head. "You used to love it, remember?"

A tremor went through Libby. *I used to love so many things. And suddenly, they weren't part of my life anymore. You weren't part of my life anymore.*

"Scared?" Tate asked, without moving.

She saw no point in denying it; he obviously knew. She nodded, swallowed.

"Of me?"

"No," Libby said, letting herself be held, just as she had during the night. It felt so good. She'd never feared Tate, but she *was* afraid of what he could make her feel, and what she might be willing to risk because of that. "Of course not."

"Then, what?"

She shook her head, unable to answer.

Tate kissed the crown of her head. Sighed.

"You can call Julie and Paige," he said, after a long time.

"Give them my cell number. If they need to reach you for any reason, they'll be able to do that."

"I don't know…."

Once again, he lifted her chin. "Just for once, never mind what you think you *should* do. Concentrate what you *want* to do. Do you even know what that is anymore, Libby?"

She swallowed, her throat suddenly full of tears, shoved back her bangs with one hand. "Of course I know what I want—"

"Okay. What?"

You and me, together for good. Kids and dogs and horses and a garden…

But there was another part of her, with other dreams.

She'd never seen the Eiffel Tower, or the Great Wall of China, that other Libby. And she wanted to.

Libby looked away from his face, looked back. Some of the anxiety she'd felt drained away, but another kind of charge sizzled in its place. "I want to go riding with you and your little girls," she admitted. "But what I *should* want—"

Tate interrupted, grinning and shaking his head. "Let's go downstairs and have breakfast," he said. "After that, we'll ride."

Libby considered that. "But my mother—my sisters—"

"Are all grown women," Tate said, taking her hand. "They don't need you with them to survive the day, Lib." He gave her a little pull. "Let's go."

She let him lead her downstairs.

To her relief, the big kitchen was empty.

Breakfast awaited in various chafing dishes, the kind Libby normally saw in buffet restaurants. There were blueberry pancakes, scrambled eggs, bacon and sausage to choose from, along with yogurt cups arranged in a bowl of ice.

Libby surveyed it in amazement.

"All this is for us and two six-year-olds?" she asked.

"And some of the guys from the bunkhouse," Tate said, handing her a plate before taking one of his own.

Libby felt her eyes go round. "You mean, a whole bunch of *cowboys* might come walking in here at any moment?" she asked, horrified. If that happened, the news that Libby Remington had spent the night in the main house on the Silver Spur—*again*—would circulate from the feed store to the post office to the Amble On Inn, where the old-timers hung out because "A man could still get a good beer for cheap."

"Maybe," Tate said. "Why does it matter?"

"You know damn well *why it matters!*"

Grinning, Tate took a step back and raised both his hands, palms out. "Okay, I know why it matters," he admitted. "You don't want the whole town of Blue River to hear that you showed up at breakfast."

Libby raised her chin a notch. "That's right."

"You can't possibly be that naive." He leaned in, whispered close to her ear, and even the warmth of his *breath* turned her on, for pity's sake. "We're old news, Libby. Everybody knows we're getting it on."

"'Getting it on'?" Libby jabbed two sausage links and plopped them onto her plate, moved on to the scrambled eggs. "Is that what you call it?"

Tate grinned down at her, speared four pancakes along with bacon and sausage. "What would *you* call it?" he countered, so obviously enjoying her heated discomfort that she wanted to spear him with a fork.

Libby decided to ignore the question, since she didn't want to say *making love*—that might sound sappy—and the f-word was out, too, because it was ugly. She turned her back on him, marched to the table with her plate and sat down.

Tate swung a leg over the back of a chair and sat across from her, setting his full plate down with a *plunk*. A mischievous—make that evil—grin danced at the corners of his mouth and sparked in his too-blue eyes.

"For somebody who could probably set the record for multiple orgasms," he observed, "you are pretty old-fashioned."

Libby blushed. "I consider that *your* fault," she said, poking at her eggs.

"Your orgasms are *my* fault?" He speared a sausage link and bit off the end, took his time chewing and swallowing.

"Well," Libby said, "I don't have them *by myself.*"

He laughed. "It's okay, Libby," he told her. "I don't mind taking the credit."

"You mean the blame."

"No. I mean the credit."

Color flared in Libby's cheeks. "Could we just eat?"

"See how testy you are? If you'd just let me have you against a wall before we came downstairs this morning, you'd be mellow right now, instead of wound up tight like an old pocket watch with the stem turned one too many times."

"Tate," Libby said, leaning toward him a little. "Shut up."

He sighed. "I'm just saying."

Fortunately, the back door opened just then, and Audrey and Ava bounded in, faces alight, with three dogs and a housekeeper in their wake.

"Can we go fishing in the creek?" Audrey asked.

"Not on your own," Tate answered.

"That spotted horse is trying to kick his way out of the pen," Ava added, looking worried. "He can't get out, can he?"

"He can't get out, honey," Tate assured his daughter.

Ava turned to Libby, her blue eyes serious behind smudged lenses. "That's the horse," she whispered, "that stepped on Mr. Ruiz and made him die."

Libby felt a maternal urge to gather the child in her arms and hug her. She glanced at Tate, wondering why a dangerous animal like the stallion was still on the place.

She quickly dismissed the concern. Tate was a rancher, descended from generations of ranchers; he certainly knew horses. He would do what needed to be done, when it needed to be done.

Tate calmly finished eating, stood, his gaze connecting with Libby's as he rose. "So how about that horseback ride?" he asked, and though his tone was easy, she knew by the expression in his eyes that her answer was important to him.

Audrey and Ava immediately began to jump up and down, eager to go along.

Ambrose, Buford and Hildie all barked, caught up in the excitement.

And Esperanza smiled serenely to herself.

The children—and the dogs—would have been too disappointed if she'd said "No." Or, at least, that was what Libby told herself.

In fact, Tate had been right earlier, reminding her how she'd once loved riding horses.

"Okay," she said. "But I need to call Julie and Paige first."

Mayhem broke out—dogs barking, little girls cheering and clapping.

Shaking her head benevolently, Esperanza picked up a laundry basket and started up one of the three sets of stairs that intersected on the far side of the McKettricks' kitchen.

"We can saddle our *own* ponies!" Ava cried jubilantly.

"Go and do it, then," Tate told the kids. "And take the dogs with you."

The big house seemed to let out its breath when it was just Tate and Libby again, alone in the room. He stood behind her, handed his cell phone past her right shoulder before moving away.

Libby dialed Julie's home number first, since it was still fairly early.

"Hello?" Julie answered sleepily, as Tate went out the back door.

"It's me, Libby," Libby whispered. It was silly to whisper, she decided, since she had the kitchen to herself, but whisper she did.

Julie sounded a lot more awake when she answered. "Are you with Tate?"

"Yes," Libby replied, since the only alternative was to lie. "We're—we're going horseback riding today, so Tate suggested that I give you his cell number, just in case you or Paige need to reach me for any reason—"

Julie giggled. "Wonderful," she said.

Libby bristled. "What do you mean, 'Wonderful'?" she snapped. "You do realize, don't you, that little elves didn't stop by and rebuild the Perk Up while we were sleeping, or bring the Pink Bomb back to its former glory?"

There was a pause.

Libby used it to rinse off her plate and stick it into the nearest dishwasher.

"This probably isn't a good time to tell you," Julie finally said, "that the tow-truck guy says the Cadillac can be repaired. It's going to take some major bodywork and a paint job, but the car is still structurally sound."

"Now why," Libby nearly snarled, "would this be a bad time to tell me anything?"

Hearing herself, she sucked in a hissy breath and squeezed her eyes shut for a moment. Exhaled.

"Let me try that again," she said, measuring out the words.

Julie gave a nervous laugh. "Libby, every—"

"Don't you dare say everything will be all right!"

At just that moment, Tate stuck his head inside the back door, assumed an expression of mock terror, ducked out as though he expected some missile to come hurtling his way and then stepped over the threshold.

"Horses are ready to ride," he said, just as Julie was speaking.

"Okay," Libby's sister said, very gently, "I won't say that. But it will be. You wait and see."

"Call me when the next disaster hits," Libby said, and she wasn't kidding. She held Tate's phone away with both hands and squinted at it, trying to find his phone number.

Standing close to her now, he fed it into her ear, digit by digit, while Libby repeated each new number to Julie. She felt silly, the whole time.

Everyone had a cell phone these days.

Except for her.

Why was that?

It wasn't just the money, although that was a factor in everything she did. Except for Paige and Julie, who were always either dropping by or calling her on either the shop phone or the one at home, she'd had no one to call or be called by.

Now she felt ridiculously behind-the-times.

Tate's hand rested on her shoulder, sending bolts of soft fire through her.

"Libby?" Julie prompted. "Are you still there?"

Libby nodded, swallowed, said, "Yes," in a frog-voice.

Tate's fingers began to work the taut muscles where her shoulders and neck met. She rolled her head, barely bit back a groan of pure pleasure.

For her, those particular muscles and the soles of her feet were erogenous zones. Thank God he wasn't massaging her feet—she might have reached a climax.

"I'm here," she said, croaking again and several beats late. "D-did you get the number?"

"Yes," Julie answered, and Libby could just see her smiling. "Are you all right?"

"Of course I'm all right!"

"Now, don't get your panties in a wad," Julie counseled. Then, wickedly, she added, "If you're wearing any, that is."

"Julie Remington, you have a dirty mind!"

"No," Julie said, "I'm just trying to think positively."

"Funny. Ha-ha, Julie, you are *so funny.*"

"I'll call, or Paige will, if anything important happens," Julie went on, sounding so pleased with herself that Libby's back molars clamped together.

"Thanks," Libby said once she'd released her jaw, and shut the phone with a bang. Turned and fairly shoved it at Tate.

"You *really* need that quickie," he whispered.

She punched him.

But her heart wasn't in it.

TATE RODE STRANGER, the roan gelding, while Libby was mounted on a gentle—and equally aged—mare named Buttons. The twins followed on their golden, nameless ponies, with Ambrose and Buford frolicking alongside. Hildie brought up the rear, moving slowly, and Tate was keeping an eye on the old dog, same as Libby was.

The sun was hot and high, the sky a brassy blue that ached in the heart, as well as the eyes. Grass rippled and flowed around them like light on water, and clusters of cattle grazed here and there, while horses, some of them almost as wild as the stallion penned up back at the barn, lowered their heads for creek water.

Tate stood in the stirrups, stretching his legs, keeping an eye on his daughters bouncing happily along on their birthday ponies, a few dozen yards ahead of him and Libby, the dogs keeping up easily.

When Libby reined in, it was a moment before he noticed. Buttons wanted to keep up with the other horses, and kept turning around and around in a tight circle, tossing her head, resisting Libby's efforts to bring her to a full stop.

Half in the saddle and half out, Libby had one foot in a stirrup and no place to put the other one. Back a ways, Hildie sat in the high grass, panting hard, tongue lolling.

Tate rode back, got Libby's horse by the bridle strap, spoke firmly to the animal. It settled down right away.

The Ruiz place was close—less than a mile from the main house, traveling overland, as they were—and before setting out, Libby and Tate had agreed that Hildie could surely make it that far, since she and Libby took a long walk almost every day.

For whatever reason, Hildie obviously didn't plan on going another step.

Libby had shifted back into the saddle with an ease that did Tate proud, though he could not have said why.

When he was sure Buttons would behave, he got down off Stranger and walked back to Hildie, crouching when he reached her.

"Is she all right?" Libby called, anxious.

Up ahead, the girls had stopped to wait, turned their ponies around.

Tate and the dog were eye to eye. "Hey, girl," he said gently. "You get tired of walking?"

Hildie licked his right cheek and favored him with a dog smile. Her tongue, long and pink, hung out of the side of her mouth.

"You better ride with me for a ways," Tate said, easing the animal to her feet, making sure she could stand. Her flanks quivered, but then she steadied, and he checked her paws for thorns or stones, the way he would have done with a horse.

Libby had ridden back to him by then, Stranger following, reins dragging along the ground.

"Is Hildie hurt?" Libby asked, sounding so worried that Tate looked up at her and felt his heart rush into his throat.

I love you, Libby, he wanted to say. *Trust me with your heart, the way you trust me with your dog.*

"Just tired, I think," he said. "A little overheated, too, maybe."

With that, Tate lifted the dog in both arms, careful to support her back, and managed to remount the gelding without dropping Hildie. The trick wasn't quite so easy to pull off as it had been when he was a kid, forever sharing a horse's back with one family dog or another.

Libby moved in close enough that their horses' sides touched, and her smile lodged somewhere deep in Tate's soul, a place beyond all reach until that day, and that woman.

"Thanks," she said. Her blue eyes shone with light.

Tate centered himself and Hildie, scooting farther back in the saddle so she wouldn't be jabbed by the horn and then reaching around to take hold of the reins again. "If I'd known all it would take for you to look at me like that was to ride

double with your dog, Hildie and I would have been working the range together long before this."

Libby smiled tentatively, then made a dismissive motion
with one hand.

The girls waited until Libby and Tate caught up.

"Did Hildie get tired?" Ava asked.

"She's not hurt, is she?" Audrey wanted to know.

Tate's pride in his daughters was a swelling in his chest
some of the time, a pinch in the wall of his heart or a catch
in his breath—it varied. That day, it was a scalding sensation behind his eyes.

"No, Hildie's not hurt," he said, for Libby's benefit, as well
as the children's. "She just needed a little help, that's all."

Audrey and Ava nodded sagely.

The Ruiz place—*his place*—was just ahead, gleaming
in the curved embrace of the creek. The grass was green,
and the round-topped oaks threw great patches of shade
onto the ground.

Tate rode down to the creek and then right into the shallow part, making the girls shriek with delight.

Stranger bent his big head and drank, up to all four ankles
in crystal-clear water, and Tate dismounted, set Hildie down
gently on smooth pebbles that glittered like jewels.

Hildie shivered, gave a happy woof and drank thirstily
before bounding up the creek bank like a pup, apparently re-
freshed and ready for adventure.

Tate slogged after the dog, pretending he was wetter than
he was, and Hildie waited until he was within range to shake
herself off with vigor, flinging water all over him.

Libby's laughter, and that of his little girls, rang in the
pure light of that summer morning, weaving together, ribbons of sound.

CHAPTER SEVENTEEN

VARIOUS CONTRACTORS' trucks and vans encircled the former Ruiz house—painters, electricians, plumbers, drywallers and roofers plied their trades, swarming in and out. The ring of hammers and the shrill, devouring roar of power saws sliced the air, thick with summer heat.

Libby wondered how she could have failed to notice all that noise and activity. She'd been entirely transported, watching Tate ride his horse into the creek, balancing Hildie in his strong arms. Watching as he'd set the dog down in the water and grinned that one-of-a-kind patented grin of his as she drank—while, for the amusement of his small daughters, he'd pretended to be stunned and outraged when Hildie shook herself off and drenched him in the process.

The muscles on the insides of Libby's thighs throbbed from even that short time in the saddle as she climbed down, pausing a moment on shaky legs, the balls of her feet tingling. She left the mare to graze with Tate's horse and the two ponies.

"Looks like you've given up on landing a spot on the DIY Network," Libby teased, nodding toward the house, wanting to touch Tate where sweat and creek water dampened the fabric of his shirt. *Lord knows, you've got the looks for TV, though. I can see you with a tool belt slung low*

*around your hips, like an Old West gunslinger's gear, and
breaking the hearts of female home-improvement enthu-
siasts everywhere.*

Tate's moist hair curled slightly around his ears and at the
back of his neck. His smile was white, perfect and absolutely
lethal, and the shadows of the leaves over their heads darkened his eyes, lightened them again.

"Yep," he drawled, with a shrug of shoulders made strong
and broad first by heredity, and then by loading and unload-
ing bales of hay and sacks of feed, by shoveling out stalls
and carrying sweet old dogs who couldn't or wouldn't walk
another step. "I admit it. I ran a white flag up the pole and
sent for reinforcements. At the rate I was going, I figured
the kids and I would be moving in here next year sometime,
or the year after that. I want us to be living under this roof
before Audrey and Ava start school in the fall."

"Can we go fishing, Daddy?" Ava asked, tugging at his
sleeve. "Those poles you bought us are on the back porch,
right?"

"Right," Tate said. "Dig the worms first."

The girls rushed off to do his bidding, and Ambrose and
Buford followed, leaping and bounding through the grass.
Hildie, bless her heart, was content to lie down in the shady
grass under a nearby tree, keeping Libby in sight and staying
clear of the grazing horses.

"Why?" Libby asked quietly.

"Why?" Tate echoed, eyes dancing. "Why should the
kids dig worms before they go fishing?"

Libby smiled and shook her head. "Why do you want to live
in this house when you have a perfectly good mega-mansion?"

Tate shoved a hand through his hair, turned to watch as
his daughters knelt in the middle of the large garden plot,

between rows of cabbage, an old coffee can nearby, the pair of them digging for earthworms with their bare hands.

They'd be ring-in-the-bathtub filthy when they got back to the ranch house—the way little kids should be. When he and his brothers were small, their mother used to joke about hosing them down in the yard before letting them set foot on her clean floors.

He smiled at the recollection.

The pups, never far away from the twins, day or night, sniffed curiously at the ground, tails wagging, and Ambrose lifted his leg against a cornstalk.

"My reason for wanting to live here hasn't changed since we talked about it before," Tate answered, at some length.

Libby tilted her head to one side. Her expression was friendly, but skeptical, too. "You claim you want to see how 'regular' people live," she said. "I'm not convinced, Tate. Even if you moved into a tent, or a crate under a viaduct, you still wouldn't be an ordinary guy. You'd be a McKettrick."

"There's so much pride attached to that," Tate said, still watching his daughters and their dogs in the near distance. They were sun-splashed, and their chatter rang in the weighted air like the distant toll of country church bells. "Being a McKettrick, I mean. These days, it mostly means having money." He turned to face Libby, and because the light changed, she couldn't read his eyes. "Once, it meant something more, Lib. Something better."

She waited, listening with her heart, as well as with her ears.

"When Clay McKettrick took over the original hundred acres that became this ranch," he said huskily, "Blue River was a wide spot on a dusty cattle trail, and nobody had a clue there was oil here. Probably wouldn't have cared much if they *had* known—cars being few and far between, especially four hundred miles up the backside of no place." Tate paused, as if remembering. As if he'd been there, back in the early twentieth century. The McKettricks tended to know all about their kin, living and dead—it was just the way they were. "Clay started with the help of the woman he loved and the strength in his back. Part of the Arizona bunch—old Angus was his grandfather and Clay was the youngest of Jeb and Chloe's brood—he could have stayed right there on the Triple M and nobody would have thought the worse of him for it. But he wanted to do something on his own, and he did, Libby. He did."

Libby debated for a moment before moving closer to him. There were too many people around for any display of affection, so standing a little nearer and letting her upper arm touch his under the dappling shadows of the oak leaves overhead had to do.

"There are those who start things," she said, quietly, "and those who carry them on. Clay founded this ranch, and generations of McKettricks kept it going, made it grow. You're part of that, Tate—so are your brothers. How is that a bad thing?"

Tate watched the sparkling creek water, most likely pondering what she'd said, though he didn't reply.

Libby turned her eyes toward the garden—some of it had already been tilled under, and a lot of the produce had already been removed, probably given away. Ava and Audrey were high-stepping toward them, the partially rusted coffee can in hand, no doubt with worms squirming in the bottom. Ambrose and Buford kept pace, and the old house was a beehive of activity.

"Tate?" Libby prompted gently. "What's wrong with

the other house? What do you hope to prove by moving into this one?"

He looked at her sharply, but then everything seemed to ease. His jaw and shoulders relaxed visibly. "There's nothing wrong with the main ranch house," he said quietly. "It has a long history. The memories are mostly happy ones. But it's *big*, Libby. Even when the kids are there, well, it's as if we were all staying in a hotel or something—on vacation all the time, and never just hanging out around home."

Libby nodded. She did understand.

Tate went on, his eyes fond and solemn as he watched his daughters, who'd stopped to argue over which one of them was going to carry the can of worms. His mouth crooked up in a semblance of a grin as they pulled it one way and then the other.

"Maybe we'll stay here for good," Tate went on, "and maybe we won't. But my daughters will at least have a sense of how normal people live."

"Would you ever leave the ranch, Tate?" Libby asked; for her, it was a bold question. "Would you ever leave and not come back?"

He looked at her closely then. "Nope," he said, with certainty. "I'm Texas born and bred. It's as if this dirt and this sky and these people are in my cells, Lib. What about you?"

Libby raised her shoulders, lowered them again. Sighed. "Sometimes I wonder who I'd be, away from here."

Tate squinted, as though to see her better, and he would surely have pursued the subject except that one of the twins let out a shrill shriek before he could say anything.

Shaking his head, Tate strode in their direction to settle the dispute over the worms.

"Hold it!" he said, holding up both hands.

Libby smiled, reminded of her dad. He'd been the peacemaker, the one who mediated little-girl arguments over whose barrette was whose, whose turn it was to bring in the newspaper or wash the dishes or weed the garden or sweep the kitchen floor.

Her dad had never raised his voice, as far back as she could remember. He'd certainly never lifted a hand to any one of them in anger, though he'd wiped away a great many tears and treated a million skinned elbows and scraped knees.

Who *was* Libby Remington, really?

Her father's daughter, and Marva's.

Julie and Paige's big sister, and Calvin's aunt.

Hildie's mistress, and a friend of animals everywhere.

The owner of the Perk Up Coffee Shop, now passed on into the realm of legend.

And most certainly the naive girl Tate McKettrick had dumped for somebody else.

She was over that last part—being dumped, anyway—she'd grown safely into a woman, and if there was one thing she'd learned in the process, it was that life was rarely easy, rarely simple, and often painful.

And it was worth all of that, to be here, now, doing nothing on a sunny summer day.

Libby watched as Tate dropped to his haunches, facing his daughters, after taking the can and peering inside.

Libby couldn't hear his words, but she saw the white flash of his grin, and knew he was working that McKettrick magic of his. She could imagine him saying what fine specimens those worms were, that he'd never seen better ones, that they were sure to catch the biggest trout in the creek.

The little girls listened with such earnest trust in their faces that Libby's eyes smarted. With a surreptitious swipe of one hand, she wiped them away, gave a delicate sniffle.

Straightening, Tate kept the rusty worm can, caught Libby's eye and winked, then gestured toward the house and said something more to the children. They raced around back, giggling again, the yellow dogs trotting behind them, baying like hounds on the hunt.

On his way back to where Libby stood, Tate stopped to speak with the plumber, and then the man loading a battered wooden tool chest, the old-fashioned kind, into the back of his van.

Libby knew ail the men, of course, knew their wives and their children, their mothers and fathers, and in some cases, their grandparents, too. She realized, standing there, how silly it was to think she could have hidden her relationship with Tate, even briefly.

As he said, everybody knew they were "getting it on."

He came toward her now, grinning and carrying the worm can.

As she watched him moving nearer and nearer, Libby's heart swelled and then somersaulted in her chest, a big, slow and graceful motion, like that of some sea creature frolicking in deep waters.

Bold as you please, Tate leaned in and kissed her. It wasn't just a peck, either. There was tongue involved.

She gasped, breathless and unsteady on her feet, when he drew back. "Trout for supper," he said.

"I beg your pardon?" Libby asked, confused.

Tate held up the worm can. "Audrey and Ava are fetching the fishing poles even as we speak," he said. "Here's the agenda: we catch a few trout. The guys knock off early, gather up their gear and leave. There's a fish fry. We all stuff ourselves and I catch the horses and saddle them up again, and we all ride back to the main house. The dogs and the kids are exhausted—bound to sleep like rocks. Esperanza cleans them up and puts them to bed. I tend to the horses. Then you and I take a shower together—this time I remember to lock the bedroom door—and I make love to you until all the kinks are worked out of that perfect little body of yours."

Libby's knees went weak. "All the—?"

"Kinks," Tate finished for her. "It might take some doing," he added seriously.

She thought about it.

A sweet, hot shiver of anticipation went through her.

Then she grinned, rose onto her tiptoes and kissed the cleft in his chin. "Sounds good to me," she said.

TATE WAS HAPPIER THAN he'd been in a long time; it almost scared him.

Needing something physical to do, at least until his emotions settled down a little, he spoke to the contractors, asked them to take the rest of the day off.

Then he unsaddled the horses, took off their bridles, too.

They'd stay close, he knew, because the grass was sweet and plentiful, the creek was nearby and the trees provided shade.

After that, Tate just allowed himself to marvel at what a lucky bastard he really was, and forget the oil shares and the money. His kids were healthy, and they were *here,* with him, with Libby.

Sunlight gilded his baby girls like full-body halos. Their voices, their laughter, their concern for worms and fishes, as well as dogs and horses—all those things roosted in Tate's heart, flapped their wings and settled in to stay.

The land, the trees, the sky seemed to go on forever.

And in the center of all this magic was Libby, as sturdy and practical and down-home as a sunflower, sprung up in some unlikely place, but at the same time, as dazzling as crystals glittering on fresh snow.

She helped Audrey and Ava to bait their hooks and cast their lines into the creek—and made sure they didn't snag each other in the process. She laughed a lot, and they liked being close to her, leaning into her sides when she wrapped an arm around each of them and squeezed.

"You know how to *fish?*" Audrey had marveled at the beginning, obviously surprised. Her eyes glowed as she looked up at Libby, and so did Ava's. She seemed to fascinate them.

She certainly fascinated *him,* though in a different way.

As simply as Libby lived, as ordinary as she seemed to think she was, there was a sense of mystery about her, of depths and heights, an interior landscape, a planet, maybe even a *universe,* waiting to be explored.

That was Libby.

"You bet I know how to fish," she had beamed, answering Audrey's question. "My dad used to take my sisters and me camping whenever he could, and if we wanted trout or bass for supper, we had to catch it."

The afternoon progressed, slowed down with the heat. Tate and Libby wound up sitting side by side on the creek bank, their knees drawn up and their heels dug in and each of them with their arms around one of the twins, showing them when to let out the line, when to reel it in.

In the end, there was no fish fry, though.

They threw back everything they caught.

The kids wanted mac-and-cheese, anyway. The boxed kind was Tate's culinary specialty; when he felt like swanking it up, he added wieners.

He'd give Esperanza the night off, he decided—maybe she'd like to go to the movies or visit a friend.

By the time the mosquitoes were out and drilling for blood, Audrey and Ava were finally starting to run down. Hunger made them cranky, and they began to bicker.

"Seems like they've had all the fun they can stand," Tate told Libby.

She nodded, grinned up at him. Her eyes looked dreamy; the quiet afternoon had been good for her.

If Tate had his way, the night would be even better.

For a while, it looked as though that was actually going to happen.

Once the kids had stowed their fishing poles, everyone checked out the progress the contractors had made on the house. The twins' room was coming together, and so was the bathroom they would share. The kitchen and the master bedroom both had a ways to go.

Tate decided he might get back into the home-improvement groove after all. Delegate some of his duties as foreman—not that he was real clear yet on what those duties actually were.

He wished he'd spent more time riding with Pablo now, both on horseback and in the company truck. And not just because of the things he might have learned.

The man's absence was still a persistent ache in Tate's middle, a wind that sometimes abated and sometimes howled.

He saddled his horse and Libby's, checked to see that the girls had gotten their cinches tight enough and wouldn't be rolling off their ponies' backs onto the ground.

Not that they'd have far to go, he thought, with a smile.

The ponies were about the size of a large dog.

Once Libby was on Buttons's back and squared away, Tate handed Hildie up into her arms, made sure she had a good grip. That dog looked as easy in the saddle as if she played polo on weekends.

Letting the kids get a head start, Tate took his time swinging up into the saddle and turning Stranger in the direction of the main house.

Sometimes I wonder who I'd be, away from here.

Libby's remark had snagged in his mind, beneath all the sunshine and the fishing and the easy enjoyment of a sunny day.

If she thought he was going to let *that* one go, she should have damn well known better.

"So," Tate began, as they rode slowly onto the range again, the big house towering in the distance, like the castle it was. "Who do you think you'd be, Lib, away from Blue River?"

She nestled her chin onto the top of Hildie's head, her arms stretched around the dog's ample body, holding on to the saddle horn for balance and letting the reins rest loosely across the mare's neck.

After a long time, she replied sadly, "I don't know. Maybe someone who's accomplished things."

Tate nudged his horse a bit closer to Libby's, not to crowd her, but in case holding the dog got to be too much for her. He raised an eyebrow and shifted his gaze to the space between Stranger's ears, though he was still watching Lib out of the corner of one eye.

"Like what?" he asked, very carefully.

If Libby truly believed she had something to prove, well, as far as Tate was concerned, that was cause for concern. Especially if she thought she had to leave Blue River to do it.

She sighed. She shook her head.

Gently, he took Hildie from her.

Their horses moved apart again.

Hildie tilted her head back to lick the underside of Tate's chin.

He chuckled. The girls were too far ahead, almost to the fence, the pups weaving around them.

Tate gave a shrill whistle to get Audrey and Ava's attention, signaled them to wait for him and Libby.

"Will you do me a favor, Lib?" he asked, when she didn't say anything. "Before you decide to take off for parts unknown, so you can 'accomplish' things, will you give us a chance? You and me, I mean?"

Tears glistened in her eyes when she looked at him. "What kind of chance?"

"You know what kind of chance."

"What if it doesn't work?"

"What if it does?"

Libby bit down on her lower lip and looked away. "It didn't before."

"That was before. We weren't living in the same town. And that was a long time ago, Lib."

She met his eyes, with a visible effort. "Isn't that what we're doing now, Tate?" she asked quietly. "Giving things a chance?"

"I want to sleep with you every night, Libby. I want to shower with you and eat breakfast with you and do a whole lot of other things with you." He paused, looked back over his shoulder. "The house isn't finished, but it's livable. I'll rustle up some furniture, and we'll move in. You, me and the kids and the dogs."

She was quiet for a long time. So long that Tate started to get nervous.

"You're suggesting that we *live* together?" Libby finally asked. "In the same house with your children?"

The scandalized note in her voice made Tate chuckle. "Hello? The parents of half the kids in their kindergarten class 'cohabitate.'"

"There's cohabitation," Libby said, "and there's *shacking up.*"

"You know, for someone as sexually responsive as you are, Lib, you can really be prudish."

Her cheeks glowed with pink splotches. "You're not concerned that Audrey and Ava will be—confused?"

Tate huffed out a sigh. "No," he said. "Did Ava seem 'confused' this morning, when she found us in bed together? For better or worse, it's a different world, Libby." He watched her for a long moment, trying to gauge her reactions. They had almost caught up with the girls, so he lowered his voice. "If it really bothers you, though—*living in sin,* I mean—we could go ahead and get married."

"Married?"

"Well, wouldn't that be better than 'shacking up,' as you put it?"

"What about—" She stopped, swallowed so hard that Tate felt the dry ache in his own throat. "What about love?"

"Love isn't our problem," Tate replied quietly. "*Trust* is our problem."

Libby didn't affirm that assertion, but she didn't deny it, either. So he still had a fighting chance.

For now, though, the conversation was over.

Deftly, Ava reached, without dismounting, to work the gate latch.

In the distance, the stud kicked and squealed like he'd tear that pen apart, rail by rail and bolt by bolt. The sound of that animal's rage sent a shiver tripping down Tate's spine.

As soon as he'd ridden through the gate, Tate got down

from the saddle, set Hildie on the ground and strode toward the pen, leaving Stranger to go into the barn on his own.

"Shut that gate," he called over one shoulder, "and go on into the barn."

Through the gaps between the steel rails, Tate saw the stallion bunch its hind quarters, put its head down and send both its back legs slamming into the pen's gate with enough force to shake the ground.

The gate held.

Tate swore under his breath. Fumbled for his cell phone and called Brent Brogan's direct line.

"Hey, Tate," Brent said, affably distracted, like he was doing paperwork or something. "Everything okay out there on the Ponderosa?"

Tate answered with a question of his own. "You heard a decision on what Animal Control wants to do with this stud?" he asked. "Because he's in a foul mood—fixing to kick his way out of the pen and kill somebody else."

Brent sighed. "I'll make a few calls," he said, "and get back to you."

"Thanks," Tate said. Call waiting clicked in his ear. "Later." Then, after pressing the appropriate button, "Tate McKettrick."

"It's Julie Remington, Tate. I need to speak with Libby."

So much, Tate thought, for loving the "kinks" out of Libby's delectable little body later on, when they would have been alone. He grabbed hold of the pen gate with his free hand and gave the thing a hard shake, making sure the stud hadn't sprung it.

"Sure," he said glumly. "Hold on a second."

Libby had gone into the barn, along with the twins, and when Tate reached the doorway, she and Audrey and Ava were all in separate stalls, unsaddling their horses and getting ready to brush them down. Stranger stood in the breezeway, waiting his turn, although Libby must have removed his saddle and blanket and bridle.

The old horse ambled toward Tate, nudged him good-naturedly in the chest.

Leaving Buttons's stall, Libby was smiling, dusting her hands together.

Job well done.

"For you." Tate held the cell out to her, and she took it.

"Julie," he added, opening the door to Stranger's stall and stepping aside so the animal could precede him.

Libby nodded, looking mildly troubled, and headed for the open door at the end of the breezeway.

Tate closed the stall door and began brushing down his horse.

"I'M *NOT* KIDDING," Julie said. "Marva is leaving. For good. The movers will come in a few days and clear out her apartment."

Libby rounded the corner of the barn, keeping to the shade, and gazed at the stallion in its big metal cage. The creature had quieted, but its flanks and sides were lathered as though it had run for miles and miles. It stood with its head hung low, its sides expanding, drawing in, expanding, drawing in again.

She thought about Pablo; how startled and afraid he must have been when he fell under the stallion's hooves. The pain, though probably brief, would have been horrendous.

"Julie, what do you want me to say?" Libby asked, backing away from the stallion now, resisting a strange and probably suicidal desire to reach between those steel slats and try to comfort it somehow. Speak softly and stroke its sweat-drenched neck. "If Marva wants to leave, she can leave. Hitting the road is her forte, after all, isn't it?"

"Nobody's denying that she left us, Lib," Julie said so quietly and so gently that Libby was ashamed of herself. "We were little girls. We needed her. She abandoned us and she abandoned Dad. But—"

"But?" Libby snapped.

On some level, she was still that terrified, heartbroken and *furious* kid who wanted her mother.

"Look," Julie went on, when Libby was silent for a long time, "she wants to see all three of us, tonight. At her place. She says it's important."

Libby wanted to scream, though of course she didn't. That would have alarmed the kids, and Hildie, who had followed her out of the barn and sat looking up at her now, pink tongue lolling.

"Why does it have to be tonight?"

"Because she's flying out of Austin tomorrow," Julie said. "Libby, I know you have issues with Marva—valid ones. We all do. But the woman *is* our mother, and I think we can do this much for her."

Libby's head began to throb. She dug into her right temple with three fingers and rubbed.

Returning to town meant she couldn't pretend the Perk Up was still standing.

It probably meant no sex with Tate.

And she'd been looking forward to that, to getting naked in the shower with him. To soaring outside herself.

Love isn't our problem, he'd said. Trust *is our problem.*

Did that mean he still loved her?

Dammit, she wanted to know. She *needed* to know.

"Just come," Julie said. "Please, Lib. Six-thirty, Marva's place."

Libby looked at her wrist, realized she wasn't wearing her watch, and asked, "What time is it now?"

"A little after five," Julie answered. "You're with Tate, aren't you?"

"Not for long, it would seem," Libby lamented. *We were starting to get somewhere, Tate and I.*

"I'm sure he'll understand."

"Of course he will. *I'm* the one having a hard time understanding."

"Well, *that* was certainly cryptic," Julie remarked. Then, barely missing a beat, "You'll be at Marva's, then?"

Libby nodded, glummer than glum. "Yes." She looked up, and Tate was standing maybe a dozen yards away, waiting, looking pensive.

And so deliciously hunky.

"See you at six-thirty," Julie said.

"See you," Libby answered, and closed the phone.

Walking up to Tate, she handed the device back to him.

"I have to go back to town," she said. "It seems my mother is leaving Blue River again—her work here is done now that my business is in ruins—and she wants to say goodbye. Tonight."

Tate sighed, took Libby's shoulders in his hands. "You're okay with this? Her leaving, I mean?"

"It's not as though she's been an integral part of my life, Tate." Libby spoke without bitterness; she was simply stating a fact she'd accepted long ago. Mostly.

He drew her close, as she'd hoped he would do, and held her, resting his chin on the top of her head. "Let me make sure Esperanza can look after the kids tonight, and then I'll drive you to town."

She nodded, wanting to cling to him, forcing herself not to clutch at the fabric of his shirt. "I don't want to go."

"Then don't."

"I *have* to, Tate."

She felt the motion of his jaw; knew he was smiling even before he held her a little way from his chest so he could look down into her face.

"This was a good day," he said.

"It was a good day," Libby agreed.

But the best part was over.

Fifteen minutes later, they were in Tate's truck, headed for Blue River. Hildie rode in the rear seat, but she wasn't any happier about leaving the Silver Spur than Libby was, evidently. The dog sat backward, looking out the window over the truckbed, and every few moments, she gave a small whimper.

Libby wanted to reassure Hildie that they'd be back, but she was strangely hesitant to make such a promise.

At home, she took a quick shower and put on a simple cotton sundress. She tracked Tate to the kitchen, where he was leaning calmly against the counter, arms folded, watching Hildie gobble up her kibble. He'd refilled her water dish, too, and even brought in the newspaper and the mail.

Libby, her hair still damp from the shower steam, searched for her car keys until she finally found them—hanging on their hook near the back door, where they were supposed to be.

"It always throws me," she admitted to Tate, "when things are where they're supposed to be."

He chuckled at that.

"You don't have to stay," she said, hoping he would.

Which was crazy, because he had children at home. He had

a ranch, livestock. Responsibilities. It was just plain wrong to expect him to sit here in this house until she got back from Marva's at whatever time, in whatever emotional condition, just because she might need someone to talk to later on.

He crossed the room, opened her refrigerator, shook his head. The pickings were slim; she had to admit that.

"What do you live on?" he asked, and from the tone of his voice, he was only half kidding. "You have three green olives, a box of baking soda, and I don't even want to think about the expiration date on that cheese. It's not supposed to be blue-green at the corners, is it?"

Libby laughed. "I depend heavily on canned goods," she said.

"Yuck," Tate said.

The wall phone rang.

Libby grabbed the receiver, hoping for a reprieve. In a fraction of an instant, she came up with the perfect scenario: Julie was calling to say that Marva was still leaving, soon and for good, but tonight's visit had been postponed—better yet, canceled altogether.

"Good, you're home," Julie said. "Can you pick me up? Paige is still at work, so she's going to be a few minutes late, and—"

"Sure," Libby broke in, deflated. So much for perfect scenarios. "I'll swing by and get you. But chill out a little. This isn't a rocket launch, Julie. There's no second-by-second countdown."

Incredibly, Julie burst into tears. "Maybe you don't want to know *where the hell* our mother has been all these years," she blurted out, in a very unJulie-like way, "but I do! *By God,* that woman isn't going *anywhere* until she gives me *some* kind of explanation!"

"Julie," Libby said gently, her gaze connecting with Tate's, "where's Calvin?"

Julie sniffled inelegantly. "He's spending the night with Justin."

"All right. That's good. I'll be over in a few minutes."

Goodbyes were said, and both sisters hung up.

Tate jingled his keys at Libby. "Hildie and I are going out to pick up something decent for dinner," he said. "We'll be here waiting when you get back."

"It might be late," she warned.

He approached, kissed her lightly. "We'll be here," he repeated. "Hildie and me."

She nodded, too choked up, all of a sudden, to say more.

Since the Impala was parked in her garage, off the alley, Libby couldn't avoid getting a glimpse of the caved-in roof and tumbled-down walls of the Perk Up.

It wasn't enough that Marva had abandoned them all way back when, she reflected bitterly.

Six months ago, with no warning at all, she'd returned to Blue River, rented the condo, furnished it and begun trying to "make up for lost time" and get to know her daughters.

But an invasion of their lives wasn't enough for Marva. Oh, no. She had to destroy the one thing Libby had to show for her attempts to jerry-rig some kind of career for herself. She had to reduce the Perk Up to scrap metal and firewood.

Libby climbed into the Impala, started the engine, calmly backed into the alley, remembering those early days after Marva's sudden reentry into her and her sisters' lives.

She'd seemed genuinely baffled, Marva had, when they resisted her overtures—the phone calls, the unannounced visits, the gifts.

Julie had been the first to give ground.

She wanted Calvin to know his grandmother, she'd said.

Paige, to Libby's initial surprise, had fallen under the spell of Marva next. Of course, Paige was the baby; she'd still been wearing footed pajamas and sucking her thumb when their mother bailed.

She'd cried the longest and the hardest. Climbed into Libby's or Julie's bed at night, dragging her tattered "blankie" and whispering, "Do you know where Mommy is? When will she be back? Tomorrow? Will Mommy come home tomorrow?"

Remembering, still the big sister, Libby ached with the same helpless fury she'd felt back then.

Julie was waiting by her front gate when Libby pulled up, the diamond-paned windows of her pretty cottage alight behind her. Flowers climbed trellises, tumbled, riotous, over fences, and the fierce dazzle of the setting sun glowed around it all.

"I can't believe she's just going to take off again," Julie said, instead of hello.

"Believe it," Libby said grimly.

CHAPTER EIGHTEEN

AFTER A SHORT SPEECH, Marva produced three envelopes from her handbag and, with a flourish, presented one to each of her daughters.

To Libby, it seemed that the floor of the condo's living room pitched from side to side, like a swimming raft bobbing on choppy water. She squeezed the bridge of her nose between her thumb and forefinger, trying hard to stem the headache beating behind her eyes like a second heart.

The tick of the mantel clock was hypnotic—steady as a metronome—and it didn't help that Marva kept pacing back and forth in front of the cold fireplace, arms folded, the hem of her wildly colorful silk caftan billowing at her heels.

Julie, seated in the wingback chair, was the first to open her envelope, the first to speak. Staring down at the check inside, she whispered, "This is—this is *a lot* of money."

Paige, perched on the edge of a chintz-covered ottoman, couldn't seem to speak at all. She pressed one hand to the base of her throat, shaking, her eyes squeezed shut.

Libby didn't move so much as a muscle. She was too stunned.

Marva stopped pacing and stood still, sweeping Libby, Julie and Paige up in a single cheerfully magnanimous glance.

"Paige? Libby? Don't either of you have anything to say?" their mother demanded, her voice a touch too high.

Paige opened her eyes, swayed slightly. "Holy crap," she said.

Libby straightened her spine. The headache receded slightly, and the floor leveled itself out and stayed still. "Please, Marva," she said, in a near whisper, "sit down. You're making me dizzy."

Marva plunked down next to Libby, on the couch. Took one of Libby's hands between both her own, as though the two of them were as close as any mother and daughter, ever. "I added a little something to your share, dear," she said, in a whisper no one could have helped overhearing, even if they'd been in the next room. "Because I crashed into your little coffee shop and everything."

And everything.

Did I mention that Dad kept asking for you, right up until the day he couldn't talk anymore, because the hospice nurse and Doc Burt put him on a ventilator, and there was a tube in his throat, and even then *he asked with his eyes?*

That until the middle of first grade, Paige thought every ring of the doorbell, every car stopping out front, meant you were home?

Oh, yeah, and Julie saw you everywhere, for years—in the grocery store, in other cars at stoplights, on the River Walk in San Antonio.

Me, I just wanted to talk to you. I was so pathetic, I would have settled for a few more phone calls. Letters or postcards.

Hell, I'd have settled for smoke signals.

And everything, indeed.

"I can't accept your money," Libby said stiffly, after finding her voice and pulling free of Marva's grasp.

Julie glared at Libby from across the small room, fanning

her flushed face with her check. "Lib," she said, "this is *no time* to let your pride do the talking."

Marva fluttered a hand, the gesture taking them all in. "It isn't *my* money, anyway," she said, in merry dismissal. "It's *yours.* I had a sizable insurance policy on your father's life— he and I took it out together, soon after you were born, Libby—and when he died, I collected. Winston—my present husband—is very good with money, and he invested the proceeds and—" She beamed, flinging her hands out wide. "*Voilà!* You are women of means!"

Women of means, Libby thought. Bile scalded the back of her throat.

"How—?" Paige paused, started again. "How could you leave us like that? We were *little kids,* Marva."

"I've never claimed to be perfect," Marva said, mildly indignant. The brilliant smile was gone.

A short, bristly silence followed. "I should have listened to Winston," Marva continued presently, frowning thoughtfully into the middle distance. "I thought if I came back to Blue River, well, we'd all get to know each other and bygones would be bygones. After all, we're all grown-ups, aren't we?" She sighed, causing her shoulders to rise and fall in an ebullient shrug. "Winston said you wouldn't react well, and he was right. I miss him terribly, and frankly I'm tired of being the only one around here who even *tries* to build a relationship. I want to get on with my life. I want to go home."

Home, Marva had explained earlier, before the ceremonious presentation of the envelopes, was a condominium overlooking a beach in Costa Rica. Winston was a retired proctologist and, apparently, a very indulgent husband—as well as a financial whiz.

Since responding to the things Marva had said would

have amounted to crossing a conversational minefield, none of the sisters said anything.

The evening was, for all practical intents and purposes, over.

Libby left her envelope, still unopened, on Marva's coffee table.

She said goodbye, travel safely, and other things she couldn't quite recall later, when she looked back on the experience.

She had almost reached the Impala when Julie caught up to her, shoved the envelope at her. Her name was neatly inscribed on the front, in flowing cursive.

"Don't be an idiot," she said. "Marva destroyed your business. And, anyway, Dad would have wanted you to have this money. He probably kept up the premiums the whole time Marva was away. *Take it.*"

Libby swallowed, snatched the envelope out of Julie's hand, shoved it into her purse as Paige joined them, shivering a little, hugging herself, even though the night was warm.

"I wouldn't make any investments or impulse purchases if I were you," Libby told both her sisters, as she opened her car door to get in and drive away. "Not before these checks clear the bank, anyway."

With that, she got into the Impala and started the engine.

"Are you coming with me?" Libby asked Julie, who was staring at her as though she'd turned into a total stranger.

"I'll go with Paige," Julie said, recovering enough to offer a thin smile. "She's a little shaken up."

Aren't we all? Libby thought wearily.

When she got back to the house, Tate was waiting for her, just as he'd promised he would be. He'd been to the store, too—supper was grilled chicken breast from the deli at the supermarket, along with potato salad and biscuits. Almsted's, which had abutted Libby's building, was closed until inspectors could determine whether or not there had been structural damage.

Hildie, resting contentedly in her usual place in front of the stove, rolled her eyes open in greeting, then closed them again. She'd had a big day, out there on the Silver Spur.

They all had.

Once Libby had washed her hands, dried them and sunk into the chair Tate held for her at the table, the day caught up with her, too. With an impact.

She was exhausted.

"So?" Tate asked, sitting down across from Libby. "Are you going to tell me what the big summons was all about?"

"Yes," Libby said, helping herself to a piece of chicken and some potato salad. "She's going back to her husband, Winston, the retired proctologist, in Costa Rica."

"I see," Tate said.

They ate in silence for a while.

"There's money," Libby said. "Sort of."

Tate raised an eyebrow. "Sort of?" he echoed. "How can there 'sort of' be money?"

Libby got up, rummaged through her purse for the envelope, handed it to Tate.

"See for yourself. There should be a check inside. I'm not getting excited until it clears the bank."

Tate chuckled at that, started to set the envelope aside, still sealed.

Libby's heart climbed into her throat. "Open it," she said, almost in a whisper. "Please?"

"It's yours, Lib. You should be the one to open it."

Libby shook her head. "I can't."

"Okay," Tate said. Slowly, probably giving her time to change her mind, he inserted the blade of a butter knife under the flap and slit the crease, pulled the check out without looking at it.

Libby closed her eyes. Waited.

"Tell me," she said.

Tate gave a long, low whistle of exclamation.

When he read off the amount, she gasped.

He handed it across the table. "Looks legitimate to me," he said quietly.

Libby briefly examined the check, groped for the envelope and shoved it back inside. Then she put the envelope on top of the fridge, under the cookie jar.

Out of sight, out of mind.

As if.

"I suppose it's too soon to ask if you have plans?" Tate ventured, when they'd both finished eating.

"Plans?" Libby echoed. He seemed to have withdrawn from her somehow, pulled ever so slightly back into a space she couldn't quite reach—but maybe she was imagining that.

Tate stood, began clearing the table, putting things in the fridge, scraping bones and other scraps into the trash bin. "Yeah," he said gently. "You could do a lot with that kind of money, Libby. You need to think about this." He sighed. "Without me distracting you."

"Distracting me?" She felt the floor tremble beneath her.

"Libby, you have some new options now, that's all I'm saying. You need to explore them."

To think *she'd* been hung up on Tate's earlier statement that he planned on asking her to move in with him, once the house was ready. She'd pretty much decided she'd say "yes," when and if the time came, but now—now Tate was talking about thinking and options and explorations.

For Libby, the money hadn't changed anything, really.

But maybe it had, for Tate. Maybe he'd liked her better when she was running a failing business, living on a shoestring. Or maybe he'd just felt sorry for her—poor Libby—and now that she was a "woman of means," as Marva had put it, he could cut her loose, with no strain on his noble McKettrick conscience.

Dammit, was the man looking for an out?

She loved Tate.

She loved his daughters, too—that hadn't taken long. Two minutes, maybe.

Yes, there had been dreams. She'd wanted to travel a little, perhaps take some courses online, buy a decent car…

But all those were things she could have done without leaving Blue River, or at least without leaving Tate.

"I'm not even sure the check is good," Libby reiterated, after letting out a long breath. If Tate was having second thoughts, looking for an exit, she could deal with that. She could survive it—just as she had before. "Marva could be delusional—or even some kind of con artist, for all I know."

Tate leaned back against the counter, watching her. Sadness illuminated his eyes. "But if it is good?"

"I don't know, Tate. Do I have to decide tonight?"

He crossed the room, leaned down, kissed the top of her head, lightly, in a way that said, See you later. "No," he said hoarsely. "All you need to do tonight is get some sleep. We can talk tomorrow or—whenever."

Whenever? Libby thought. Her disappointment was out of all proportion to the situation. *Whenever?*

"Lock up behind me," Tate said.

He bent, patted Hildie on the head and started toward the front of the house.

Just like that, he was leaving.

Going back to the ranch—alone.

Libby waited until Tate was down the front steps, through the gate, on the sidewalk—until he'd actually driven away in his big-ass redneck truck—before she engaged the dead bolt on the front door and stormed back to the kitchen. Shot that dead bolt, too.

Hildie hoisted herself up off the floor, yawning.

Libby shut off the kitchen lights and led the way down the hall toward her bedroom. By then, she was absolutely certain she'd been dumped again.

Slam, bam, thank you, ma'am.

"Never trust a man," she told the dog.

Hildie plopped down on the rug at the foot of Libby's bed, while Libby peeled off her clothes and flung them away. Shimmied into an oversized T-shirt and hauled back the covers on her bed.

"He's probably got you snowed," Libby said, heading for the bathroom, where she washed her face and brushed her teeth. On her return, she resumed the one-sided conversation. "All that McKettrick charm. 'You're too tired to walk? Poor old dog. Here. Let me carry you, on my horse—'"

Hildie sighed, dog-tired.

Libby climbed into bed. Switched out the lamp.

A tear trickled down over her right temple, tickling.

"What exactly did Tate do to make me so angry, you ask? As anyone would. He *left*. As soon as a challenge comes up—*poof!*—Tate McKettrick is out of here." She paused, pulled up a corner of the top sheet to dry her cheeks. "The thing is, Hildie," she finished, staring up at the darkened ceiling, "I'm in love with the man. What do you say to that?"

Hildie, of course, said nothing at all.

Somehow, against all odds, Libby slept.

HE HADN'T SEEN—or spoken to—Libby in four days.

Cheryl called on Friday morning—early, even taking the time difference between Texas and New York into account.

Tate, sleepless since leaving Libby's house the night of the meeting with her mother, had just started the coffee brewing. Having glanced at the caller ID panel, his usual greeting was gruffer than usual.

"Tate McKettrick. What do you want, Cheryl?"

"My," Cheryl said. "Aren't we testy?"

Tate drew in a breath, let it out slowly. "You don't know the half of it," he said.

"How are my babies?" The chirpy note in Cheryl's voice made him instantly suspicious. He hated it when she wheedled, and that chirp was the equivalent of a fire alarm.

"Audrey and Ava are fine," he said evenly. "Looking forward to seeing you tonight. A whole weekend with Mommy. Audrey wants to show you the routine she's been practicing for the Pixie Pageant. What time does your plane get in?"

Cheryl was silent for a few moments. "You're letting Audrey enter the Pixie Pageant?"

"Yeah," Tate said. "I might have been wrong, saying 'no' out of hand the way I did. She's giving it a shot."

"*You,* Tate McKettrick, were *wrong* about something?"

"I can think of several," Tate answered. A pause, during which he restrained himself from listing those things he'd been wrong about. It would surprise Cheryl to know she wasn't number one on that list—that slot went to screwing up what he'd had with Libby in the first place. "Can we cut to the chase now, Cheryl? You didn't call to shoot the breeze. It's not even four o'clock out here—the girls are sleeping."

A short, stormy silence, during which he could feel the bad mojo building. "Dammit, Tate," she finally burst out, "you *know* why I called, and you're *deliberately* making it all as difficult as possible!"

Since there was some truth in her accusation—he *had* known why she was calling—Tate decided to chill out a little. "Okay," he said. "I'll stop making things difficult for you. Go ahead and say it."

She sighed, and her voice sounded moist; either she was crying, or she wanted him to think she was. "It's the job— I'm new—low man on the totem pole—"

Tate suppressed a sigh. His knuckles tightened around the cell phone. God knew, he didn't give a rat's ass if Cheryl *ever* came back to Blue River, but the girls did. They were only six, and they loved and missed their mother.

"I'd suggest that Audrey and Ava come here," Cheryl went into her bravely-carrying-on routine. "But there wouldn't be much point in that, when I'll be at the office all weekend."

"No," Tate said. "There wouldn't be much point in that."

"I'll come *next* weekend," she promised, rallying. "And bring presents." A pause. "Will you tell them that? That I'll come next weekend and bring presents?"

"No," Tate replied. "They need to hear it from you."

Cheryl sounded pained. *"Why?"*

"Because this is between you and the kids."

He heard her draw in an angry breath. "You *love* making me look bad, don't you?"

Tate closed his eyes, held back the obvious retort.

"All right." He nearly growled the words. "I'll explain—

this time. But you still need to call Audrey and Ava yourself, Cheryl. They're your daughters. They miss you, and
they'll want to hear your voice."

"I'll call," Cheryl said, after a long time.

"Yeah," Tate said, and hung up without a goodbye.

Right about then, Austin meandered down his private
stairway, wearing nothing but a pair of black boxers. Scars
from two different rotator-cuff surgeries laced his right
shoulder, front and back.

He ruffed up his already mussed hair and gave an expansive yawn.

"Tell me you stayed out all night," he drawled, "because
nobody in his right mind gets up this early, even on a
freakin' ranch."

Tate chuckled, but the sound was rueful. "*You're* up," he
pointed out.

Austin all but staggered to the counter, took a mug from
the cupboard and poured coffee into it, even though the stuff
was still percolating in the fancy steel-and-steam apparatus
Garrett had donated to the cause when their mother's old
electric pot finally conked out.

"Hell, yes, I'm up," Austin grumbled. "The bad vibes
were practically bouncing off the walls."

Tate shook his head, exasperated. "Cheryl isn't coming
home for the weekend," he said. "I knew things would come
to that eventually, but I thought it would take a while. The
girls are going to be let down, Austin. Big-time."

"Are they?" Austin asked, after rubbing his eyes. "If
they're missing anybody, I'd say it's Libby." He took a
cautious sip of coffee, made a face at the taste. He'd been
doing that for as long as Tate could remember.

"Why do you drink coffee if you don't like it?" he snapped.

Austin chuckled. "Is your tail in a twist or what?" he countered, clearly amused."And what the hell are you talking about?"

"The way you grimace."

"I grimace?"

"Yeah. When you drink coffee."

Austin laughed, shook his head again. "It's just something I do," he said. "Who cares why?"

Tate sighed. "You're right. Who the hell cares why?"

"This is about Libby—this weird mood you're in."

"What makes you say that?"

Austin lifted his cup in a half-assed toast. "I'm psychic. I might just set up my own toll-free number and start telling fortunes. Here's yours for free—If you don't get a handle on things with Libby Remington, once and for all, you're going to wind up as one of those crusty, grizzled old sons-of-bitches who grouse about everything from taxes to the breakfast special at the Denny's three towns over, train their dogs to bite and post No Trespassing signs on every other fence post."

Tate couldn't help a wan grin. "That was colorful," he said.

"What's the problem between you and Libby?"

"What if I said it was none of your business?"

"I'd keep right on asking," Austin said, smiling over the rim of his cup.

Tate sighed. "She came into some money."

"And that's bad?"

"I suppose not. It gives her a lot of options, Austin. She could leave, start herself a whole new, Tate-free life someplace else."

"And you'd rather she didn't have any choice but to stay here with you?"

For all the chewing and mulling he'd done, Tate hadn't

thought of that. "No," he said hoarsely. "I just want her to stay. To *want* to stay."

"And she doesn't?"

"I don't know—I don't think *she* knows, either. Libby is deciding what she wants. I'm trying to give her enough space to do that."

"Space is good," Austin agreed. "But too much of it might make Libby think you just don't give a damn, one way or another. Talk to her, Tate. Tell her what you feel, and what you want. *Then* say you'll give her space to think things over."

"You might be the next Dear Abby."

Austin laughed. "I applied," he joked. "Too much bull on my résumé."

"Hilarious," Tate said.

"Yeah," Austin said. "I'm a one-man tailgate party. Bring your own six-pack."

"Speaking of bulls," Tate said. "You've given up on the idea of tracking Buzzsaw down and riding him, haven't you?"

Austin shook his head, set his coffee mug aside with a thunk. "Nope," he said. "I know the stock supplier who owns him. Buzzsaw and me, we have a date with destiny."

Tate's gut tightened. "Let this go, Austin," he said quietly. "That bull almost killed you before. Why give him a second chance?"

Austin's eyes were grave. "You know why."

"All you have to do is turn your back. All you have to do is walk away."

But Austin shook his head again, and Tate knew that particular conversation was over.

MARVA LEFT TOWN, ON SCHEDULE.

A day later, a moving van pulled up in front of her condominium, and her furniture and other household goods were removed.

Just like that, she was gone.

Again.

Libby, Julie and Paige drove all the way to Austin in Paige's car, just to deposit the checks Marva had given them. That way, they had each other for moral support, and it would be considerably less embarrassing than walking into First Cattleman's Bank in Blue River and finding out there was no money, carefully invested by a fiscally minded, retired proctologist.

The checks were good.

They plunked down on a bench in front of the bank, the three of them in a row, stunned.

"We're rich," Julie said.

"Not rich," Paige clarified. "Comfortable."

"I'm a teacher," Julie countered. "You're a registered nurse with state-of-the-art skills. Maybe this kind of money says 'comfortable' to you, but it says 'rich' to me."

Libby laughed. "Hot damn," she said.

She could go anywhere, do practically anything.

She had choices.

"What are you going to do with your share?" Julie asked, probably relieved that Libby hadn't torn the check into little pieces and tossed them into the breeze.

"Buy a new car," Libby said.

"That's all you want?"

"It's not all I want," Libby answered, smiling to herself. *And sometimes you have to go after what you want, and have confidence that you'll get it.*

The clarity was sudden, and it was glorious.

"Let's get lunch," she said. "I have things to do at home."

"Don't we all?" Paige agreed.

They had salads at a sunny sidewalk café.

Libby bought a cell phone and, between Paige and the salesman, figured out how to operate it.

And then they drove back to Blue River.

"You look like a woman with a purpose," Paige said, dropping Libby off at the back gate.

Inside the house, Hildie began to bark a relieved welcome.

Libby merely nodded; she knew her mysterious smile and wandering attention had been driving her curious sisters nuts all morning.

Waggling the fancy phone, which was probably capable of polishing the lenses of satellites deep in outer space, she smiled and unlatched the gate with her free hand.

"Call you later," she said.

Paige honked her horn in farewell and drove away.

Libby hurried up the walk and unlocked the back door.

Hildie spilled out gleefully, greeted her with a yip and squatted next to the flower bed.

While the dog enjoyed a few minutes of fresh air, Libby changed out of her go-to-the-bank-in-Austin dress and sandals and pulled on comfy jeans, a short-sleeved black T-shirt and tennis shoes. She brushed her hair and pulled it back from her face.

She put on lip gloss.

"Come on," she said to Hildie, grabbing up her purse and the new cell phone and the keys to the ratty old Impala. "We're on a mission."

During the drive, Libby rehearsed what she'd say when she reached her destination.

I love you, Tate McKettrick.
Let's give "us" a chance.

Now that we're all grown up, let's make it work.

She'd done a lot of thinking in the days since Tate had left her to consider her options. She'd realized he hadn't so much dumped her as assumed she was going to dump him. But she wasn't, and she trusted that he'd respond to her rehearsal speech just the way she wanted him to.

She stopped at the small house first; there were signs that Tate had been there, pounding nails and splashing paint onto the walls, but he wasn't around at the moment.

Libby called Hildie back from the creek where she'd been exploring, and they moved on to the main place.

There were trucks everywhere, parked at odd angles, but Libby didn't see anyone, either by the barn or in the spacious yard.

She was standing there, beside the Impala, trying to decide whether to knock on the kitchen door or check out the barn, when she heard the small, shrill scream.

Libby's heart actually seized in her chest.

For one terrible moment, she couldn't move.

Couldn't speak.

The scream came again, smaller now, more terrified.

And it was followed by the sound of the stallion trying to kick his way out of the pen again.

Libby broke into a run. "Tate!" she yelled. "Somebody— anybody—*help!*"

She rounded the corner of the barn.

The stallion was kicking in all directions now, raising dust, a whirling dervish.

And through that choking dust, Libby saw one of the twins—Ava, she thought—wriggle under the lowest rail and right into the stud pen.

Jesus, Libby prayed, *Jesus, Jesus, Jesus...*

She slammed against the side of the pen, grabbing the rails with both hands to steady herself.

Ava huddled within inches of the stallion's flying hooves, sheltering one of the pups with her little body.

Raising her eyes, the child spotted Libby.

Libby flopped to her belly in the dirt, but she clearly wasn't going to fit under that fence. She bolted back to her feet and started up the side, hand over hand, rail to rail.

"Tate!" she screamed, once more, as she reached the top.

And then she was over, landing in a two-footed crouch in the churned up dust and dried manure, Ava within reach.

The stallion froze, quivering all over, sizing her up.

Libby knew the respite was only temporary.

She could barely see for the dust, and her eyes scalded. Her heart pounded, and her throat felt scraped raw.

Moving slowly, she got Ava by one skinny upper arm, pulled.

Ava held on to the puppy.

The stallion snorted, laid back his ears.

A bad sign, Libby thought, strangely calm even though her body was stressed to the max. A very bad sign.

She pressed Ava and the pup behind her, against the rails. Pinned them with her back, spread her arms to shield them as best she could.

"Easy," she told the stallion, hardly recognizing her own voice. Her nose itched. She thought she might throw up. But she didn't dare move her arms. "Nobody wants to hurt you."

"Hold on, Lib." The voice was Tate's. He was just behind her.

Thank God he was there.

Thank God.

"Daddy," Ava whimpered. "I know I gave my word as a McKettrick, but Ambrose dug a hole under the stud-pen fence and got inside and I—"

"Hush," Tate said, very gently.

He started up the rails, making the same climb Libby had.

Libby became aware that Austin was there, too, fiddling with the padlock on the pen's door. A rifle rested easily in the crook of one of his arms as he worked.

Everything seemed to be happening in slow motion.

The stallion began to get agitated again, tossing his head, snorting. Pawing at the dirt with one front hoof, then the other.

Tate was over the fence, in front of Libby.

Shielding her and Ava and the little dog, he spoke to the stallion. His words were quiet, and their meaning innocuous— it was the tone of his voice, the energy Tate projected, a sort of calming authority, that made the difference.

The pen gate slowly creaked open.

The stallion turned his huge head in that direction, then back to Tate.

The danger was by no means past.

The pen was small, the stallion still riled. Sweat glistened on his hide, and his eyes rolled, all whites except for tiny slits of dark along the upper lids.

Libby let her forehead rest against the back of Tate's right shoulder.

Behind her, Ava and the puppy squirmed.

Austin moved away from the pen gate, wide-open now, and cocked the rifle.

Dear God, was he going to shoot the horse?

She must have wondered aloud, because Tate answered her. "Only if the stallion turns on us, Lib," he said.

Libby closed her eyes, clutched at Ava and the pup, holding them in a sort of backward hug, and waiting—waiting for the stallion to make up his mind.

Had Pablo's heart pounded like this?

Or had death come too swiftly for fear to take hold?

"Come on, now, horse," Austin said mildly, backing farther out of the path of freedom. "You come on now."

The stud took one step toward the gate, then another.

Quivered again, from behind his ears, laid sideways now, all the way to his flanks and down his haunches.

Then, with breath-stopping suddenness, the enormous and terrifyingly beautiful beast kicked out his hind legs, high and hard, missing Tate by inches.

And bolted and ran.

Cowboys stayed clear, though one rider opened a series of corral gates, clearing the way to the range beyond, the hills beyond that.

Tate finally let out his breath, turned around to look into Libby's eyes.

Ava set Ambrose on the ground, and he promptly fled.

"Daddy," she whispered, as Tate hooked an arm around her, lifted her and held her tightly against his side. She buried her face in his neck, sobbing.

Tate's gaze was riveted to Libby's.

"I love you," she said. "Maybe this isn't the right time to say so, but I do. I have choices. I can go away or I can stay here, and this is where I want to be. I really, truly, forever *love you*, Tate McKettrick."

The white flash of his grin made a dazzling contrast to his unshaven face and the stud-pen dust embedded in his skin and lightening his hair.

"I'll be damned," he said, throwing back his head, giving a whoop of joyous laughter.

"Hardly romantic," Libby said, pretending to be indignant.

"I'm saving the romantic stuff for when we're by ourselves," he answered.

Austin handed off the rifle to another cowboy and took Ava from Tate. She clung for a moment, then attached herself to her uncle.

"Where is Audrey?" Libby asked.

"Rehearsing for the Pixie Pageant," Tate answered, taking her hand.

Hildie was still shut up in the Impala, crazy to get out.

Tate opened the door for her, and promptly hoisted her into the back seat of his truck. He did the same with Libby.

"What about Ava?"

"She'll be fine with Austin and Esperanza," Tate answered, getting behind the wheel and starting up the big engine.

They drove to the other house.

Not a contractor in sight.

Tate lifted Hildie to the ground, and she immediately settled under a shade tree, the picture of canine contentment.

Progress had been made on the inside of the house—the kitchen was coming together, boasting granite countertops, glass-fronted cupboards and travertine tile floors.

There was still no furniture, but the shower in the master bath was working fine, and a sizable blow-up mattress stood in the center of the largest bedroom.

Tate opened the etched-glass shower door, reached in to turn the brass spigots.

Water shot, like a hard rain, from the matching showerhead, which looked as though it was roughly the same diameter as a manhole cover.

When Tate was satisfied with the temperature of the

water, he tugged Libby closer, hooked a finger in the neckline of her T-shirt.

"I love you, Libby," he said gruffly. "I mean to spend the rest of my life proving that to you but, for now, it'll have to be sex."

"Oh, no," Libby joked, kicking off her shoes, unfastening her jeans, wriggling out of them.

Tate laughed, pulled her close.

They began to kiss.

And undress each other.

And the water from the big brass showerhead poured down over both of them, washing away the worst of the dust.

Washing away, it seemed, the mistakes and the heartbreaks and the disappointments of the past.

The foreplay was brief; they were both too desperate for contact to drag things out. Tate teased Libby to the absolute verge of a climax, then took her against the slick wall of the shower, the first thrust as hard and deep as the last.

Long minutes later, they both erupted, mouths locked together, tongues sparring, shouts of release ricocheting from one to the other.

They sank to the floor of the shower when it was over, leaning into each other for support.

"Will you marry me, Libby?" Tate asked, both of them kneeling under the fall of water. "Please?"

She nodded, traced his jaw with the tip of one finger, tasted his mouth. "Yes," she said. "I want a big wedding, on New Year's Eve." She nibbled at his lower lip. "In the meantime, though," she said, caressing him intimately, loving the way he groaned—and grew—in response, "let's keep working on sex until we get really, really good at it."

Tate gasped. "We're—pretty—good at it now."

Libby kissed him. "Practice makes perfect," she said.

September...

"You look like a princess in that sparkly blue dress," Ava said, a mite wistfully, as she and Libby made their way backstage at the Pixie Pageant, just a few steps behind Tate.

Libby smiled, squeezed the little girl against her side. "Thank you, sweetheart," she said. "You're not unlike royalty yourself, as it happens."

Up ahead, she saw Tate lean down to catch Audrey up in his arms. Libby's heart clenched with love as he straightened, this man she would marry on New Year's Eve.

They caught up, Libby and Ava; the four of them were together.

After tearful explanations over the phone, Cheryl had sent an impressive bouquet from New York; she was working on a big case and hadn't been able to get home for the pageant.

She and Libby e-mailed each other fairly regularly, always about the girls. Libby took a lot of pictures, uploaded them and sent them to Cheryl.

"I lost," Audrey announced cheerfully, as Tate set her back on her feet.

"Nobody wins all the time," Ava said consolingly.

Audrey shrugged. "It was fun," she said, "but I'm ready to move on."

Libby and Tate exchanged smiles at that.

"Could we get pizza?" Audrey asked her dad.

"Yep," Tate said. "We can get pizza."

They stopped on the way home, picked up the steamy,

fragrant boxes—Hawaiian with extra cheese. Back at the house, Hildie, Ambrose and Buford greeted them with a lot of barking and jumping around.

The meal was happy cacophony, around their kitchen table. Audrey was still wearing her tutu, leotard and full stage makeup.

"So," Ava asked her twin, with real interest, "what are you going to do next, now that you're not into beauty pageants anymore?"

Audrey gave the question due consideration, even though it was clear to Libby that she'd already made up her mind. "Rodeo," she said.

"Rodeo?" Ava echoed.

Tate put down his second slice of pizza and opened his mouth to speak.

Libby laid a hand on his arm.

"Barrel racing, I think," Audrey went on.

"I want to do that, too!" Ava decided.

"Mom won't like it," Audrey warned. "Not unless we get to be rodeo queens."

Libby hid a smile behind a paper napkin.

"Barrel racing," Tate repeated, after clearing his throat.

"We'll need lessons," Ava said, ever practical.

Tate caught Libby's eye. *Help,* his expression said.

"You'll be fantastic," Libby told the girls. "You're McKettricks—rodeo is in your blood."

Tate gave her a *This isn't helping* look.

"Can we call Mom and tell her we're going to be barrel racers?" Audrey asked excitedly.

"Yeah, can we?" Ava chimed in.

"Go," Tate said.

They raced to the cordless phone on the kitchen counter, and Ava got there first.

"Don't you dare dial Mom's number," Audrey cried, "until I have the phone from Dad and Libby's bedroom!"

"Thanks for jumping right in there and taking my side," Tate told Libby, a wry grin tilting his mouth up on one side. But he took her hand, moved the big diamond in her engagement ring back and forth with the pad of his thumb a couple of times, and then kissed her palm, sending fire shooting through her.

"Don't do that," Libby whispered.

An impish twinkle lit Tate's wonderfully blue eyes. Where he'd been kissing, he flicked his tongue.

Libby groaned.

He laughed, tugged her onto his lap. Nibbled at her earring.

"You look hot in that dress," he murmured.

"Like a princess, I'm told," Libby said.

"You'll look even hotter when I get you out of it, of course."

She blushed. "Tate."

He slipped a finger under her low neckline, inside her bra, found her nipple. Grinned. "Do we have to wait until New Year's to get married?" he asked, his voice a low rumble, his gaze fixed on her mouth.

Libby removed his hand, afraid the girls would come back. "Yes," she said. "We have to wait until New Year's. Why?"

"Because I want to make a baby with you."

He kissed her, long and deep.

She forgot they were in the kitchen.

"You'll want to get it right, naturally," she whispered.

"Absolutely," he responded. "And that means we need to keep right on practicing."

They kissed until the twins burst into the room again.

"Mom says we *cannot, under any circumstances,* take up barrel racing!" Audrey announced.

"Does she, now?" Tate asked. He didn't move Libby off his lap, or even stop kissing her, really.

Ava heaved a big sigh. "Come on, Audrey. Let's go watch TV."

"Yeah," Audrey agreed.

"They're practicing again," Ava said.

Audrey nodded. "And that's so boring," she replied.

They vanished into the living room.

"Boring?" Libby asked, against Tate's mouth. "I don't *think* so."

* * * * *

The Texas McKettricks aren't done yet. Watch as city boy Garrett McKettrick comes home to slow down and take stock of his life.
Little does he know Libby's sister, Julie Remington, is just the change he needs.

Look for
McKettricks of Texas: Garrett
by Linda Lael Miller